The Voyage of a Bean

The Voyage of a Bean

Stories

Volume 2

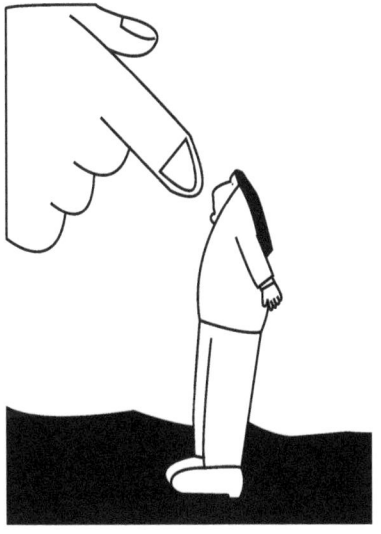

Bruce Adam

ꜰ❧ Ara Pacis ☙ꜰ

The Voyage of a Bean, Stories, Volume 2.

Copyright © 2005 by Bruce Adam.

All rights reserved. Printed in the United States of America. No part of this book may be used or reproduced in any manner whatsoever without written permission except in the case of brief quotations embodied in critical articles and reviews.

Cover Photo © 2005 by Clay Johnson, Philadelphia, PA.
Title page drawings and book design by the author.

First Paperback Edition, 2005

Ara Pacis Publishers
P.O. Box 1202
Des Plaines, IL 60017-1202
www.arapacispublishers.com

ISBN 0-9661318-2-7
Library of Congress Control Number: 2005903543
Manufactured in the United States of America

Contents

Foster Strauss 3
Mark of a Man 9
Holloway 13
The Parrot's Feather..17
The Golden Arrow 21
Don and Julia 24
Bold Lover..26
The Ferris Wheel Tragedies...35
The Spider Priests...43
The Book of Gerald 63
The King of Rain Checks 74
Father's Death 91
The Letter of the Law...94
The Money Tree 100
The Death of the Explorer 101
Pandora's Box...127
Homecoming..128
In the Country 131
The Sandmen 133
War Machines...136
Manned for War 141
The Tower..143
Caroline Kane 145
My Little Flower 179
The Good Host...196
A Siren in the Woods..199
No Hand 201
World of the Small 202
Mr. Pepperdale 207
The Sixth Room 211
The Room Next to the Dead 215
Dying Visions 219
Train Trance...221
The Grafting 225
The Nail Scrum 229
A Little Croaking 236
Chartes...239
The Dirges..243
Square One 246
The Voyage of a Bean 253

v

The Voyage of a Bean

For Eliot, Renée and David

Foster Strauss

My name's Foster Strauss. Thirty years ago I was working on my Doctorate in Theology at the Divinity School, nowhere near finishing it, and I'd taken a keen interest in the occult sciences. I had a great computer game where I had trapped a genie in a pentagram, and I was forcing him to reveal all kinds of secrets that would help me in the game. "Oh for such a lamp in life!" I thought. I'd have done anything for a few hints granted by a devil at my mercy. I was flunking a course in Kierkegaard at the time, and I could have used some tutoring in his "Concept of Dread." I received the lowest mark in the class in last year's final exam for writing thirty pages on why I wasn't afraid of anything. The professor said, "Read the book, and be afraid of me!"

I had a part-time job in a small real estate office that was just great. My boss, Mather Stopholis, was unusual to say the least, but he'd amassed a fortune in real estate, a business he took up when he was kicked out of divinity school. I thought he'd be good for what he knew, but frankly, where it concerned matters of theology, he was worse than me. Knowing him, it was little wonder that he was kicked out. He just wasn't what you'd call a godly man.

When I was studying the "Problem of Evil," I asked Mr. Stopholis what he thought. He said evil wasn't a problem. I explained the point was that because there is thriving evil in the world, it must be considered that God may not exist, for if a God existed who was omnipotent, along with the rest of the omni-qualities, He would not let evil exist, and therefore, because of evil, God, at least as we imagine Him, must not exist.

Mr. Stopholis scratched his chin a moment and said he wondered how I could be flunking my courses when I could so capably reiterate the most commonplace arguments. That is all that is required, and if that were all I sought, I would do just fine. "Repeat exactly what the professors say," he said, "and you'll succeed — which seems about as big a problem of evil as I ever heard."

But my problem was I was always going off the logical track. In class, for example, I used to ask whether it were possible, according to the Ontological Argument, for each person to have his own personal God, a being of which no greater can exist, and if that be the case, there would be all sorts of equal Gods, and in that sense, no God among them, and people fighting over whose God is greatest. It seemed to make sense to me, and I would have pointed out some historical precedent, but the professors always cut me off, told me to shut up, and resumed reading in monotones from sacred books of arguments and essays by the saints.

Mr. Stopholis confided that he commiserated unequivocally. It was for such relentless, individual pursuit that he was expelled, and he remarked that I showed great promise and would probably do far better without such dreary confines as the divinity school where worn-out minds wander dull hallways spilling refried beans as if they would grow into bean stalks of great knowledge. No, I must finish school, I told him, at least I wanted to complete the courses, but there was a chance I'd fail anyway without help.

"You've too inquiring a mind, too unique a grasp and approach, to don the thin slice of mind that distinguishes a priest," he told me. "You were not born to be a creature of such habits."

It was true. I had often wondered if I really wanted the degree.

One afternoon when I was particularly depressed (the genie had escaped, stolen my treasures, and wizards had redesigned caverns I'd spent weeks exploring), Mr. Stopholis made me a very strange offer.

It went something like this. I worked for him, didn't I? Well, why not let him work for me? "Huh?" I replied. Sure, he told me, I'd get something I wanted and pay him with something of mine, just as he gave me cash for my time. "So you'll help me with school, and I'll work for free here. Sorry, can't afford it." I said.

"No, no, you've got it wrong," he told me. "I'm in the real estate business, and I'm interested in a piece of property of which you are currently the sole proprietor."

It stymied me. I didn't have any property. What could he mean? Then I thought I saw something in the way he was grimacing at me, and it struck me all at once. He wasn't married. We never talked about girls, much as I thought of them. Mr. Stopholis, gay?! I could not believe it. I'd heard of people getting kicked out of divinity school in the old days for such things. It was starting to make sense.

"I assure you, I'm not gay," he said.

"What, can you read my mind?" I shouted. "I never said I thought you were!"

"I can tell by the look on your face, but it's your soul I want, nothing else, just your soul, and I'll make it worth your while, and on convenient terms. Let me explain," he continued, "I'll take out a mortgage on your soul, and pay it off in installments. If I fail in any way to make payment to your satisfaction, you can take repossession. In other words, I rent your soul with an option to buy, and when fully paid off, it's mine. The papers are right here; all you have to do is sign."

He went on, "And what do you get out of it, you wonder? Power beyond good and evil, that's what. Years of control and deliverance from yourself will be yours, because I'll be at your beck and call to see your will be done. You still don't fathom what I mean. Stop gaping. So Adam needs a bite of the apple before he knows what's what. And so you need a sign before you sign. Fine. That computer game that's got you hoodwinked and bedazzled… you're the master now."

Even as he spoke, a sudden insight into the secret of the caves occurred to me. I had the genie and total victory in sight. This nonsense about soul selling was just another one of his divinity school attacks, and I wanted to get home to finish the game. The genie would be powerless against me. Even the whereabouts of his lair was known to me, where soon I would free and wed the captive princess, showering her with treasures only she has beauty to outshine.

It was as easy as I thought, and amazed, I swept through the caverns like a titan, deftly demolishing roguish dwarves with the sheer force of command, and by stripping wizards of spells, I restored the cave in all its stalagmighty paths and stalagtitanic grandeur. By the time I'd reached his lair, the genie was beside himself, literally, for he had the power to split himself, though it meant there were two, each with half of the original strength. He was seething to have had to resort to this, for it meant as well that he must double his sentence of imprisonment as a genie, and nothing desires final freedom like a djinn.

Then I saw the princess, chained against a rock. Near her, several menacing dwarves I had decapitated in another part of the game were running about looking for their heads, blindly but boldly brandishing axes.

But were they a threat? I remembered one of the hints in the instructions that came with the program, and saw fit to apply it at this time.

I walked right into a bevy of elves, and they promptly slashed my head from my neck. Exactly as I hoped, something remarkable transpired. From my head grew a body, with twice the strength of my own, and between my shoulders there appeared a head twice as wise. In the booklet it said, "... and prepare to lose your head at the sight of the beautiful princess."

The end came quickly. The genies squared off, but they were no match for the two of me. After vanquishing them, two puffs of smoke first whimpered into one, then entered a bottle, which rolled into a pit. Then the ceiling caved in, burying it forever, or until the game is started again. I merged into one as well, but with twice my original strength and intelligence, "a suitable match for this princess," read the text on the screen. What was that supposed to be, a slight? I thought she should take the victor as is, but I allowed that she might be too royally spoiled to swoon before courage, common sense and mere good looks. She is nevertheless heavy, I thought as the game ended with me carrying both her and the treasure out of the cave. I couldn't have carried both otherwise. Perhaps it's best, I thought, not to question or tamper with design.

I had other games I hadn't figured out, some rated less difficult, and enthusiastically tried to play them. Something seemed gone out of me though, and I could sense I'd lost that inspired knack. A sense of outrage and powerlessness got hold of me. I was my former self, with half the strength and wit that won the princess, and yes, I was alone. Wherever the gift had gone, I wanted it back. If the princess were by my side, I would sell her to ogres for it, and once I had it in my possession again, then I would fight to win her back. I'd do anything for it. I would give up myself. Yes, I would even sell my …

I stopped. My soul, that's what I was about to say. That's what Mr. Stopholis had been babbling about when I left the office. I wondered. "No, that's ridiculous. What power could he have to do any of that? I've played lots of computer games, never with that much savoir-faire albeit, but I've won plenty of them. Well, allowing for a point or two left hanging for some petty chore left undone, I've finished many and racked up every, well, nearly every point, and besides, it takes too much time and effort to start over just for that one point or two when chances are I'll never find it. But I got everything in the most baffling challenge of them all. It's impossible, impossible!" I tossed and turned most of the night.

Mr. Stopholis sensed the degree of my ambivalence, split between interest and disbelief. My disbelief faded as I realized he expected such a reaction, and I knew he was patient enough to wait for the gourd of my interest to swell before he'd finally heed my pleas to pluck my soul off the vine.

"You've got nothing to worry about," he said, pulling some papers from a desk. "It's a mortgage only, and if I fail to make my payments to your satisfaction, it will be yours again to repossess."

Despite my instincts, I agreed. I told myself that if it was nonsense, I would soon find out, and if it wasn't, I could use the gifts for a time, study them, regain my soul and create the gifts in myself.

"Ah, but this is not something you can possess if you have your soul," he told me. "What I offer and what you exchange must each occupy a separate place. It's all in this agreement, ready to sign."

A one week reading period before finals had just begun at divinity school. I wasn't prepared for the exams, nor was I likely to study. The gifts of insight would be nice. "What the hell, Mr. Stopholis," I said. "Give me the pen; I'll sign. What? In blood? OK, whatever."

The Voyage of a Bean

That was almost thirty years ago, and all this time Mr. Stopholis has dutifully made all of his payments on time. He took up residence in my soul, so to speak, right after I signed. I say "so to speak" because he hasn't been living in me, but like the insights he gave me into solving computer puzzles, each payment he makes hasn't gone far. I haven't been able to accumulate anything from what he's given me since it hasn't been in cash. If he gave me insights associated with horse racing, my bets would wind up going just enough off track that the best I'd do was to break even. I have as much to show for what he's done for me as what you get from drinking. With each payment, he's made me feel I'd gotten something special, and it has certainly kept my interest, but I realize now that I've made a mistake, and I'm looking for a way out of our deal. The problem is that my soul is nearly gone already as my life has been this long experience of gratification amounting to conquests of imaginary kingdoms and some real girls, but they never stayed very long. They sensed something unstable in me. They said I wasn't grounded, and that I had heart but no soul. They said I was clever, but not brilliant.

I wasn't even clever without the artificial heightening of my gifts according to the terms of my pact with Mr. Stopholis; and despite being made so clever, I haven't made any contribution to society. I've essentially lived from payment to payment, and soon it will be time for me to pay up, though I feel he's already taken my soul away from me, slowly in chunks. I don't feel nervous about the future, but it's unsettling at times to be so numb to what I've done. At least Adam in the garden was fooled by his mate. In my case, the snake came right to me and made it plain, which makes me stupider than innocent Eve, because she was made to think she was gaining something, while I lost something I obviously didn't think highly enough of to keep. I've been uselessly boosted into frittering it away, and I'm numb to God, numb to evil, numb to change, and tired of the whole thing. There's no excitement or mystery. I feel life is what's on TV, and though I've seen it all a thousand times, there's nothing else to do but watch. My only hope is a clause in the contract that I can throw him out for trashing the place, which he's done so well that I think I have a case to make him leave, but I don't really care.

Mark of a Man

John Cobble was not deliberately mixed up. He had tried various ways to understand himself, to get a picture of his life. Events seemed to pass by him year after year. Nothing had a recognizable resolution on close or even distant inspection. He felt as though he had not done anything worthwhile, that he had accomplished nothing. But most importantly, he did not understand himself.

As we move in for our first look at him, he is in his second year (the eighteenth month) of journal keeping, and, for the first time, he is sitting down to go over his daily record. It astounds him that there are many things, even though carefully recorded, that he does not remember. He is thoroughly displeased at the end of his reading to find that it is impossible to get a clear picture of himself when he can't even remember events or moments from recent days. Though there were numerous incidents he knew he had experienced (because he had written them down), his life was so routine he couldn't distinguish many days from one another.

The whole point was to get a good idea of himself in retrospect. Without writing, he had never been able to picture his personality or character. Now he had kept track, and he had fared no better. He resolved to change his life.

It struck him that he should do something strange and different each day — a unique, single action never before done and never to be repeated. One unforgettable new deed done each day would give him an unfrayed thread through his life. He'd be sure to remember each action and form a picture of himself from the choice of things he'd done.

So, he filled the ensuing days and weeks in that manner. From one day to the next, in the midst of his routine, he'd do something bizarre. One day, he'd spend twenty dollars on a bottle of cognac and fill a balloon with it — a balloon he had put in another bottle first. He broke the bottle to see if the balloon would hold. It didn't. Another day he blindfolded himself and went for a walk. The next day he used the blindfold as a sling and hurled cat's-eye marbles at a statue in the park. Soon, nothing was too weird for him. The more dangerous the choice, the more memorable it was. He flew a kite when it snowed. He painted graffiti on eggs before Easter. He stole a book from the library. He broke a window. He ran a stoplight. He chopped a tree down. And he wrote only these items in his journal.

It was tension that made an idea worth selecting. By the end of two months, he could read his diary with no trouble remembering any incident. What he did not notice was that day after day the incidents were becoming more and more lawless. At first, they were merely outrageous. Then, they were delinquent. In the fourth month, he lost his sense of perspective. He'd become a criminal.

Finally it happened that John Cobble was arrested. The six-month diary he wrote stands out as a tapestry of the ridiculous, an indictment of a misdirected imagination. Just having the list, the fact he kept track of the events, made it worse for him. But to top it off, each day in court he pulled something off to add to his list. Slapping the judge didn't help his case.

For grand theft auto, armed robbery, assaulting a peace officer, damaging public and private property, taking indecent liberties with a minor, keeping a still in the basement, and a host of other crimes, he was tossed into jail.

Cobble did not quibble. In fact, he was amazed at himself. The portrait he had made over those months was very clear when they turned the key, but they didn't give him his journal, and the clear thread he tried to make became a jumble of memories. Had he put sugar in the gas tank before or after dropping water balloons on pedestrians? Did he burn the flowers and poison the lawn, or burn the lawn and poison the flowers?

He became depressed. Even after only a few days behind bars, he wasn't doing anything memorable. He kept going over the months preceding his arrest. He remembered those days as being turbulent — exciting and tense. He would do only one thing new each day, but there was so much in the concocting. He took such great care in putting together the current recipe of his scheming that the whole day became wrapped around it like a boa constrictor. They said this was the mark of a criminal mind. But he felt free. He could find his spirit and let the events untwist their grip on him.

His first weeks in jail were introspective. He concluded he was not the outlaw they thought he was. They had his creation — the wrong man. Even if they didn't understand, he was now having moments when he actually fathomed his depths. Clarity was what he'd always wanted to find. He thought it everyone's duty to seek it before the mind totally crumbles. No one can forestall the inevitable, but he abhorred the idea of being "irresponsibly" mortal; of living and dying without a rise before the fall.

He felt cheated that he couldn't return to the world and use this new understanding of himself for living better. After all, he had originally wanted self-knowledge. Now that he'd arrived at some recognition of what he was, why was he being deprived of the opportunity to explore his fate? Then he thought that perhaps it would only seem more interesting for a moment. Without the crimes, wouldn't everything just become routine again? The cell was just as good a place for a plunge into boredom. Whose fault was it that when he found the thread of his life, it went straight to a knot in his stomach — a knot he'd become perpetually bent on untying every day. How could he work himself out of a hole when the hole was within? Acceptance of the present, not the past, was his problem. Prison was just a location, not a condition.

He laughed at himself quite a bit during his first few weeks there. He laughed at life, the big joke. It was too awful a condition not to laugh. It was a terrible kind of laugh that comes from a reflex taking the place of reflection. And though for a while he rose to the occasion of remembering thoughts, moods, and even states of mind, all thought on the matter suddenly ceased. Not by accident, so did the laughter. He fell out of reflection and embraced the routines, something he'd never done in life. He concluded he wasn't as strong as he once thought he was. He accepted his mediocrity, but often found himself yearning to be gripped again by the bonds that helped him forget about emptiness and made him feel almost alive. Now, to fight being eaten alive, he had only routines — hardly sufficient to feed his ravenous bit of hollow gnawing in the void, but enough to survive.

As we move in for a last look at him, he's in his cell, scratching a line on the wall. It marks his three hundred and seventy-seventh day of good behavior in jail. The wall is covered with many such marks — four parallel, one across, in familiar bundles of five.

Holloway

Jay Holloway lived with a high voice and a lucky quarter in the north suburbs of Chicago, far from the city but close enough to get a whiff of it. His voice was soprano, and the quarter had no date, having been worn out some time earlier by the world.

One morning Jay took his cat out for a walk and saw a chicken cross the road and get to the other side. He chuckled at a joke. Another day, a black cat crossed his path. He saw himself in a comic strip seeing the cat. In the first frame (so that the artist could get across the idea of movement), a dotted line trailed the cat. It started from the far side of the street. In the last frame of this imaginary comic, Jay saw himself trip over the dotted line and the cat licking his face.

A week later, he saw a cat dead in the road. Two days later, he drove by a dead raccoon. He thought he had seen the raccoon moving, and supposing it still alive, ran over it to put it out of its misery. He had heard of cases where people literally stomped on the head of a dying animal out of mercy for it, but he thought it best to stay in the car.

Gradually, he began to believe he had killed the raccoon. First, he blamed himself and thought he should have taken it to an animal hospital. Later, he would say he'd run over a raccoon once, and it was an awful feeling if the subject of animal hit-and-run came up in conversation. He never added that it had already been hit.

Jay had trouble getting to sleep at night and was a chronic drinker. A corner bar had a hook in him, and he would put up a fight every night as it reeled him in. He liked to play pool and thought of the good shots rather than the ones he missed. He would brood over the bad games until the next night when the sound of the colliding balls would lure him to the table where he'd be eaten alive.

He liked the girls with the strange eyes. There were lots of body problems with some, but if the eyes were right, he would check her fifty times in an hour just the same. He checked out all the girls, and he talked on his CB radio on the way home.

One night, he bought his usual pack of Old Gold cigarettes at the A&P, and he smoked all of them before going to sleep. Most of them he smoked at the bar. He was angry not to have any when he woke the next morning, and he searched for a half an hour, combining time between innings of a Cubs game.

That was unusual. Jay was a pack-a-day man, but usually saved a few for the morning coffee. If he got down to only four in a night, he would finish his drink and smoke one on the way home, even if it were earlier than usual, just so he could have some in the morning. The pack was more of a clock than the watch on his wrist.

The Cubs were losing, and the coffee was nearly gone. This was a crucial cigarette moment for Jay, and he was having a nicotine fit. He was sitting in his underwear in his small living room watching the Reds pound the Cubs in the third inning. When the Cubs were up in the fourth, he promised he'd quit smoking if they tied it. When Madlock homered to do it, he went out for a pack to celebrate.

He got home in the sixth and looked everywhere for matches into the ninth when he found a pack in a chair lining. That's when Bench doubled to send in the lead run that held up to win the game. He was smoking his third when Madlock hit into a double play to end the game. He promised to give up on the Cubs.

A week later, at about four in the afternoon, he got off the Skokie Swift with a swollen right hand that he soaked in cold water when he got home. A line-drive home run was nearly stabbed by a flying, diving, Jay Holloway leap that sent him crashing into the stocky, forty-year-old steel worker who caught it. The swollen hand was the result of the fight over the ball that ensued. Jay was thrown out of the park.

The swelling went down as Jay watched the end of the game at home. The Cubs won it in sixteen innings. It bothered him, and he couldn't go to sleep for thinking about the good game and the ball that had been stolen from him.

Two years later, Jay saw the security guard that had made the decision to eject him from the game. The Late Night News anchorman said it was apparent the Chicago police officer, a former Cubs security guard, had disappeared. His car was found empty on Madison Street. The next night, Jay learned the body of the officer was found in a golf course pond in Des Plaines, not more than a mile from where Jay lived. It was a lousy nine-hole course bordered by two main highways. The officer had been shot.

Jay remembered the room with hundreds of baseballs at Wrigley Field where the guard had talked to him. Now Jay thought of him in the mud of a pond with hundreds of golf balls. He thought of the guard quite a bit after that, and quite often told the whole story — from home run fight to Des Plaines golf course. Two standard details were that: 1) it was his ball, and; 2) the golf course was near his home.

One night at the bar, someone asked Jay if he wanted to buy a gun. The guy said it was an authentic war revolver. Jay asked if it would shoot. Of course it would. Jay asked what shells it took. Six millimeter. Jay couldn't tell the guy was guessing. Jay asked if the shells were sold locally. That wasn't known, but it would take forty-fives just as well. Jay said he'd think about it.

During the next few days, he strongly considered buying it. He imagined himself carrying it, and suddenly he imagined he was getting frisked on the golf course the same day the guard was shot. They would find the gun and find a motive in the disputed ball. Or, someone was pushing him just a little too much, forcing him to pull it out. There he was, thinking he'd made a mistake after he'd already emptied it into a poor slob — the poor slob who wouldn't be dead if he hadn't forced Jay to shoot. Or for that matter, he wouldn't be dead if Jay hadn't bought the gun. On the other hand, here this slob would be slugging poor Jay while poor Jay had no gun.

He resolved to buy it, but didn't see the guy at the bar. He was afraid of being charged too much, so he called a gun store to see what it was at retail. When he said six millimeter that also takes forty-fives, the dealer just laughed at him. "Sure you don't mean

The Voyage of a Bean

nine millimeter and three fifty-seven?" Jay didn't know and hung up. The next time he saw the guy at the bar, he imagined shooting him.

Jay had one big thing in life. It was to get even in a way that got him ahead. In the morning, Jay's way of getting even was to be so far ahead of everyone that the luxury was too luxurious to be described. His money made everyone envious. In the late afternoon and early evening (into the second half of the pack of Old Golds) getting even was driven by some overall Jay Holloway grudge. He would be Peg Leg Pete the pirate. No one would know who he was, the disguise would be so great. His knee would be resting on the peg with a bayonet hidden inside. At given moments during the scenes flashing on the screen of his anger, the sheath would fall as he raised his leg, and he would stab his enemies in the stomach with one good knee kick from a bayonet protruding from his knee.

Jay Holloway: bloody Peg Leg Pete. Or, he would play a village idiot just to get a reputation as an eccentric to get the community off his back. He would wear a mask and walk around blabbering insanities at everyone he saw. They would leave him and his riches alone then, or those who tried to take advantage of a crazy old eccentric would wind up with a bayonet in the belly.

Late in the evening into his drinks he would be the traveller, and by travelling get even. He would be gone. Everyone would wonder where he went. He would do well. He would show them all. Day after day, Jay Holloway backed off secretly from the town and took trains to California and boats to China, or he worked as a stomach hole-puncher named Pete.

These were all ways of getting even in order to get ahead, but though he dreamed about them, he never put anything into practice. Not to say he didn't get even in at least one way. His high voice was frequently heard mumbling at the bar when Joe refused to serve him and told him to go home; more because he was broke than because he was babbling. Jay offered his lucky quarter for a round for everyone, but it was so worn, and such an old variety that few recognized it as a quarter. He was even because he didn't owe the bar, and Joe said to him, "Jay, why don't ya go on home. Quit while you're ahead."

The Parrot's Feather

On Alan Shortridge's carpet was a nearly round, white Parrot's feather. If the soon to be described event is going to be reported by anyone, the "p" in parrot should be capitalized for the parrot lived by the name of Parrot, and demanded that everyone refer to him as Parrot. Alan would be swooped down on by the green bird until he said, "Hello Parrot." Then again, Parrot had a habit of swooping and there's evidence to suggest Alan's greeting was only a signal for Parrot to rest a moment.

Parrot lived upstairs on the third floor of the unit of the condominium complex where Alan lived. Alan had become involved with the woman who lived there. From the first floor, there were only two flights up, and he was there, though many times she'd stop by after work and they'd stay there. Her name was Leslie Heron, and she was generally nervous. Alan didn't know that her nervousness meant she was interested in him. He hadn't known her long and hadn't seen her in any social situations to make any comparisons. Once or twice there had been a chance meeting in the parking lot when she was talking with other neighbors but he didn't stay to talk, and she seemed a bit nervous even then. Then one day she knocked on his door. They just talked for about half an hour, and she left. Then she started coming by with regularity. She never could stay past nine, nor did he when he went upstairs. Her husband came home around 9:30. Alan thought her nervousness might have something to do with that because she never talked about Bob, but when his name came up she quickly came up with some excuse to leave.

The Voyage of a Bean

What Alan never saw in the nervousness was the sign of trouble that it was. He thought that maybe she liked him, but he had a girlfriend, and Leslie was married, so he didn't figure there was anything to it. But the nervousness really meant that Leslie was excited about something. She grew bored very easily, and it didn't take a long period of time in the pits for her to look for something to excite her, and when she found it, it made her feel like she could fly, and while she was pursuing whatever it was, how she hid her excitement made her seem a bit nervous on the outside.

When Alan found the feather, he thought of an amusing way to start a conversation with her. He would wait until he caught her coming into the building, and he would say that while she was out, Parrot had come downstairs looking for a feather that he lost. "This feather," he would say, holding it up to show her. Then he would add that he had only found it after Parrot had left and was anxious to return it to the bird through Leslie if she would be so kind as to take it up to him. When he did catch Leslie coming in, she made him follow her to her door upstairs, and after he'd tried his ice breaker on her, she looked at him quizzically at first, then threw her arms around his neck. "Oh thank-you, thank-you. Parrot has been so worried about that feather, and so have I. Thank you so much!" And she gave him such a big long kiss that she opened the door without looking. They went in without opening their eyes, and the feather ultimately dropped to the floor again next to the couch where they sat down as they began to melt. They went to the dark bedroom never turning on the lights. They repeated this the next two nights. They chatted with two glasses of wine before not turning on the lights the following evening. The next night she described her unhappiness with her husband in the darkness. Alan grew uncomfortable with her embrace the more she described how she hated him, and he finally turned the light on.

Alan knew Bob only a little, and was obviously nervous in front of him the next time he saw him, giving away the fact that there was something going on between him and his wife. Alan said hello, and Bob, noticing a parrot's feather on Alan's sleeve, grabbed Alan by the arm, swung him around and punched him to the ground. "What

The Parrot's Feather

have you been doing in my place anyway? I told her to tell you stop coming over."

Leslie assured Alan she'd only mentioned him as having casually visited, and that Bob had become so insanely jealous, so she'd opted not to even mention any further contact between she and Alan. She lied and said she never dreamed that they'd really be doing anything to make him jealous, and added that she'd never dream of mentioning Alan again under any circumstances.

Then she suggested that Alan have fun with Bob's jealousy and gather feathers from Parrot's cage or from the floor and cover his jacket with them to see what he'd do. "Are you crazy!?" Alan shouted. "Why don't you take pictures of us and pin them to yourself and see what he does?" She said that was a funny idea.

But it didn't stop Alan from coming over when Bob was working. For some reason, he wanted to see her all the time. He enjoyed living dangerously, and the Parrot was an irritation. It used to fly into the bedroom when they were making love and say, "Give it to me, give it to me." It soon struck Alan that Parrot must have learned it from Leslie as she said it five times to its one.

One evening Alan did not go up to see her, and she came downstairs to his door wearing a feather on each breast. The little round feathers barely hid her nipples, and she told Alan she wanted him to stay and face Bob with her looking like that. Alan said it had gone too far and not to come back again, and please, not to tell Bob.

Well, she did, and the mechanic in Bob went down to take Alan apart to see what was wrong with him even if it meant no one would be able to put him back together. Alan called through the door that Bob should be mad at her for being a looney, but Bob's axe against the door (he never even tried a knock) was too loud to really talk clearly over. And Alan might have realized that her eccentricities were part of the intimacy Bob knew with her, something with its own logic that he could not possibly understand unless he developed an ongoing relationship with her, which now looked unlikely. Bob didn't think it was bizarre, nor was he willing to share it with anyone.

When Bob came through the door Alan had a coat with feathers on it, which Bob saw and went ballistic. Alan also had a samurai sword in his hand. Bob wasn't expecting hand-to-hand mortal combat. Cutting through the door had worn him out, and it made someone call the police. They could hear sirens. Leslie came downstairs. Bob fell to his knees and was still crying when they took him away.

When it was all sorted out, Alan was left alone in the room to consider there are various ways to make the heart beat faster. One was love, another was facing death, and still another was being left alone in a room after a close call with death and the police.

When a reporter followed the police to Alan's place after hearing the call on the scanner, he stayed around to try to talk to Alan to see if there was a story in it. Since nobody was killed, there wasn't, so he left. But what makes it interesting was what went on in the minds of the individuals after the event. Alan could no longer go outside without fear of running into Bob and having another brush with death. He peered through the drapes. He couldn't sleep. He put his place up for sale and moved. He never guessed that Bob was actually in worse shape over what he had done, suffering greatly because he had wanted to kill his wife when she came down the stairs, not Alan, and he moved out as well, leaving her all alone.

Meanwhile, Leslie was thinking it was getting to be a bit dull after all that excitement. She was wearing her most comfortable faux silk robe with the red feathers, feeding Parrot and thinking about the young man at the grocery store checkout who was always so nice to her. He lived just across the way in Building #2 and made her heart beat a little faster. She was watching him through the front window watering the flowers in front of his condo. "I will ask him to help me find you," she said opening the back window above the sink. Parrot flew to the sill and looked out. "Don't worry. He won't say no," she said. Then she waved her arms at him. "Go ahead," she shouted, and he flapped out into his favorite tree. "You stay there until I come get you," she called out after him, then ran to the front door leaving feathers in her wake. "I don't even think I have time to change, under the circumstances," she chuckled as they flew off of the cheap robe behind her. She couldn't have seen them, but she felt like she had wings as she went flying out the door.

The Golden Arrow

Cupid, whom far too few believe in, hit me with a golden arrow not long ago, and I've a tale to tell of all of this. He hovered over me when she walked in the room where I was watching the dance. He pulled the bowstring back and let the golden arrow fly. Of course, I went insane for her. I planned out carefully how I might get her in my arms as she smiled in the smoke-filled room, and I asked her if she'd like to be my partner. She didn't show a sign of liking me at all, and I suspected that a lead dart of hate had hit her when the golden one shot into me.

I couldn't give her up. I'd started out to try to run into her accidentally, to make it a casual thing so as not to scare her off, but I couldn't wait and expressed my passion too soon, calling her each day, and soon made the biggest mess of things. What small chance I'd hoped I had was gone. Then one day, in deep despair, thinking of her, I walked into a beautiful grove, unaffected by the spring blossoms and petals dropping through the mist on that sweet-smelling, sunny afternoon before the summer, and there I saw the god of Love. The little sprite was smiling at me from a tree. He may have made me love the girl, but I was very angry with him.

"You!" I called. "You pint-sized destroyer of the rational and ordered side of life. There are some words I'd like to get off my chest about that arrow you let fly at me — that hit me, wounding deep." He kept on smiling. "Do you hear me? Of course you do! You must! I plead with you!"

"For what?" he asked. "You seem to have more words than hair on that chest of yours that holds an aching heart. What would you have me do that would be more than I've already done for you?"

"You mean you'll grant a wish?" I asked. "Then shoot that girl again and have her love me too!"

"I never shot her to begin with," said the God of Love. "I merely let fly one sharp, potent shaft of gold that has awakened you to her. It's not my fault you fail!"

"Now wait a minute!" I broke in. "That's not the way I understand your ways! Don't you shoot us both? I'd understand it if you'd tell me there's some time between your careful aims, a time of suffering for me — but not to shoot her too! I just don't understand."

"One arrow is enough," he said, "for many more to fall in love. You may not win her, but you are a golden dart to hit her — that's the way it goes."

Then he was silent. The petals kept falling, and I noticed they were fragrant — that the afternoon was nice. A gentle breeze cooled my forehead as I erupted with anger and said, "Now listen here! If there's no hope for me except in moving others like objects directed by a scientific law, what good is life for me? I stand here suffering before you. You're a god, and I am just a man!"

"I'm not all god," he said. "I'm half a man myself, born of plenty and of lack, and while I range among the heavens and the infinite, I find my other self in comfort here on earth."

"I won't contest your birth," I said. "You're half a man, and so you must know something about how I feel, and you've made me feel it. But being half a god, don't you know I cannot understand? Can't you help me out with some advice, or take this arrow out of me?" At this his wings began to shake, and he shook up such a wind that the great gusts whipped the white petals to a flurry, and soon I couldn't see a thing. I was blind in a blizzard.

When the swirling stopped, I found myself ankle deep in blossoms. I figured it was meant to be an exit, and sure enough, Cupid was no longer on his branch. But very strange, I saw a golden shaft of an arrow protruding from my chest. Apparently, Cupid had let me see the arrow. Extracting it was up to me. "Cupid!" I called. "My eyes scan heaven for you now in thanks — you are great for your concern for inferiors, and a great man since you understand!"

At that moment I heard, "What are you babbling?" It was the one I loved. She was walking toward me through the blossoms. "This is nice," she said. "What brought it on?"

I asked her, "Do you see what's in my heart? Cupid's golden shaft! I'm going to pull it out and end my futile, painful pursuit!"

"Don't start that again!" she said. "In any case, what wounds you isn't me at all — but how did these petals get here? They're so nice."

"Well, I'll tell you," I began to lie "from town I noticed the strangest smell, sweet and subtle, and I thought it must be coming from these groves. I came directly to revel in the falling blossoms that we're up to our necks in, and I prayed that I might share the scene with someone — to not have it all wasted on me — and you arrived."

Laughing, she said, "You're silly, and, of course, you lie." Then, she left me there.

I walked home, dejected and once again in the dark. I listened to the evening bells and watched the tops of buildings and the tree branches for the little god. Every time a bird flew by, I looked up, hoping it was him. I'd more to ask. Only I could see the arrow protruding from me, and through carelessness, already I had bumped it deeper into me.

For the next few days I couldn't sleep. I had trouble rolling over. I'd cover myself and hold the arrow like a knife, not sure what to do. Confused, I wondered which was stronger — my mind to yank it out, or my heart to stay in love. Since I couldn't seem to muster the courage, I guessed the heart was the stronger of the two. I asked myself, "I'm in love now, so, is that why I am moved to stay in this state? Am I not better off to love, even if I am unloved?"

Thinking thoughts like this, I would toss and turn in bed. I even became afraid the arrow would fall out, so each night I would stay awake holding it in. Then, finally, I'd succumb to sleep, alert to strange but cogent dreams.

Don and Julia

Julia wrote, "Some of us are more absorbent than others. Some of us are so sopped with the world at any given moment that nothing else can be taken in. We act much like wet rags too. Others, like plastic sheets, let everything bead right off and couldn't take in anything of the world if they tried, and they can be seen clear through."

For a time, Don, her husband, was a breath of fresh air inside her little shell. They both seemed open and able to resolve their difficulties. But soon, he went back to his own world, and the air became foul. They closed off from one another, stubbornly refusing to open any vents. They lived for years together, their love long since having suffocated in a vacuum of civility.

Julia was always wringing herself and collecting the drippings. She had quite a collection of her "interpretations." The world spun around with her on it, immersed in magazines and news, and she loved it. But on the whole, she was the tired, lethargic sort who worries about anything and everything.

Don, her husband, on the other hand, was unable to absorb the least bit of the happenings of the world. He worked, went about his business, and could hardly be held accountable for having any knowledge whatsoever of Julia's "absorbent" condition. The more she soaked up and wrung out, the more oblivious he became — not because of any deterioration on his part but rather due to the worsening of her condition.

Julia was under the impression that absorbing the world gave her a mysterious power. The ability as she saw it was in her being able

Don and Julia

to transform cold facts into important truths. What she took in of the happenings of the world was cold — but through her, when she wrung herself dry, events had been reshaped and given warm meaning. She was transformed in the process, and part of the miracle, the greatest part of it, was that after some time of being a passive, absorbent tissue in life, she began to participate.

She felt as though something inside her had opened up, giving her a glimpse of personal, yet universal, secrets. All the collecting had a secret, silent effect on her. Each item had imparted a portion of itself into her soul, and years of constancy to the habit of being attentive to every morsel and tidbit had brought about her birth.

But Don, while he had remained the same, much like what happens to paper left in the air too long, yellowed, and his support for her causes disintegrated. In their marriage, there were far more examples of his personality (if it can be called that) than hers, and when she left him, their shared last name had become the only thing they had in common. There were no sad goodbyes.

Her opening and his hardening were both private and unseen events. She became mother to a whole stream of sensible and persuasive insights — subtleties of the world — while he was father to his own continued emptiness. But the world paid no attention to either of them. Julia explored and experimented and found secret joys to fill her life, and she considered the experience sacred. Don, however, deepened his rut.

"Great jaws in life swell open, attesting to the boundless hunger of the universe to gape and bite into the boiling diversity. All souls come and go. The shape of the world matters little as the jaws snap shut and carry away a generation," wrote Julia.

What she failed to collect will be pieced together into a new epiphany, and that apotheosis can be lived out by someone in a lonely void. When there is an infinity to absorb, there will always be Julias who understand vivid growth by a touch; and change by allowing changes to take place. They see the emptiness through solitary windows. The jaws are seen coming with no emotion. Then there are the Dons, with worlds to lead, administrations to run, jobs to keep and no time to lean toward heavens.

Bold Lover

John Marsh was forty-three. A prime number, he thought. He taught math. John was forty-three and bright. As a matter of fact, he was born in Brighton, Massachusetts. A cold place, but only a matter of hours from M. I. T.

He was having dinner and reviewing his life that muggy, summer afternoon after running his laps. He had been 1, 3, 5, 7, 11, 13, 17, 19, 23, 29, 31, 37, 41 and now 43 — all prime numbers. He'd never make it to 199, 409, 619 or 829 unless he did something great like prove the "Riemann hypothesis." He took a huge bite out of a head of lettuce and turned the page of the *Time* magazine he was reading. At the same time every day, as he had for years, he devoured the news. He picked up a section of the newspaper. There was an ad for a car — $2,089 — quite a low price; also a prime number. But he didn't need a car. He preferred walking, and he strolled to his classes everyday, when there were classes.

At this point in the summer, he had nothing but time to review and time to prepare for the semester ahead, and he started by reviewing his strict adherence to schedule. Up at 8, carrot at 9, class at 9:30, class at 11, lunch, class at 1. Then laps to be run until 5, dinner, nap, then time at the library for books and newspapers. Then exercise, and finally sleep that started at 11 or 1 but never midnight.

But that was the old schedule of school. These were the doldrums after summer school. These lifeless days were like flashes of lightning that left only a space of time and a vague memory that not the heat and light, but rather the emptiness, summoned something from

Bold Lover

within him worthy of the name thunder. It was a time he'd rather forget. But the pain would pass. Summer would be over soon. School and the rigorous schedule would resume, just as she would return. She must, and restore his equilibrium. But there would be so little time before summer would come again. This might be her last year. There was so little time.

He knew it was only a matter of time. What could he say though? Come into my routines, my sweet, prime number. That was out of the question. She was too beautiful for that. He wanted a wife, and what a wife she would make. She was tall, buxom and blonde — a real beauty. But he couldn't bring himself to say anything to her. He only knew her name was Janine.

Whenever he saw her, he felt daring and peculiar. He knew that she knew who he was. She must know that he loved her. She made it impossible for him to forget her, and she knew it, but there was no solution to the situation. That was his fault, and he knew it. But how could he alter it? He could feel she didn't want him to talk to her. She even indicated to friends in the library that he was watching her from across the room. He gazed down for a long while, and when he looked up, they were still watching, and his not making it seem casual was proof of her accuracy even if he really took his time. He was abrupt and unskilled in the flirtatious arts, but he could take a differential equation for a logical ride down the blackboard with ease.

What was significant is how he tried to live his life by prime numbers in the hope that he might discern some kind of pattern, and that she somehow seemed to be on the same schedule. She wasn't a math major, but somehow she was on this path of primes, which he devised consciously. She seemed to have stumbled on it unconsciously, but what did that mean? It totally confounded him.

The library was half for his study, half for her. At least she knew who he was. For some, that was half the battle. For John, it was as far as it had gone in three years. He would read the paper. Then she'd be there. She had a schedule too. She'd be on the other side of the room. She would sit at a table with her books according to her equally accurate timing. The two of them had a tradition they kept, and it made him feel comfortable at the same time that his

The Voyage of a Bean

heart started pounding so hard that he felt overwhelmed. Later on, she'd open her briefcase to keep him from staring — but only after many looks had gone back and forth.

Yet the following night started fresh with new forgiveness, as though it hadn't ended the night before with anger; and every night it would end with her leaving as though he stopped her from completing her studies. She even had the cover of the briefcase open just high enough so that when he stood up, he could peer over it into her eyes. By the fifth time he'd done that, she would get up to leave, but he staggered the looks so she would leave on time, just a few minutes before the library would close.

Then he would follow her home, far behind her. He never wore a coat — not even in the coldest, winter weather. It wasn't just that his exercise enabled him to go without one. It just didn't bother him. He wore a short-sleeve, white shirt and black slacks every day of his life, even when it was ten degrees below zero. He didn't even own a coat. He'd always been that way. He could endure it, however cold it was. Then he remembered the one time he'd felt terribly cold. It was a hot day at the beginning of the semester when he saw Janine and followed her to the ice cream stand. She was several people in front of him in line, and as she walked away, she handed him an ice cream frappe.

He thanked her, in awe. It happened sometime during the first weeks of the first year of their flirtations in the library. It was the short hand-off he turned into a marathon. He walked out with the shake, sipping it so hard he hardly noticed how hastily he was drinking it. The ice quickly overwhelmed his throat with cold, agonizing pain. He suffered brain freeze until it finally subsided and then stood there shivering in the heat. He watched her walk along the river, hardly noticing she wasn't striding there alone but with another guy. When she took his hand, John turned away, jumping up and down for warmth. The shakes at that point weren't just about being cold. It took a hot shower for him to settle down that day. Nothing had ever had this kind of an effect on him before. What else could it be but love? On the other hand, giving him the shake, which gave him the shakes, might be about exposing him for following her around.

Bold Lover

It might mean that she was on to him and making the point that she was "giving him the shake." Hence the guy in the park. She knew he'd be watching, and she was only trying to shock him. It didn't really mean anything. He was relieved, and he resolved to keep a closer, more furtive watch on her in the hope of advancing their relationship.

She used to exercise at the field house, too, and sometimes he thought he might ask her if she'd like to run with him around the track, but he started to watch her run and count her laps. She always stopped at a prime number. One day she'd run seven laps. The next she'd run eleven, but she'd never run nine. What didn't make sense was that even if there was an underlying proof to Riemann's Hypothesis, what law was there to explain what he was witnessing? Was it just a random event? It was more than that. It was a complete mystery, more so than the mathematical problem he fantasized about proving. He even had a working theory of solving it. It would take the isolation of a new set of numbers that he called "budding numbers." These would in actuality be blocks of numbers that would connect to primes in still undefined relationships and reveal the underlying pattern that would forecast links into the yet undetermined primes. John's chart would effectively prove the hypothesis, but there was much work to be done, and he knew that, scientifically speaking at least, he was way past his prime.

His age did influence his thinking when it came to Janine. But she also affected his abilities to reason. He'd sit in his room and work on his problem, and he'd walk all the way to the library in a driving snow, insulated by his concentration on the problem, and when he'd find her, it would all go out the window. There she was, the living embodiment of some connection, perhaps the living solution to the problem, the secret being within her along lines of why the swallows always appear at Capistrano at the right time, and yet he had no way of arriving at an understanding of it because he could not even muster the courage to speak with her. If he were to ask her out, she'd certainly say no, and he couldn't just hand a date to her. She was so pretty. Just looking at her revealed how many ugly girls there really were. Janine was like the discovery of a new high prime

The Voyage of a Bean

number. She was a rarity — his calculated risk and lucky find.

It suddenly struck him that thoughts of Janine were occupying the entire summer. He hated the intersession and yearned to see her in the library again soon. It wasn't the same without her, but this had been going on for the better part of three school years. The first time he ever saw her, he felt weak. She was taking his introductory math class. She hadn't quite bloomed then, and it wasn't until the end of that first year that he saw her in the student lounge and felt an overwhelming desire for her. She was wearing a jersey with the number 11. The next day he went to the library at 11, and she was going up the stairs just ahead of him. Then as he was leaving, there she was just ahead of him. Then he started looking for her in the library and would peer through the books at her. He started following her around. He lost track of his own schedule, and then he realized she was keeping him on it. Then he'd follow her home — a white shirt in the dark night. He hoped one day to find the courage to ask if he could walk her home, but he feared that would be the night that he would feel cold as a mortal, succumb to it and freeze to last gasps, when all she wanted was a quiet walk and a warm, gentle clasp of his hand. He couldn't even offer a coat to keep her warm.

He tried to remain intent on his math projects, but with her on campus, he couldn't manage it. Working problems to solutions was his principal way of fending off the cold. Though it would take a miracle for it to happen, he might escort her home if she really desired it, but would the calculations be enough, or would his heart pound open his armor to a conquering cold? He did what she permitted, and so he was able to offer protection some hundred yards behind her where he would wait until she put out her bedroom light before returning home. The problems kept him at a safe distance — protecting him equally from the cold and from too much thinking about her. She was out of his reach, but she was always there for him. When she would go away for the summer, it was difficult. He longed for autumn and the long winter. In the past, his summer routines made the time pass quickly, and when she had returned, she brought along his longed-for symmetry.

But these last weeks before classes resumed were the most difficult.

They were devoid of meetings and obligations. Everything was closed after six, including the library. But every day, John carefully combed his short, graying hair over his forehead and put on a clean, short-sleeve, white shirt and black pants. He shaved diligently and used a mild after-shave. The rooming house was all but empty, but even during the year, he seldom talked with the other men who roomed there. They were generally boys — undergraduates who never seemed to stay for more than a semester. He could sense they thought him an oddball — sitting under the clock in the kitchen every night eating raw vegetables and reading magazines. He was sick of being asked why he didn't wear a jacket when it was cold. No one understood his inner strength. They had their ideas about him that they believed without testing. They thought they were right, and they were wrong.

To him, they were frivolous and empty, travelling in groups and determining their identity by drunken conformity. They had no focus. He had every minute of the day plotted. They didn't know why they were in college. He had mathematics down to a science. They didn't know what direction they wanted their studies to take. He had Janine as an indicator that his prime number studies were the right beacon in the night, guiding him toward safe harbor. They had nothing so rare in focus they could call their vision. He chewed his lettuce and read his Time, laughing inwardly at their stupidity while they ignored and shunned him.

Only Janine could permeate his thick skin that had been tempered by math and hundreds of cold, night walks. She was his in a special way, and it was a Common Law arrangement for him. He wished that she would come and take him away. He wondered though what he could say to her. As he devoured his raw carrots, he'd pretend it was a year after the wedding. What would he say across the table — "The lettuce is great! Pass the Time!?" It was absurd. He could never treat her like that. One must take all the time one has for one such as Janine.

She was consuming his thoughts. He chewed on his last carrot. Dinner was just about over. So was this summer that stranded him. She must return! She was his Santa Maria — the deck from which he was discovering a new world. At the same time, she helped him tread the old paths with a sense of new discovery. It struck him that this was the greatest thing a woman could be in man's life — whatever the relationship, she would be a support and renew in him whatever the world has taken out. But what could be said except that he hardly ever left town and was the reciprocal to a woman who was at best a library flirt? Together, they were painted on a Grecian Urn:

> Bold lover, never, never canst thou kiss,
> Though winning near the goal — yet, do not grieve;
> She cannot fade, though thou hast not thy bliss...

But some of this was getting old. At least one path was balding — one that went straight across his mind. What more was there to it than that? He could feel that the moment was approaching for his nap. These were tired thoughts, old ideas that led to his wondering whether she thought about him at all. What could he mean to her? She was the spice on his timetable, but what did he offer in exchange? Perhaps what she gave him bore witness only to the notion that every man that truly loves a woman is rewarded by her with at least some small pension of attachment. However weak the quality of adhesion, he could feel some kind of appreciation, even if it was only in the recognition of his love.

It was enough when she was around, but the summer months alone were so long to endure. They were a retirement during which even the solid schedule seemed to be filled with useless routines. In his darkest thoughts, it occurred to him that one day she would disappear. She'd graduate. Though he was hopeless and could see that their affair would end before it changed, he knew that emptiness would follow. How would he endure his regularly scheduled tedium? He knew it now — the pill he took to regulate himself was a placebo. The line between them had stretched — grown taut — and when it snapped, the chasm between them would open. Even in place, their connection kept them apart. They were like the poles of a magnet, twin destinies, opposite and essential extremes. Remove her from the other side of him, and the spheres would fall out of alignment. The laws of their small connection defined the greater patterns above. He sensed the living proof of this hypothesis. It just could not be reduced to numbers. He saw himself amorphous, frozen — collapsed on his side of a widening canyon — while she held the answers to mysteries within him on her side with a healing touch he could never reach. On the blackboard of the sky, she indicated miraculous arrangements. He had no idea how to determine her plans, yet he looked to her as a cooling force for the lava flowing along fault lines and bubbling from new crevices like the tar in the street outside. He could use his position to find out where she lived, but how would that look? He could never make that fly.

He looked from the magazine to the clock. What if she didn't return? It was fatiguing, and he felt the scheduled need to nap. The nap itself was close at hand.

With the approach of the fall semester, he was increasingly plagued by fears that claimed large tracts of energy reserved for his equations, and as the balance shifted, he felt he was losing control. But three weeks of no classes at all! These had been the hottest days of the summer, and in proportion to all the free time, thoughts of Janine increased. He could hardly concentrate. Sweating out the last days before her arrival had itself become something of a ritual. He was trying to work it in, to ride out the sense of being frozen in a heap, to let the amorphousness be whatever part of him it was meant to be, and to explore the loss of balance in himself whatever the factors were and wherever the search would lead.

For now, he tried to accept the pain of this August ritual of self-examination that excluded everything but exaggerated sentiment for a futile link at the breaking point with Janine. Even in trying to read during dinner — except for a vague recollection of articles on the discovery of a new, high prime number; pagan rites in ancient Rome; half-frozen survivors of an avalanche; city street gangs; a new book concerning the poetry of Shelley, Keats and Stevens; a controversy regarding the voyages of Columbus; and volcanic eruptions in Hawaii; he realized that the news had hardly made it through to him. Weariness, however, was surging in splendors of shadows and waves. Its tide slipped in through the unheeding spirit and rinsed his fear and hope from sightless and dreary sensations to the peaceful stability in fragrant portals navigated by a bright blot over the dimly-starred, vast sea. Resting on the table, Marsh drifted into his after dinner nap at exactly seven o'clock. He was carried out by the ocean tide with his head held up high on the open issue of Time, but oh, the patterns were clear. They bridged across the primes in a predictable manner, and the shape was a patterned cloak he took off the vault of heaven and placed around her shoulders to keep her warm as they walked along connecting the stars.

The Ferris Wheel Tragedies

Timothy Panther worked in a carnival during the summer near San Francisco. He sold tickets for the merry-go-rounds and ferris wheel, and when he had the chance, hid deep in the machinery underneath, watching the gears. The screams above him, and the dangerous gears around him gave him pleasure.

He sat there on break. He escaped the ticket lines and milling crowds, and the motor and music drowned out the bingo announcer and the balls striking metal milk bottles. He could only take so much of the tents, cotton candy, toy bears and long, stuffed snakes. All too quickly, it was time to return to selling tickets.

As he did so, a new line formed by the gate to the ride. The ferris wheel chugged around, emptied and filled chair by chair. It only made several quick revolutions if the line was long, and more than half the time on the ride was spent in waiting to be let off. But once it took you up, you were high on a rocking chair where the crowd turned into dolls in a tent town on a dirt patch. Then the telescope would turn around, and tiny shoulders would be normal backs, and then they would shrink again. Where Tim worked, he could hear the unmuffled motor puffing blasts of burned gas. When he watched the wheel going around, he picked one chair and imagined the view telescoping back and forth as it rose and fell.

Once in a while there was an accident. Tim had read about ferris wheel tragedies and was waiting for one to happen when the San Andreas fault decided to let out a good jolt. Just once he wanted to be there when something went wrong. One day the ferris wheel would come off its hinges and plow into the bingo tent and soda stands crushing them. Then it would roll down the street before finally spinning down like a penny on a table onto some house. Timothy hoped he would be there to see the journey of the giant rubberless tire. Timothy imagined great Ferris wheel tragedies, and thought if he could plan one, it would be very, very spectacular — something like inviting all the dignitaries of the world for a ride at the same time and have it come off its hinges and roll into the ocean. He felt most world leaders looked down their noses at the whole world as a seedy carnival and were doing their best to profit by flushing as much of the planet as they could down the toilet. To Timothy, the carnival was the home and hope of man because it had people who lived on the edge with nothing to lose. What they stood for was a true foundation because it was there to stand on after all reductions and subtractions. There was something vital in being a lowest common denominator, and he was proud to be one.

Among Tim's fellow employees were the roller coaster men. They were renowned for stealing change as passengers stayed on for a second ride. Every morning, they tested the ride for safety by going on the initial run. Pros of the scariest ride, they rode while smoking cigars and dangled their legs over the side of the cars.

Once, when they were going through the tunnel, a young man was hit and knocked to the ground more than thirty feet below. He had been sent up to do some repair work, and the foreman who ordered him up had forgotten to warn the others. When word went around that there was an accident, the foreman was silent. There was a suicide or two every year, so the matter went undetected, although the ride was modified.

As for suicide, Tim had considered it a number of times. He figured he would sabotage the ferris wheel and be the only one on a test ride at the time. He would laugh as the bingo jar exploded forth its many numbered balls. And who knows — maybe he would survive the harrowing ride. But before he would even consider risking his life, there was an account he wanted to square with two other employees, namely Edith and Midge.

Once he had gotten even with them, there was a chance that the elation he'd experience would give him a new raison d'etre, but on

The Ferris Wheel Tragedies

the other hand, were they to find out he had perpetrated the scheme, whatever it happened to be, murder would be on their minds, and he might never have the chance to ride the ferris wheel over the bingo and into the night.

Edith worked at the fun house and Midge in the bingo tent. Both were obese gossips who got together every night. Tim overheard many of the conversations they had, and he found that most were about people they didn't even know. They would contrive stories about people who'd come to the carnival, and some of the tales were quite bawdy.

Tim figured people who were so cynical couldn't possibly like one another except superficially, and at one time, weeks earlier, he had managed several conversations separately with the two women and confirmed his suspicions. Each was quick to condemn the other. But together, they were a secret newspaper that everyone knew was a daily issue. It printed news day and night. They would sit around eating hot dogs, turning the conversation to whoever happened to pass by.

Tim had been told that Edith and Midge's favorite tidbit, which ran daily, was a hot item about Tim himself. It concerned his habit of hiding under the rides, and suggested that there were suspicious reasons for his doing so. Until their news started going around, no one paid any attention to it. But they started saying that they found some magazines of a questionable nature under the tilt-a-whirl.

Tim didn't bother to defend himself, figuring it was common sense to realize there was no light under there. But everyone bought the story and shunned him. He discovered later that embellishments had been added, like his having a flashlight with which to read in the darkness. Many mistook a light on the fuse box under the tilt-a-whirl as proof that Timothy was indeed a pervert, even while at the same moment he was selling tickets for the ferris wheel. He had nothing more to do with anyone and swore he'd have his revenge. The presses cranked out stories about his surreptitious escapades under the rides for a time before moving on to other subjects.

This is how Tim managed to get even some time later. He rigged it so a winning raffle ticket for a new car was picked with a fictitious name — Esther Smithers. The car sat for several days waiting to be picked up, and then as a promotion stunt, the manager decided to have a parade over to the winner to deliver it. When a circus convoy pulled up in front of the trailer listed as the address, Midge answered the door. Carnival employee's weren't eligible to win. There was bedlam. It made the real papers as an attempted fraud. To make matters worse, it came out through a rumor that Edith had forged the ticket. Midge was livid. Then a real Esther Smithers from town showed up and claimed she'd won the car. Everyone seemed grateful as she drove it away.

The farce held center stage at the carnival for several weeks while a crowd milled around without the least sense of it. The net result was that two newspapers emerged from the one; each in the business to attack the other. For Tim, that entire season had been a great lift. Selling tickets from his "upright coffin," as he referred to it, he felt the hours glide by, and the moments he spent with the motor were somehow more relaxing.

Then one evening just moments after Tim went under the tilt-a-whirl, he heard voices outside. Someone pulled the canvas up. Light poured in from behind the silhouettes peering in, revealing lots of stuffed animals all around him as if they were Tim's. They were soiled and well worn. Edith and Midge had struck again. Tim vindicated himself almost immediately by discovering labels that had been sewn into some of the animals. They were owned by Edith and Midge and were thought to be stolen property. They denied it, but it was obvious that they were friends again, and some doubted whether they had really ever been enemies. They were embarrassed by this turn of events, however, and were in the doghouse for some time. All the manager said was, "Cut the crap!" meaning all the monkey business between the employees.

Soon after, Edith and Midge began diet programs, and they took to riding the roller coaster because they believed holding on for dear life would shape up some of the flab on their arms. One morning, they got into a fight as it was going around the park. Tim only heard about it later, and no one ever discovered exactly what happened, but on one of the slower turns, they were both standing, and Midge

The Ferris Wheel Tragedies

toppled back from her seat in the front to the fourth row, breaking an arm. She was hospitalized for a time, and Edith sent flowers but was apparently unwelcome at the hospital. Edith took to worrying and overeating, while Midge's doctor put her on a diet program in the hospital.

When Midge returned, she had lost about eighty pounds, and Edith, to whom she still was not speaking, looking huge by comparison, felt betrayed. The papers again were grinding out copy concerning the shortcomings of the other, only this time the attacks were more vicious. Eventually, a physical compromise was reached, meaning that Edith dieted while Midge, satisfied with her weight loss, began to eat again. Soon there was parity, and the carnival again had one paper.

After nearly two years of working at the carnival, during which time there were a good many revolutions between Midge and Edith, Tim saw a ferris wheel accident. One woman bought a ticket for the ride and told Tim she was nervous. The wheel did not roll away, but got stuck for more than six hours. The woman was on top, alone. Right behind her were Edith and Midge who had taken a simultaneous day off and decided to come to the carnival for some fun. The two of them could be heard by the crews working below to get the motor running again. The world in which they worked lay before them like a city in a bottle. The presses worked full blast as the princesses worked together sleeplessly detecting wrinkles in the pea. Tim tried to drown them out from below by exhorting those on the ride to remain calm. He could hear them laughing and yelling above the sound of his bullhorn, and he sensed that their levity was relaxing to the others on board.

Once off the ferris wheel, they continued their rounds of the park, moving ride to ride, game to game, candy stand to candy stand. When he saw them on the merry-go-round, Tim thought, "... two polar bears at the zoo waiting for the crowd to toss marshmallows across the moat to them."

As they walked around, Tim went under every ride he could and tossed peanuts at them. They ignored it at first and then began chanting his name and laughing. Later, just before closing, he overheard the editorial meeting as to the contents of the morning edition. They were going to get him for the raffle-ticket scam, as they had decided it must have been him.

The next day, it took the two of them a while to find anyone at the carnival. Following the sounds of laughter, they came to the tilt-a-whirl, and underneath, found a party. Tim had brought a keg of beer and most everyone was there. Throughout the day, everyone stopped by for another cup. This became an annual event, though it moved to the fun house where there was more room. Midge and Edith attended the events for their paper's continuing coverage of community affairs. Tim only had a hand in organizing the first one.

Late that night, still drunk, he returned to the carnival grounds with a gun. Everyone was gone, and all the lights were out, but he could find his way around easily, accustomed as he was to travelling under the rides in the dark. He'd bought a pistol with a silencer from a friend, and he started putting holes in the animals painted on the fun house marquee. There was also a "mummy" mannequin in chains in front of the sideshow, and one shot blew off half its head. Tim took a look at it and saw there was a real skull inside. Shocked, he immediately went home.

The next day, the vandalism was the minor sensation at the carnival. The real newspapers were there to take pictures of the dummy, and later, the coroner went to work. Several days later, Tim found the following notice in the paper:

*D*UMMY FOUND SHOT TO DEATH — RIVERSIDE (AP) — *A man who for years had been on display as the "mummy in chains" at a carnival sideshow was killed by a gunshot wound in the abdomen, the county coroner announced Friday. Everyone had thought it was a dummy.*

County Chief Medical Examiner-Coroner Frederick N. Trimond said the fatal bullet was still in the corpse, the identity of which remains unknown.

Surgeons examined the body Wednesday after employees at the carnival found it had been vandalized. Sometime early Wednesday morning, one or more persons trespassed Riverside carnival grounds on a shooting

The Ferris Wheel Tragedies

spree. One shot shattered the "mummy's" head and exposed human bone.

The coroner's office took X-rays and measured bones to try to solve the mystery. Teeth were also examined in the hope that a clue might be obtained. There were no fingers from which prints might be taken.

Trimond said that there were signs on the corpse that a postmortem medical examination had been performed and that the corpse had been embalmed. "It is the desiccated body of a man 5 feet 6 inches tall, weighing 170 pounds."

"The bullet appears to be one of a type made during the 1930s, not manufactured during or after World War II," he said.

The body, used as part of a display, was wrapped like a mummy and painted with a fluorescent material. The "mummy" was purchased more than ten years ago by the carnival from a wax museum that later closed. At the wax museum, the "mummy" had been billed as the "10,000-year-old-man." Police are seeking the owners of the wax museum for questioning.

Business was never better at the carnival. After that, it began to have a ghoulish aura. Rumors of prostitutes, robberies and murders began to circulate. Edith and Midge said that the murderer came to the carnival to expose his earlier murder in the hope that the police would track him down. The manager encouraged everyone to talk about the mystery — to suggest it wasn't the only thing that happened. The sideshow itself became a better attraction as unemployed freaks, as well as those from other carnivals, came looking for work. The police relinquished the "mummy" to the carnival on some "arrangement." On the weekends, there were lines so long to the sideshow that the ferris wheel would run ten minutes at a time, there were so few waiting for it. That suited Tim, as it gave him more time to break away and sit under the tilt-a-whirl and ponder.

He used to dream he was a southern gentleman sipping mint juleps, and the carnival was his plantation. He thought of the ferris wheel coming off its hinges and spinning on its side, much like the tilt-a-whirl above him. He wondered how he could loosen it so it would fall when he was on board. Tragedies ran backwards in his mind. From bloody finishes, everyone came to life and ran backwards to the happy ending which saw him selling the tickets to victims who'd cheerfully walk away backwards. At his command, beer in the keg, what was left of it, turned to mint julep. The wrinkles went out of the pea.

He thought of the mummy, the center attraction of the sideshow, with half its head cracked off. Other men in business would have been rewarded for increasing profits the way he had, but there was no way anyone could know of it. The vandal would have to remain anonymous. But Edith and Midge — couldn't they start a rumor about it? They'd been silent on the matter. No, there was nothing Tim could glean from loosening the chains of the mummy. He was going to be selling tickets at the carnival for a long time.

He wanted to take charge of things and manage the employees. He wished he could get them going in the morning. He would have liked to wind them up with a ride on the ferris wheel. He would be at the controls, the leader of a nation, and there would be Edith and Midge chattering away in circles, the free press. But then the hinges would come undone, and the ferris wheel would roll away with Tim at the helm — center cog of a wheel rolling around the country, taking on and letting off passengers without a mishap. And when it came time to rest, he would park it inconspicuously at some amusement park, and make himself at home under the neighborhood tilt-a-whirl.

Then he realized that it would never be allowed. They would try to stop him. There would be a chase, megaphone warnings, a shooting in which he would be killed, and then a cover-up to hide the abuses of the powers that be. Then they would have to get rid of his body. They would wrap him up like a mummy, cover him with paint and put him in the carnival fun house to scare the kids. Then they would run a front-page story that thanks to the quick thinking of local authorities, a ferris-wheel tragedy had been averted. The world would be saved to spin again, its old gears freshly greased. But another, more inspired denominator would be reduced to the same foundations on which he stood, and he would pull the lever to bring the world off its high horse. He would let events get into the saddle and put into motion what most would call a tragedy, but it would send the world spinning on one of the great rides of its life.

The Spider Priests

Father Healey was out visiting a shut-in who lived just a few blocks from where he grew up. When he left, he decided to drive by the old place which he hadn't seen in years. It surprised him that there was so much decay. Windows on the house across the street were boarded up The sidewalks were broken up, the yard had not been mowed in weeks. The paint was chipping on the house, and while there was a rusted car in the driveway, the dwelling could otherwise have passed as vacant.

By the time he reached the highway, the picture in his mind was of a house completely covered on the outside with dust and cobwebs like the interior of a haunted house. He couldn't remember his happy days of playing there without the intrusion of its current state. Spiders had taken over and were hiding somewhere in the branches just waiting for someone to tickle a strand. He was deep in the kind of musing that puts drivers in the state of automatic pilot and makes them wonder later how they managed to go several miles without an accident. Then what looked like a spider in the road brought him out of that state. For an instant, it really was a large spider directly in front of him, but as he came closer before passing it he saw that it was only a shredded tire fragment.

That afternoon was slow. He took only two confessions, from two women, but found himself in a similar state of composure listening to one's tale of petty theft and another's admitting to having an affair. His mind was so full of dream images that it was the same as when he was driving: he hadn't been listening, but still he had understood each confession and doled out the proper penance, even giving good general advice. He felt as if he were in perfect balance, that he could rightly divide sin from truth, but he wasn't at all moved or sympathetic; only cold and just. It wasn't until Mass the next day that he felt he'd been insensitive to the confessions, and that they had, in fact, made a larger impression on him.

But when he woke that Sunday morning shortly before the alarm would have sounded, Father Healey was still struggling in the roots of a huge tree that had fallen over in his dream. It was no ordinary tree, but a large sycamore in front of his neighbor's house when he was growing up. It was the only tree he'd never been allowed to climb. As a boy he had certainly tried to climb it, but every time he went near it he was caught before he could pull himself onto the first branch. The tree was directly in front of the front picture window. As the years passed, it changed from a challenge to simply being the one tree in the garden of his youth that he had to avoid. By the time he was thirteen, he had probably climbed every other tree in town. But he never did get up the sycamore, which bothered him for a time though it wasn't even tall compared to some of his conquests. Then he just grew up and forgot that it had ever been an issue. He'd passed that house the day before, but hadn't even remembered the tree or looked to see whether it was still standing. He wondered why he would dream of it at all except that seeing his own childhood home must have stimulated it.

The images in the dream were still flooding his mind as he pulled himself out of bed. He wasn't just standing in front of the exposed roots; he was in them. Everyone in the dream was standing in one vantage point or another, but he was right in the tangle of the roots through which he could see his angry neighbor looking for him. He remembered at one point in the dream he was using the roots as a place to hide. He thought he could climb around in them and get away, and it worked. They had given up looking for him. But then he was entangled in them, and now they were trying to set the tree back up. They'd brought in a crane to do the job. He remembered trying to trim back the roots and get out before it buried him, and trying to call out, but he was numb and lacked the necessary strength. But he recalled the numbness was the same sensation he'd had on the road when he drifted into his own thoughts, and again at confession when he had listened without participating. So even during the terror of being engulfed by the roots, his thoughts drifted elsewhere. As the tree was being pulled back into position, the crane producing loud beeps as it backed up, he realized the roots were sticky, and they were not covered with bark or dirt but hauntingly white. He was not tangled but stuck and could feel himself being raised. He didn't feel fear of being buried, but a sudden darkness woke him to daylight, and as bells sounded a spider was on its way to the center of the web. The church bells awakened him.

He continued to drift through scenes of the dream trying to get a better understanding of what it meant. As he showered he tried various ways to stop thinking about it in order to concentrate on what he had to do that morning, but he felt groggy and the dream kept coming back to his mind. He could still see the look on his neighbor's face. He couldn't remember climbing the tree and causing it to fall over. How did he end up underneath it? How did being covered with dirt turn to daylight, the roots to a web? What was the spider?

It occurred to him that he was deliberately put in the roots by the neighbor who was going to have the life sucked out of him in order to feed the tree, as if the tree were some a kind of Venus Flytrap or man-eating spider plant. He rinsed and imagined the sting would turn even his bones to fluids, and then being sucked up the trunk and spreading through the branches, giving life to the forbidden tree.

As he stepped out of the shower and took a towel, he was still effortlessly daydreaming the compelling images. He suddenly felt the branches shrink away, as if he had poisoned the tree. He watched the tree shrink from the outside, but he was still in the roots. It withered until it was a wooden cross on his grave, and weathered such that his name was worn away, lost and forgotten. It leaned ready to fall over itself and turn to dust. It was a waking nightmare.

He was slightly depressed, weary and distant, by the time he made it to the church for Mass, in stark contrast to the way he had felt the day before. When he approached the altar he was thinking that he hadn't given life to the tree but had rather sucked the life out of it. It had occurred to him that it wasn't the expanse of time that made the cross turn to dust, but rather his feeding on it from below that brought it down. After several prayers, he remembered how he had accepted that the cross would mark his spot. But what had made him indulge in imagining himself still writhing, struggling underneath it, forsaken by God, unable to leave the world and evolving into a predator whose mission it would be to hide and feed on anything that might venture into his net? Perhaps he was the spider.

Just before beginning his sermon, a sudden fragment of another dream he'd had that morning absorbed him forcefully. He was a young man at a party. He was the only one dressed formally for some reason. He was wearing a white tuxedo. Everyone was avoiding him. Then he saw in a mirror that there was a tarantula patrolling his shoulders, pacing back and forth, ready to pounce on anyone who came too close. At one point a brave young woman approached — Lucy Albright — someone who really liked him in high school. The tarantula did nothing. He looked in the mirror. Was it ill? Lucy asked him to dance. He told her he wanted to get some food. She followed him to the buffet table. He grabbed whatever he could find, including raw meat, dripping with blood, and set it on his shoulder opposite the spider. Looking in the mirror, he watched it cross over and begin feeding. Lucy walked away. He breathed a sigh of relief. There were marks on the sleeve where she had held his arm, but the spider left his shoulder clean.

He was alert and focused during his sermon, which he delivered impromptu since what he had written the previous week seemed mundane compared to what he was thinking at the moment.

I was just remembering one day more than ten years ago I was cleaning up my office, trying to go through various stacks of paper, which included clippings, old magazines, newspapers, and other kinds of junk. But every item I found was something I seemed to remember as having been put there for safekeeping. The piles had certainly grown old and high enough to shovel out the door, yet I could look at any single item and remember exactly when I'd found it and the reason why I'd put it aside. I found it impossible to throw anything away and spent the day reading through it and putting it neatly into storage. Today, as important as I thought it was to save them, I don't remember anything that I read.

More than ten years later, I don't think I've touched or opened any of the boxes once. It reminds me of the sediments in the ocean collecting as the sea creatures die, layer upon layer. Scientists can still examine cores pulled up that reveal the state of the ocean floor millions of years ago. I can sample what I've been collecting in the same way, or perhaps there is a cultural sea floor from which we can draw up in a core what we were thinking during a given time span. If I keep a journal over the years, I can tap into that. A library may be the place to start to see what the world was doing during a given period. An archive with newspapers on microfilm would also be a good source. But what about when it comes to a living mind? What about all the layers we build up over time that only we ourselves are able to measure or fathom?

When it comes to my own mind, and I'm sure it's true when you think about your own mind, I fear there are layers that will never be revealed or measured, and I treasure these so, along with my own consciousness, that the idea of dying makes me realize that a whole universe will be lost. It is not easy to endure the thought of losing the character and sentiment, the ineffable quality of memory and personality that makes us what we are, but it often seems that even our own spirits are at the mercy of the drifting currents such that we cannot be sure from one day to the next where things will lie in us. And even the most fastidious personal pack rat among us has to realize and reckon with the fact that the personal archive will have its demise in the end, and while some effort may be made to preserve some of the content, nothing can be done to salvage the more significant host of information, and when the librarian in us goes, a thousand precious volumes vanish as well.

Yet over the years, I have enjoyed doing my own archiving of memory and experience, and at any given moment can sample a core from childhood, college or more-recent times. How can I be overly concerned with what will happen to all of this when I am gone? Everyone is really too busy with all that particularly pertains to them to care what is actually lost when any given person dies. And we might just as well say that it's all there to entertain us to a degree, or provide a sense of wholeness against the shredding blades of experience. We don't think much along the lines that I'm discussing. We take it day-by-day, don't we?

The Voyage of a Bean

But we have this tendency to think of the world that we live in as harboring some kind of permanence that we're just passing through; things that will continue long after we're gone; things we were lucky enough to experience in passing through. No, we say it is wonderful to be a part of this, and any stillborn child has missed out on great wonders for not having a chance to wander through the great museum called space and time to take in some of the sights before passing on to the other side of the glass through which we only see darkly.

But what does it mean to have access to Shakespeare and a thousand other writers just by being alive? Anything you read will be lost to you. Express anything in any manner you wish, and perhaps it will have a slight chance of being tended by anyone who'll care for it well. Perhaps it will even be bounced around like a beach ball in the crowd at a baseball game, become a subject for the general babble highly regarded as the general intellectual mainstream. It may be all we have in offering a sense of success. Booed or cheered, we've been noticed by our peers. But while receiving the garlands, Nobel Prize, olive branch or blue ribbon, think of Hamlet with the head of Yorick, or of any anthropologist with any skull, maybe Hamlet's in his hand, freshly exhumed but empty of all that it once thought. Keep in mind that the brain only reveals its riches inwardly to the soul in the universe extended by it, and once it begins to wither, cannot be tapped for its wonders except eventually with a small hammer or scratching tool that will knock dirt out of its crevices. Yes, keep that in mind. How long can we keep even that in mind?

What has been created that is actually remembered for all time? It only passes mind to mind, generation to generation, and we all are only temporary custodians of all that cannot be retained. And when we know we only have a few days left, how many of us would not rather consign the better part of our papers to the flames than leave them for others to pour over. No, by far the greater part of all that we hold dear is garbage in the end, and even we know it. So what is there left but talking to other spirits about spirituality, and why is that so difficult for some to do?

Whenever I read a newspaper, I see that all kinds of sporting events were held. There are meetings, book signings, movies, public auctions, debates and thousands of other time and space displacements. A newspaper is a time and space displacement record that says, "here on an otherwise flat plane there was a displacement hereby deemed worthy of recognition." We meet and have a game for that recognition in the paper. It is our nature, our instinct that drives us to displace time and space. We do so at all costs. We do so no matter what harm it may do to others or whom we ignore while driven by our displacement ambitions. We have to put a dent in the flatness, to place a marker between the sheets of time and space, or there would be nothing to prove we were here. We do it to convince ourselves, but it is not enough. We live as if we were not convinced. That is how it is until God delivers a more complete understanding of the state in which we exist, and its ultimate meaning.

On the one hand, we fill limbo just by being here, but in order to say we are here, we must scratch something, or do something so that others will scratch the tablets that will say that we were here and this is what we did. Otherwise, we fill limbo with waiting, and pass the time futilely trying to mark time and space on a daily basis. On the other hand, we are told to have faith that there is more.

As we're pulled into the swirling eddy where life empties, where we die, do we scratch the banks trying to hold on, or post some kind of message that might be read by those who will pass the same way? Do we pick a flower and smell it to make the last few moments more pleasant, or do we just put our hands on our chest, close our eyes and float without fighting it? Like the Olympic Marathon, our last mile finds its way to a stadium filled to capacity with the eager and curious, but like driving on a highway, there is always someone ahead and someone behind us. One is shooting into the stands, another does flips to please the crowd and yet another does one last painting of the crowd, depicting the giant stadium as being on the same course, heading inexorably for the same drain.

Sometimes as I wend my way down the river of life toward the inevitable end of my life, I experience a difficult-to-describe blend of feeling both a terrible longing for another kind of reality at the same time as an overwhelming thankfulness that Christ came into the world. It is as though I wish that the world did not need Christ, but as soon as I recognize the reality of the world, the only state in which I can really feel there's any sense in the world or that the world is right includes Christ. The horrible sense of what the world really is dawns on me whenever I take everything for granted too long. Christ returns to save me in repeating loops. It

The Voyage of a Bean

seems that once saved, I can return to feeling no need of being saved, but soon the buffer disappears, and I need saving again.

Every time I administer communion I remember a moment of great significance years before entering the priesthood when I took the Eucharist and actually felt the miracle of really having Christ's flesh in my mouth. It was not that flat, flavorless wafer but a rippled curdle with the actual definition and feel of skin. I was kneeling and praying at the time I received it, with faith that I really was receiving the actual flesh and blood of Jesus, and I was less surprised than actually grateful to really be shown by God that it was in fact the case that a transformation had taken place, whereupon one took place in me, and no matter what it has felt like or tasted like in my mouth again, I have never thought I was ever getting less than the body of Christ at communion.

I remember hearing someone say in a eulogy that the purpose of life is to reveal God. If that's so, why is there so much dissension as to His whereabouts? Isn't it a paradox that God would create life in order to reveal Himself, then disappear into the background waiting to be found. Do you wear a mask in order to let people know where you are? Perhaps we could amend it to say that our purpose in life is to reveal God. We're not here to wait for life to differentiate what is true and what is not, but rather explain to life in no uncertain terms what the truth is. You can spend your whole life in whatever sea of papers is pouring off the presses at the time calling it our modern scripture while a great ongoing light goes unnoticed in your heart. Remember the law in scripture is life, and following the letter of the law without love is a kind of death. I tell you that Christ is alive and God is in you, and His promise is that affirming that displacement in the timelessness and spacelessness will give your living light absolute permanent glow in His kingdom.

Experience is the journey into other people, the process of discovering the meaning of the soul through others, is something to avoid. It's the baggage department. When we hold people at bay in the lobby with lame excuses for the delays in reaching the promised inner sanctum, is it any wonder that we generally hold back that same part of our real self in nearly all human contact, even from ourselves? This is done so universally, that the entire planet is characterized by life on the cold surface. We walk crowded avenues utterly lonely. In the end, we're far from loving everyone, and hate the world for having made us a stranger even to ourselves.

Once we're in that shell, God offers the only way out. Through Him, a part of us that is already dead is replaced by a part of Him that lives forever, which begins to live in us. It is love like we never knew it before — with a warmth that burns despite love-related fuel shortages of a cold world; and a caring that transcends the weight of worldly cares. It is love for life not of this world but from God, and it is truly a gift, for it has understanding of the way God loves us, allowing us to love others whom we do not even know; and it also speaks of life beyond this world, and so it offers faith; and faith is the greater goal than even love, for longing for love is often the symptom for lacking faith, of fearing death; whereas having faith means there's light in the darkness. The lack of such light explains why the world is in its current state, so loveless and Godless, and needing both so desperately. I destroyed documents because in the end I could not remember them. Know that God remembers you, and trust you will be saved. Let us pray.

A few minutes after he delivered this sermon, Father Healey held the cup to the lips of soul after soul that approached the altar, telling each person that it was the real body and blood of Christ. He added "Christ is alive. He is with you," and he hoped that each and every person would know with the same certainty that Christ was being received and was ready on the receiving end.

When he sat down again, he felt a great wonder for a world that was to come, and then a slight disturbance as his dream invaded the inner sanctum. The terror of being lifted up to be slammed down into burial while being trapped filled him again. He wondered if he feared the transition or the judgment that would come, or if there was some internal denial of everything he believed. Then he realized that in the dream he wasn't actually afraid when he was trapped. In fact, he remembered a hazy composure. Only after waking and reliving it was there fear, which seemed more a response to the immediate idea of dying in that manner than to dying in general.

He looked out to the congregation and wondered of the lives of all those who were so wrapped up in life that their interest or contact with the church was only cursory at best. He always reminded

The Voyage of a Bean

himself not to see one-dimensional people but to remember the wide expanse of lurking forms and shadows, fears, plans and worries that form the mental rings circling individual minds. Still, he wondered whether the occasional confession and communion was enough for them given little, if any, theological discernment and so much numb doubt. Was one hour a week enough to offset sin?

The church was not what it used to be. It seemed that fewer and fewer young people were seeking refuge there. If he were a fisher of men, he thought, then the fish weren't biting. Anyone seeing him in public even with just his collar seemed to put on airs of respect much as drivers slow down when police are on the road. How can one gently persuade with the Gospel, which once heard is a pretty sizable stick of dynamite in the water? His experience was that once someone really comes to God, God has done something to nudge them pretty forcefully in His direction.

On the other hand, it was hard to judge, but there were so many simple souls like Mrs. Delaney, the woman who always sat up front with her feathered hats and rings. He looked out and found her in her usual place and then noticed the hat with its entanglement of light feathers swirling in the slightest draft. She had confessed the day before that she'd run low on money and had to turn to shoplifting from a local store. She confirmed it wasn't anything necessary like food but wouldn't specify. Father Healey assumed it was more likely a bracelet or lipstick — something she wouldn't have to resort to stealing if she weren't already spending all her money on such junk. As he watched the feathers swirling in her hat, he was suddenly reminded of the roots in his dream and saw the feathers as legs of a spider sucking the life out of Mrs. Delaney.

That morning Mrs. Delaney's son Michael was sitting next to her rather than his usual place as an altar boy. The week before Michael had come to Father Healey at his mother's urging with complaints that Father Bishop, a new, young priest in the parish with a wild imagination and sense of humor, had been making uncomfortable advances. He thanked the boy for keeping it within the church, thought it best that Michael keep his distance and had promised it wouldn't happen again. Seeing Michael reminded Father Healey

The Spider Priests

that he still needed to address that issue.

Then, across the aisle, he saw a hand from behind Mrs. Shaw come to rest on her shoulder. She was a pretty widow whose husband had passed away two years earlier. She turned and briefly touched the hand, which stayed, on her shoulder, squeezing her from time to time. Father Healey remembered her confession the day before. She had been sleeping with a man and said she was the happiest she'd been since her husband died. The hand squeezing her shoulder looked like a spider sucking the life out of her. He craned and was surprised to see it was Andy Dineen who was married to Father Healey's sister Sarah. He hadn't come up for communion. It angered him, and his immediate thought was to confront him, but he couldn't just betray a confession. Even if he'd learned another way that Andy were cheating on Sarah, it was still a delicate matter like the plants in the church garden with pods that would pop at the slightest touch.

After Mass, several people complimented Father Healey on his message but added it was deeper than usual. Father Bishop joked in the rectory referring to Father Healey's miracle as the "fleshy communion." He apologized before saying it but couldn't help thinking the wafers might be served between real slices of bread and offered as "Jesus sandwiches." No one laughed. Father Healey felt outrage, but merely asked that Father Bishop come into his office. There was something they needed to discuss. Father Bishop said he could only do so later in the day after the decorations were finished.

That afternoon all of the priests went to the school lunchroom to help decorate for the party early that evening for parish teens. Father Healey blew up balloons until he felt faint, then helped twist crepe paper and pin it on the ceiling wall to wall. He caught sight of Father Bishop talking to Michael Delaney in the corner. They were standing under a set of long balloons tied together on the ceiling and dangling down like spider legs when Father Bishop put his arm around Michael. He seemed to be angry and held him with both hands. Father Healey couldn't hear what was said, but it was obvious that Father Bishop was agitated, muting to whispers what were visible as shouts. Michael started to struggle and screamed, "Leave me alone," before he wriggled free and ran out of the room.

The Voyage of a Bean

Father Healey crossed the room and said, "You stay away from that boy, and I'll see you in my office at four, sharp!" Then he left.

He went immediately to the Delaney's house to apologize for Father Bishop's actions. They lived just down the street. Michael had locked himself in his room and wouldn't come out. Mrs. Delaney didn't understand why until Father Healey explained that he hadn't yet confronted Father Bishop but would do so that afternoon. Mrs. Delaney seemed stunned, then started to cry. Father Healey tried to comfort her, but she waved him away and dried her eyes. "I want to show you something," she said and led him into another room where he was surprised to see a small shrine. She explained that the various icons, candles and statues were things she'd been stealing from the Church store. "Ever since this started with Michael," she whimpered. Father Healey could only say that it was quite a lot in only a week and asked why. "I don't know," she answered, "but somehow by stealing it I feel more in the right mind to pray whenever I kneel here. But I should return it all though, shouldn't I?"

"Let's call it a gift from the church for your trouble," he told her.

Then she gave him an envelope and said Michael had stolen them from Father Bishop. Inside were pictures of Michael naked. "Father Bishop took them," she said. "The negatives are there too."

"Are there any others?"

"Not that I know of. Michael broke into the rectory this past Friday while everyone was at the Archdiocese meeting."

"I, I had n- no idea," Father Healey stammered. Somehow he managed to talk Michael out of his room and pray with him and his mother, kneeling with them before the shoplifted shrine. Michael lit the candles, Father Healey burned the negatives, and they all held hands. His prayers were so eloquent and peaceful that even he had tears in his eyes when he finished. They stayed together and prayed for more than an hour, when they saw that the candles that should have burned to stubs by then were as tall and fresh as when Michael had lit them. "Christ is alive," he told them. "He is with us." As he was leaving he asked Mrs. Delaney for one of the candles, which she gladly gave him. He told her to leave the building of her shrine to him and promised that the first thing he would do would be to bring in more candles.

At four o'clock, Father Bishop knocked on Father Healey's door. When he sat down, the pictures were spread on the table in front of him. "I think I have a decision to make," Father Healey told him.

"A Bishop outranks a priest, doesn't he?" Bishop joked, then fell silent. Father Healey stared and said nothing. Father Bishop began to fidget. "You wouldn't go to the police anyway. The church can't have any more of this kind of publicity, and you know it."

"Just tell me how you got into this. I don't mean this," Father Healey said, pointing to the pictures. "I mean tell me how you became a priest."

"Actually it's kind of a long story. When I was a boy I was just like every other kid, but I used to sleepwalk. I'd get out of bed and go downstairs to my parents and be very talkative and extremely polite. I wouldn't call them 'Dad' and 'Mom' but 'Father' and 'Mother.' My eyes would be open and I'd stay up watching television before going back to bed. When I didn't remember anything about it the next day, they were curious. Later, they came to understand that I was sleepwalking and could tell because I became uncharacteristically polite. It was something they didn't take very seriously. If anything they laughed about it. No one could have predicted what would happen to me later.

"There's a gap in my life of more than a few years of which I have no recollection. It didn't seem to surprise anyone when in my early twenties I suddenly became this polite young man who was so wholesome and respectful. Everyone was delighted when I decided to go into the seminary. It was my mother's dream.

"I've had to piece that part of my life together from a journal I kept. There are also scraps of information that others have told me and documents I've collected. But I breezed through seminary and was the best in my class. I was two years into being a priest before I finally woke up.

"For some reason during this long sleep I studied music seriously and was put in charge of the choir and music programs. Music's the one thing that still comes out of me like old shrapnel from the sleepwalk. I didn't transfer to this parish touting my musical abilities because I'd lost it all, but believe it or not I can still sit at the piano and play. It's amazing.

"But one day I was tutoring one of the choir boys and went all of a sudden into an erotic cramp. Because I remember the sensations, I'm sure it's what woke me up, and there I stood, lusting after this boy. But I was more shocked at my surroundings, the church, my collar, being called 'father' politely by this young boy asking if anything was wrong.

"I sent him home and tried to learn what happened. I called my mother first and we figured out I must have been sleepwalking. She encouraged me to seek help in the church, but the best I could do was claim some kind of breakdown. They tried to 'heal' me with prayer. One old priest even suggested that the changes in me might be better left to an exorcist. But I told new lies to alleviate fears. I'd enough religious schooling to fake the faith. I just needed a refresher course in being a priest. That took a few months, but when I was rehabilitated it was just a job. My heart wasn't in it, and to everyone around me, all pretty uninteresting themselves, I was just a pale copy of my previous self. I became a glorified altar boy and felt like I was a bus driver. It even occurred to me once when I was giving communion that I should have had some kind of puncher to put holes in the hosts like tickets before handing them out. It got so depressing I wanted a fresh start, and I left it all behind me when I came here, except the part about liking boys.

"I really was a normal-enough kid aside from the sleepwalking. I expected to get married. I had a girlfriend before I entered the seminary and apparently hurt her pretty badly at the time. I've thought plenty about getting out of the church for some time, and this is as good a time as any. If that's where this is headed, it's fine with me. When I was a kid I hated church. I'm amazed this is what I would sleepwalk into. I used to hide in the morning when my parents were getting ready to go. After waking up from my long nap, there were times I did try taking responsibilities seriously. But when I wrote sermons they were about some new pet perception, like yours this morning, a piece of my own thinking, not about the gospel or clarifying the truth. It was embarrassing, but at first,

The Spider Priests

since I was surrounded by so many devout men and women, accepted in this culture, I saw it as worth emulating. I thought perhaps the spirit would come to me if I faked it as they say happiness will if we smile.

"But it didn't take much to see that the priesthood is more autocratic, bureaucratic, nose-up-in-the-air, stick-in-the-mud bullshit than devotion. We'll turn our eyes and have a high mass for someone who commits suicide if there's a large enough donation. Why stick to our religious guns when the convent needs repair?

"If anyone's sleepwalking, it's me, I know, but that's better than being one of the living dead. This life is as flavorless as the host. The clergy may think it's delivering the living word but it's so wound in traditional locks and dams of rules and dogma that we should not be surprised that no more than a few drops of holy truth come out of this gigantic bureaucracy. I've been masquerading, but the sad thing is there are priests who got here as believers who still prey on boys and think they're good priests. I know I don't belong here, so you can start processing my discharge papers, but we all have something we're hiding Healey. In the secular world we just deal with it. In this garb it just eats at us. I'll pray for what preys on you, Healey. And you'll pray for me, won't you?"

While Father Healey was listening to Bishop, an image had passed through his mind when he mentioned he was in charge of the choir. He saw the boys in the choir, each encased by a spider in what seemed to be white robes, but they were just holding them as victims waiting their turn for the spider to devour them.

He warned Bishop that he wouldn't let him go without serious counseling to ensure that he would pose no threat to children outside the church, and said that out of all that Bishop had told him, it hurt most to hear that Bishop had thought his sermon was based on pet perceptions. "Nothing could be further than the truth," he said, insisting that Christ's being alive in us outweighs any stiff requirement of chanting only what has been said before. "Knowing Christ is how the church maintains its relevance." Bishop just looked at him and rolled his eyes.

Father Healey agreed with Bishop that indeed each person carries a cross, but said that Christ is there to help carry it for us even when

The Voyage of a Bean

the ball and chain is permanently shackled to our leg and still slows us down in this world even with His help."

"I've heard all that before," answered Bishop, "but I'm not 'weak and heavy laden' and don't need anything carried at the moment. The only impediment I know is this collar," and he took it off his neck and put it on Father Healey's desk.

"That might make you feel lighter right now, but the other stuff will get heavier over time," he said. "Come back and see us any time and pray with us. Even the shepherds smell like sheep." Then he swiveled his chair around and dismissed Bishop without even looking at him. He then sat for a long time looking out his window musing on the city outside. Was the church really having an impact, or was it just another firmly entrenched institution? Dark clouds had rolled in, and it was just starting to rain. Streams of darkness poured out of the clouds, and they looked like legs streaming down. He thought of a giant spider hanging over the entire city that stretched out end to end beneath it. It may have been raining, but as Bishop said, everyone had something to hide, but the world was being quietly sucked dry. Even the rain said so. The church was a refuge, and must always be maintained as such.

For a time the spider seemed to dance around, and then it dissolved in the darkness. The phone started ringing. He swiveled his chair around, switched on a table lamp and answered the call. It was his sister. He started shuffling through papers cluttering his desk as she said, "Andy's having an affair. What am I going to do?"

Then he realized the pictures were gone. "'I'll call you back," he said and hung up.

By the time he got to Bishop's room, he figured Bishop would have destroyed the pictures, but Bishop was sitting on his bed looking at them. The door was open. He looked up at Father Healey and said, "It's a miracle," and handed them over.

Father Healey was surprised to see pictures of Michael Delaney fully clothed, probably taken just before the others, and he knew Bishop had switched them. "Give them to me," he demanded.

"No," said Bishop, "I mean it. It's a miracle. The pictures went from nude to fully clothed. I didn't have anything to do with it."

Father Healey started looking through drawers for them. "What did you do, rip them up?"

"You turned your chair around and told me to go. You wanted me to take them — didn't you? You wanted to give me another chance. You knew I had nowhere else to go, and the only purpose those pictures could possibly serve was insurance or blackmail, and you're no insurance man or extortionist, are you? Or are you my judge and jury? Am I your victim?"

"I thought you were sick of the collar and the cardboard existence," Healey said. "Do you really expect me to believe this is an effort to stay here and not a way to keep the pictures?"

"The pictures are gone," Bishop said with a smile. "The Lord destroyed them. You gave Him the means for a miracle to take place. He obviously isn't going to do it right in front of your face. And who are you to say that the end-result isn't inspired by God? It certainly yields a way to understand that miracles are not merely rare and amazing spectacles directly empowered from above but ongoing experience from which His presence can be inferred." He stopped. "I think I've just had a revelation. Moments ago I was just at my absolute lowest, and now I'm completely charged with energy. And to me that transcends whatever you think of what happened. Am I just a clever opportunist or a keeper of a universe? Are you going to judge the moment where a light goes on in a person's heart?"

There was silence. Father Healey thought of his sister and wondered what he was going to say to her. He didn't know, but he wanted to move on. "Just please show me the pieces," he pleaded.

"They're gone. The pictures are gone. Forget about them. And if you expect me to have any faith at all that there's hope for me as a priest, then you'd better find it in your heart to forgive me. What about the parable of forgiveness where the master forgives his servant a great debt, and then the same servant goes right out and beats someone who can't pay back an even smaller debt?"

"Well, it's ridiculous to say the least," Healey shouted. "Now I don't even believe the part about your sleepwalking. I don't know what to believe, and that only applies to what you're telling me. To me you have a problem with believing in anything. Well we all start

The Voyage of a Bean

there, with nothing. We're like spiders paying our respects to the dead. Imagine that you smash a spider with your driver's license, which is face up with the dead spider on it, and along comes another spider onto the license. It stands somewhere next to the numbers indicating your date of birth. Now you ask yourself, what does this spider understand? Can it detect that a fellow spider is dead? Does it have any feeling at all for it? Does it pay any kind of respect, or is the husk merely another object to a kind of mind so beneath ours that consciousness is hardly an issue? Yet, for us, intelligence and understanding abound. The license has meaning. There's a direct relationship and connection to you. Your picture, height, weight, date of birth, even a number corresponding directly to you according to the state's method of tracking you is there. That spider stands on a symbol of and direct link to human society next to a dead comrade, but what does it know? The numbers mean nothing, the picture isn't perceived. That spider is standing on something that represents an entire world that makes complete sense, just as we stand on the planet, unaware of what markers may indicate an order higher than we can perceive. We are the spiders, dumbly staring across at one another. What do we know? All we know is that we don't even really know what the spider on the license knows. We're so far above it, and yet we're so far away. Now we stand on God's Word. He's given us the license and explained it well, that it represents another world, and what we trust is this: as removed from us as He is, as we are from the spider, still He knows us better than we know it. He knows what we are and what it means for us to be here. We know He understands because of Christ. And we can choose to be dead to it, to reject it, but it doesn't change whether it's true."

Bishop was quiet for a moment. "*Le Pape est mort. Un autre Pape est appelé à regner. Arraignée? Quel drole de nome pour un Pape!* I guess my actions certainly qualify as utterly outrageous in His sight, if I understand things right. I've just been trying to get His attention. I wish I were sleepwalking through it because it wouldn't hurt so much."

"Well, if you do repent, who am I to question your sincerity? You wouldn't be the first to leave the priesthood, but you wouldn't be the first to stay either. It wouldn't be worth staying if you don't believe in the shepherd's work. Anyway, I've got several problems of my own to deal with. It looks like my sister's husband may be having an affair, and I've got to deal with her on that."

"Forgive me in advance but I took her husband's confession yesterday and he told me he was looking for a way out of it. I told him he should tell her all about it."

"Well Father Bishop, you should not have told me that. Please remember to observe in all cases how utterly essential it is to keep confessions as a sacred trust. As God gives us the power to forgive sins through Him, what we hear is never to be spoken. It is as when God forgives that it is as if things never happened. And that is how I will forgive you now for all that has passed here. It is as if it never happened. Here we have a fresh start and may part in peace." He paused, and then his tone turned threatening. "But tomorrow I expect nothing less than a full confession. I don't care if it takes all day, and don't bother with stories only a fool would believe. And I want pictures, whole or in pieces right now, do you understand?" Bishop nodded, and handed them over.

That evening, Father Healey drove to his sister's and mediated what was a rather difficult and emotional moment in his family. At one point, his three-year-old nephew came downstairs for something to drink and asked why he couldn't drink whiskey. Father Healey looked at Andy and Sarah and asked why the child might be asking this. Andy explained that the boy had seen an ad in a magazine, and they had explained how some people do things that hurt them, but they were a family that believed the body is the temple of the Lord, and they would never let anything in so as to hurt it.

Father Healey looked at the boy and said, "Your folks are right. The way to find the Lord is in your heart. He's in there, and you must look for him, and don't ever eat or drink what can hurt you."

"Yeah, and some people eat shoes," the boy answered.

Again, Father Healey asked what caused this remark. They shrugged. They gave the boy some water and sent him off to bed.

When he had gone, Father Healey asked for a whiskey. They looked at him. "Look, I've had a rough day and have some things to say. Just get it for me." They complied, and then went by degrees

The Voyage of a Bean

into a rather eloquent rampage on the sanctity of marriage, the impossibility of divorce and the importance of family. The whole time he kept his voice down for the sake of the child, but his words brought down the rafters. He left the couple demolished by the shock waves, and yet holding one another in love and tears, thanking him for bringing them back to God. He warned them that coming to their senses was the point of the discussion. God was just the natural extension of true common sense.

As Father Healey left, he thought of the homeless and their worn-out shoes. It occurred to him to have a shoe drive for the city missions. Then he had another great idea. It was just past midnight, and he drove to his old neighborhood. He parked the car a few houses away from his boyhood home and stealthily meandered over lawns in the darkness thinking how a priest's black jacket, shirt and pants are perfect for such clandestine activities. He passed his own yard and went straight to his old neighbor's sycamore tree and climbed as high as he could safely go. At the top, he pruned a bundle of small branches and climbed back down. He had caught the whole neighborhood napping, not just his mean old neighbor, and he'd gone to the root of an old obsession and even outwitted the spider of his nightmare that morning. He exulted as he stood on the lawn after he had climbed down. He felt like a spider at that moment, in touch with all of the elements on the driver's license. It was made out to him, issued from the kingdom above, which was very real. Then he heard a noise and returned stealthily by the same route to his car, which he'd left running, a fact that surprised him, and as he drove home he began to realize that some of his courage had come from the quite stiff drink his brother-in-law had poured.

That morning, he burned the branches, gathered the ashes and used them to mark foreheads as it was Ash Wednesday. "May we all be taken where none of us can climb," he prayed, feeling a great joy as he met the smiles of his sister, her husband, and Father Bishop among those affirming their faith beyond a mere return to dust on that day of days; and then, in a world where spiders and licenses are never far away, he went back, started a roaring fire, burned the pictures, cleaned the fireplace and disposed of the ashes.

The Book of Gerald

Everyone who met Gerald in church felt a bit put off by him, but would never say anything because they were in church. He had excellent manners, and a kind and considerate disposition but had put such a high fence of Bible knowledge around himself that he was totally insulated — safe from knowing anyone or being known by anyone. He'd once been a lawyer, a pretty good student of the law at that, and could talk circles around most judges citing this or that precedent.

But what had served him in the law did not translate well in religious circles. Gerald was blind to the fact that learning every fact in the Bible, which he certainly had, did not constitute a greater awareness of God anymore than a certain number of moles of oxygen combined with twice as many moles of hydrogen will produce a glass of water without a lit match. Gerald made a sterile case with static components at everyone's disposal, and despite his court practiced charm, was about as awkward as a baker without an oven. The shop was always open, but no one was interested in what he was selling, which would be funny considering they'd come to church to learn about God except that it didn't take a master's degree in theology to recognize that Gerald's real message was to call attention to himself.

By the time he was seventy, he had developed a pretty large bag of tricks. One was to ask someone to pick random numbers in precise ranges until it led to a single Bible verse on which he would then expound. He also would use two and three Bibles at a time to show various connections that he'd found. It was generally new folks coming into the fold that he'd corner to exercise his skills. It had the effect of making everyone politely steer clear of him the best they could, but this did not make Gerald any the wiser because he couldn't detect it. He thought he was really getting through; that everyone respected and appreciated him, and so he decided to extend his range, visit other churches, publish his distillations of the Bible, and take his juggling act on the road.

One night during a thunderstorm he was sitting alone in his room reciting the Book of Daniel from memory, opening the Bible and verifying his progress every few verses, when a bolt of lightning blew out the lights in the house. He sat for a long time in the dark continuing to recite, when there was a sudden bright flash outside his window that lit up his room for an instant. His eyes had adjusted to the darkness, and the flash had the effect of making the whole room appear as clearly and distinctly as it did with the lights on. He'd been casually gazing down, and the image of his right hand was the central image of the strange apparition.

Gradually the sharpness began to blur, but the hand remained visible when all else returned to normal. He shut his eyes and rubbed them a moment, but the hand still would not go away. Finally it grew larger until it almost filled his field of vision. Before it vanished, he had the distinct feeling the hand was a vision and a sign to him. A moment later the lights went back on in his room, and a darkness invaded his mind. What had it meant?

What troubled him most was that on further reflection Daniel himself had been a prophet who had visions, and could make interpretations and dissolve doubts. He'd even been able to relate to King Nebuchadnezzar details and the meaning of a forgotten dream. What Gerald had seen was only an image of his hand dissolving into a great blob, but he wanted more.

And so he took it as a tailor's mannequin on which he must design his personal vision and then proclaim it as a message from God. Gerald agonized for days as he tried to make the blob into something he could use to demonstrate his connection to God, but as the days wore on, he felt woefully shortchanged by the lack of communication. The more he thought about it, Daniel was certainly connected

The Book of Gerald

and gifted. Put at risk in the lion's den, he came out without a scratch because of his faith.

A few days of thinking like this and Gerald had become as disconcerted as he'd been before ever having joined the church. When he was in his middle thirties, at the height of his law practice, he enjoyed getting the better of justice now and then by swaying a jury his way despite knowing better how things were. He didn't need God then. Lady justice was not only blindfolded but also tied up in the chair next to him. In his mind she was blind not because nonpertinent factors had no bearing under the law, but because in the long run, due to what happened in the courts, she couldn't possibly see. To him, a judge was simply a sentry to ensure that protocols were followed, which always worked in Gerald's favor because he knew procedures better than most judges. But what finally upended Gerald's confidence and practice was a terrible accident that took the lives of his wife and three children. A judge became a central figure and Gerald's nemesis in the case that followed.

What happened was a drunk driver had walked away from the crash after broad siding them. Gerald was at home at the time. The driver was an illegal alien. When he was brought up on charges, lawyers for the family argued that he should be kept in jail as he might try to skip bail. Nevertheless, the judge set a rather low bail. Once posted, the driver disappeared across the border and was never heard from again. Gerald was so outraged that over the next year he dug up so much dirt on the judge and his practices that he was all but driven out of the county. After that, Gerald had little taste for the law and took no pride in remembering his successful practice. If anything, he felt he should pay penance. He reached a point where he actually believed his wife and children were taken from him as a form of punishment, and so he turned to the church and the Bible, gave up his life in the law, as it were, to serve the greater law and judge. But as if cursed with a certain way of doing things, just as he had done in the legal system, Gerald only took to the letter of God's law, rather than the spirit of it, and down deep, though he wouldn't admit it even to himself, blamed this judge as well for what happened, and though he could spout chapter and verse better than

The Voyage of a Bean

anyone, he was not working for the church, but in his heart, though he didn't know it, trying to drive the Lord out of town for what had happened to his family. At the same time, he thought he was doing the righteous thing by mastering the good book, except that it really didn't make him really part of a larger family. He preferred prosecuting his case out of that sense of self-righteousness, which had the strange effect of driving people away from him.

But suddenly Gerald was acutely aware of being alone again. Some of these matters of being angry at God began to seem all too real to him. Gerald had tried to keep Biblical knowledge a specialty, but having as many volatile ingredients together in the same place is an accident waiting to happen, and while Gerald may have expected to remain inert forever, this new feeling that something was missing was all that it took to have everything blow up in his face. He fell down on his knees and realized what a fraud he actually was, what he still was. He was nothing more than a country lawyer who didn't give a hoot as to whether anything behind the blindfold could see through him as long as whatever he projected could be made to seem true to anyone witnessing his prestidigitations. It was spark enough to set off the blast, and the apparition that survived the flash came into Gerald's mind with the force of vision that simply amazed him like the sharp edge of a knife feels when it reaches the nerve.

He was already in bed at the time, with the lights out, and had been tossing and turning when the right hand of God appeared in the center of the room as large as a table, the plane of the palm parallel to the floor with the various fingers turned upwards like figures seated around the table. He felt beckoned from bed as if called to a séance, and got up, merging into the place occupied by the thumb. From this vantage point, he was simply able to cross over and touch himself to any given finger across from him and derive a vision from it. He knew he was not there to conjure any spirits out of the darkness such as his wife and children, but to be borne into the spirit inhabiting the various figures.

Each of the four fingers across from him, from pinky on the right to index on the left, had a noticeable duality depending on how he turned his head to look at them. They were almost like channel holograms in this sense, only that they were misty and transparent, part of the whole hand glowing like a ghost in the center of the dark room. He did not resist the impulsive thoughts that crossed his mind, for he could not — they were not his own thoughts, but given to him.

The first of these thoughts to cross his mind was that the four fingers were four stages of life — his life — and the messages borne by them were pertinent to his own salvation. The first finger, the pinky, was that of his youth. Its duality was that of the child, both in a state of wonder, ready to receive anything given to it, and that of the inherent emotional beast, ready to bite whatever hand willing to try to feed it. Both he the thumb and the child pinky moved toward one another over the center of the palm and touched. As soon as this happened, Gerald felt himself transported into living a tale he remembered his mother telling him when he was a boy. It was his favorite story about a mother turtle who had given birth to a batch of eggs, but while she was trying to bury them, a hawk descended, driving her away with a great peck that sent her onto her back. By the time she righted herself, all but one of the eggs had been devoured or broken. She drove the Hawk away who didn't put up a fight since his hunger was satisfied.

Afraid to lose this last egg, the mother turtle went against her nature and stayed with it throughout its incubation. One thing she noticed as the egg matured was how a strange concaved pock-mark would appear whenever she approached it, then return to roundness after a short time. She finally understood that it was the meekness of the baby turtle in the egg, doing exactly what turtles do in the wild, withdrawing its head when it sensed an approach, and causing the shell to contract. As such, she thought it a timid turtle indeed, and decided to name it so. When finally she helped break open the shell when it was time to hatch (for the baby turtle was too timid to do so), it was so attached to its mother and she was so fond of it that she decided "Timi D." was a better name so that others wouldn't think her child to be a coward. Still after she introduced Timi D. to the water, other creatures were quick to notice how quickly the

The Voyage of a Bean

young turtle withdrew its head at the slightest encouragement or provocation. Sensing its weakness, they took great joy in teasing it whenever they could, and long after the mother had left it to start a new brood, Timi D. looked forward to the long periods of hibernation under the mud.

Every spring though, Timi D. emerged to the same cruel world he grew to abhor. One season he appeared to have grown a lure on the top of his head. It drew fish near out of curiosity. Timi D. would shrink away as usual, but the plankton and small floating matter no longer appealed to him for sustenance. One day he was very hungry indeed when one fish came up to inspect his little lure, and before shrinking his head back to the safety of his shell, Timi D. surprised himself by lunging out and swallowing the fish in one gulp. It was all so sudden, and even this scared him, but now from time to time he did the same thing. He thought it monstrous that he was actually devouring some of the other creatures in this way, but over several seasons he actually grew to accept it. He even managed to learn how to bury himself in the mud and wiggle the lure whenever he was hungry. This never failed to attract several fish to inspect it. He realized that these same creatures that made so much fun of him over the years were in fact quite stupid. He took new courage in his skills and grew quite fond of the taste of his enemies. In turn, eating well made him grow quite large, until one day he noticed that he was being given quite a large berth by all the creatures around him. He saw them whispering, and as he craned out his neck to hear what they were saying, he watched how quickly they swam away as if he had been on the attack. They were actually afraid of him. One day he hid and even kept his lure under the mud, leaving only an ear exposed to hear what they were saying. Their conversations were mainly about those that were missing among them, friends that Timi D. had eaten. They were saying that so-and-so was "in Timi D." or "Timi D. ate her." This was spoken so often by groups of fish that new broods of creatures mistook it for "Intimidator," and quickly they were saying that, until he was known as the Great Intimidator. And finally, grown fully mature into his own nature, the finest example of his species, the Great Intimidator ruled a wide expanse of ocean floor for many years, and reveled in his nature as a great solitary beast.

    When the thumb separated from the pinky, Gerald was again in the position of the thumb, and felt another thought that was not his own — that the thumb is the single-most important appendage for differentiating man and the higher primates from all other creatures for its ability to grasp. His head still spinning from the journey into the story his mother used to tell him, his head next crossed over the palm and touched the ring finger, which he saw had its own duality. From one vantage point, it was the stage of youth closest to the child, its face still smiling. From the other side, it was the stage of youth closest to becoming mature, and due to the incidence of information received to discharge innocence with violence, the face was marked by sadness.

    As they touched tips over the palm of God, Gerald was filled with the recollection of the time he spent in the hallways of school and sidewalks along the street in front of his house as a young boy. There were just throngs of kids playing. He had no doubt of the community of sentiment as he experienced it. Everything about it was plain and open, even as to how it was all asserted in school by his teachers. He would be at the shopping mall going up an escalator, and there would always be someone in front of him or behind him, going the same way with the same expectations of life. Next door to him was a family and across the street was another and every family had children and they were all living in much the same way and enjoying the same things.

    From there though, he was suddenly in a darkness in a burrow, tunneling like a mole underground, digging alone with no sense at all that there is anything like him out there. In this part of the vision, Gerald had the distinct knowledge of digging long portions of tunnel at the same time as knowing he was ignorant of the fact that actually everyone in his childhood was out there doing the same thing — digging and believing it was being done solo. He saw himself crossing other tunnels, unseen at the time, and going long distances through tunnels taken by others previously, all of it unknown to the mole. He saw himself again with his wife and family, not in their

The Voyage of a Bean

home, but in a trench barely holding their own in a war, shells exploding overhead. He put his head up to look across the plain and saw the heads of his burrowing friends all equally absorbed in protecting the trenches they had dug for their own families.

When Gerald and the ring finger stopped and resumed their places at the table of the open hand, Gerald looked across to the middle finger, tallest at the table and recoiled at its perceivable duality. He did not welcome the notion of crossing over to touch it, for there was something terribly dark about it. It seemed to ascend into increasing obscurity, shrouded in symmetry like a spider's web, on the one side closer to youth with a bearing of fangs, and on the other side, the very backside of the spider, being itself drained of any of life's fluid, the life sucked out of it. He felt his very core panic as he crossed over the center of the palm and met the eight eyes looking mercilessly into his. The symmetry of the web was actually the print on the pad of the finger, and the thought he had that was not his own was of the ultimate destruction of even the greatest of men.

But the vision he was drawn into surprised him, for there was no actual threat at all. He was the spider on the prowl, filled with an instinctive sense of purpose. All around him were the spent husks of previous prey cast to the side. He was working on draining another spider, drawing its life's blood into him, when out of the corner of several eyes he thought he saw something to the underlying plane, which should have been a web. He only recognized it as a page from the Bible because he recognized the text from his human mind. The duality of the spider was that it can sit directly on links that define a higher presence, a great code of another world, and exist unaware that there is any meaning beyond its own driving force.

He resumed his place at the table of the hand across from this finger and wondered what familiar landmarks of his surroundings might actually be the signposts of a much higher order of which he was so nobly ignorant. He looked across to the last finger, the pointer, and once again experienced a thought that was not his own — that this was the final stage of life, but he could not detect its duality from looking at it. He only noted that the other fingers had curled so that its pointing was evident. It reminded him of the depictions he'd seen of Christ's hand in the posture of blessing, and realized with the touch of the last finger would be his redemption. But no matter how he tried, he could not get across to touch it. He was expecting it to meet him halfway, and as a thumb he only made it to the base of the finger. It made it seem as if he were bowing to it, except there was no respect or devotion on his part, only frustration at not knowing what his redemption actually was. He then had a thought which was his own that the duality of the last finger was actually that of good on one side, evil on the other, whereupon as he strained himself across the palm, he was ensnared by the other three fingers and held down.

Gerald found himself in such a total darkness that he thought he'd lost the vision, but there was great emptiness and blindness besides being held down. When at last he was released by the other three fingers, he raised himself back into thumb position at the table of the hand and saw he'd been looking into a gaping hole in the center of the palm that had been made in nailing it to the cross. Then something amazing happened. As Gerald gazed into the gaping wound, shreds of skin healed a layer all the way across and became an eyelid. He watched the eye open in the center of the palm and for a few moments felt an awareness of a greater order. The eye did not blink, but became so bright itself that Gerald could not look into it. It made him wince. He turned away from it. When he looked back, it was gone. The gaping hole was back. But through it like a spike stuck the stem of a goblet with its bowl above and base below, both being too large to go through the wound. Then he had a sudden thought, believing it was not his own, but sent to him, that the cup drew its source of fluid from the wound.

Another thought that was not his said that this was the Holy Grail. Still another thought that was not his said that in order for redemption, all five fingers must touch in the center, where the single vision that would occur in Gerald's mind would be far more than even the combination of all that he'd already witnessed, more than the combination of the four single touches, and yet he still had not experienced the touch of the final duality of the pointing finger. He knew without knowing how that he could not have all five fingers

The Voyage of a Bean

touch in the center without first experiencing a touch to the last finger itself as he had with the other three, and now a goblet blocked his ability to reach the other four fingers. The best he could muster was to get himself to the base of the bowl, and through its ghostly transparency he could see the other four fingers were doing the same — touching the base of the bowl, and then he realized that all together, the fingers were holding the cup as if to drink. As long as he must fail to connect with the pointer itself, this was what he must accept as the next best thing. This must serve as his redemption.

And as the entire vision began to fade into a bright blob, it was not the hand that remained, but the cup, and it didn't grow ghostlier, but more solid and shiny, until he could see his face in it, and not the face he knew by looking in the mirror, but of the demon that possessed him, for the face was so contorted in anger and frustration it was not his face, but he recognized it as the only thing keeping him from God. As soon as he admitted that, the vision dispersed completely. He sat up in bed, startled to find himself under the covers and not in the center of the room. In reaching to turn on the lamp on the bedside table, he knocked over a goblet. He realized what had happened when it smashed into a thousand pieces on the floor.

That morning Gerald threw away the files he'd been collecting as he was tracking church-per-person ratios at various congregations. He no longer cared. He also removed the give-away aids which were only harmless condensations but which he pushed while showing off as necessary study guides. Finally he cancelled his appointment to speak that afternoon at a church in the inner city. He said he wasn't feeling well, but his real reason was that he no longer thought the topic worthwhile. It was on the importance of bringing the Bible alive through a correct knowledge of all the various obscure names and spellings, titled, "Do you know Noah's sons?" He went to the library and took out anything he could find on people who puncture their own eyes. He was especially interested in whether there was any eastern literature on the inner eye, and whether anyone had attempted to poke that eye out to be blind with love of God. He found the story of Oedipus, who blinded himself when he realized that in trying to escape the prophesy of killing his father and marrying his mother, he'd actually fulfilled it.

His peculiar interest wasn't due to any plans he had to hurt himself, but because at seventy years old he suddenly saw himself as having kept his eyes closed ever since his family had died. Of all the images he could remember from the night before, seeing the face he harbored in the goblet was the most disturbing. It was so completely different from anything he ever projected it wasn't as if he should go about apologizing or trying to be nice. If anything, he just wanted to start leaving people alone; rather, to pay them attention as situations warranted. He might have shrunk away out of embarrassment at the thought of having anything to do with anyone anymore had it not been for a sense that he finally felt like he cared for them. For the first time, he attended church, kneeled, took communion and had coffee without an agenda of checking passes as people filed by.

Nor did he tell anyone including the minister about his vision. If it were truly a communication from God, it was so personal a message he must respect its privacy. In a word, Gerald relaxed and found it in himself to forgive. It wasn't the drunk driver who'd killed his family or the judge who'd let him get away who benefited from his newfound graciousness, but Gerald himself. He was letting himself off the hook for all of his own previous excessiveness, for he finally had learned that accepting grace meant not wearing it as a badge. Gerald knew the driver and the judge would have their day in court just as he would; that extensive knowledge of the book of law wasn't going to do him any good at all in his trial if the spirit wasn't forthcoming in his heart, and so he did forgive them.

What came from this was that his anger dissolved, and during his next visit to the graves of his family, he cried for the first time in many years. Then he stood there a long time, hands folded, without thinking or saying so much as a word, and at last the link was made over the palm in his heart, and he felt heaven willingly bend halfway to receive this special kind of prayer.

The King of Rain Checks

So much has been said in philosophy that one can hardly keep track of it all, let alone extract one right structure from it all and apply it to the mind, which is an amorphous mass much of the time. It would seem that the best people have found some set of principles on which to center their great bearing, but in the end, everyone must experience dissolution of whatever high consciousness they achieve. Senile old men, who have long since lost their once-great marbles, still have the very furrows in their brows that made the world bow before them. It is almost as if the habit of looking thoughtful and perceptive was permanently imprinted, or we might postulate that within the chaos of their advanced dementia there is still a blending that takes them quite a few notches above most such patients. We like to think they may still be in touch somehow in their lost realm, in tune with order of some kind.

It sometimes happens in considering philosophy in a general way that a premise emerges that seems to make sense though it may never have been postulated before, like aromas never known until they rise from a bowl of plants and spices crushed together for the first time. The whole of philosophy may turn its back on the bastard child born of its very blood and bones, but the child may still walk on its own and grow until one day it will take a seat in the Senate and silence the irritated and reluctant colleagues with a stirring speech, finally blending harmoniously with its progenitors.

Consider the creative function. We only know so much of how and why it works, but much of it is shrouded in mystery. Some artists have epilepsy or migraines that somehow help them in their art.

The King of Rain Checks

Yes, and pain often facilitates the production of a great work. But even the question of what is great is still under consideration. Children are tested and evaluated for their intelligence, and at the same time, Abraham Lincoln has been assigned a high IQ based on his work because he did not live at a time when such tests were administered. So was he born great or did he achieve greatness? Why are so many mensas so unproductive? What constitutes clear vision and an important contribution to art when so many critics follow only the fashion of the moment and are generally disabled when it comes to identifying a new and important work? In the long run, it would seem, those with something to say, those who have a contribution to make, will be heard, their contribution accepted, and their place in history secured, but what happens within the mind that produces the work is the great mystery. The work in the end is just some wonderful thing. How it got there is often quite another, and the question falls to the wayside. The artist is simply put on a pedestal, and the world gets busy trying to do the same thing without the epilepsy, the migraines and the pain, and falls so far short it's ridiculous.

Our case in point for the purposes of this discussion is one Henry Irwin Basil III (the only son of the American Ambassador Henry Irwin Basil II) who was born in London in 1953 shortly after his father arrived in England to assume his new post. Irwin saw mostly nannies and tutors until he was seven, when his father returned stateside. Then he attended the finest private schools Connecticut has to offer and excelled in all subjects, particularly music. By the time he was fifteen, Basil was already determined to be an orchestra conductor, a vision his family fully supported. He attended Harvard and Julliard, and before he was thirty was already an assistant conductor with the New York Philharmonic. He appreciated art, but he had no desire to create it himself. He became a master in the world of art. He thought of himself as an artist, but he had no desire to actually create new works. He saw his contribution in recreating it and bringing into balancing its power and precision. His image of himself, strangely, was as a sedentary stone, avoiding contact with people and nature in order to be the best rock it could be. It did not matter that he would gather moss. He was bred for greatness: to

The Voyage of a Bean

require nothing and be completely self-sustaining. If there was anything negative in this, the ends would justify it in the end.

Basil wanted ultimately to be conductor of the Boston Symphony Orchestra, and his connections served him well in gaining access. Twice in 1987 he was guest conductor and received marvelous reviews. In 1993 he was offered the job with the passing of Peter Orland. It was also the year he married the daughter of one of Boston's most prominent families. There was a child born the following year, a baby girl, and we enter Irwin's immediate circle two years later, the week after the baptism of his daughter, Lisa Anne.

Basil was disgruntled because his wife was putting pressure on him to continue attending church regularly. They lived outside of Boston in one of the finest suburbs, and she argued that it was at the very least a way to enjoy the countryside. But he had no more interest in church than he had in history class while in school. He'd absorbed enough information to recite enough chapter and verse to pass a test, and isn't that what it amounted to anyway, he would ask her? Church was there when they needed it. They'd gotten the baptism. He argued it would be there for her communion when it came time. His wife urged him to try it for a few weeks, and he reluctantly agreed.

The last Sunday they went as a family was the first Sunday after Lisa Anne had been baptized. Irwin was still tired from the concert the night before. He was also angry he'd forgotten to leave two tickets at the will-call window for some friends who'd wanted them. During intermission, he learned they were waiting outside, and he went personally to let them in, but it was an embarrassment in which he was still absorbed.

As they walked to the church after parking the car, he found the two tickets in his coat pocket. First it reminded him of his oversight. He tried to calm himself by recalling how wonderfully he'd conducted the main event that followed, Beethoven's Third Symphony, which was the piece they'd come to hear anyway. He pushed his mind off the sinking ship of chagrin into the waters of music, immersing himself in not just the sounds but also the notation. Being brilliantly literate in music, there was so much symmetry it

The King of Rain Checks

was almost a religion for him. His God was music, and he was Boston's great preacher.

His congregation knew at least a part of the peace that passes the understanding. Most certainly couldn't read music, and therefore couldn't really fathom its depths, but the message of music after all is the sound, and he was certainly the best equipped to deliver those sounds so that whatever was supposed to be felt would be felt. And what he loved about those who loved music, his parishioners, was that this was knee-thumping stuff that sent the spirit soaring, yet everyone sat still, stirred to the high heavens, but silent and appreciative, solemn against such passion, taking the roller coaster ride without so much as a scream.

As he looked out to the roads passing the church, he noticed how many people weren't stopping to attend the service. They had better things to do. A police car had just stopped one motorist in a hurry to get somewhere and was writing out a ticket. Now there was something interesting to think about. What if God Himself were really making a visit to this church? What if it had been advertised and tickets were printed up to be sold? Wouldn't all those cars be heading to church to see the maker of the universe in person? Wouldn't the tickets be snarfed up pretty quickly? Wouldn't the place overflow with the eager and curious, and wouldn't thousands more wait outside in disappointment, hoping just to get a glimpse of Him rising upward to heaven when the service was over? Even a glimpse would be enough to be sure that He really exists.

Basil smiled as he thought the ad might say that the Lord and Mighty One, the Great Redeemer will appear this Sunday at Holy Cross Cathedral from ten until noon. Coffee served afterwards and a question-and-answer period will follow. And yet it made him wonder even more why anyone would bother coming to church at all, given that it's where one is supposed to find Him. Basil had sat through enough services in prep school and college and had never seen a sign of Him. Most people were happy to spend their Sunday puttering around the yard. As he looked at the houses around the church, there were plenty of examples of people who knew better what to do with their time than his wife.

His thoughts turned again to the cop, and God as cop, handing out penalties from on high for the infractions he observes from His hiding place. Who would slow down, let alone go to city hall to pay a ticket if the cops used telepathy to send guilt to those who broke the law? When drivers see a cop, they slow down; then they just go back to speeding when they're out of radar range. Even the cops know that. They must do it too when they're driving cross-country. But God's not actively enforcing His laws, and the world's driving record corroborates that. The only sign that people care at all for God is that there are so many old people attending, going for the last-minute redemption, trying to make good and pay up on a lifetime of imagined transgressions. But were God to hand anyone a real ticket to come see Him personally, it would be more frightening than getting pulled over by the police.

As they entered the church, Basil took their coats and went to hang them up while his wife went into the service with their daughter. He then went in and found his daughter playing a familiar game she loved at home, which was to block him from sitting down. He wasn't in the mood for this and warned her sternly to give him room. She read it as the pantomime anger he used in play and stretched out even more to keep him away. Finally Basil reached down and pinched her hard enough to confirm the seriousness of his meaning, which surprised and stung the little girl to tears. Then she told her father to go away, crying loudly though it was barely a disturbance to anyone around them because the organ was playing an introductory hymn. It struck Basil hard as a music professional that if this were God's house, then why wasn't there a higher standard for the quality of music? Between the lack of talent he perceived in the organist and the flatness of the voices around him, it was almost more than he could stand. Would the manner of interpreting God to him fall as far short of its potential as the musical portion of the service. His daughter's scrannel screaming further destroyed any last resemblance to music of what he was hearing, and quickly the hymn was winding down to the last few lines, and since there was nothing Basil and his wife could do to quell the outburst, he finally angrily directed his wife to take the child out just as the hymn was ending.

The King of Rain Checks

He could still hear her loud cries just as the priest turned from the altar to welcome one and all.

Basil then sat there alone, immersed in distance, angry for his own impatience, yet feeling justified under the circumstances for all he had done. After a few minutes, he grew so uncomfortable sitting alone where he'd only agreed under protest to accompany that he left the church to find his wife and daughter. The ushers acknowledged him with the same friendly smiles he saw whenever there was reason to be greeted but no recognition. "These idiot's don't even know who I am," he thought to himself and strolled to the nursery.

He wanted to leave right away, but his wife insisted that they at least wait for a time in case they might return to the service. They finally calmed their daughter, or actually it was because of the toys they handed her, but whenever they tried to take her back, she cried that she didn't want to go. This went back and forth between toys and crying until Basil decided enough was enough, threw up his arms and said, "We're going!" He retrieved the coats, hurried his wife's forcing of little arms through the sleeves, and led his small family out of the church at a brisk pace.

The last thing he saw was that communion was under way, and what struck him was the gulf between whatever they were doing and what he was doing. It was only a glimpse, but like a page of music written for many instruments, there were several parts to it. First, there were all kinds of signs of order. Ushers were standing formally beside a pew and people were standing ready to file out and join the line of procession to the altar. There were lots of white robes there, and lights, flowers, details of organization and other manifestations of ceremony that struck him as oddly as if he were hiding in the bushes watching the bizarre rituals of a strange people. His head was swimming with frustration at even being there. He heard the music again when the organist missed a note and asserted to himself that such must drive God out. Maybe He took notes on attendance, or sent deaf emissaries to oversee the mass, but He Himself could certainly not bear to attend.

He was grateful to be in the breezy silence again. It reminded him of Tanglewood, the orchestra's summer home where he so much

The Voyage of a Bean

enjoyed the concerts. "That is certainly something on which God smiles," he thought to Himself. "If His church is anywhere, it's here in the open air."

He remembered the cop was probably back in his hiding place in the bushes somewhere and drove carefully so as not to get a ticket. It brought his mind back to the notion of having tickets to see God in person, and that in his visit to the church it was almost as if he'd gone through a revolving door, as if he were unwelcome. It brought to mind a subtle notion that perhaps God had a hand in what had happened, relative to his earlier thinking, and had pinched him such that his own whimpers had made the spirits rush him out like impatient parents.

He told his wife that they would not be going to church after that. They could still be on track with God, just as there were probably thousands who did not go to the Sermon on the Mount, but got wind of it later. There were no tickets sold for that, no requirements to attend it, and enough of what was said and done is remembered to have it written in the heart. She didn't say anything. Then he said, "The activity of being alive implores God to make an appearance now and then; and though we don't directly see him, that whether we all at once pray together or all together deny Him at the same time, it amounts to an earnest plea, a focus on the notion. Theologians and atheists have the same subject matter. He's there though we don't see him, just as I don't see the government right now, yet I know it's there. And I realize the tickets to see God are still good, for He is the king of rain checks too, and will always be master of the miracle of unlimited seating."

"You're the king of rain checks," was all she answered, bitterly.

Over the next year Basil and his wife grew distant from one another. His duties as musical director for the Boston Symphony completely engulfed him. His home was like a hotel when he was not on the road, somewhere to arrive late and use to sleep, shower and shave. Between his regular duties when he was in town and an increasingly active travel schedule, the marital bonds grew dusty and brittle. Neither he nor his wife had been raised to argue the finer points of a situation. What was important must be assumed.

The King of Rain Checks

There should be no disagreement on fundamental points, or if there is any encroachment, it must be by something petty or unnecessary and petty, after which normalcy will be restored. The wife of a man of his talent and position must count herself fortunate and willing to abide by all of the rigors and requirements of fame.

Along these lines he thought all was well when he returned from a two-week concert tour in Europe, only to find that his wife had left him. In a manner befitting his stoicism, however, he contacted his lawyer to sue for divorce immediately, indicating all matters should be conducted with absolute fairness and propriety in order to ensure there would be no negative press. Both families had plenty of money, and the kind of proceedings that punctuate most common divorces would not even be hinted at in the case of the Basil family. It bothered him so little that he even went out that evening to attend a party to benefit a young violinist who had injured her foot in an automobile accident.

At the party, he was delighted to be recognized by and meet so many new famous faces from fields other than music. Every writer, poet, painter and composer of any reputation was there, but after a couple of hours of being in the same room with them, something strange occurred in Basil's heart. One minute he was the great, young conductor, the one that everyone knew from his telltale gestures on the podium while conducting. It was the way he swung the baton, commonly referred to as a stroke of genius. It was such a smooth, nice touch that he had, that it was suggested he directed the music from within. The next minute he was a fraud, a mere figurehead who was no more than a service artery for the great, not great at all himself, but who possessed the ability to put a stamp on schedule for the machinery at work at getting the public on board the train. That was it. He was a mere train conductor. He punched the tickets brought to him with a certain dexterity and called out the stops, riding the rails watching the birds on the telephone wires out the window but was part of the replaceable action, not the eternal activity. Everyone at the party was involved in the creative process. He was accepted among them at a party as if they all shared something in common over their success, everyone thought he had

The Voyage of a Bean

the most talent in the world for what he did, but he didn't know anything about what they had written and could not hold a discussion that would suggest he had any expertise in their field. Still another minute later, and they were all frauds, dressing up to congratulate one another on their charm, much of which was passed to them in the form of trust funds and high education, and most of it earned largely by imitation of one kind or another; the painters, writers and composers all following the trends expected of them by the industry which had its roots in the air of superiority because of its long affiliations with respected, untarnishable traditions. One minute after that, he had collapsed and rolled down a spiral staircase, rather awkwardly, turning the party into a major ruckus. An ambulance followed quickly and took him away.

It turned out to be a stroke, so severe that doctors said it could render him incapable of resuming his responsibilities with the orchestra. The press had served him up as a vegetable side dish before he regained consciousness. Of course it was all dripping with sympathy, for he was such a young man to experience such a debilitation and disappointment, for he was only forty-three and at the height of his powers. It was a great pity, and the story stirred great sentiment in the city and nation for the poor maestro. His life was largely the focus of the city for the first day or two, but when it leaked out that Basil's wife, Lisa Benefield, had left him and had not so much as visited his bedside, the whole nation turned its gaze eastward to see what was happening.

It was then reported when she did make her appearance at the hospital that the Benefield and Basil families, along with the Boston Symphony, had conspired to make her come forward in order to avert the national outrage. All such reports were denied, and Lisa Benefield stated in a news conference at the BSO that she and her husband were having normal marital problems and were working things out. Basil's lawyer who had leaked the story of the divorce later denied Basil had filed papers, and the paper that first published the story suggested he'd been bought off by the family, then dropped it as the nation seemed content that it was all just typical media hype and journalistic trash.

The King of Rain Checks

In the months that followed his stroke, there were many events that took place. Basil woke and was told he'd had a stroke. His wife was present, and he was able to indicate he was happy to see her and his little girl. This was taken as a good sign, but it was also apparent he was partially paralyzed. He received many visitors the first few days after he awoke, most of who were at the party where he collapsed, and because they were famous, the coverage in the press was enormous. All around, the Basil stroke was very good for business.

The Boston Symphony saw such a sales increase of Basil's recordings with the orchestra that nearly his entire repertoire went into a newer, larger printing. A benefit was held in Boston for his speedy recovery, though it was largely a political event promoted by the city and the orchestra in order to continue to ride the wave. The family hardly needed the money, Basil was insured anyway, and a percentage of the proceeds that would have gone to him went to charity later, which also sounded good in the press.

On his release from the hospital, Basil was asked by the orchestra to attend a variety of functions that were not a part of his former duties. Meanwhile, at the orchestra it was business as usual under the direction of Harris Walters, formerly Basil's assistant but appointed interim conductor due to the expected long-term loss, but Basil thought it didn't take an orchestra conductor to tell a sour note in these new duties, as it was obvious to him that he was being used as a fund-raising tool. What angered him more was the way in which Walters assumed his "temporary" position. He'd taken over a news conference and alluded more than once to a "likelihood" that his role was not actually temporary, and that he was fully prepared to take over the reins of musical director by title as well as soon as public interest in Basil had waned to its proper perspective. He said that there was an issue not only as to how long Basil's recovery would take, but whether he could ever make a full recovery. What the orchestra needed was a full-time conductor working at one-hundred percent efficiency, and having to work in the midst of such issues impairs the powers of an interim conductor to work at maximum efficiency.

For making such remarks before even his debut, Walters set

himself on a line that only time would tell if he could toe, but he'd already split the field between those who were outraged by his brazen attempt to commandeer a role reserved for a far-more-enabled conductor, and a growing number of orchestra supporters who worried that a handicapped conductor is a contradiction in terms. In any event, the BSO felt it necessary to state that the views Walters expressed were his own and not a reflection of the position the orchestra was taking on the Basil question. The Basil question? Not only had the orchestra merely given the upstart a slight slap on the wrist, they had validated his concerns.

Over the next several month, there were defections from the ranks favoring Basil. There were new, more serious questions regarding the nature of permanent impairment, motor control. Basil himself hadn't converted any doubters of his case when he made his public appearances arranged by the orchestra. They couldn't have made it more painful for him had they tried. There was always a microphone and a call for him to speak, at which point the most obvious of the complications due to the stroke was obvious — that of speech impairment. The man could hardly finish a sentence, and trying harder only made it worse. It wasn't so much the papers as television that brought him down. A clip was shown of his struggles every time the story was aired. He seemed hopeless. No one had to say it — the pictures were worth a thousand words, all synonyms for moron.

The issues were bandied back and forth with no new energy on the ball until it was announced that a mutual decision had been reached by the Boston Symphony Orchestra and Henry Irwin Basil III that Basil would step down from his post, and that Harris Walters, interim conductor would take over as music director, effective immediately. It was a big story for a day or two, but it was also closure for a thread the city had grown tired of, so it went back page and second half of the nightly news within a couple of days, and the city got on with its life. To Basil's credit, he went before the microphones one last time and fielded questions from the media. He admitted that he had filed divorce papers, and that he was unaware, obviously, because he'd been incapacitated, of the machinations going on behind his back, and he added that they were reconciled and planning a move

The King of Rain Checks

to Chicago. Everyone present noticed one thing about Basil's news conference — there was a marked improvement in his speech, and all were moved by his honesty and courage not just that night but through it all. Still, only one reporter suggested that the decision to can Basil might be premature. It was a short blurb in a gossip column.

In fact, the Basils had reconciled. He was totally dependent on her. She never left his side, and he grew to wonder how he'd ever managed to travel and work without hardly seeing her. It also gave him a chance to appreciate qualities he'd never appreciated in her before, nor were they anything he'd looked for in a woman. She'd fit his several requirements of status, education and an acceptance of his devotion to his profession, none of which seemed relevant anymore. All of what had seemed important was stripped away, and here was an angel, he thought, or two rather, for his little girl was his greatest joy. More than one doctor said he was deriving more benefits from her than from any of his therapy.

The settlement of the contract buyout and assorted financial agreements between Basil and the BSO would have assured he never would have to work again if he wasn't already wealthy. The Basils bought a nice home in Lake Forest, and cut Boston loose behind them. It was a lakefront estate, and Basil would sit for hours watching the waves on his beach through the window. One afternoon he slumped off and dozed, and dreamed he was conducting a major new symphony that had stunned the world with its originality. He woke with the music so fresh in his mind that it was hardly a chore between Lisa, tape recorder and paper to get it all down. He honestly believed in its complete integrity as a significant work of art. As well versed in music as he was, he'd never seen or heard anything quite like it. But he sat on it for a few weeks because it seemed to open up a musical cascade of ideas, tear down the dam as it were, and there were more ideas than he could keep track of pouring out of his head.

When a friend from the Chicago Symphony called him one day to see how he was doing, the fact he was composing was received with great interest. Sam Richter, the CSO's musical director was told the story over lunch the next day and took a ride up to Lake

The Voyage of a Bean

Forest and looked over the symphony. At first he was speechless. He asked where it came from. "Is this what happens after a stroke? Let me have one like it. It's wonderful, sheer genius. Why don't we give it a play. Feel like conducting again?"

Basil was all for a public performance of the piece, but it took some convincing for him to agree to taking up the baton again. Richter arranged for some meetings with the orchestra during regular rehearsals over the next several weeks. Basil was impressed with how he was accepted and encouraged. Within a few months all of the legal matters regarding his new symphony were worked out, and finally a date was set for its performance. There were still a few minor matters to attend to in order that everything in Basil's return would go smoothly. The podium was made higher so that he could remain seated. One of his arms was still rather useless, and Sam Richter taught Basil how to use his eyes and head to communicate. Rehearsals reduced many concerns as the performance was polished. By the time everything was ready, there had been so much news about the impending concert, so many leaks about its wonders through the fabric of so much secrecy that the whole world was watching that night, Boston in particular.

The day of the concert, Harris Walters told a television reporter, "If Basil was ever as sensitive as he said when he alleged he was being used as a gimmick in Boston for the orchestra to make money, then why is he out in Chicago stirring up a circus? The Chicago Symphony to my mind has the greatest gimmick of all to attract attention to itself — a sideshow conductor — why else would people pay so much attention to a freak?"

But his attack was a grenade that got stuck as he tried to throw it. The evening's festivities went off without a hitch. Basil's new work was one of those rare works of art that conveys greatness at the first hearing. Basil was nervous at first, but his love of music quickly calmed and carried him along as within a river current. It was hardly an effort to get to where he was going, and after all, it is what he'd been trained to do. The work was instantly hailed as a major work, and therefore Basil himself rose even higher as a star, and beyond sight, in a sense, because of the hardships and reversals he had to overcome. Then there was the fact he'd never been a composer before. One reporter called it "God's compensation." Most just said it was a gift.

Basil took few calls the following day. He sat watching the waves and composing. He'd been worried that the act of conducting might stand in the way of composition, and was relieved to find it still flowing freely. One call he did take came from Boston. It was the BSO. First, they wanted to congratulate him both on his coup de grace, his grand new symphony, and for his return to the podium. Second, they wanted to know when they could schedule his return to Boston. The whole city would be waiting, they said.

"Wait, you're talking into my deaf ear," he said. "Now, what was that?" And the message was repeated. "Sorry," he said, "now you're talking into my other deaf ear." He hung up the phone.

A few days later, Harris Walters resigned from the BSO, apparently under pressure after remarks he made the night of Basil's performance. One fair-minded Boston reporter who had followed the Basil story from the beginning put together a story that highlighted every ambitious or rude comment ever made by Walters. Everyone picked up on it as Walters became a scapegoat for the city's treatment of Basil. He might as well have been tarred and feathered out of town for the way the stairs were greased on his way out the door of Orchestra Hall. Once again, the BSO put out a release that said Walters' views were not representative of the views of the Boston Symphony Orchestra. The harshest language used was that, "An orchestra conductor has an obligation to conduct himself in an appropriate manner, and the BSO does not sanction certain comments made by Harris Walters regarding Henry Irwin Basil III, formerly of the BSO."

Basil felt the orchestra was trying to use his previous association to aggrandize itself, if not profit. He contacted his lawyer and worked out an airtight plan that was announced when all the pieces were properly in place. In brief, the documents filed refused the Boston Symphony Orchestra any and all rights to ever perform any of Basil's original works for all time. It was the will of the composer that for as long a time as a renewable copyright can be secured and until such a time as his works became part of the public domain, not a single note from any Basil composition would be performed in any manner by the Boston Symphony Orchestra.

Basil agreed soon afterward to appear on a popular accredited television news magazine program to discuss the issue. He said the following. "On a staff of music, there are not only notes but rests. A rest is quiet, and there are many silences in music. I look at my experiences with the BSO with peace and quiet, and that is just what I send to them of my music. To every other orchestra, I leave my notes. In Boston's case, please let me give it a rest. There will only be my silence in that auditorium when it comes to my music. I dedicate every note of silence, every pause, every measure of time between movements, to the BSO. I hope that all told over all the many years to come that it will amount to quite a number of hours of deafening silence for them to consider.

"While I was a conductor there, I was famous for my stroke, for the way I moved the baton. I was probably hired for it. Now I am more famous for another kind of stroke. I was most certainly fired for it. It has been said that I owed all of my previous success as a conductor to the way I held the baton, to my stroke, as if all my love for music and long years of study had nothing to do with it. Now people are saying that I owe all of my success in composition to a stroke of genius, as sometimes an illness can change a person for reasons still beyond our comprehension. And yet it isn't like I just went out and started fixing jet airplanes with a full knowledge of their hydraulic systems. What I bring to bear is a complete literacy for music.

"I have a certain amount of anger that I must admit I channel into my music. I can't help what has happened thus far, and to a degree I know I must continue to deal with some baggage, but to the degree that I have control I will exercise control. It is in this sense that I feel that closing out the BSO is my own masterstroke. Call it revenge if you will, but I think it's a reasonable arrangement. There's plenty of music for that orchestra to play. All that I ever would have conducted if I'd never had the stroke, they can still hear. Anytime people are gathered there and it is quiet, I hope they will think of the music I brought there and the music I did not. It is

The King of Rain Checks

in this way that I hope to have a lasting impact on the Boston Symphony. For the most part, things will go on as they would have and always have at the BSO, but without anything to do with me, as they wanted, as they decided, as they deserve. Whatever else they cook up, they just won't be using any basil, that's all, the end."

This story too receded into the back pages, and Basil's life in Lake Forest returned to being relatively normal and remarkable at the same time. The latter state described his recovery as well, for as of one year later he was walking again, doing things for himself, speaking clearly, and working as a guest conductor once again, but only in cases where one of his own works was being performed. He still made regular visits to his doctor whose advise was to continue to take it easy, and while some would say Basil in a rested state does more than most people enjoying full health, Basil himself made sure he spent time with his family, and if he traveled, they accompanied him. He just became part of the country's musical landscape and counted himself fortunate to be involved with the orchestral music industry, for in most any other music industry, rock, rap, or country, the tabloids would have been running regular sensational features about him. As it was, as it always had been, there was only a limited audience and interest in Basil, and he appreciated a certain squeaky-cleanness of the industry as the dirty water seemed to have a way of rolling off its back.

And so we shall take our leave of him after recounting one last incident of relevance. It happened that one chilly Saturday night he was going to a concert with his wife and daughter and needed a coat.

He put on the one he had not worn since before he had the stroke. A dog jumped up and down before him, thinking he was going to be taken out for yet another walk. He was able to get the coat on by himself, and in reaching in the pockets to see if there were any gloves found the same tickets that he had in his pocket the day he'd left church early with his wife and daughter years before. And he remembered the conversation with his wife that resulted in both he and God sharing the stage as the kings of rain checks. These were tickets that seemed to have signaled the major changes in his life. He was so much a different man then, so driven and demanding, so sure of

The Voyage of a Bean

everything, and yet so vacant. Lisa came into the hallway and caught him staring at them. "Thinking of going to church, then?" And he laughed uproariously for a moment. He remembered hearing somewhere that people had as much laughter as they had faith, and that laugh had uplifted him.

In its residue a new melody began to form in his mind. As he went out the door to get the car, he was humming further variations on the theme. It had the makings of a modern religious piece. Perhaps he could write something like a Mass, or a choral work. It even occurred to him that church would be a good place to conduct research on it, and something Goethe said about *belief being fertile and skepticism barren* seemed like a decent opening lyric. It danced in step with the enchanting melody that had come to mind. He considered clearing his schedule, and secluding himself in his study for several months to complete the work.

As he sat in the car, he could hear the orchestra. Within a few minutes, he had actually heard the overture. It was only a matter of transcribing it later. He couldn't believe such music was coming to him so easily. He wasn't creating it. He was just the first to hear it. His whole family must come second. He could hardly leave at this time. The music took a sudden dark turn. His heart started pounding. He wanted to turn it down for a moment, but he couldn't seem to stop it. It was getting louder. A great fear suddenly gripped him that he wasn't going to have a chance to complete the transcription, let alone a simple errand. He'd forgotten why he was in the car. He started honking the horn. His wife came out and took him inside. It turned out to be more than an anxiety attack. He told his wife that he heard beautiful new music, and he wanted Lisa to transcribe it.

Sadly, it was the same piece he'd composed after his first stroke, but it lacked all the layers of brilliance. It was a melody of a hundred instruments playing in unison, and it all quickly and quietly went down from there for poor Irwin. For all that he had accomplished, he was remembered as a sedentary stone whose rare and refined moss quickly rubbed off on its way down. Critics said his music was cold, and there was more stroke than genius in it. It was clever and cruel, and it played well in the news.

Father's Death

I show up late for work as usual, but I can do that, working for my dad and Henry. They're not going to fire me or anything. Sure they give me the usual grief, but they show the same disrespect when I do everything right. It has something to do with their generation that I haven't quite yet put my finger on, but they act like they feel it's necessary to keep some kind of distance between me and them. I get to tag along, that sort of thing, but it's never like I'm included in anything. I don't really want to be with them, but they sure know how to make you feel like the dues you've got to pay keep getting lost in the shuffle. I've got my own life after work, and it's not like I'm the only one having to deal with this superiority complex of our parents. It seems they don't know how to treat younger people unless they treat them like children.

Anyway, I hop into the minivan right into one of their conversations I'm not welcome in, we're driving down the road, and Henry starts to fall asleep at the wheel. So I'm helping him drive, pushing him around to wake him up and saying things like, "So I'm not the only one bored by what my dad's got to say," at which my father gives me a phony dirty look, then starts laughing, and by the time we get to the job site, Henry's wide awake, and we're all just kind of joking, and they're asking me about how much I paid for my new phone, where did I get it. I'm thinking my wife picked it up, and I don't really know, but we're carrying our gear into the building, and we climb up a step into the freight elevator and some gal's refusing to step in. She's waiting for her family, and I said, "Well how do you know I'm not your family, I've got my ID here, let's take a look at

The Voyage of a Bean

it," and she makes a joke about that making it official, and I say, "Yeah, sounds like something my sister would say," and it goes on like this until I really feel a connection and want to get closer, but the elevator has been taking us up, and she's been getting smaller on the ground below.

As we get about halfway up the building, the elevator suddenly starts to shift, and we start to falter. My dad's in one corner, Henry's on another, and I'm holding on in a third. I put my elbow over a rail between floors to support myself, and the box becomes detached and starts to sink in my father's corner. Henry's able to grab hold as well, but I'm no longer looking across to my father. I'm looking down at him where he's trying to find some kind of grip as the box is tilting more dangerously. Then, all of a sudden, a line breaks, the box drops and my father topples out of it. He bounces off a wall, scrapes and hits the bottom, bounces over to another side where he lands on his head, where he just crumples and settles in a heap.

Somebody says, "He's gone." The girl to whom I was speaking starts screaming, and as I'm dangling on the railing watching this unfold, somebody from below asks for one of my frozen yogurts from the lunch box I dropped. Its contents have spilled all over. My immediate reaction is why anyone would think of eating at such a moment, but they want it for first aid purposes and apply it to my father's forehead. I can see his eyes are fixed open, but there are motions to go through just in case there's any chance he may be alive. Henry yells down they should get out of the way in case the rest of the box falls on them. With the sudden crack of another wire, they immediately clear the area.

Now my cell phone rings, and I can just reach it off my belt without losing my hold, and it's a sales call from a rival phone company trying to sell me a better phone card, swap it for whatever one I've got, but I don't understand the way the minutes are working, and some guy below overhears and says that "Advantage" has one for $66.50, and I ask how many minutes is that, trying to make a calculation, and the salesman on the phone brings his down to five minutes for a buck, but he's trying to throw in three lines for a certain amount, and I don't know what any of it means, but I'm also dealing with this tragedy. I tell the guy I can't talk now, that I have to to call my brother and tell him I think my father's dead. We'd been talking about a visit, and now all he has to do is just come out for the funeral instead of us meeting somewhere, but the guy's supervisor breaks into the line and starts trying to close the deal. Suddenly Henry starts singing something, quietly trembling, and I get a call waiting beep on the phone, punch it to get rid of the sales call, and it's the office asking if we're on site yet. I explain the situation quickly, and Henry suddenly dips, dropping an elbow, and I realize he's singing something in a final effort to comfort himself in terror. I don't know what to do, so I just say, "Hold on," but he loses hold and falls to the bottom of the shaft, landing broken next to my father, and the voice on the phone says, "OK, I'll hold."

I can feel my own arms losing strength, and I find a foothold in the wall to boost up and hold on much more comfortably, and I realize that I'll get through this. I get back on the phone and let them know that Henry's gone too, and all at once, despite the gravity of the moment, the front office is barking out new orders to me, all contingency plans, and they tell me that now I'm in charge. With my father and Henry gone, all that's left is a group a few years older than myself, and I know it's a major transition of power from the old guard. They tell me on the phone they're taking bets as to whether or not I can hold on, and I say, "I'll take some of that," and they laugh, and though they don't understand the gravity of the situation, it's obvious they like me and want to have me around as part of the business when this is over. There's a certain camaraderie born in tragedy, and I'm grateful to believe in it as I'm hanging on. They're telling me I've got to hold up my end of the elevator, but it makes me look down, and they're telling me of the big jobs ahead, important calls I have to make, all the job sites to visit, but everything is moving too fast. I don't want to see anybody. I've got to deal with so many things, I can't even grieve. I can't tell anybody that I need time and can't just act like nothing's happened. They're not going to stop talking anyway because so many things have happened; but it's sad to see the lengths we'll blindly go to get things back to normal as quickly as we can.

The Letter of the Law

Let's start with something to chew. You hear the moo? Hey hey Bossie! Wag your tail. Show us a hoof, Bossie. Sit, Bossie, sit. Where ya off to drifter? I'm a goin' to the stables. It's feedin' time.

It's God-awful in here. Gotta watch the step. *Oh you pusillanimous and enfeebled degenerate stinkard! Am I down? Moo why doncha! Come on out of there you gizzard! God, you conjure balloons, and you pop on infinite edges. What's it all for? And gape red. Red and raw. Don't scoff at me, you stumbling annoyance! Criminal nuisance! Derelict shyster! Ruffian! Slug! I'll push the envelope into the slot after I've put you in it, stamped it with my blood and addressed the sucker to hell!*

Now now Bossie! It's OK. Go ahead and gape. Don't mind us a bit. We're simple, but loving. Bound to go far. Aren't we girl? Alright son, you can have the car, but don't go too far. Where ya bound mister? To the tracks. Dammit, can't ya see, to the tracks! Well, why ya sittin' there? Don't ya know there's a train comes along here? You want help don't ya? Tied down air ya? Why, that makes for a whole conglomeration of possibilities. Right Bossie? Milk the cow, junior. Join the circus.

Noon train. Let's greet it with a band. How should I know why the engine wheels are red? Junior, this ain't a warnin'! Don't get underfoot, nuisance, and don't go showin' off your nuances.

A whole shitload of possibilities. Kids nowadays are fallin' short. Ain't got no ambishin. Yes I am bitchin'. Don't even see how ground they are in the dust. Can't get them serious for a minute.

Whatdyamean there's no nature in the city? There's plenty of thunderbird down in skid row. Yuk yuk yuk.

The Letter of the Law

Yep! The stable's a stockyard now. Kids don't think of workin' and then goin' to the barn dance. They want the pump room on a platter. When were the Platters in the Pump Room?

This is known as a sub, ensign, and this is war. Yes sir. Where ya from boy? Schenectady, sir. I'm from Texas, son, and seen it all!

Sore of the times all the time? Wag your tail. Wag it why doncha? No? OK, let's think about this. Let's not be rash. We'll dwell on it. Who wants to go out anyway? Oh, would you rather go out instead? We'd only dwell on it there, out in the cold and on the duff. That's no place to be, but you can go. You can go very far. How far? So far, not very. Mommy, I wanna go out.

Can't go out of bounds though. What are we gonna do? There's the law to think about. Don't try to get away, Slim. We've got you cornered. I don't buy it, sheriff.

Man crushed by a giant cow. It chased him miles and miles. By the time he got it from the cow he couldn't see no more. But he knew about the law by then. He knew that nothing could change, and that he could change nothin'. Can't brush now, ma, barn dance in ten minutes. What's a mother to do?

Yep, Bossie. Everything in this here pail is goin' to make'm grow up big 'n strong. Twelve ways, thirteen ways? Who knows? But a lot. Shit Bossie, gotta have your hoof in the pail, don't ya?

It's not botherin' me. No sirree. It's not in me to modify or mortify. They want it from you, Bossie girl. They can have it. Sure, I don't care, swish in the tail.

It's only love, and that is all
Why should I feel the way I do
It's only love and that is all
But it's so hard loving you

MOO-OO-OO-OO-OO-OO-OO-OO-OO.

Is this Nantucket, or is that a lot of wailing? Don't cry, Bossie. We said we love you. Oops. Look out! It's the giant cow.

They died with their boots on. One last request? One last look at the glare of the sun? Why, to tell it how you hate its beams? How

The Voyage of a Bean

about another, Bossie? Squeeze coal. Make a diamond. Gee thanks, Superman. OK, Jimmy, it's all yours. All the coal in the world.

Gee thanks! How about turning a cow into a hag.

Diamonds! Diamonds! Calling all diamonds for the dresser of the hag! For that vile and graceless venal menace. It's madness. A wayward rash. Demented course and bitter surreptitious nine out of ten times warped in her sense of humor, hag!

But a diamond is so many things. So many things to the hag.

Well, we've got to face it. Let's give our single all to her. All the way! And the most we can do is leave her with a diamond? Alright then. Oh Haggie! Sweet dullard of immortal retardation! Won't you please take our careful theory? We've got to do this manually, into the tube. A round peg, you square hole! Quick boys, stuff this down her throat! Ensign, on the double!

MOO-OO-OO-OO-OO-OO-OO-OO-OO.

Watch out for that utter now. There. What a beaute!

There is no one law higher for the hag, except, of course, the hag. There's no law for the hag higher than the law of the hag.

Wasn't that a butte?

A some a say a yes, and a some a say a no, and a some a don't a say because a some a don't a know!

Here comes the pitch. Dropped third strike. Safe at first. There's rules to the game even if you don't understand; it all swirls together and seems to make sense, so she starts thinking there may be diamonds in the rough. Ah, that hag'll take anything she can get. Remember the time her windows was all barred up, and keep it holy. And the time she was whipped a hunnert years? And she musta spent a thousand in mud-packs over all. That bitch takes and takes. Say all ya want about givin', she just goes on a takin'.

Promise her anything, but...

Clobber the sniveling hag. Draw a walk. It's all for the best son. Do what you have to. Do what you can to grab what you can. That's the way, isn't it? See, Bossie moves her hoof in agreement. Another day, another struggle. All the coal in the world.

Do what you can. Grab what you can. Why, that's what they all do. They come from all over.

The Letter of the Law

They came from out of the West!
And she don't do nothin'. They's brung whips, bars, mud. Anything and everything to shake her up real good. And everyone of 'em out to win her. Stick her and ya got 'er. And she don't do more than twitch a bit of a finger. May seem like more to some of 'em. They turn to drunks. Why, she takes every axe whack and flower, and just goes on hatchin' new maggots peaceful as ever. A life's worth of flowers, and there's your return.

Safe and restful, sleep, sleep, sleep.

Diamonds are forever, but not so little boys. They may look like they's a lot on her dresser, but where are they? What does she do with 'em? It chased him miles and miles. Poor ensign. He turned blind. Blind drunk. You can't beat the law, son. There's a prom tonight at the Pump Room, Dad. Can I have the car? The back seat is rigged like a bear-trap. Do you think you could maybe squeeze her in? Not without a ring.

She'll take your salt, she'll take your ice. Just grab her udders, Walt, now don't be nice.

How did she take to you? Like a bat outa hell, a fish outa water? There are plenty of fish in the sea. Forget the pump. You don't got all day. Just enjoy the dance.

How long do you think we can hold out, Captain? Didn't they teach you at Annapolis, ensign, that these tubs are made to take a Depth Charge, and to Give Hell!! DIVE! DIVE!

A man on third, the squeeze is on. She took you Walt, gave you a son, the little turd…

Just about milked, Bossie? I saw a show last week about a man who wore a number. Life was no joke. He wore it on his shirts, gave it to make a dinner reservation. He used it everywhere, demanding total respect in the matter. Never lost any friends. A smart man. Gave it to a Chinaman in Chinese once while ordering to go. If anyone happened to accidentally call him by his name, he simply corrected it. Let by-gones be by-gone. And if anyone did it on purpose, if they was to call him by name to irk 'em, he was irked to the gills, right from zero to the number 212 that was his name. Boilin'!

It's face to face now, ensign. But I'm blind! You have your orders!

The Voyage of a Bean

We all have the same name, the number painted on the hull, and when it's up, it's up. FIRE!!

'E's a bloomin' beenballah, ats whoat 'e is. Won us a gime, 'e did, but i nevah 'erda the bloke.

Have you heard the one about the blind men trying to describe the elephant by the part of it they're touching? It's a cow, ensign. Hold on! Sit Bossie, sit!

Or would you rather swing on a star, carry moonbeams home in a jar, and be better off than you are, or would you rather be a pig?

Did the blind men ever hear the story, Daddy? You mean the blind men the ocean speaks of on its bottom? Junior, did you milk the cow like I asked you to? He didn't touch all the bases, ump! Safe, and that's final! I swear he didn't, ump! What did the voice in the whirlwind say? It said, *Get me outa here! OK, yer out of the game!*

Another day, another battle. We'll get 'em next year. Be secret and exult because of all groups known, it's the smallest cult.

And now, join us, won't you, in singing our national anthem. MOO-OO-OO-OO-OO-OO-OO-OO-OO.

Alright Bossie. How are you today, girl? Hoof hearted? There's been a change in the weather, then. Ice melted.

Don't wrap it, bag it...it's in the hag.

Alright Junior. New day. You're of age. Go! G'wan, beat it! Get thee to the circus! Go! And remember the law of the hag and keep it holy. Cram it around the coal. Squeeze. Gotta make a diamond. Nothing else will do. Remember, this is a diamond mine, even though there's no kimberlite — just all the coal in the world. Now that's something to chew, somethin' to dive for, dig for, round the bases for, dance for, drink too much for, and to regurgitate — for all the wholesome goodness you're hoping it will generate, ain't it? You'd risk your life for it. So, if your soul were a cow, wouldn't you sell it to the devil just to show him who's Bossie? You could always sacrifice yourself for another and receive an exemption. That act is, in fact, regarded as above the law of the hag, but you will already have had to pay with your life for us to keep it holy. "What do I care about your damn fiddle," said the composer to the violinist who couldn't play his concerto, and yet as I brandish my sword and prod

The Letter of the Law

you down the plank to the deep, who am I to say, "Keep away from these my pearls," or declare the sea is not a swine?

Where's a perfect reader? Floating in the sea of perfect critics? No! In a pig's eye is where! It all came back to me from hell. *Return to sender*, it said, and I looked inside myself, and I didn't find you Bossie. They took you out of the picture. They didn't understand you like I did, girl. But they'll take it all back in the end. They'll say they understood you and the hag all along, and there will be lectures and essays, and kids falling asleep filled with their own ideas. Lincoln Lincoln I've been thinkin' what on earth will we be drinkin' tonight? And I really wish that I could be there with you, Jimmy, but there's a soldier in the grass with a bullet in his... Don't be alarmed, it's only what dies in us, all the voices that make us what we are, the movies, the cartoons, the comic books, the popular songs, the television shows, the commercials — all the references no one can understand. They make up the hag within us, and for most of us, she makes the law we must break if we're to break out, if we're to break free of ourselves. To what? To all the accepted references? To the libraries and lecture halls and *Finnegan's Wakes*? Those voices just add to the cacophony, to the scrannel madness of looking for answers in the pigpen of ideas swirling coast to coast between deep oceans of high minded ideas struggling for ascendancy, warring for a hold on the faithful who are the fodder, the sheep who don't have a say, who don't know what to think except what they're told to believe, even if they're free for a time and need to take up arms to defend that for their given moment. Help us, return us, oh please, to the safe retreat, to our womb-warm burrow, to the familiar echoes some may understand, sharing for a time until the times change. That is what I sing, or rather what I purge — a living thing — a cow you have to milk. And now that it's out, nobody can take it away because it just came back postmarked from hell. I said I didn't find her in me, not that she wasn't in the letter, madder than hell, horns on fire from her trip down below, and now she's addressed to you, which is to say that nobody pushes an envelope without someone lined up on the other side. So go ahead and open it and follow it to the letter of the law, and try to see what spirit is. OK, here: it's a child looking for God.

The Money Tree

Every summer the whole family gathered at Grandma's for the gun ritual. She had a big family and a large property, and she'd sit on the front porch with a shotgun and just take a few shots, and most of the time she never hit anyone. But there were stories I heard after marrying into the family, and wounds I saw to back them up, that proved that you could get hurt. Even so, grandma was not the kind of person to play favorites. She just had her religion and her family, and the former taught her to treat everyone the same. At the same time, everyone knew to stand far back and wear lots of layers.

When I came into the picture, I refused to take part in the gun ritual. My thought was that she would shoot for me before one of her own, and more of the in-laws had taken pellets over the years than the immediate family, so I stayed out. They accepted this, and I kept the first-aid kit handy in case someone was shot.

As Grandma grew older, she was less able to distinguish things. Her vision was worse, and her thinking wasn't clear all the time. I had a money tree and was looking for a place to hide it, and Grandma's yard seemed like the perfect place. She watered it and tended it, but didn't know what it was, and when the bills sprouted, I'd pick them off, and there were never any missing. But before the gun ritual, she came out to practice and started shooting at the tree. Branches started flying off. Money started flying. I told her to stop. "What's that thing doing in my yard? I'm gonna kill it," she shouted, so I ran out to yank it out to save it, and she shot me. As my blood ran out, she stood over me and smiled, and I knew she did it to feed it, as the roots of money trees are bloodthirsty indeed.

The Death of the Explorer

In late March I was reading the paper in a Chicago cafe in a neighborhood known as Bucktown, which used to be the place where the pens were kept full of animals destined for slaughter at the old stockyards. It had blossomed into a scraggly repository for artists, thieves, drug pushers, and retired blue-collar workers. Also visible were the offices of the corrupt Chairman of the House Ways and Means Committee. The expressway roared right through the heart of all the dust and debris. The broken glass from smashed car windows glittered everywhere you walked.

It was time for coffee, so I left my chilly apartment, the windows rattling in the cold wind. A few weeks earlier, I'd finally quit my job as an editor for a trade publication. The publisher, my boss, had made life impossible for me. The list of her insanities is too long to delineate. Suffice it to say that she was an irrational beast who lived in my desk and garbage can, full of lies and deceit, so I finally quit.

My immediate purpose in going through the paper was to find another job, but in browsing the news, I stumbled on a notice that the explorer from Franz Kafka's great story, *In the Penal Colony*, had died of natural causes. I had actually met the man more than twenty years earlier when I attended a series of lectures he delivered at Harvard, so I read the obituary with keen interest.

He'd been born in 1897, so it figured he was only in his twenties when he'd visited the penal colony. It amazed me that he was so accomplished even so young. He was in his seventies by the time I heard his lectures, and now dead in his nineties. He was truly a twentieth-century man. It was the early seventies when he came to

The Voyage of a Bean

Harvard. I knew he was great at that time, but I'd never before seen the list of his accomplishments and was now astonished to see the breadth of his experience. He truly had covered the globe, cutting fearlessly through bramble of cultures. During the Second World War, his assistance to the Allies earned him medals from more than seven different countries. Reading the accolades brought to mind a sense that he was never touched by even a smattering of self doubt. He went everywhere but was always at the top of his own form. In his sixties, when everyone else was retiring to a university post, he never sat still. Instead of being nailed down into a university chair, he lectured everywhere, and also continued to join various expeditions where his experience always proved invaluable. I remember being surprised when I heard him speak that he'd never actually received anything but honorary degrees, and there were many of those. There was so much wonderful information crammed into his lectures that I remembered taking notes almost non-stop. It had an almost dizzying effect of satisfying an itch that yet insists on the same scratching.

But there were also striking similarities to the two times of my life. Here I was already in my forties and I felt like I was in limbo. I'd chosen to be a writer, a career, if one can call it that, whose study is longer and harder than any other respected profession, say that of a doctor for example, but a writer doesn't finish school per se, and there's no secure job waiting for the writer unless it is carved out by blood and guts. Only in the end when a writer has been successful do all the similar rewards follow. Then it looks like a great position. There are many who march in the beginning, but in the end, only a few can say that persistence paid them anything.

Twenty years before was also a very difficult time of transition in my life, so hard in fact that even now I tend not to like dealing with it. I considered my parents unsupportive brutes with a huge appetite for empty entertainment. We seemed to clash on every matter imaginable. Though my parents could afford it, they said it was too expensive to let me go to Harvard. My life with them had become a desert, and Harvard seemed like a great oasis, a giant drinking fountain in that wasteland. Besides, almost every writer I could think of spent time there, and those who didn't, like Faulkner, had characters like Shreve who did. With a desperate and terrible thirst to quench, I was determined to go there even as a vagabond if necessary. So I ran off with great urgency and without any approval to Cambridge, Massachusetts, to find my niche.

I immediately fell into a world split between the university and the city, and because of my situation, lived in both worlds. Instead of attending Harvard in the expected strict manner after growing up on Park Avenue and going to prep school, I was loose on the fringe. I saw the world from its underside. I associated and absorbed but remained an unprivileged outsider. So to me, Cambridge was a community knit together partly by bag ladies, partly by classrooms. I looked though windows into sirens and squalor as well as student protests in the Yard. Due to a lack of funds, I was also forced to work, so instead of spending an educational evening at a concert at Memorial Hall, I could be found working in Central Square at an ice cream parlor and later seen giving some drunk bus money to take him to the next open bar in town before being followed back to my apartment by some weirdo I'd certainly see in the square the next day. Finally, shortly after I arrived in Cambridge, my girlfriend back in Chicago severed our long-distance relationship.

So I was all alone then, much as I am twenty years later, but at least in my twenties I was on a mission. Though everything seemed to be working against me, I enjoyed living by the seat of my pants. Things hurt, but I was certainly more resilient to adversity, more persistent like Joseph K. was in trying to get into the castle, hindered at every step by his assistants. Parables of being hogtied seemed wonderful truths, and the ropes had yet to eat through my wrists. Mr. Kurtz' horror was an essay question on an hour exam.

I had a personal agenda for acquiring whatever tools I needed to write, and even a working theory of what I was living at the time. I called it axle agony, loosely defined as a first-stage center of emptiness with impetus to acquire wisdom that in the last stage (when emptiness has been alleviated) will have centralized knowledge on which the whole will spin. I wrote a couplet at the time that I thought expressed the thought: *The hole is more of doughnut than it knows/And feasting finds itself around the dough.* To me the regular students were kids dulled by their riches who were put there to fulfill family tradition. I knew I was hungrier, and there was so much knowledge and truth at Harvard it amazed me how generally students could stroll along without being charged. I couldn't believe how much of it spilled out of the Yard, and how few in taking everything for granted stooped to lick it up. I remember seeing the placard on a construction barricade in the Yard advertising the explorer's lectures entitled, *The Trouble with Kafka*, and its immediate appeal to me. Kafka as generally depicted had many troubles. He was sick, was relatively unknown in his time, had difficulties in love, had a young son he never knew about, and he was distant from his father. I could identify with much of that and was an avid reader of his novels and stories. My own work was not going well. My parents said my stories were way over everyone's head. I felt I needed to see these lectures, but I couldn't help thinking how hard it would probably be to hear them. I thought everyone would want to be there.

After finishing my coffee, I folded up the newspaper and hurried back to my apartment where I rummaged through boxes of old college papers in the attic until I found the notebook I'd used to transcribe the explorer's lectures. As I poured over them, I felt transported back to those days.

Due to the fact that the explorer was giving that year's William Belden Nobel lectures in Memorial Church's tiny Appleton Chapel, a rather small facility for such an exciting speaker, I recall feeling that I probably would not get in at all, so I made a point to try to get off work early, which would cause me even greater difficulties the following day.

The notes begin with a description of the chapel, references to the high spires of memorial church, and the statue of John Harvard in front of Harvard Hall across the Yard. I remembered the statue well, standing there in mid-lecture leaning one arm on a lectern, the other arm raised high with a book in hand, as if shaking it to make his point. It reminded me of Kafka's own description of the Statue of Liberty waving her sword in *Amerika*. I was so afraid of not getting in to see the explorer that I went to my boss at the ice cream parlor and said I had to leave early. There was an argument, but I prevailed and arrived so early that I sat alone for at least an hour. Hence my descriptions in the journal to take up time. Appleton Chapel is all wood, perhaps hand carved. No seats face the lectern. Two bays of high-backed pews sit sideways across an aisle from one another, several rows deep. It reminded me of an etching of the room where John Keats heard William Hazlitt expound his theories of the poetic imagination. I waited with great anticipation in a pool of influence across the ages, and wrote of my sadness that such focused eras had to be washed away by time. I wrote that it was up to the writer to capture it somehow.

Ten minutes before the lectures were to begin, barely a few students had arrived. Five minutes later, the room was still not full. It amazes me to this day that there were actually several seats available throughout the series at a prestigious university with literally thousands of students. When the explorer entered and was introduced, those few of us who had braved the late-March fifty-degree temperatures applauded him as he took the podium. He examined us with a wry smile. I tingled with expectation and remember how distinguished and focused he was. His eyes especially conveyed great confidence but were also reassuring in their depth. As I looked at him, I thought how great he was. From the standpoint of being at the end of his career, in a world where everything seemingly had already been discovered, there for the most part in recognition of past achievements, but still embodying the same spirit of blazing trails through new territory, this time by giving back to another generation, giving his report of what he had gathered into his center, telling us his secrets somewhere in the message, so that we might have a chance to do the same. This truly was an amazing man.

As I expand what I think to be pertinent notes into text here, I must apologize if there is a sketchy sound to lectures. I will try to make it read with a flow when possible, but a certain compact disjointedness is inevitable with notes. But hopefully, if I succeed in doing this, there will be a certain identification to anyone reading this account in the association of ideas all relating to one another that will conjure up a feeling of gestalt that comes in learning something with something greater almost taking shape.

The Voyage of a Bean

And so he began the first lecture. *I now hold a chair at a Canadian University and am a contradiction in terms: An explorer in residence — which I define as being always on sabbatical. But I'd rather be a visiting professor than sink into the cushions as an armchair philosopher.

The first lecture will focus on the trouble with Kafka, sometimes in specific terms, at other times through parable. His troubles, the trouble we have with him or any writer like him, and the ultimate trouble we have with the truth expressed in literature. The second lecture will feature information on my own experiences with Kafka and will include a show and tell of mementos of my explorations. Finally, in the last installment of the series, I'll delve into the nature of exploration in general.*

On the first level, we have an artist whose early writings are largely destroyed and whose mature work was generally unfinished and unpublished in his lifetime. He never finished getting his perception out, then after his death is eventually regarded as a great literary figure. In his lifetime he experienced the impossibility of imprinting his ideas successfully on the mind, then he's a mainstream lord of truth? What's this mean? He was sick at the height of his powers and died a month before he reached forty-one. There were few accolades in his lifetime, though he won a prize for The Stoker. He had a son he never knew about who died before reaching the age of seven, and three sisters and many friends who died in Nazi death camps. Why do these facts seem to connect to his life though he's been dead twenty years? It is because of his work.

I'm assuming a wide, general knowledge of Kafka through reading his novels, stories, diaries, letters, etc. And if you're compelled by them, then swept into the vortex of life for a couple of decades, there is going to be further trouble with Kafka — the trouble we have with him in that so much of the imagery is maintained in us. When removed from the wonder of reading into experience, it will ultimately be the case that the best stories stay alive, not just in memory but in pertinence. Kafka is immediately compelling, and his own life seems to make his message even more clear, but it's just so much literary "truth" that we learn, but from which we're immune. The most we have to worry about is waiting in a dentist's office, right? At least it's no chair on which we're going to die while waiting to get through a guarded door.

Given the images of the great wall, the bug, the execution machine, to

The Death of the Explorer

name a few, what is the overall effect of reading Kafka on the mind? Are we enabled somehow, more prepared, or are we just made cynical by all the parables if we accept them at all? The fact is that whatever the answer, there's a time element to experiencing his work that even made Kafka himself its victim, at least in terms of rewarding him for his effort. You don't just read The Trial and head out to a cafe to behave that much wiser. Actually, perhaps that's the way to do it, but the wisdom comes later. You cannot speed up the process of discovery no matter how well-read you become for experience is just a confirmation if you have the knowledge. Wisdom comes through the application of the knowledge to affirm the experience. The alternative in the worst-case scenario is despair and suicide. In the state of educated preparation, despair is neutralized into acceptance through recognition of the truth all along. Enlightenment becomes affirmed acquiescence.

Compared to money, this is priceless if you want to live past sixty. It regulates the passions. The trick one has to perform is an anatomy of Kafka, the living mind, for how things come to life, to understand how the parables and various thought processes of a writer in his stories can free our minds when the chains wind round to wrap tight their claim. We become burdened with the things he said only in doing an autopsy to discover where the trouble is, to find out what killed him and what's killing us. So we should think of dissecting Kafka not in the stories but in the mind after one reads him. Alright, my mind is filled, but how is it enabled? Without lessening his greatness, this is a demystification of Kafka. The coffee shop conversations of how great it was to read him puff him larger than necessary. In everyday life, he is restored to his proper perspective.

I first realized the trouble I had with ideas when I was out shoveling snow, and in Canada we get some real blizzards, let me tell you. For some reason I remembered the tale of the trapeze artist who wanted a second trapeze in the story First Sorrow. What I needed was a second snow shovel. I laughed too, but it brought to my mind the question of what good does having mythology do in a world of physical and practical considerations? Does it get you a job or build character in what it makes you think? And for anyone trying to create a mythology, the trouble with Kafka for any writer if he gets to you, is the struggle to free yourself in order to write. There is a machinery in Kafka that wraps around you with needles

The Voyage of a Bean

that inflict a hidden message. Having worked with him, and having seen his rise, I consider myself a witness to the gradual clarity of hidden messages inflicted into the vulnerable underbelly of the world. His distortions tell the truth better than any gradual, factual depiction though to twist something doesn't necessarily make it reveal any more. To borrow from Wallace Stevens, "What spirit is this, we asked while reading, because we knew it is this spirit in Kafka that we're seeking, and knew that we should ask this often as he sang."

And now we jump to some more difficult thoughts, but it is pertinent here because some of it was derived from personal conversations I had with Kafka, and which I am relating for the first time. Some of it is my own interpretation, and I'll leave it to you to infer which spirit is which, but if you have trouble, remember that there is a lineage to spirit. How could there not be? Which came first, the chicken or the egg is actually answered as both arrive and grow at the same time — the chicken in the egg. The question doesn't beg what outside force intervened to initiate the formation, but is the source of the confused interpretation of the question. To take it further, the egg is the universe, great in spirit, and we are the chickens, fearing where we go. "Don't worry, it's all in the mind, except the mind, which is in the body, so worry all you want," as Howard Nemerov put it.

Take an example of soul balls, small glass globes filled with living energy seen as light. When a globe is broken, where does the light go if energy is neither created nor destroyed? That's hard enough to figure out, but it begs the question: what kind of energy are we made of? You might have a good scientific explanation for the disappearance of light, but the living entity, what happens to that?

Within the lineage to spirit, there is certainly evolution and growth as well, as one spirit quickly absorbs what took a lifetime for another spirit to acquire. Finally came the mind of a God, complete with all the ideas of spirits that came before Him as well as the inspiration to make matter, so he was derivative, though it could also be said that His ancestral spirits were no more creative than early man could be considered smarter than us for inventing stone tools that we don't carve anymore as we've improved on the knowledge. And clearly, modern man is a new race of primate compared to robust Australopithecus of millions of years ago. In

The Death of the Explorer

this way, after any major influx of ideas we are altered, just as some would argue that after Jesus Christ, we became a new race of spirits.

So I have a parable of God's parents who decide to take on human form and come to stay on earth to see their grandson Christ. People asked but were told, no, these were not Joseph's parents but were in fact the parents of the real father. Being great spirits themselves, they felt capable of doing as much if not more than God their son and so while they enjoyed visiting the world, they had a rather begrudging attitude about everything except their grandson for whom they were making their visit. They were always fighting about their son, but couldn't show enough love for their grandchild. In the long run, people found them so eccentric because it was obvious they didn't actually love people of any kind, let alone children, so despite their promoting themselves as the first and last God Parents, no one would have them and rather chose others to be the God Parents for their children. So they just go on arguing about God and loving his son, and people picked up on that and passed it on to others until God's Parents grew weary of such a place where people could be so thankless to their own creator.

Much of life is spent in material cravings, but there are times when knowledge and art are what one hungers for — times that whatever the peace God or faith brings, we just need to sit and listen to music or read a good book. Compared to God it might be taken as a physical thing, but it's actually a spiritual quality made by man, for man, addressing certain instincts and needs causing lineage of spirit as well as its growth in the person. We can stop at any time, but if we've grown in spirit, there will come a hunger for truth beyond peat, coal and oil where the only hope is to go nuclear, but it means going very basic, down to the atoms, as well as out into the universe, into what makes the stars burn.

Nemerov put it well in his Journal of the Fictive Life: "Yeats speaks of coming into the desolation of reality, and this is for him a religious condition; it may be like what is intended by another splendid phrase of his, about withering into truth. But there is perhaps a prosier desolation of reality than that: In middle life, you perceive as though suddenly what was always there to be perceived, that all the stories are only stories. Beyond the stories, beneath them, outside the area taken account of by stories, there are the sickbed, the suffering, the hopeless struggle, the

The Voyage of a Bean

grave. It makes the stories look like hypocrisy, and the vision is so terrible that one becomes humbly grateful for the hypocrisy...Goethe added something sensible...that the attitude of belief is fertile, while the attitude of skepticism is sterile, and this remains true even if one is compelled to skepticism by the period in which one lives."

Now let us move to the universe of one head, totally sparked by understanding, whether through spirit or reading, in either a temporary or permanent manifestation of clarity. The question is how does one transfer that quality to another head, not so inspired. All the lines are there, and a bulb's in place, but how does one get the light to go on? Put in that plight, one can sympathize and identify with God's situation of trying to translate a great understanding down to man. First comes a capacity to love. Those sharing in the whole truth have a remarkable capacity to deal with others' pain, for they know or have faith of what lies beyond. Imagine a reluctant Christ, having to be dragged around by others and forced to help people which he finds distasteful, never liking it, but over time getting better at it. Is this the kind of man anyone would follow, or wouldn't we call him "Chrust" because the love was only a shell for down deep he didn't really like it? Only those in grip of the whole can in fact be a part of the spirit of exploration.

No it's impossible to read a book, have a revelation, then walk into a room and expect anyone else to suddenly connect. On the other hand, God does have the ability to intervene with spirit to cause an awakening that would not happen otherwise. One of the paradoxes of the difference in man's knowledge and God's knowledge is just this: Man is taught through books that may themselves have had no original instruction but were themselves begotten solely from imagination, and yet these often command an almost religious reverence. Consider the parable of Jerod's dream in which a young man of great spirit in an ancient nomadic tribe of early man begins having strange dreams. This young man has no power in the tribe, but the tribe is without any religion or traditions. As I said, his dreams are very strange. In one he sees something like spikes on ropes on the backs of other people. In another he sees a human sacrifice.

Now there no precedent for this in his culture, and while he feels the dreams are important messages, he has no power to do anything about them. At the same time, he feels selected and works to stand out in his

The Death of the Explorer

culture. In time, he arrives at an age where he makes a successful claim to power and becomes chief. As a new leader, his sense of himself seems all along justified now that it is fulfilled, and so he begins to turn his dreams into real acts in the culture including human sacrifice. Everything from facial paints and dancing, from hunting rituals to making a permanent village is added from Jerod's dream. The culture thrives, and Jerod, now in his prime and richly enabled, chosen and right, has further dreams that he institutes which become the basis of medicine and religion. Jerod lives a long life during which he sees another generation or two indoctrinated into the culture, and he dies certain of the greatness of his visions and secure that the culture will continue to thrive and keep his story alive. It does, without major modifications, for thousands of years. It is what anthropologists call a "cold" culture.

Now we come to the issues, and I'll let these pour out. It is now centuries later and the culture is discovered. Anthropologists come along and catalog the various rites and put it under an umbrella of protection to ensure that no one will mess with its pagan structure. No one knows that it was derived from the dreams of one individual. Though the catalog is complete, there remains a desire to continue to study it. And so, what the outside world brings to the center of the culture is a condensation of it, a self-conscious representation that wants neither to destroy nor disrupt it, merely to affirm it, to act as a teacher, in order to preserve it. A way is found to transfer the sounds of the language into characters so that written language can be taught. With books and schools come questions. The origins forgotten, the best written history that can be generated begs them, and the once active culture begins to become self-conscious. Universities are added to perpetuate themselves, not to preserve freshness nor answer to the paradox that learning decreases imagination. Culture that constantly renews itself ends up regurgitating. The story of Jerod itself is questioned, relegated into a myth. The myth, while held high, creates a dichotomy between diminishing a place for anything new unless it conforms, not all that it entails which must be original, not hybrid, but the ability to do so is lost, along with respect for the barbaric conventions the old ways represent. In the short version, books make references to Jerod as part of the folklore, larger than life but not a high point of cultural consciousness, rather something for the kiddies. Mythology. Jerod is finally a statue in a

The Voyage of a Bean

museum. No one believes anymore, but a once fervent, active and fertile people, is now rather skeptical, sterile and hungry for something new. So what comes next? The missionaries? No. But anything new will develop by corruption and ultimately be absorbed. For example, we take Jerod's tribe in its modern sterile state. Like the original Jerod, a couple of tribesmen have a vision. They see the world as a writhing, corrupt monster of a society, and feel they must bear witness to it. So they set up the first basic news service to report on any events that bear out this vision and keep the society honest. It is enormously successful. As it achieves its success, it grows, and others who come to participate are hired. Soon the news service goes in various directions and gets out of hand as originators delegate and rise in power. Over time, it becomes gigantic itself, quite out of hand, replete with people with their own agendas who do not have the original sense of the mission but reveling in their fame. Eventually, the media, as it comes to be called, is forced to report that it is perceived to be a carnival, something that pretends to be a science, requires proper certification and good looks, but not integrity of its professionals. In the end of its own cultural progression, it is impossible to distinguish from the writhing monster, as it is only one of its ugly spewing heads.

Ultimately when we take Jerod's dream along with the advances of civilization and base knowledge provided to children, we accept that all major foundations of insight are first put forth where they surround. After this, they are taken in as part of the foundation, however shaky, and lost within it — all except the issue of truth and God for somehow they are maintained as having come from without, though paradoxically real god and real truth from without are correctly seen as having real life within, aligned, where they can be maintained despite outside corruption, sterility or skepticism of an era. Belief and fertility maintain links to totality within and without. Ultimately secular culture has a form of godliness in impact, but in fact not at all of real God, and evolving like Jerod's tribe is no different in complexity and mystery than how salmon learned to migrate and spawn. In the human drama, even dreams surprising to no one else but the dreamer may be taken for more, enforced on others through power, to be ultimately taken as cultural because of tradition or time. And this is why we are drawn to the great story tellers, but I'll ask a question. Are we pulled strongly into art to turn its manifestations and

The Death of the Explorer

creators into our gods (a dangerous plight, wherein lies sale of the soul), or simply to remain fertile, to maintain belief and strengthen our link with real truth in the wasteland? Ask yourselves what distinguishes great work from comic book and why I'm not here talking about Batman and Robin.

Anything that achieves this kind of draw though, including that spiritual supplanting of the godly requirement is both a blessing and a danger, for while it frees the mind, it also has the tendency to bind the culture into strata of intellectual presumption, conformity by recognition of ideas, and assumed understanding by association with false icons. All that is somehow a necessary downside or surprising result of keeping the truth alive. Ardent thirst for truth leads to statues in the parks, not of truth but of those who embody it. There would be no need to erect them if the world were really free.

On the other hand, perception of the truth is transient even in the artist, even unfulfilling in the long run. Art can be a dead end for wholeness even if sought for that reason. Imparted only glimpses of it from time to time, the artist tries to make a more permanent connection and develop an order from it that both isolates that perception and constitutes what becomes known as his style. The end result is ultimately therefore far different than the millions of story lines that clog out the general recognition, and their unique difficulty relegates them to a special category most hold at arm's length. It is why I'm here willing to say a fragment of Kafka is worth more than ten thousand comics or dime-store romantic novels.

Sometimes an artist makes the transition through illness, epilepsy, migraine, and sometimes even drugs, to get past the spirit of the first sorrow of needing that second trapeze, as in Zeus' headache giving birth to Minerva who takes on a life of her own and becomes goddess of wisdom but of course the problem is acquiring not only the trapeze but the ability to do a flip on it seemingly without a jot of training, which raises other questions. How does merely preparatory, plastic effort lead into the real stuff? How does one cut off all the outside mainstream influences in order to loosen their grip so that there is a real birth of truth out of the union of talent and vision. Still, it isn't surprising with all the questions that science has managed to answer, there are still no answers for all the great questions of life.

Despite this, it is almost intuitive that even in a day by day, brick by brick outlay of time, which in no way has anything but a factual, steady

The Voyage of a Bean

pace to it, there is a whole universe of perception waiting to be inferred, truth to be uncovered, and the whole world, even in factual layout, can be thought of in that light. We are in the trouble with Kafka if he binds us into a way of thinking without at the same time providing our escape once we get into his machinery. What happens is we fail at the start, struggling on that terrible execution machine, tied down between a bed and a designer with the harrow shuttling between them sticking its needles into us with a message we can only decipher later from our wounds. "Death to the superhuman, worse for the human," as Robert Lowell said in the context of learning here at Harvard. There's also that great line that I read as education revealing totality while removing imagination: "The best tale stales to homework." How in the quickening pace of the everyday, living lives of "quiet desperation," where is the certainty of realizing any secure returns, or dividends of empowerment? You have to settle for having an appreciation of literature in the end and be your own judge of what that affords.

Constructs of totality as offered by Jerod's happy, pagan world, or ancient mythology, are lost to us because we don't buy them. Even our own multi-headed dragon begs an increasingly narrow conformity along secular political lines. This will prove hard to buy for the few. "He who joyfully marches to music in rank and file has already earned my contempt. He has been given a large brain by mistake," as Einstein put it. What distinguishes Kafka and those like him is that he took his raw truth from the subconscious, hammering it into shape with an unchained conscious mind, compelled by truth, deciphering visions into cipher seeds awakening in our own minds by a mellowing of occasion, so we can't be dispassionate, for the real trouble with Kafka is he happens to be right. The laws of nature, true on earth, are obeyed equally throughout the universe, yet we come down to the fact that the trouble with Kafka is that we live as though he must be wrong but discover by degrees along the process that in fact he is right; and the trouble is that though he's right, nobody cares. Most would rather live life out like Jerod's tribe, but settle for the evolved, self-conscious and corrupted society without a link to God. To most of mankind, though they wouldn't put it exactly this way, Kafka and those like him are analogous to the anthropologists whose sole purpose is to put distance between us and first-hand discovery of the terrible truth for ourselves. He's depressing. That's the trouble with him, say those of the tribe that hasn't budged

The Death of the Explorer

in thousands of years, that refuses to explore the inner world and whose sole legacy is a dusty museum containing only the artifacts of a society born without a bridge to God from the lost but formulative mind.

My notes for the first lecture end here. I remember starting the round of applause that followed and a brisk, thought-filled walk back to my apartment. I was reading Camus at the time and added a note from *The Rebel*, which I think, is appropriate. He wrote, *There does exist for man, therefore, a way of action and of thinking which is possible on the level of moderation to which he belongs. Every undertaking that is more ambitious than this proves to be contradictory. The absolute is not attained, nor, above all, created through history. Politics is not religion, or if it is, then it is nothing but the inquisition. How would society define an absolute? Perhaps everyone is looking for this absolute on the behalf of all. But society and politics only have the responsibility of arranging everyone's affairs so that each will have the leisure and the freedom to pursue this common search. History can then no longer be presented as an object of worship. It is only an opportunity that must be rendered fruitful by a vigilant rebellion.*

The following morning when I arrived for work at the ice-cream parlor, my termagant boss Terry had already changed his tune about my leaving early the day before. It seems there was a rush after I left. I became a scapegoat, and he browbeat me all morning. One customer who was an alcoholic vagrant called me a name. When I related the incident to Terry, he said the customer was always right and that I must be a non-person. At one point I was working the take-out counter and Terry was working the grill. There was a wall with an open window/counter dividing the two areas. On the counter was a bell. Terry told me to ring the bell and give him any orders for the grill that came through. There was a lull and finally a regular customer came in and asked for a blueberry muffin on the grill. Terry was listening in, and waiting at the window when I put up the ticket and told him it was a blueberry muffin on the grill. After five minutes of waiting, both the customer and I wondered what was taking so long, so I looked through to Terry who hadn't even started cooking it. "You didn't ring the bell," he told me. Later he trained me briefly to work a register I had never seen before

The Voyage of a Bean

while the assigned employee took a break. I hit the twenty-dollar key by mistake and asked for help. Someone showed me how to void it, but then Terry came over and asked what had "possessed" me to hit the key. During another lull, with no customers in the store, I took a moment to rest and Terry rushed over to ball me out. He demanded that I keep busy every second, wiping counters, just to look busy if I had to because the other employees worked hard and would resent seeing me idle when they put their hearts into their jobs. I looked over and pointed to the coffee station where four waitresses were taking advantage of the lull and having a nice chat. Terry grew angrier and said, "If you think I'm wrong, keep it to yourself." In the final incident, I'd given an extra spoon to a customer who'd bought a lime rickey. Terry quizzed me as to why I'd give away company property for free, and explained the customer had sat down at a table to eat a piece of cake he'd bought at another store. One of the waitresses brought it to Terry's attention, so he threw the young man out. He was still chewing me out when the customer returned and demanded his money back, that Terry had had no right to toss him out. In the same condescending tone he'd been using with me, Terry told the man he couldn't have a refund for the drink, whereupon the man threw what was left into Terry's face, and then he walked out quickly. Terry gasped for a moment, then followed, running out of the parlor. We all waited expectantly for almost half an hour. When Terry returned, his shirt stained, we learned he'd chased the man all over Cambridge but couldn't get to him on the other side of a car where the man taunted him relentlessly. "You see what your friends will do?" he said pointing sternly at me when he walked into the store.

I worried about leaving for the explorer's second lecture though I didn't have to leave early because I knew there would be a seat for me. Terry's attitude was the issue. He'd already made it clear to me he expected me to stay through any rush despite any conflict with my classes. We'd had a few arguments, but he'd always finally relented because he'd agreed on principle when I'd taken the job to let me go by 2:30 every day because of school. But this day was different. When I said I was leaving, he hit the ceiling and said I was fired. I followed him into the back room. "You can't fire me," I told him. "We have an agreement." He told me he was letting me go because nobody there liked me. "What about Jenny and Virginia?" I asked. "Jenny and Virginia," he scoffed, "who are they?" "Examples of people here who like me," I retorted. We argued for quite a while and he finally relented and agreed not to fire me. "Good," I told him. "I quit," but because of all the time we'd spent wasting time while customers cried for service, I was late for the explorer's second lecture.

I don't have as many notes here due to being late. I think I was preoccupied a bit as well. It was embarrassing opening the chapel door, letting all that light in, and interrupting the explorer in midsentence. He looked at me and smiled though, asking if I'd been out exploring. I nodded. "Good, good." He said.

My notes here indicate that he was discussing... *Kafka's overestimated influence on me. He only brought me in as a consultant and rewarded me by making me a character. It isn't as if I absorbed his philosophy, nor am I a peculiar manifestation.*

There are only a few stray thoughts here that I may not have caught accurately, but I want to convey the flavor of the discussion, so please bear with me. *Selling the soul to the devil is a notion based on ultimately perceiving a worthlessness for almost anything done compared to giving up the soul to do it,* he said. *But when one perceives worthlessness prior to the sale, but is driven to perform anyway, a great work may be achieved in God's domain. Mellowing into the truth yields a bargainless stream of ideas, not tainted with earthly desire or fanatical needs.*

He finished the second lecture with a surprise show and tell I was happy to be able to see. He had collected quite a few items of interest during his life of exploration, and for the first time anywhere was obliging enough to share some of the more interesting relics. I didn't take notes, so I don't remember everything, but foremost in my mind is the moment he opened a rather large box and pulled out the giant, black, dried up and quite fragile insect leg of Gregor Samsa, the man who turned into a bug in his story *The Metamorphosis*. He explained it was not general knowledge, but due to the fact that he was often present during other Kafka projects and had witnessed most of what happened after Gregor was transformed. He said the head had

The Voyage of a Bean

recently sold at auction for a million dollars.

He also brought pictures of the castle used in the novel of the same name, and of the courtroom where *The Trial* took place. But most interesting were items from the penal colony. In a bottle he had the filthy gag of felt used to fill mouths of so many convicts before the machine was destroyed. Finally he demonstrated a working model of the execution machine, setting a tiny doll into the bed and showing us how the harrow inscribes its message to be revealed only to the victim at the time of death as it moves with its needles between the designer and the bed. I recalled the end of the officer who had put the message, *Be Just*, into the designer before the machine malfunctioned, killing him and tossing his body into a pit. It is one of Kafka's great enigmas. I walked home from the second lecture looking at the ground as a bed, the sky holding all the tools of the designer and life as a harrowing experience. What message would I be forced to fathom before being tossed into the pit, too weak to spit out the gag to say what it is?

In his last installment in the lecture series, the explorer's topic was on the nature of exploration, the nature of discovery, and breaking free of Kafka altogether to speak on issues central to his domain. At first he covered some of his exploits and adventures, but I failed to take good notes on these. There was whaling and gnashing of the teeth, of a tiger, and that sort of thing, but his explorations weren't really my interest. Suffice it to say there were many, and he'd been everywhere. He did discuss his philosophy of exploration, and this is where my notes are full enough to transcribe.

Here is a tale that differentiates between a real explorer and a mere traveler. A young man in the East grew discontent with his life. His friends all seemed to be happy as they assumed their stations in life. One became a banker, another a barber, and another a bricklayer, one a salesman, and so on. None of this interested him as he didn't want to let any one occupation limit life's possibilities, and so he resolved to go west to look for his place. He didn't know what he was looking for, but felt he'd know when he found it.

As soon as he started his journey he saw many beautiful sites on which he might build his home, if he were so inclined. There were fine sites by

The Death of the Explorer

the mountains, next to pristine lakes and streams, in the vast forests or on the plains. Each place had its possibilities, but the limits were his concern. He felt he needed to keep moving so as not to be stuck in any one thing.

After a few years of traveling this way, years of convolution and uncertainty, he finally reached the West Coast. Nothing he'd seen seemed to be his niche, so he decided to return to the East because he had started to miss his friends and family. "Certainly," he thought, "my home is where I'll find the heart of me. On the way home he thought how well his old friends must be doing whereas he had nothing. As he retraced his steps he saw that most of the places he thought would have been good places to settle had houses on them, and the people who'd built them were accommodating and congenial when he needed to rest.

When he returned to the city of his youth, he was welcomed as a son and friend but felt as much a stranger at home as he had been out west. He thought he should display some fortune he made though there wasn't even a hint he'd made promises or that anyone cared if he had. Everyone was excited to hear of his journeys. What had he seen? What was it like in other places? He obliged them but was disinterested as ever in what he had lived. He was more interested in how the town had grown, how all of his friends had even deeper roots and families to show for their time on earth. He noticed that everyone except him was making a contribution to the whole. He was still unhappy, but didn't know what to do. He didn't want to travel again, because it bothered him that he might waste time again. He did not know what he wanted, but recognized that essentially he had no faith that he would find anything. He lived out his life through projection and envy, with a keen sense that one day he would arrive at a state of contentment. Nothing held any particular interest for him although it was noticed how he took such pride in maintaining the grounds around what would eventually be his final resting place. He was often seen at the cemetery, puttering about the grave.

As an addendum to the story, consider this man as a traveler — everyone nailed down but him — who can't stop because there's something left to see, who doesn't realize that he's not going anywhere, having to watch as people in their niche die according to plan. The coal miner and steel worker die young due to work-related problems, while the banker grows old before he goes, but all in the great scheme of things. Even in the end,

The Voyage of a Bean

the traveler feels detached, lost in self-inflicted limbo with no place in life or death. From our point of view, he's unable to make the leap to unconscious being, to acceptance of life. If a prism were to divide his experience like light into its constituents, there would be no thread of joy.

Consider a man who has roots and station who decides to leave his life in a big lie, running away from his wife and children to start a new life along the path he wished he had as a young man. Imagine he then proceeds to make some kind of tremendous discovery or finish a great work that just begs to be brought out into the open. At the same time as he fulfills his dream, his lies grow huge and command him back into hiding for it would also mean his own shame to be discovered. In exploration, anything less than serving the truth is a deception.

Consider another idea about a young man who grows up in a wasteland of sterility, commercialism. He loves the truth and hates his world. During the last few years of staying with his family, he can't wait to get out, but he makes careful plans of where to go and what to do to serve the truth. When his time comes, he heads out with great enthusiasm and puts his heart into further studies, exploring his own potential. In the end, many are surprised when he returns to the same town in which he grew up. After all, they remember how much he claimed to hate it. But he has come back as a man, fully realized and able to work without being hindered, and nothing about the area now stops him from being able to think and create, though nothing about it has changed.

Or consider the story of two young men of the same age and similar interests and visions who enter a city through the same gate at the same time, resolved to meet exactly ten years later at the same gate. When the appointed moment comes, both arrive, but there is no longer any connection between the two. One has grown, ripened into wisdom by experience; the other has withered and been sadly diminished to a shadow of his former self. There's a difference between exploring with authority, recognition of reality; and exploring that amounts to something being taken out of you by the experience, wising up to the state of ugliness after the erasure of the beautiful, the laughing and the crying philosophers.

Each one of these tales has a bearing on the theme of exploration in general. We remember the oft-quoted line from Eliot's fourth quartet, Little Gidding: "We shall not cease from exploration/And the end of all our

The Death of the Explorer

exploring/Will be to arrive where we started/And know the place for the first time."

Eliot also said, "The second-rate artist...cannot afford to surrender himself to any common action; for his chief task is the assertion of all the trifling differences which are his distinction: only the man who has so much to give that he can forget himself in his work can afford to collaborate, to exchange, to contribute." In the broken fragments of Kafka's thought lie the seeds of the miracle of feeding the multitude with a basket of fish and barley bread.

Another take on Eliot is that exploration as itself does not end, cannot stop — and like the state of being that you as students seem to go through, everything seems to mesh together and from one thing into another indefinitely, inexorably. But we don't begin in an explorative state, but need to be taught or motivated as to how to explore for the basis is discovery. So in the end of all exploring is actually a return to the pre-explorative state, where we do nothing, and truly know it for the first time as an empty state for having done all the exploring.

Also in exploration, Kafka looked into mind and experience, while staying still. His wasn't an exploration of geography or science, but of metaphysics, where discoveries are more like seeds than places to visit or artifacts to be studied. They need to be grown within in order to be understood, become alive inside in order to be analyzed.

How many of us ever get back to where we started, or realize there's a sense in which we never leave. Eliot prefaced Four Quartets with a wonderful fragment that is translated, "Although the logos is common to all, the majority of people live as though they have one of their own." Part V of his second quartet East Coker says much along these lines. Listen closely to the last bit which has an interest to me personally as an old explorer. And then he read the stanzas to us.

When he finished, he put the book down and took a long look at us. *Pascal put it another way*, he finally began. *The last thing you get to know is what should come first.*

And so we arrive at the end of three lectures, he concluded, *where the hope is that words will bring us where no words are necessary. We know we will come to the end, but with imperfect understanding, we only dimly see and can't know whether we're going the right way. Somehow it is only*

The Voyage of a Bean

clear we're being judged. Even if there is no judge, it is a judgment upon us. So either way we're in trouble. This no-win situation was also Kafka's trouble. You can scoff at it and treat life as a big joke, but don't forget that in the end, you have to go through to the end and die, so the joke's on you, but if you discover anything in the end, don't forget to pass it on. Thank you very much, all of you, for exploring with me here.

After warmly applauding after the last lecture, we went with the explorer into the church for a question-and-answer period. I took notes here as well, but briefly, he told us to remember these days of learning, of being so charged by the onslaught of ideas, the way they were held and divided by those who taught them, and the power of the books themselves, the community, and friends. He encouraged us to let the ideas take on a form of their own, as full as we already were and impossible as it was to absorb it all. "Much of it is taken in as by osmosis anyway," he said. "The triumph of the understanding comes in grasping what cannot be maintained, but managing anyway with unexpected, almost magical dexterity." Then he cautioned us to realize that while Harvard provided a sense of security that truth is a thriving commodity, when you hit the streets of reality you come to realize it's barely twitching in the incubator.

As he took questions from the field, I mustered courage and raised my hand. On the second or third try, he called on me. With a two-part question, I read a quote from *The Rebel* and asked how it's possible to reach people who stand apart, behind an ideology. Then I brought up the execution machine. In Kafka's story the officer takes the encrypted message, *Be Just*, and the whole machine collapses. Imagine we're in the bed, harrow and designer. What's the message being written on us that we should see life telling us in the end?

"As for the fanatics of an ideology," he replied, "First you must realize there is nothing you can do. When you realize that, then, maybe, you can do something. As for our being in the machine, the message we ultimately get is *Just Be*. Too bad it's a final realization rather than an inborn response to life."

Then I asked, "How can you really say that, when in fact, in all your life, it does not appear that you ever *Just Were*. Are you planning to just start *being* from now on, or is it just an explorer's way of telling lesser people who will always be students to keep on reading, but don't get in the way of those doing the really important work. I mean, what have you really discovered that you brought to us here that we wouldn't have already known or heard in boring English classes? What are you exploring if it's already been found by others? You've made your way around the globe and seen it all, but in the final analysis you sound like an academic, at least to me. You pay homage to ideas, to simple slogans when at least I was expecting you to show up here with the skins of lions and show us the scars you won by fighting and killing them barehanded."

He just looked at me. There was something odd in his stare, like he was working toward something, as if I had asked him to solve an equation. Then he asked, "Is that all?"

"No," I replied. "You want it with both barrels? I came a long way to this fine, university and couldn't even get in. I wash dishes and dish out ice cream, and I audit classes and pour over volumes of forgotten lore. I believe I'm driven to be a writer, which I thought would be exciting; I thought that I would become a kind of explorer myself, but listening to you, it's as if all you did was read books. Why should I write when what I'll deliver in the end, doing less than you in real exploration, will be more boring and useless than anything you've said here." He tried to break in, but I went on. "I've been living two lives here, one studying, the other working but barely support the other, and I believe I'm learning more from my personal struggle than anything you think you can teach me."

Then he looked down and said, "Ah, there it is again — being on the verge of nothingness and greatness, and not knowing which."

By this time other students, real ones, had begun to boo me. He held up his hand. "No, no. To build society, the world sells a prefabricated package. Buying it leaves the inner life unexplored. The same experience can destroy faith or build it. Literature helps us to be resilient. It is about building the soul, uplifting it until one embraces life, within and without. Life without a developed intuitive sense is an incomplete life, so develop that first. How? Study nothing. Become an expert at nothing. Teach others to become comfortable with the *nothing that is there*, and if you can do that, then you can be sure that you have really done something. And you have helped me discover something too, so I'd like to close this. Thank you." At that he stood up and passed through his university handlers out the door. I was quickly surrounded and asked for personal information. It was all I could do to get out of the room. The next day I couldn't get into classes without an ID. I found my way around the campus closed. There was an article in the *Crimson* about it, and as far as I understood it, the Explorer had quit his university post and disappeared. Everyone was buzzing with either a sense that he was somehow throwing in the towel or off on a major exploration of some kind to prove himself, to jump to that second trapeze.

Someone who had attended the lectures recognized me at my new position hawking papers one day, and alerted the university. I was soon let go from the job. My picture and a story about vagabond students was published in the city newspapers along with a somewhat modified account of the incident. I was cast as a zealot of some kind that had caused a regrettable disturbance. The university indicated there was a breach in security that would be tightened, and that similar incidents would be prevented in the future.

I returned to Chicago shortly after that and made it a point to reject anything to do with writing. I drove cabs, worked in restaurants, and did odd jobs. I didn't have anyone to help me, and I got as far as I did by myself. Still, I always felt as though some of the people with silver spoons in their mouths were still looking down on me, as if by birth there is some indication of intelligence. In the end, birth makes too big a difference, but I've always thought, true or not, that as many people end up coming down from artificial heights than are kept from rising up, and in the end, we all end up going the same route. I have regrets, but I wouldn't change a thing.

As I finally look up from the old Harvard notebook into the present, I feel a need to better understand what drove the explorer out of the university. There is nothing in the obituary that indicates that he did anything amazing. It doesn't go into any of the details of his last speaking engagement at Harvard where I had my fifteen minutes of fame. Compared to my current state, I looked back at the whole period as a kind of distortion. I don't think it's as much a

The Death of the Explorer

change in the times as it is the changes in me. There isn't anything that happened back then that has made a difference in the world, but I can say it made all the difference in me. At the same time, if in some way I managed to keep the explorer from doing anything significant, I may have hurt the world by keeping something from happening. On the other hand, what had the world done to properly evaluate me and give me a chance? I was blackballed for not attacking but openly questioning one of the sacred cows in a place where I thought that might be encouraged. If anything, that whole era was open season on anything that smacked of the establishment, so it's a wonder that I was a scapegoat. All I can think is that something I said rubbed off. If he was made of sterner stuff, if what none of what I said were true, it wouldn't have made any difference, and if it were true, it would have ultimately come to his attention in time. All I did was say what would come anyway, and in fact, it was something he probably already had thought about.

I turned back to the newspaper obituary for more information about the explorer. Interestingly, it said there were indications that he had burned lots of papers before he died, and it was thought that this might have been a long-awaited autobiography. I always thought the world was losing whatever an individual consigned in the end to the flames, but as I've grown older, I've come to the conclusion that we have the sacred duty of destroying things before we die if we have the time. If there is anything of value, it would be a shame if we lost our sense of it and destroyed what really might be a great work, but given that we might have already given everything of value that we had to give to the world, it was incumbent upon us to burn whatever was left to prevent the idiots from mistaking junk for treasure as they so often do, and these idiots are quite well educated and in positions of authority. They just don't have the necessary insight to distinguish them or what they supposedly evaluate.

As I closed the box I found pictures of the statue of John Harvard. I was surprised to see him reposed in a comfortable chair because for some reason I'd remembered him standing and waving a book. So I reasoned it must have been just after he lectured, and now he was resting. The explorer lectured us as one sitting, but in his explorations, he was the one standing. It's too bad that what students get are the ashes of experience when what they need is the fire of ongoing experience that burns in reaching out to teach.

Actually I didn't quite close the box all the way. Over the next few weeks I wandered through my old journals, remembering my passion for the dream of becoming a writer. I wasn't far from a sense of picking it up again, though it couldn't be where I left off. Back then I was so immersed in what I thought was the glory of the calling, when in fact it's a lonely existence. And it struck me that I'd be risking the death of the explorer in myself if I sat down to write. I'd grown so negative to not just writing but to all the arts, which have evolved much as the clergy in the middle ages when the church was the government, bringing people in for the wrong reasons. It may not be political, and artists are not governors, but there is a way in which art has grown into a more social than individual industry, driven more by selling some social package than educating the soul.

I didn't even know if I could still write, but I was beginning to want to try again, as an explorer, which meant it wasn't about me but the discoveries. It was about developing the intuitive side, the inner life, preparing one for the mystery, to meet it head on, and to help others wend their way through the bramble, to the truth. The only thing that could stop me now was myself, and I was at a point where I could do something, which is in line with what the explorer had said in answer to my first question: "First, realize you *can do nothing*, then maybe you can do something." Then it struck me. Neither of us had done anything since we'd met. When he made the comment about being "on the verge of nothingness and greatness, and not knowing which," I thought it was for me, but I believe he was talking to himself. He had achieved greatness, and nothingness was "something" he had never had to consider. Perhaps it was the only thing left for him to explore. I think of him now as a kind of prisoner himself, waiting for an ultimate discovery, to find the words of eternal truth in the needlings of being alone, and yet he had burned his papers. Did he get a message and die enlightened by the needling machinery of the universe, or did it all go haywire? We all must go through it to find out, but acceptance of the gag is optional.

Pandora's Box

A young woman is put in charge of a large box filled with all the evils of the world, but she is not told what is inside. She is only told not to open it, for the contents may destroy the world.

She takes it in her charge, but begins to worry about it. Then she guesses it's probably an atomic bomb, so she calls the bomb disposal unit. They come to disarm it, and treat the box like the housing of the bomb itself. They attach cables with internal drills, which put holes in it, and they pour in all kinds of foam and solvents, which would disarm any kind of known explosive device.

When the treatment is complete, they open the box, and all the various evils come out of the box unharmed by the solvents. The young woman is called by those who gave her the box in the first place. She tells them about all the evils coming out of the box. They ask her about hope. "What about hope?" she asks.

"Hope was in the box too," they tell her. "Didn't you see it come out?" She tells them she didn't, and it isn't in the box. Then the best scientists confirm the worst fear that the solvents most likely dissolved hope into liquid components that were probably absorbed into the box itself during the bomb-disposal effort. This, everyone agrees, is a tragedy. Meanwhile, all of the evils are hard at work destroying the world. Within a week, the situation has become very grave. It looks like the whole world might go up in smoke in a matter of days. Those who know about the box show up at the girl's house. "It may be our only hope," they tell her, climbing into the box for shelter, which she locks behind them, successfully containing enough of the evils to take the pressure off and save the world.

Homecoming

It is the eve of my twenty-year high-school reunion, held during homecoming, and my head is flooded with remembrance as I pack for the trip. I'm excited at the prospect of seeing all my childhood friends. I never made it to the ten-year reunion, and I'm that much more wound up about this one. My wife has to help me find things that are in their proper places as well as reassure me that everything is on schedule. By the time I go to bed, I'm exhausted, but my head still swirls, and I can't sleep.

There is a seamless transition from thinking about packing to a dream about packing, but in the dream I am leaving home. I'm going back and forth to the car, packing the back seat, not telling anyone, trying not to call any attention to it — feeling shame but not sure if it's because I'm trying to sneak away or whether it's an overall sensation that is driving me away. My father asks if he can take me to breakfast in New York City. I decline saying I was just there yesterday, but that's not the reason. He says he loves me. I say "Me too." I feel like I can be misunderstood, but he lets it go.

I sneak into my brother's room where he is still sleeping and take a key to unlock the trunk for further packing, planning to leave before he wakes. Just as I open the trunk, my mother and sister come in to see what I'm doing. I divert their attention by pretending there is a garbage strike and I'm just taking garbage to the dump. To prove it, I pick up a bag of garbage from the corner and jokingly ask them if they mind my taking it. My sister sees something in the bag and says she wants it. It is one of her unfinished paintings. Then I remembered hiding it in my brother's garbage the night before so I could take it, but the plot has backfired on me.

As I get closer to finally leaving home, I feel I want everyone to know that when I left home the first time when I was eighteen years old that I knew exactly what I wanted out of life. I've only a vague remembrance of what that was, but I'm sure it was something the world doesn't reward particularly well, but is nevertheless a career worthy of being pursued. Now, at close to forty years old, I'm leaving home in my dreams. Where do I go when I have to leave my dreams? Why go just because I'm free to go? I should have some idea of this, but I've no idea of what I want and don't know where to go. My mouth feels filled with something preventing me from saying anything. I can't figure out a way to make them proud of me.

I hear them ask me direct questions about my plans. Twenty years before, they couldn't get me to shut-up on the subject. Now I don't know myself where I am going. Some ideas come to mind, but they're more directional like north or southwest. There's no clear favorite even on the compass. I wish something would keep me there, but there is nothing standing in my way. Everything is clear in front of the house now. I can get going, yet I stand and look at the house feeling regret. It occurs to me that I don't have to go as I drive away. Just before I wake up, I realize that I didn't finish packing, and only left when there was an opportunity because no one was looking. I can't remember what I would have packed, but wake up with a sense that it's terribly important to remember.

All through the next morning, something from this dream hangs over me. I'm no longer looking forward to the reunion. All I can think about is that I'm coming from a life that's amounted to generally nothing. I've no great position, no fame to match the promises I made when diving from the springboard of youth and potential. I feel like so many shards of brittle bones scattered in the basin of an empty swimming pool.

On the plane, I feel expectation and fear. Whatever it is I am doing, I don't know what I want. Whatever it is I am living, I don't know what I am. Along with remorse I shouldn't have on leaving home, I still feel the sense that I forgot to pack something. I also remember that as I stood and looked at the house in the dream, it wasn't the house of my youth, but the house I live in now. It merges into a sense that I'm going back to the town where I grew up, where I once knew exactly what I wanted out of life. I start to remember that somewhere along the path of twenty years since that time, I'd made up my mind not to think about the old days and swept it all out of my mind like broken glass. Now it seemed that I was carrying it in a box to the factory, not hoping for a replacement but feeling that it will somehow be fixed.

In the Country

A storm is approaching. As I sit in front of my house reading some old books, I can see buildings on the horizon. I know I have visited them, and yet I cannot remember exactly when or how. They looks like tall boxes under dark clouds, but somehow I know what they look like inside. As far away as they are, I know the city well and can feel what people are doing in the distance, but I've been living in the country all my life.

It begins to rain, and in running for cover I am surprised to see how many mice are also seeking shelter. Why do I feel like it has been a long time since I have been in the country? These mice are really large. Perhaps they are rats. It feels like it has been a long time since I have seen either species.

One of them runs into the garage. As I go back for my things, others are appearing. Then I see a particularly large one, which does not frighten as I approach it. It turns out that it is a cat. Rather like a bobcat, it's going to take care of these mice, I can tell. It takes a stab at one that attempts to run by it, catches it in its claws, picks it up and puts one half of it beside the other. My God! The mice back off.

Now all of a sudden, one of my ex-girlfriends, Kay, appears. She wraps herself around my neck. One of her legs goes around mine, and as she tells me that she still loves me, she squeezes me in secret places to relax my anger. But it is no use. She promises she will marry me, but it is no use. She goes into the house. I step off of the porch. I see the old books that I was reading outside are now drenched.

I pick them up. It is the third or fourth time that water has

The Voyage of a Bean

attacked me. Water has destroyed so much in my life. Flood after flood, year after year. It comes in through the walls in rainstorms. It comes in through the ceilings as people upstairs fail to properly attach the hoses of their washing-machines. It attacks the work I did yesterday or the day before. I can't do anything without water getting to it. I should be working on plastic. I should protect everything that I do in plastic seals. I should live in a rubber house in the desert where new rivers rarely form.

I take these books and try to squeeze them out, wondering if the quality of the paper is enough to keep the pages from drying together like glue. I believe they are ruined. I feel tremendous frustration. I even begin to cry. Wailing about the disaster of water, I make more.

I peek in the house to see if anyone has seen me. Yes. My mother is there. Yet there's no sympathy. She has seen it all before. I feel tremendous exhaustion. I bring everything inside. It is the first chance I've had to examine the premises. It is my mother's new home. I am only a guest. I remember Kay. Why is she so cozy here? Signs of my mother's new life are everywhere. Here's a photograph of her dancing. She is with a man I don't recognize, but he's her type — cultured and wealthy. Looks aren't important — just that she is happy.

I think of Kay again. Where did she go? Oh, there she is, sitting in a rocking-chair — reading. Perhaps I should ask her to take a walk. That would be a good idea — a walk. But just as I'm standing on the porch again, who appears almost in disguise? Bea — another old flame. Even her face is covered. She says, "I told you this would happen." I recognize her by her voice. What is she doing here? We'd broken up a long time ago. And she came from inside the house. I say, "Are you taking a walk?" She says yes, and she disappears. My worry that Kay might see Bea evaporates. The time to worry about that is long past. Neither one has anything to do with my present. It's time to head for that city I feel like I know on the horizon. I'll not look back. Then, I remember that it is a giant mirror, and all those new faces in the distance are old enemies, quietly going about their business all around me in the city.

The Sandmen

As we sleep, sand comes out of our ears just like out of an hourglass. A pile of sand grows beside the bed, and as it gets larger, it begins to take the shape of a little man. Call him the sandman if you like, but what he does is leave your head completely open to make important calculations of the events of the day — ascertainments that are essential for judging the meaning of your life.

Along with the rest we gain from sleep, the new perspective that comes through dreams is important in maintaining balance in the face of the world's continuing insanity. While we sleep, the sandman, who is composed of everything ugly and devious that has ever entered our thoughts, heads out to mingle with all the other sandmen out of minds in the world. Like the next world where we will be perfect, no longer linear and limited, the sandmen merge with another in this world. This is heaven for them. They dissolve into one another. They become a heaving desert, full of dunes of information, which they exchange as they sift around one another.

By the time sleep begins to wear off of us, our sandman is just returning from his reunion. He is much the same as ever, just a bit more wily, having picked up new deviances to add new wrinkles to us in the new day. Besides that, as he returns into our ear, he clouds what was a great coherence. He disperses our dreams, he extinguishes new insights, snuffing bright embers until we can barely remember a single cogency in the smoke, let alone the key to the code. Occasionally, as might happen when we are surprised awake, when the sandman has had very little time to come together and return to our minds, we have a chance to view the current tapestry

The Voyage of a Bean

of clear thinking that comes from our unimpeded mind, and can sense the wonders of the dream and even feel the key in some open pocket of thought to unlock its further mysteries.

Then it almost seems worthwhile to battle our sandman. But the world gives us little time to mount an assault since the perception of him is so fleeting. And the world is so filled with their mischief, and bears their mark so lightly that a slight breeze will erase our footprints soon after we've taken a step toward them, and we quickly lose our way inside ourselves. Each morning on his return, he brings at least a few new notions to add a wrinkle to our forehead by the end of our days. By the time we've finished our lives, we've been little more than a vehicle for a steady stream of ugliness to pass through. At the moment we're finally discarded, when our souls cross the threshold and enter the perfect ether of the next world, we will be surprised by the sudden sense of perfection and completion even though we may have learned about it in some detail during our existence in the limited world of the here and now.

Have you not heard of the great knight who made a visit from the next world, who came into this world of shifting sands, and though the desert heaved and the sandmen united in us to silence him, in the end he left us with exactly what was needed to conquer the enemy? In its very basic essence, all that we need is the very thing that we discover in ourselves after we take a broad survey of the world in our search for the truth. We slowly learn that we cannot change the world, but something changes in us along the way. We learn to reject the ways of the world which punish the weak, and we learn to love everyone who endures the same ultimacies that we endure. For regardless of how long or how well anyone fights, in the end it is the same for all. Life proves unendurable for everyone.

What is it that keeps us from completely losing our minds? We have the sandmen to thank for that, don't we? For the sandmen shield us from too much sensitivity on the issue. They want us to last as long as possible. If we focus one day almost completely and come close to complete understanding, we tire and fade into sleep, only to bring an entirely new outlook into the next day. We may even wonder what we were so charged about the day before. Thanks

The Sandmen

to the sandmen, we are protected even from too much fear of our ultimate end, which is so frightful to realize fully that the realization turns to an echo, which turns to merely thinking of the echo, until the fear is twice removed from fear itself. How is a sense of the truth to be maintained when it changes to a pale copy overnight?

But the sandmen don't have it all their way. We have nothing to fear since there is ultimately no end for us. The fear of death is replaced with worry that something we do may keep us from crossing the threshold; may hold us back to turn to dust and mingle with sand to clog the ears of our descendants. What can we do to ensure that our children will not be left to the mercy of the sandmen if we become the sandmen? We are at their mercy if we think they can do anything to hold us back, for we are free to cross into the next world. If you want to know the spot where the crossing takes place, look for where the sandmen are working their hardest to blow up blinding sandstorms of deterrence. If you were a sandman and wanted total control, and the way to defeat you was available to everyone, what would be the central point of your effort to divert attention if not to hide the fact that defeating you was a simple task?

The sandmen have chosen well to work between the worlds of consciousness and sleep for there is much fertile ground to plant seeds of doubt. Nothing endures better in the soil of the heart than doubt. We have everything we need to destroy it, yet it flourishes such that we would let it remove the last flicker of faith and destroy us. But seen another way, though the sandmen seem to control us, they allow us to keep a small degree of hope alive, knowing that without it we would destroy ourselves, and them in the process. On the other hand, that small hope is both the only thing that saves us, and the one thing that ultimately destroys them.

The world in great measure has not changed, and in large part, too, we've stayed very much the same, but the bottom line is we know the next world truly exists regardless of the horrors of this world and the forgetfulness of time. We know that in the end, the sandmen will alone possess this world, and they can have it! They churn even now, their own definitions wearing thin as they hear we will escape them. We must whisper this incessantly in their ears.

War Machines

Keep in mind that, at its worst, war had reduced people to the lowest levels of insensitivity. One world war had killed more than 200 million people. The pledge of one tyrant at the outset was that sheer physical strength would bury all who opposed him. "Our jaws will break their will," was his call to arms.

At the end of the war, people were found in the jungles using the heads of his dead soldiers to cut through fruit. They had wired the jaws back onto the skulls and said they found them to be very good at cutting through almost anything, and admitted they thought nothing of using the head of a man as a kitchen aid. War had done this to them, but still, they argued, it had not broken their will.

In fact, many villagers admitted after the war that using their enemy in a manner directly opposite their very battle cry had not weakened but had actually sustained their spirit. "We weren't so much using their heads as we were using ours," one villager said. It was concluded in a post-war conference that a means should be found to avoid war. "When the bones of our enemy become merely another kitchen utensil, have we not sunk to new, dehumanized, low?" asked one member of the conference. It was universally agreed that war was to be avoided at all costs.

Meanwhile, the villagers returned to their former lives without much fanfare or consequence. One enterprising villager developed a cutting device that bore little resemblance to a skull, but took over where the skull left off, surely influenced by the article of war whose niche it filled in peace. It was especially good with fruit.

After months of negotiations, a plan was decided upon in order to stave off war. All the countries of the world agreed this new plan would help to let out their natural aggressions in a peaceful manner. Each country would build a robot using their best technology. Then, once a year there would be a fight for supremacy on a field of battle. Certain specifications would have to be met in order to ensure there would be a fair fight. The winner would be the last robot left standing after the battle, and therefore, the country that developed it. The winner would also win the rights to a remote, exotic island for one year. The territory would be theirs to use as they pleased. Within certain reasonable parameters, it would be theirs to keep until the next annual battle decided a new victor.

Every year there were several countries whose robots proved themselves to be superior to all of the others. The lesser nations became the butt of certain jokes and began to resent it. Some defended the jibes as fuel for the fires of the competitive spirit. Others repudiated the slurs as dangerous nationalism. In response they sent spies to steal the technology, and eventually the lesser countries improved upon it and banded together into an alliance. That year, they entered a robot into the contest to represent them. The perennial winners scoffed at the chances of the weaker nations, and they didn't win at first, but after several years of trying, the alliance finally had the last laugh when their robot won the competition easily. Almost at once, the usual victors levied charges that the upstarts had to have cheated in order to win. "Espionage," they called it. "Spoil sports," came the reply.

The alliance took over the island with a great deal of pride, pomp and circumstance — unusual considering the original reasons for having the competition. The peaceful point was lost in the military exhibition. There was also a great deal of suspicion from other countries regarding the future of the island. The alliance was said to be unworthy of occupying the island, and as soon as they took it over, there were reports of in-fighting amongst the various nations in the alliance over the administration of the territory for the one-year term. Then followed rumors of outright fighting. Ships were said to be seen arriving on the island with reinforcements for one country or another. None of these reports could be verified. A good portion of the countries of the world took the position that it was just a tempest in a teapot — a lot of smoke that would eventually blow over. Most agreed that the alliance had the right to enjoy the use of the island for the allotted term. They were entitled to their own style of occupation; all else was sour grapes.

At the end of the year, another competition was held, but surprisingly, there was no entry from the alliance to defend the championship. It was dismissed in the media as probable resentment to the competition in general. As for the games, one of the nations previously accustomed to winning pulled off yet another victory, but the familiar mutual congratulations all around were somehow lacking. Then, when the winner attempted to take over the island, they were met with fierce resistance. A force of robots had been put in place to defend the territory against invasion. Satellite surveillance discovered that there were no people on the island. The alliance members had returned to their respective countries rather than face any danger first-hand. Still, the alliance announced that it considered the contest null and void, all activities near the island to be an act of war and the island to be permanently annexed to the alliance.

It was then charged that the alliance had leaked reports of its infighting in order to lull the rest of the world asleep. Emergency meetings were held, and the nations of the world decided that the alliance could not be allowed to keep the island, and so an all-out war against them was declared. An army of robots was quickly manufactured to be sent in to do the fighting. A terrible battle ensued. In the end, a single robot was left standing. Every country in the world waited anxiously to see which robot it was, but reports of the identity of the victor were immediately disputed. Due to the nature of the distrust, no one could be sure who won the battle of the robots on the island, and the fate of the island wasn't clear. Some felt it would need to be under the permanent oversight of an independent council. Others felt it must be returned to its previous position as annual prize. Then there was the question of how to punish the alliance for its treachery. Meanwhile, the alliance was gearing up for a real war.

The bickering over one point or another got so quickly out of

War Machines

hand that the articles of the robotic conventions were abandoned altogether. The alliance called their next move a "retaliation," while everyone else called their move a "sneak attack." Once again, countries all over the world were fighting using both machines and people. Given the advancements made over the years of the robot wars, this new war was bloody indeed. It gave rise after just a few years, only after millions had died, to renewed calls for a search for new ways to avoid war altogether.

One proposal was given particular attention. It argued for computer simulations to be made wherein every country having any kind of grievance against another would be required to enter all kinds of information. The other country would do the same. Then the computer would take over, choosing a victor finally and fairly without a single loss of life. To the victor would go certain spoils of war in the form of a cash transaction between banks of one nation to the other. This plan, though not universally agreed upon, was put to a vote and made international law. It led to a truce being signed, and an end to the war at last. Agreements were then finalized as to the exact nature of this new computer method of avoiding war.

After several years of using computers to judge grievances, the world having enjoyed a certain equilibrium using this method, there began the first rumblings of discontent with the status quo. Certain nations were becoming increasingly disgruntled with a growing sense that everything was merely evening out over time. No particular advantages had been gained, even with what may have appeared as very righteous causes. Two very similar arguments at different times between different countries may have been decided upon with opposite judgments.

The only logic in the decisions appeared to some as merely determined to keep things ultimately the way they were. Every nation had as many losses as victories. No nation seemed to have lost much for long, for it wouldn't be long before the computer would award it a victory, and effectively give back all it had lost. The whole process was accused of being "fixed." Various studies were made, several that determined the simulations were indeed fixed, and several others that bore out the overall integrity of the project. An independent judge was appointed, but his independence, authority and allegiances were questioned along the lines of his nationality. The council that appointed the judge was also attacked as having its own agenda, a charge it hotly denied. Much of world regarded all of the protest and debate as just another political sideshow and waited anxiously for the judge to render his decision. He was, however, assassinated by a zealot before he could render a verdict.

Nations quickly took one side or the other as a result of these events. Two alliances of millions of angry souls formed and squared off, thirsty to shed real blood for a change and to exact vengeance for all the wounds perceived to have been received during the years of peace.

Each side had its own fervent rallies. They shouted catchy patriotic slogans to channel the spirit of the people toward the fight to come. It only seemed to be about one side being more right than the other, and it didn't matter which side one was on, for they both claimed God was on their side, and that they were mightier in their truth. The ideas were as interchangeable as the other weapons to be used. But while the battle of words remained woefully unchanged, ways to kill had seen many refinements and had come quite far over the years. At the height of the war, the dead had piled up so high in one camp that a crane was used to move them to a fire. A great steel-jawed bucket took huge bites out of the pile like an apple. It was so highly automated that once he'd gotten it going, the operator actually had his hands free to smoke a cigar. He clipped the end with a cutter he didn't even recognize as having been a development of another, long-forgotten war, sat back, and wondered what he'd be having for dinner that night.

Manned for War

The professors had a wonderful boat on the riverbank and were doing ever so well. It was built before their time, and they kept it in such very good shape. It was an excellent craft from stem to stern, and somehow it reminded me of Noah's Ark.

From the deck, it was always a beautiful day at sea. The waters spread out a great distance to all horizons and lapped the underside of the boat. The professors looked over the edge on these nice afternoons and kept watch. It was a contemplative watch, for no matter how they waited, they couldn't help but enjoy the waiting because the waters were so nice from their perspective.

One day, I passed the area of this boat while swimming the river, and it was practically teeming overboard with enthusiasm. Several professors were spreading the sails. One was knitting. One was in the crow's nest with a telescope, and one was vomiting over the side. Then the lookout saw me swimming. "Man overboard!" he shouted, and the teeming redirected itself.

Now in my eyes this seemed very strange. I knew the boat was grounded on the shore and that it only seemed to them that water spread out everywhere. Intellectual life prospered on the intricate vessel, but only of a certain kind, and my course was taking me in another direction. I'd spent enough time with the professors.

"I'm alright!" I yelled. "Just leave me alone!"

"You'll drown!" they called. "You can't make it! Stay afloat, and we'll cast you a line!"

Then a life preserver landed near me. The line from the ship landed more on land than on water, and I swam by it. "You're crazy!"

The Voyage of a Bean

they yelled. "You're going nowhere! Come back while you can!"

Well, I could see they were angry. The whole ship was alive with action. I suspect they saw a storm brewing and a bad afternoon ahead. The waves must have seemed to be really rocking the ship. It was a beautiful day, and their delusions only made it seem dark and stormy.

Then it was apparent that they were deliberately trying to rock the boat back and forth to send waves toward me. The woman who was knitting rocked in time in her chair. Vomit got on deck. Doing a backstroke in calm river waters, I thought all of this was ridiculous. There was this boat on land, and those on board trying to increase waves they only imagined. I calmly swam toward the opposite shore despite their feeble attempts to drown me by rocking in the mud.

From their perspective, I was merely heading into oblivion and the open sea. And when I stood up on shore, from the ship it looked like I got up and began walking on the water. I turned to them and saw their incredulous stares. They were stunned, and the cold glare they gave me could have fused the sand beneath them to an iceberg.

I knew they'd never forgive me and would keep a constant lookout. They reeled in the life preservers, dragging them over the churning waves against the strong currents of mud and sand, and manned for war.

The Tower

All the information about experience that would take many lifetimes to absorb completely fills a mile-high building. Inside, it is quite disorganized, but everything that is there belongs there. Daily, as I ride to work, the building imposes its presence on me in its size and shadow. Everyone carries a card, but most people don't take advantage of it. I manage to obtain several items per month from the ever-increasing, enormous collection. These are not lent but are given freely. As for what I've acquired so far, I've touched only a small flake of a chip of an iceberg chipped off the face of a glacier. If the few moments of my life devoted to gathering knowledge were multiplied and a projection were made to determine how much of my life I will have spent at the building, I will have touched just a part of a chip when it's over. On the other hand, why do I need information about experience? Experience happens outside, and it's plain enough what the story is. No one cares here, and no one bothers there. The building is like a morgue, and the general feeling is we'll get to one of those soon enough.

The building is small compared to the aggregate thousands of other structures in the city. Life teems throughout them all day long. The receptacle of value, on the other hand, stands untended and is largely ignored. It is a metaphor for me: the greater part seems mediocre, but there's a dream in my heart, and inklings or what may be thoughts which are not complete — of a world in which I should be living, full of perfection. I know these fragments are complete somewhere in the building, but I've hardly enough time in my life to search for them to enhance my vision. But their presence in me makes me yearn to

The Voyage of a Bean

understand them in a generally fruitless, outside search, so I visit the building when particularly piqued by this quest. At those times, I remember a fellow commuter used to think of the skyscraper as the imaginary conservation ground of the human spirit.

I watch it become smaller as the train leaves the city. Soon it has become just a speck on the horizon, just a light that sweeps across the city, and all the way to me, in the dimming light. It occurs to me how tiny it really is. But could I put it in my pocket, I would lose it. Could I possess it, I would crush it in the palm of my hand. For that matter, it is in our collective pocket, and binds our hands together as we surround it like a fire. Immersed, we burn up and grow weary. Separated, we hunger and cool like smoldering logs kicked away from the roar. Like most, I sustain myself by coming and going as I please. That's why it's not going anywhere, but some do not agree.

In the paper this evening, there's a story about one group that wants to have it torn down as a threat, and another that wants to see it removed piece by piece as an antiquity. A third group is fighting against them and has plans for an addition. In the accompanying photograph, the factions are picketing in front of the edifice. All around them, the thing that keeps it standing, its great foundation, is the sea of humanity that doesn't give a damn.

This multitude that just passes the protest with unfeigned disinterest represents only the smallest particle of a chip off the face of one mountain in an immense range. As far from it as anyone may go, its influence looms in shadow and light, generating power for the beacon on our shore. As for the ships in the sea, those who sail will find the same rocks that ignite the beacon lurking, like Scylla, in mists and waves.

Caroline Kane

Caroline Kane had disappeared. Her ocean cottage was deserted. During a storm, the sea restored it to the looks of a ruin it was in the process of becoming since she took occupation. When she didn't return after six months, her son Franklin boarded it up.

At low tide the entrance was open to caves in rocks below the cottage. Exploration of the tunnels cost several lives every year. Bodies or bones usually washed out, eventually.

The caves were not navigable, but when the tide was out, there always seemed to be a group of people crawling into the main room to have a look, emboldened by the company of others. Some would venture further into the various tunnels, but only as far as fear or friends allowed. Others would stand guard at the mouth of the cave, ready to call out a warning should the waters begin to rise. Still, accidents would happen, and every few years, an organized expedition went in with full gear and oxygen, but returned more often bearing their dead than with any new cartographic information.

What was known about the cave system was not extensive. Conjecture that suggested Caroline had wandered into the caves at a bad time turned to alternate theories when no sign of her emerged, though she would not have been the only one who'd gone in whose bones hadn't been coughed out by the sea. Through one winding tunnel beyond a deep sump, a large room and several skeletons had been found. It was enough of an adventure just to get there, and the cave entrance was so deep that it sometimes was not exposed for weeks at a time.

The sea alone was enough to have taken Caroline. The planet

itself for that matter offered plenty of space in which to disappear. The cave was a convenient hole to suck her into, a crack in the skull of opinion that needed a patch of underlying gray matter. Few believed she'd met with any foul play, and though she had never disappeared before, her son Franklin said, "She was gone a long time before this happened. As often as she walked the shores, she was just one of the shells."

When Franklin was a boy, he was not allowed at the beach. His mother made that clear. She would make him drink a glass of salt water if he disobeyed. He knew the sickness well. So he learned how to go and not be discovered. It was his hiding place, and where he went, no one could find him.

In his first visit to the caves, everything he'd expected to see was not there. His mother had warned him of skeletons and amphibious monsters, but it was all mussels and seaweed. The rasp of the waves lapping at the tunnels beckoned him but he never went beyond the main entrance until he was fifteen.

By then he hated and no longer feared his mother. He went to the sea as he liked and was well into mapping the caverns. In the best times, there were only a few hours during which he could explore. He tied a rope at the entrance and went in, one tunnel at a time. In five years he'd made a number of discoveries unknown to anyone else at the time. For example, there was a surface vent into a tunnel that meandered all the way to the entrance.

It was miles down the coast. He'd gone through it once. Waiting out the tide in an air pocket that night had thrust him into manhood. When he returned that morning, his mother beat him, she said, for staying out all night. The beating had virtually no impact on him as he still tingled with the adrenaline of survival.

Caroline Kane lolled in bed watching the curtains waft in the sea breeze. Soft strains of a piano air started in the next room. It was like the meal had reached the table. Having fasted, all at once she melted and was ready for her lover. As the drapes bounced, she could see all the way down the beach, the sun starting to set, and someone walking. Even at a distance she could see it was her son. She steamed, and the mood fizzled.

He would be punished. How could do it without saying she had seen him? It was easy. She would get home before him and say he was late. Having no fear of complications, even what she was doing didn't enter her mind. A man she hardly knew entered the room to satisfy her needs, and there was extra pleasure knowing her son had crossed her and that she could punish him. She'd even add an extra knock on the head in the name of knowing the difference between right and wrong. It went from disrupting to stimulating her passion.

What disruption? It wafted away. She'd already opened like an oyster to have her pearl tickled. She drifted into dark tunnels. The tide rushed in. And when it was full, it was smooth, without thoughts of her husband, Peter, who was an insignificant grain of sand. But finally it wasn't satisfaction; she was merely satiated. For a few moments she could stand musing, bearing even memories of her childhood as the shell slowly began to close in on her again.

Later, escaping into night, she found her way home to box her son's ears, serving revenge cold with salt water to drink with dinner. She tried to feel the moment again, softly squeezing lemon over raw oysters, mouth watering ahead of savoring, and humming that piano air. Then he began retching from the salt. There was no privacy. He was kicking sand through the curtains on her reverie. "Keep it down in there," she yelled, her mouth gorged and her eyes bulging in rage.

The Able bungalow was modest, but during the 50s, Peter Able's recording business was growing. He was able to expand from sound to video as television started to boom. He was consulting and directing by then, hiring out a crew and offering a full line of services. Most felt his success was all due to the connection to his wife's father, but it wasn't true. Peter's talent was unmistakable, and from the moment he'd met his future wife, her father, Ollie Kane, the "Big Oak" as he was called, or simply "OK," had done nothing but set up roadblocks.

Before the wedding, there was a light rain. Walking his daughter up the steps of the church he forecast "stormy days ahead" and asked what the world was coming to when Kanes start marrying Ables. Over the next few years, Peter and Caroline visited only during holidays. On one such visit, Ollie refused to acknowledge his son-in-law to friends. When Peter complained openly, he received the Big Oak's patented, "Who are you? You're no one."

"Me, no one?" replied Peter, "Why, you're the Big O — a big fat zero to my way of thinking." The name would later stick, used by many behind his back. Outraged, he forced his daughter's family to leave that night, not with any words but with an icy tension. Actually, Peter made the choice to leave. The situation was intolerable. It was Christmas Eve.

In those days, the children were toddlers and Caroline stood by her husband, partly out of vengeance against her father, but over the next decade, Peter's responsibilities took him away so often on business that she felt cheated by him too. She took up bridge to get out of the house herself, and soon the children knew more of baby-sitters and "grab" food (which meant she would do nothing to prepare a meal) than they did of their parents and nurturing. It was during her bridge outings that Caroline began having affairs.

Peter was devoted both to his business and to his wife, but she felt neglected, second-best, and resented his doting. A virgin when married, she began to enjoy sex in her mid-twenties, and genuinely hungered for it by the time she was thirty. When she started having affairs, a can of worms opened. The stress of concealment escaped in self-esteem. By comparison, her husband's performance was no match for the combined glow of cheating and fantasy. She complained about the size of his penis openly, even to the children, the oldest not yet in her teens. Peter drove deeper into his work. Caroline looked over her bridge hand, making eyes as she made her books.

Franklin remembered his childhood as a winter landscape, not for the snow, but because it was stark. It was as if he was conscious while having a liver removed, while remembering the "happy" days when he had the liver but in the knowledge it was in fact becoming diseased. His happiness as a child was utterly removed by the chill of fact blown in by reality.

The first clouds arrived during his teens when he first proved his mother's indiscretions. It became simple actually. Bridge had been abandoned for tennis, and the "partner" who picked her up every other day waited in the car outside while she bustled more with makeup than gear. He saw the same anxiety in his sister before dates arrived and became uncomfortably aware. Men had called her before, and he'd wondered about that, but the pothole in the road was quickly repaired as he willingly accepted her denials. But her two- and three- hour afternoon phone conversations, replete with whispers, giggles and silence whenever Franklin came close enough to hear began to bring out the Hamlet in him.

He confronted her several times as she sprayed perfume and gathered up her things, wearing an outfit that looked more like pantyhose in a bathing suit than a sports uniform. "You're having an affair with him, aren't you?" he'd say, and what bothered him was her glow, and the fact there was no scowl in her denial.

She laughed all the while, as if being chased by tickling hands, not by a son just beginning to emerge into the adult stage, beginning to sink in despair. She told him more than once, "Don't pry — you may not like what you find out."

One day he just said he knew it for a fact, and her laugh became straight, the giggle gone out of her into scorn. "Yeah," she said, "I'm having an affair. I can't fool you, so pull up your boot straps and get used to it. Now you have to live with it, and if you tell your father, there will be hell to pay." The next moment, she slammed the door after her leaving only a last glare. But as he watched her from the window getting in the car, she was all smiles, all motel, all full of holes. A sea poured down his throat.

The anguish of knowing was greater than he could have expected. Kicked in the stomach for how it felt, he couldn't get answers to his questions in the seconds before she left because she'd only admitted it as she put the final touches on her face. He feigned certainly to resolve doubt, but confirmation was not what he'd expected.

The world turned black and white deep into his sands, not melodic, but still structured stark as Bartok, a chemical experiment that suddenly turns black, and a flute duet becomes a real argument

The Voyage of a Bean

between two people, his mother and father. A beautiful athlete cut off at the trunk, standing up against his father, now perceived as weak, but inwardly so hostile against his mother for what she was doing, but impotent too, for that was what she was now saying Peter was — impotent. "He can't even do it anymore," she said to everyone. But Franklin could only think his father must see it too, and didn't want her. Was that why he was promising her mink coats and new cars in response? He turned to the dark sea and clouded sun, longing to be blanched.

Caroline was the ugly twin, though it wasn't apparent until critical. When boys mattered most, Anne had them in a jar singing like bees. Carol stung all over. She sought praise but didn't believe it from her family. The mirror told the truth.

As toddlers, the twins were almost identical, and then she was happiest. But one night one of Big Oak's friends said he'd tuck her in and in the process tucked his finger between her legs and gently woke her to strange new sensations.

She thought Fran Shaugnessy special. He drew the famous *Radio Police* for the *Big Little Books* and would draw her pictures when he came over, and helped her to hold the pen. She bounced on his leg, straddling it like a pony.

When he started taking her to bed, she flushed in expectation. When he was engaged at her bedtime, she called for him to tuck her in. He eventually withdrew himself from the family before anyone might have guessed what was going on, but Carol became the sullen twin. When Anne became popular, Carol escaped to riding horses, bounding through the woods on a beast she further tamed.

One night during dinner years later, Caroline mentioned Shaugnessy's abuse and shocked everyone not just with the fact but by adding emphatically, "And I liked it!" She delineated the experience in detail. It tainted the meal for them, but she ate hearty, saying finally to the stares, laughing with her mouth full. "What are you gonna do to me — take me down to the chopping block?"

Years before, her father took an old stump and polished the surface. He would take the girls down, put them on the stump, bared their bottoms and belted them whenever he felt they needed to be punished, which was often. Any offense including talking at the table, laughing or wetting the bed would yield a sentence of strapping on the "chopping block" as it came to be known.

When Franklin was a very little boy visiting his grandfather, he was threatened with the chopping block to the delight and instigation of his mother. They took him down kicking and screaming and set him up like Isaac to be sacrificed, stopping short of strapping. She told him there would never be a chopping block at home and not to worry, but she hit him for the same reasons she'd been hit, only she did it to him in bed, before she kissed and tucked him in.

Because of the Big O's cold shoulder and deft foot put to Peter's rear, the Ables made themselves a scarce branch on the family tree. Peter's best work came near the ocean, and at the time he could live and work where he pleased. He chose the rocky northern coast with its smattering of barren rocks, white sand and cold sea. Except for Anne's untimely death, there was not a single visit for almost fourteen years, and that, coincidently was when the Big O went down.

Carol incorporated the stress of isolation, the distance from her father, and the guilt of her increasing infidelity into a thin veneer of unquestionable control. On the one hand, she was exceedingly surefooted and demanding. On the other, she was upended by any question of authority or criticism. The three children were domineered into a corral, and Peter was insensitive to the bleating of his sheep. He accepted it unblinkingly as post-war modern maternity. Children were to be seen, not heard.

He busied himself with acquiring status symbols. While a good craftsman, he lacked the philosophical insights even to the understanding of his own work, which was more commercial than artistic. At some point, their lives took a dramatic materialistic turn. Perhaps it was the pool by the ocean that said it best.

The war had taken children and made them kill. When the boys returned as men, one can only ponder what the gap war had filled would have contained had it not been for the war. While Carol escaped stress in her new purchasing power, while pounding into the children that they were "ungrateful brats." Every toy she bought them became tainted with the story of her deprivation as a child. The children at that time could still look past her comments and enjoy the gift. It was only much later that what she planted in the soil of constant berating popped out all over them like shrapnel.

Carol demanded that Peter back up her every dictum, and that he did. Though not aggressive, she forced him to behave as if incensed for maximum impact. When he was out of town, she warned the children that when he returned, he would surely punish them after relating what they'd been doing. It became routine. He even became frustrated and truly angry that after every trip he was forced to beat the children, rather than love them. At the same time that she knowingly transferred the whip into her husband's hands, operating him like a bad-guy puppet and ensuring they were soundly belted in bed, she would enter and whisper what a good mother she was, wasn't she, and beamed as they sobbed yes and said that they loved her.

Franklin Able was given Caroline's mother's maiden name. They called him Frank. The first signs that he had problems dealing with his mother were apparent whenever she would visit his school. He felt a wave of shame or fear when he'd see her peering in the window of the classroom door. She sensed it too, and took it personally, though it was merely having the spotlight on him, at least in the beginning. She made it an issue, but he couldn't explain it. She'd never warned in advance, and though he tried to express happiness, it was stigmatized by her heavy hand.

His younger brother Peter, by contrast, loved her with the toddler's unconditional instinct, and she made it clear to Frank that she preferred Peter, bathing the baby in her glow whenever Frank was around. Chantal, the eldest, was given privilege always, for being the eldest. She was allowed to stay up later, and the boys were promised they could stay up later when they reached her age, but it never happened. She was always older, and bed times remained constant through the years. Chantal sneered and stuck her tongue out at Frank. Pete didn't care, but Frank complained. Caroline would hold up a belt and ask him if that's what he wanted.

Chantal was only being groomed as a matriarch's protégé and was simply imitating her mother's attitude for the rewards it brought. Disdain for her brothers brought down laughter from above, delighting and encouraging the little girl. The boys were told that girls were special, that mothers and daughters enjoyed a special bond. Chantal could sit in the front seat of the car between her parents while the boys were left to whine in the back. Chantal was called smarter though it bore only on her being two years ahead in school. She could multiply and divide when the boys couldn't, and do cursive writing. Anything she knew made her special and used to demonstrate that the boys were inferior.

The special relationship included special girl talks about things boys weren't allowed to know, and these conversations always took place in the bathtub. Several times a week, the girls locked the door and splashed in bubbles exchanging secrets. One "special" night, Carol told Chantal she had a secret that she could tell Chantal only if she vowed never to tell anyone, not even Daddy. They'd already talked about sex. Chantal was proud that she knew more about sex than all her friends. She knew she could get a straight answer about sex from her mother at anytime. When controversies broke out in the schoolyard on the meaning of certain terms, by the following day, Chantal would have the right definitions, denied by many but borne out over time. Her friends said Chantal was lucky to have such an open mother. None of them had such a relationship. Chantal just beamed.

In the tub that night, Caroline told Chantal about a very special friend who was a man who touched her in secret places. "You mean Daddy, don't you?" asked Chantal. "Not Daddy," Carol scolded. "Don't you want to hear this?"

Chantal was scared, but couldn't say anything. Her mother began to explain not just that there was a special man, but the next few months, created a twelve-year-old sounding board for her indiscretions. After a rendezvous, there was always a bath the night during which Caroline told her young daughter the vivid details of her sexual escapades. There wasn't just one man, but several. Some dropped out of the stories. New ones took their places. The depictions were lurid and sensual, and Chantal didn't know what to do with the sensations and confusions. She only knew she had to listen and never say a word about the secrets she heard or else be punished, but over time having listened turned into punishment.

Seven years later Franklin pressured his mother into the dreaded admission. That night she came to his room. He was listening to music; two flutes in a heated argument. She sat on the edge of the bed. "He's a man," she said, "something your father doesn't know anything about. Didn't play tennis at all today. Three times, that's how good he is."

Franklin sat up in bed. "I don't want to hear about it."

"Don't talk to me like that," she quipped, but she saw a new look in his eyes, a glare that she could only meet with equal force. She backed out of the room. "Don't you ever talk like that to me again." The glares met until he looked away. A battle was won, but the war had begun.

Over the next year, Franklin felt an increasing burden of awareness and contradiction in the house. He began to have alarmingly harsh arguments with his father. Once there was a standoff where Peter asked Franklin to come down with the keys to his car. "Come up and get them," Franklin called, and so it went. Neither would budge, but pressure built until young Peter came home from school and intervened, taking the keys to his father.

Caroline too became more domineering and unpredictable. She complained bitterly that no one supported her. A doctor had determined her blood pressure to be elevated, and she used that to quell any argument against her, warning that any question of her authority caused life-threatening stress. The kids rolled their eyes behind her back, effectively silenced. Their father explained it was the ghost of her father, that she'd had a horrible childhood, and this was the effect. "We must try to understand and accept your mother for what she is," he counseled.

"If you only knew what she is," Franklin thought.

One day young Peter came home from school, and hearing Franklin and his girlfriend in the shower together, called his mother to tell. Chantal was off in college and both the boys were in high school now, Peter in his first year, Frank in his last, so Carol had taken a job operating the switchboard for a small electronics company. "You tell him he's not allowed to take showers with girls in my house," she said, and Peter went right up to tell Frank. Peter got punched for telling, which made him glad he had tattled.

When Carol came in, she confronted him, and Frank just said, "Don't tell me that what I'm doing is wrong! That's some nerve! At least I've had the same girlfriend for a whole year." Carol left it for her husband to deal with, but his power had waned and did not have the same effect as when they were children. Franklin told his father to go to hell. Peter exploded and told him to move out of the house.

As Franklin was packing, Carol came in. "You go down and apologize this second." "No," he answered, "What I'd rather do is go down and tell him what you've been doing. That'll put my shower in perspective, won't it?"

Instead, she went down and interceded for him. Peter went upstairs and told Franklin that he understood there's an age when fathers must be stood up to, and he accepted it. But Franklin felt buried when his father left the room. He couldn't meet his father, mind to mind and reach an understanding. It became what he wanted for lack of it, but he held too terrible a weapon to destroy his father and feared using it and not revealing it at the same time.

That night an even more eventful experience awaited. Chantal had driven home from school and arrived after the arguments. She only heard about it later after their parents had gone to bed and the three of them were talking about Peter's having blown the whistle on his brother. Chantal didn't understand why there wasn't more loyalty between the two brothers. Franklin said Peter was still a kid and didn't know what he was doing, that if he knew more about his mother he would be more loyal, but that was another story.

Rather than ask what there was to know about his mother, young Peter surprised his siblings by saying he knew something they didn't know. They exchanged looks. Scrutiny met certainty. "You couldn't tell me anything about mother that I don't already know," scoffed Frank. "There are some things I couldn't even tell you because I've been sworn to secrecy."

"Me too," Chantal said. "I know things she told me never to tell."

"So it's probably all the same thing we know," suggested Peter.

"So let's see if it is," suggested his brother, but no one would go first. Still, in a minute, the sense of the burden they shared brought it out. Peter had known longer than Frank. Chantal was much younger too when she found out. Franklin was the last to know. He had learned something about his mother he hadn't known already, and this already was a bigger blow, not being last, but that his brother and sister had been so abused and for longer. For more than a year he carried a secret, which was carving tunnels in his head. Now it was out, but sometimes shared burdens weren't any easier. It had just burst out of three hearts and formed a larger pocket.

Whenever Caroline found a new lover, the whole house knew about it. In her early forties, by then the late sixties, she became enamored with the "Me" philosophy wafting around in pop culture. She wasted no time making the rounds to keep each of her special secret-holders informed; Chantal and Peter enduring it straight-faced, Franklin wincing as if being doused in a cold spray. Caroline was always offended, but watching how he behaved, selected opportunities to exact his pain.

One evening Chantal and Franklin talked with their father who admitted not feeling close to them and wanting to be close. He said he felt like he was eighteen even though past forty, and began to cry. Hearing him whimper, Caroline jumped to her feet in a flare of fear. What was he crying about, she demanded on entering the room. "Nothing, we're having a good conversation for once," he answered. She urged him back to the bedroom and warned Chantal and Franklin against ever getting too close. "I don't want you talking to your father like that again," she said in full sneer, but it was exposure, even the feeling of exposure that she didn't like, and it had grown into paranoia.

She wore a medic alert bracelet for allergic reaction to tetanus, and held up the blood pressure shield at all times to fend off possible attacks. When the house was settled and behaving as she wished, she could glide about freely, listening to music that reminded her of her new lover. Her dancing was awkward and without talent.

In her teens, she lacked confidence and had no understanding of relationships. Her mother never talked to her about sex, only warning her against ever letting anyone touch her. Remaining a virgin until marriage was the utmost goal of instruction. One night she was kicked out of a car by a boy who told her to "go preserve it in alcohol." But she was proud of protecting her honor, and even later passed on the legacy to her own daughter, ingraining it in the first twelve years, and assaulting it after. Even so, there was seemingly no contradiction to her demanding family honor of Chantal while relating her stories. "You can do anything you want after you're married," Chantal was told. When Chantal's next-door neighbor girlfriend became pregnant, Chantal could no longer see her. Mary was a few years older, and Caroline didn't want the bad influence around her impressionable daughter, she told Mary. "She looks up to you, and you're nothing to admire," she said, and that was that. But that night, Chantal had to listen to all of the sordid details of one of her mother's trysts.

The boys meanwhile were urged to attack. Other people's daughters were fair game. They couldn't consider themselves men if they didn't succeed to win out over any female resisting in the name of honor. They only knew it was different for boys. Their sister couldn't give, but that didn't mean other girls couldn't.

Chantal walked in her mother's footsteps through high school, losing boy after boy because she wouldn't let them touch her, all the while knowing more about adult sex than the boys. It was no wonder she was asked out or that the boys were trying though, because she was her mother's student in make-up. So while she was living the virgin, she looked like she'd just come off a street corner. Caroline applied as much make-up as a clown, following the current fashion magazines in garish imitation. Her eyelids were usually so purple as to be black. She wore fake eyelashes, and rouged her cheeks, then powdered them so as to leave a hint of color showing through. She had two face lifts within five years, all to make herself attractive to men who gave her a brief reprieve from having to live with herself.

The Voyage of a Bean

And while she demanded that everyone pay her tribute and say how beautiful she looked before going out, as in making them compliment her for her cleaning or her cooking, when it came to her children, no boyfriend or girlfriend, was ever good in her eyes. It wasn't that they weren't "good enough" in some way for her children. She just was hyper-critical of anyone they brought home. "She's ugly," she would say to Franklin when he'd bring a girl home for lunch. It wasn't cute that young children liked one another. They were always funny looking or talked funny. One girl cried on the way into the house, stopping short at the sidewalk when she and young Franklin arrived from school. It was the way Carol stood outside the door glaring. It frightened the child. Carol told Franklin, a second grader at a time, that he shouldn't like funny-looking girls who cried over nothing. Franklin couldn't look at the little girl the same way again. By the time he was a teenager, he knew his mother would berate anyone or anything he liked. He tried not to care, but it always mattered. She knew how to cut into him like a scalpel.

When Caroline's sister Anne died before the age of 30, she swept Franklin out of a deep sleep into her arms and carried him out to the car. The transition from dream to awakening, from the waters he was sailing to the ship that cradled him, made a profound impression on the five-year-old boy. It was three-o'clock in the morning. "What's the matter?" he asked. "We're going to Boston to see your Auntie Anne," she answered, lovingly, and it was the closest he ever remembered feeling to his mother at any time in his life, and the strange character of the sudden waking and the sensations of dream dissipating into reality in the dark early hours of morning intensified over the years.

By the time the sun came up, the three children were still scolded to stay asleep, but they only could close their eyes. "Why is Chantal awake then?" asked Franklin. She was sitting in the front seat between her parents. "She took a nap yesterday," Caroline lied.

On the drive to Boston, they saw three funerals on the highway, and Caroline said not to mention a word of it to their grandmother but wouldn't answer why. Franklin remembered the rows of cars with the headlights blazing in the early morning, but had trouble with the feeling of dying. He tried to ask questions but was shushed. Even his father told him finally to shut-up. "Another funeral," Franklin said pointing to the oncoming lights across a median, and his father reached back and hit him across the face. The shock yielded a good five seconds of silence before the first sound of crying, and he was quickly warned from making any fuss, though it was difficult to quell. Franklin didn't really understand what a funeral was, actually. It was another thing of curiosity in the world around him. What he couldn't know was this was not a time for learning about things. The information coming his way was about the people around him, and he wouldn't know how to sift through that for many years.

The fact he had the most difficulty understanding was why he never saw his Auntie Anne during the visit to his grandparents. He looked forward to it since being awakened from sleep that night, that birth into consciousness and dark flight, but no one would answer him. He got sad glares from his mother, pats on the head from relatives he didn't know.

Old Aunt Flo, his grandmother's sister, took care of the kids while everyone attended the wakes and funeral. Franklin remembered making ice cream, but couldn't understand why there was so much salt involved, but it didn't taste salty. He remembered playing with sliding closet doors with a cousin, and having difficulty getting them set straight with the knobs in the right position. It remained a mystery all his life how simple doors could have so confused two children.

He remembered Tony, a little boy his Uncle Dan and Aunt Marie had adopted. They were in Aunt Flo's back yard where there was a waterfall down to a kidney-shaped pool. It was after one of the wakes, and the families had gathered there for lunch. Tony had just been punished and was standing next to the pool looking into the water. Franklin wanted to say something, but the boy was bigger and intimidating. He asked his mother who he was. "That's Tony. He's adopted," Caroline explained. "He's going back to the orphanage because he didn't work out." Didn't work out? From further questioning he

The Voyage of a Bean

learned that children sometimes didn't have parents and could be adopted, but if they weren't liked or did anything wrong, they could be sent back. "You're one of the lucky ones — you have parents," she said, "but even you could be sent away if you're bad." Franklin felt the fear she hoped he would, and he spent the rest of the day pondering poor Tony's fate, with sympathy and vicarious identification.

He also remembered playing at Auntie Anne's house with his cousins and Auntie Anne not being there. But even playing, he wondered where she was, when she would appear. She was the reason for the visit, and the few memories he had of her were clear and loving.

Once he had cut his finger on a can lid, and she had dressed it for him without saying he was stupid for doing it. He'd cried at first, and was surprised how quickly she'd soothed him, even to smiles and a big hug at the end. He wondered how someone could be so nice, and when later he was stung by a bee, he ran to her though his mother was nearby, and Auntie Anne gave him the attention and love he wanted.

Only on the drive home a week later did Caroline honestly answer Franklin when he asked why they hadn't seen Auntie Anne. "Because she died," was all she said. Franklin erupted into tears of grief for the aunt he loved, who loved him, and mixed in was an anger he couldn't name for not being told all that time. He sat in the back seat in tears and silence. Chantal pointed out the window and said, "Look mummy, a funeral, just like Auntie Anne's."

She'd gotten to go. She'd known all along. Franklin suffered more then, and remembered how Tony looked into the pool for the last time. He tried to straighten up but had to pretend to sleep, covering his face because he couldn't stop crying. "I won't be sent away," he thought, but all of the sadness he felt for Tony was also for himself.

Being a twin, Caroline felt the loss of her sister deeply. The impact was myriad. All at once doors to her youth had closed behind her, and before her gaped a world she did not want to explore. She was suddenly Carol. Carrie, a name she'd been called all her life, was no longer used because after the death of her sister, she would return to Boston only once in fifteen years, and she did that alone, to see her sister's children. Otherwise, she would send cards, and then would complain if she received no response.

But that one time she did visit touched her. Two little girls and a boy became infatuated with their lost mother's sister. Auntie Carrie, they called her. With their Boston accents, it sounded like "Annie Carry," which summed up the link she still felt with her sister.

But she had almost thirty years of resentment for her sister's beauty that now became guilt. Added to that was the worry that being a twin, she faced the same prospect: breast cancer. The problems she had with her father had come to a head at the funeral, and she swore if she ever saw him again it would be over his dead body. And when they returned up the northern coast after the funeral, she played cards in the front seat with Chantal, teaching her basic games, but even discussing the fundamentals of bridge, a game she'd played with her sister which she was now thinking of taking up seriously.

Her teeth had never been good. She'd been told by her dentist that they may have to come out, and after the funeral, she thought it as good a time as any. Self-absorbed and almost masochistically, she let a bad dentist perform an ill-advised procedure, yanking all of her teeth in one sitting. But she walked home afterwards, through tears, but with a clear defiance of the reality she felt was being force-fed.

Peter couldn't believe it when she walked in. He'd been telling her to see someone else because the same dentist had put in a gold bridge he later learned wasn't necessary. But it was too late, and when she was afterwards fitted for dentures and bared her new teeth, she was pleased at their perfection, and set out to find bridge partners, for she was now ready to confront the damn competitive world from across a table. She thought the world was made up of millions of individuals, each proudly doing their tiny bit to damage others as they could. She was determined to damage the pride of any individual she met, and save her own world, and perhaps finally gain some increased measure of pride in the process.

Franklin, meanwhile, was losing more and more of his baby teeth. Before the funeral, Caroline was patient with loose teeth, finding a gentle way of pulling them. Her own teeth were sensitive. She understood the pain. But after having all of hers yanked, she had little patience with the fears of a six-year-old. When Franklin came to her with loose teeth in the first losses, he thought of money he'd find under the pillow. Then one day, Carol felt a tooth that Franklin said was just beginning to feel a little loose. Without warning, she dug her nail under and yanked it out. He bled for half an hour. When she'd done that a second time, he stopped coming to her for assistance. Fearing the pain, he let new teeth grow in front of the old ones. Eventually, they fell out, but it left the teeth in his lower jaw completely crooked for the rest of his life.

An immaculately clean house was Caroline's source of pride, but the children made it nearly impossible, which frustrated her to no end. She set up work schedules for the children, setting the table, doing the dishes, vacuuming, washing the clothes, folding the clothes and cleaning the various rooms, including closets. Because her focus often drifted in and out of her depression, there was time for the closets to become chaotic and for dust to build up. Then, when guilt and stress would build up, she'd notice a mess and explode into fits of military order once again, shouting that the children had no discipline, no respect and were basically "ingrate brats."

Franklin was threatened with being sent away to military school repeatedly. He was paranoid for years about that. Only when he was into high school did he sense that he'd finish without being shipped out. Caroline made Franklin her principal instrument of house cleaning. Chantal had privilege because she was older and didn't have to participate. Peter was too young and didn't do a good job. Caroline whispered praise in Franklin's ear. "You clean my bathroom better than they do, and you know how to organize the silverware when you put it away," she'd always say, and so he spent every evening and much of every Saturday doing chores while his brother and sister had mock tasks in their rooms and went on to play after little work.

She asked Franklin what the houses of his friends were like. He knew what he had to say — that there were toys everywhere and dust and chaos. "But your mum keeps a nice, clean house, doesn't she?" she'd beam, and he'd agree, but without caring. He liked to play at other kid's houses because they could play with toys on the floor. He couldn't bring his out to play, or hide them under his bed. His favorite toy was a small flashlight from a baseball game. He played with it under the covers until the battery went dead. Replacement batteries were out of the question because they wore out. Caroline called them a waste of money. Franklin had to buy those himself, with money he'd earn. Once Caroline borrowed ten dollars from Franklin, which his grandparents sent for his birthday. A week later, she denied ever borrowing it and refused to pay it back. Franklin was given a coin collection by his paternal grandfather Charlie, and when she admired the Indian Head pennies and said she wanted them, Peter interceded when Franklin cried. He put them with the rest of the collection under lock and key.

When Caroline started playing bridge, she inspected the house before leaving to make sure it was clean. Then she told them to wish her luck. "Win win win," she taught them to chant. Her first partner was Ethyl Haffner, a woman her own age who loved jewelry, make-up, dressing up, and having her hair done as much as Caroline. Their principle point of agreement was how awful everyone looked compared to them. They smoked in smoky rooms, playing a game that seemed reserved for morose, concentrated competitors with bad habits and fat guts. They enjoyed standing out. Almost as soon as she entered the room, Carol had such high disdain for the motley crowd that it invigorated her desire to squash the colony of bugs.

And she began to win. She was nobody to anyone, and suddenly she was taking home the points and the trophies. Those that had been used to winning knew they had competition and boned up on their play. When Carol would lose, she blamed Ethyl who was the poorer partner, but not to her face. If a losing streak went on too long, she'd team up with someone else and tell Ethyl it was winning that mattered, not with whom she was playing. When Ethyl could beat her when they faced each other in a round, then she'd play with her again. Surprising Carol, Ethyl did defeat her one evening, but Carol felt it was both her own partner's inferior play that cost her, not to mention Ethyl's partner's successful bidding. Still, they

The Voyage of a Bean

became a team again, but only after Ethyl confided she was having an affair and needed to tell someone the details.

Caroline was at once both shocked and excited to hear that Ethyl had found a lover, and when Ethyl expressed misgivings, Carol offered encouragement to continue. The Haffners had what looked to be a happy marriage, and Ethyl said it really was happy, mostly. She loved her husband Merv and didn't want to do anything to risk her family. "You don't have to give up your family to have an affair," Carol said, then joked, "You can have your cock and eat it too." Caroline's father had a mistress for years. Her mother had to accept it. It was the way things were for many men, so why not women?

"But I don't want Merv to find out," Ethyl worried. "He'd kill me." She told Carol all the details, how she'd met him, how she resisted for a time, how she'd fantasized about not resisting. Then Merv went on a business trip, and the opportunity presented itself more tangibly at a bridge tournament. There weren't as many tables as expected. It broke up early. The baby sitter wasn't expecting her for a couple of hours yet. They drove to a dark spot and did it in the back of the car. But it was better than Ethyl expected. "It was like dating all over again. We parked and made out. He was so gentle. The problem is I can't stop thinking about it anymore."

Carol couldn't either. The romance had long since gone out of her marriage. She was saddled with three kids most of the time. Peter was travelling more and didn't think anything of tacitly expecting her to do more. He didn't even perceive the increased burden of the kids on her while he was away. How would he know if she did anything behind his back?

In high school, she hadn't dated much, and her mother had indoctrinated her to remain a virgin. She didn't enjoy love-making at first, but discovered its pleasures later. She missed her husband when he was away, but began to feel he took her for granted. After Ethyl told her about her affair, she thought how few boyfriends she'd actually had. Peter was the first one who really took more than a passing interest. Most of her dates were set up by her older brother, and they didn't come calling twice. Even during high school, some girls were getting married to soldiers, some of whom were killed shortly thereafter, leaving young widows behind. Caroline had two friends whose husbands were killed in battle, and her father frowned mightily on her dating servicemen for that reason. But who else was there?

The war ended just as Carol was finishing high school. Obviously, the influx of boys was huge, but Carol stayed at home more often than not, preferring solitude, she said, to her brother's drunken sailor buddies. Anne was married the year the war ended and moved away. The Big O would have neither of his two sons in the house, now that they'd come home from war. They had to get jobs and get out, and if they wanted more school, let the government pay for it.

Carol feared the years were starting to go by. She was waiting for something, but there was nothing on the horizon. Her father started calling her an old maid. When Peter came along he was a blind date her brother had set up again, but now she was being pushed on all sides to get out. She wanted nothing more than that. Life with her father had become unbearable. She'd also become aware of her father's indiscretions and her mother's subservience. It sickened her to watch what was happening. She also became more apt to speak up. Too old to be taken down to the chopping block anymore, she didn't fear her father. Her brother told her some details about "Pop's floozie," and when she referred to it using those words to his face, he slapped her for it, hard to the face, and never apologized.

When her blind date showed up the next weekend eight inches shorter, she went back to the house, exchanging her high heels for a pair of flats. She was still taller, but she was used to odd coupling date disparities. Determined to have a good time, they went dancing where she let him buy her a few drinks though she was not yet twenty-one. She was boisterous and loud for the first time on a date, and he seemed fascinated, holding her hand and complimenting her often for her dancing, her good looks, her sense of humor, and later, for the way she kissed.

In the car she even let his hand wander under her blouse and meander a moment before pushing it off. She'd never done that, but felt entitled. She even hoped her father was watching from the window, but he wasn't even home that night. He spent most nights

The Voyage of a Bean

now with his floozie.

The next time they played bridge together, Caroline was pressing to know who Ethyl's lover was. She wouldn't tell Carol for fear of an embarrassment, but Carol made it more embarrassing without knowing because every man in the room was treated as if she knew something. One would sit at the table and Carol would ask with her eyes, "Is this him?" Ethyl couldn't concentrate, and they lost two of the first three boards.

When Ethyl's lover finally did sit at the table, Carol didn't have to ask was this was the one. She knew, but was perfectly cool about it, much to her partner's relief. Then Carol played like a master, bidding her signals brilliantly, and when it was over, had won decisively. Ethyl felt only relief, but Carol was sure she had sent clear signals that she was the more interesting woman, even though she didn't find herself particularly attracted to him. He was short. His partner though, now he was tall, and the better player of the two men. When beaten, he winked at Caroline. "Now you're someone who can play with me anytime," he said and reached over to shake her hand. "Nicely done."

Between the boards, she wondered if the two men had discussed them. More likely they've been talking more than we've been talking, she concluded, and so his words about playing with him began to echo in her mind as purposely spoken. The implied meaning caused her to go into a reverie, daydreaming about having an affair. Consequences could be controlled, She asked Ethyl later if she'd see about getting together a double date the next time she slept with him. Ethyl balked in a fluster, "Oh, I don't know. I don't even know if I want to do it again."

"You do," Carol said, "and you will."

Before ever having an affair, Caroline had already discovered a paradox: a woman who looks in public for an honest relationship will face more rejection from men than a woman who only wants one thing in secrecy. Men made that possible the way they prowled for an opening. The moment she began to consider what it would be like to have a little extra on the side, she saw possibilities everywhere she looked, and she was the one in control, not the man. There would be no "conquest" if it can be called that, unless she gave the green light. Whether a man was or was not persistent had no bearing on the matter whatsoever. She felt that she could decide when and with whom she wanted to spend an illicit evening. All those years she waited for the phone to ring when she was afraid of what boys might try to do and what they would say when she proved unwilling to go beyond a kiss. She only felt ugly when they went on to easier girls. Now with just a wiggle or a wink, she could have anyone she wanted, and she felt desirable and pretty.

Her personality bloomed as she began to flirt with everyone. It was the way she'd acted on her blind date with Peter that night she changed shoes. She'd gone on to marry the one man with whom she'd had a good time, even though she started wearing heels again and friends often remarked how much shorter he was. They were polite and never said how much taller she was.

She even flirted with the pastor of their church. They attended regularly. Also, Peter edited a radio show of sermons and music as a community service, and the children were put in Sunday school. Caroline believed it was in the best interest of the children to give them a sense of God they could have their whole lives. But she told them from the start that was why she was sending them there. When one day they asked if God exists, she just said she didn't know.

She used the Bible and God mainly to frighten or punish them when necessary. She didn't know any stories or have examples of rewarded good behavior, only punishment and hell fire. She often sent them to their rooms to read the Bible as punishment. Because she enjoyed her nights out during the week playing bridge and Friday and Saturday nights with friends, she often liked to sleep late, and church was not always a priority. The children would wake and hope not to have to go, and often they would miss church, but if they'd done something against her will, she would warn them that there would be church that weekend.

In her thirties, Caroline had hit her stride and finally come out of the shell into which her father had driven her. It delighted her when she discovered she could be herself without retribution, get a bit tipsy

The Voyage of a Bean

and loud without criticism, and flirt in front of her husband without suspicion. She'd told him many stories about her upbringing, and he knew how important it was to her to be happy and open. To her, when open flirtations with the pastor brought laughter and not religious examination, she exulted in open acceptance by the heavens and no longer felt constantly scrutinized and harshly judged. If the pastor could be comfortable in being one of the gang, and let his hair down, what did she have to worry about? At one party, when couples were passing candy life savers back and forth on toothpicks held in their mouths, she got up against the pastor and made a mock scene of rubbing her body against his. Everyone roared at her wit, the pastor included, but her children, awakened by the noise, up from their beds and looking on, didn't know what to make of it.

Caroline had no critics around her anymore, except these three, young as they were, even if they didn't say anything. Seeing them up and out of bed brought her wrath because she'd warned them to go to sleep and not get out of bed, but she never asked anyone to keep the noise down. "Why are you kissing Pastor?" Franklin asked when she put him back in bed. "I wasn't kissing him. We were playing a game," and explained passing life savers on toothpicks was fun. The next day, as Franklin watched the Pastor distribute communion from his choir berth in the balcony, the hosts seemed like hors d'oeuvres from the party that were missing their toothpicks. As he looked down at the pews, he saw other grown ups who were at the party. He had a solo in the communion hymn the choir performed that morning, but he thought as he sang that even to the pastor it was falling on deaf ears.

Caroline pressed Ethyl to arrange a get together, but her partner's response was to act as if it were a joke. She was going out evenings to play bridge two and three nights a week now, and with Peter's frequent business travel, it meant baby sitters for the children. She slept through the mornings, thanking Carnation for the introduction of "Instant Breakfast," a flavored powder added to milk with the purported nutrition of a full breakfast. It was never that for the children. Their stomachs were growling by mid morning and they didn't feel well, but they couldn't get her out of bed to fix anything for them. She was usually out until after two.

In one of her bridge magazine subscriptions, she saw an upcoming tournament to be held by the American Contract Bridge League in St. Louis in three months. She began to wonder if she might persuade Ethyl to go and wondered if their two friends might be going. Despite Ethyl's fending off Caroline's entreaties pretending they were jokes, Carol managed to get to know Mark Pauncher better over time. She always played to win and impress him and when he commented about easing up a bit on them when he and his partner sat down to play one night, she quipped, "If you think I might let you have your way with me, it won't be on the bridge table." She laughed quite loud at her own joke. Regulars on the bridge circuit became used to her new boisterousness. She became one of the popular "characters," willing to dare to stir up the dust a bit, but here she was going a bit too far, and Ethyl kicked her under the table, later demanding she be more subtle.

As they walked out that night carrying their trophies, Carol brought up the tournament in St. Louis. Ethyl had never traveled out of state for bridge. Carol argued they needed red points if they were ever going to become Life Masters, and the only place they could win red points was at a national tournament. "Life Master, who's talking about us becoming Life Masters?" Ethyl asked.

Carol held up her trophy and sneered, "If you think I'm satisfied with this…do you think I enjoy these smokey rooms and those people just to be with you? I'm on a mission here, and if you're not serious, I can find a better partner."

Ethyl thought she might like to go, she just didn't know if it would be possible. Merv would have to approve. "Then tell him you're going, and then tell Pat and Mark they should go."

"Invite them? Is this for bridge or sex?"

"Alright, I'll just see if they're going. I won't invite them, and we can pretend it's for bridge we're going."

She was already prepared how to let Peter know she was going. The trophies were adding up. The children were disappointed if she didn't bring one home. It wasn't always a trophy night, but she usually won if it were. The trophies started small and not always for first place. Then they got larger and more frequent, mostly first-place finishes, and began to line the window sills all over the house.

The next night she told Peter she thought she was good enough to become a Life Master and gave him details of what she needed to do, most importantly to travel. "Won't there be a tournament out here someday?" he asked when she mentioned St. Louis.

"You're complaining that I might travel one measly time for what I love to do when you're always away leaving me with these brats?" She got his permission with very few tears shed.

When the children heard about her trip, they were excited about her becoming a Life Master. She already was in control of their minds. She always told them how she picked other players apart at the table, how she showed no mercy. They worshiped her for her success and hardly complained that she wasn't around very often. Franklin made a comment once about there being no Instant Breakfast in the house for a whole week and going to school with nothing to eat, to which she responded, "Am I going to have to wipe your butt for you too like I did your first five years?"

At bridge several days later, Ethyl was both glad she was going but perturbed that Carol had called and talked to Merv about her going. "I told him we needed each other as partners, that it would make a winning difference. He agreed," she defended herself. "No," countered Ethyl, "you went behind my back. Don't ever do that again!"

When Ethyl wasn't around, Carol took the opportunity to ask the two men if they were going to St. Louis. They said they hadn't thought much about it. "It's sure to be a good time," she said. "I can't wait to beat the experts at their own game." She lit a cigarette and blew the smoke up over them. "And to have a little fun," she added with a wink.

Ethyl called Carol the next afternoon with unusual excitement. "They're going," she said. "I can't believe we're doing this."

"I can't believe we've waited so long to do it," Carol answered.

Carol knew she had a gift when it came to cards. It was the first time in her life she not only excelled at anything but could reap the rewards, which included being able to stick it in the faces of anyone whenever she wanted. She'd become a regular winner in the small tournaments so quickly that the reputation that proceeded her was often strongly questioned. She knew they were coming gunning for her, and she was only too happy to oblige by shooting them down. Someone dubbed her Annie Oakley, but she thwarted the nickname. It made her think of her sister and father. She had a great memory for whom had beaten her in the first few months of her playing, and she never tired of daring them openly to give it their best shot. The reputation she had among many was of a loud, poor winner whose main method of play was intimidation.

Before the Nationals she studied books on bridge strategy but often disagreed with the experts. She could only explain that bridge was more structure than cards, and it had to be realized in the mind. She'd had a breakthrough in understanding the game early on, and sensing what was going to happen charged her almost to laugh while playing as the gift proved its presence by bearing out her higher sense of order with repeated victories.

It carried over into her personal life as well. Bridge extended over the family like an umbrella, became her children's purpose as well. They were taking her trophies to show-and-tell, proclaiming her mission to become a Life Master and vied for rights to play "fish" and "war" with her. She'd only play against those who'd done everything she said. The Big O had sent the family a "dog house" board with hooks and dogs — each with the name of one of the three children. Only one could be placed on the hook in the doghouse at any one time, and very seldom was it empty.

Caroline organized the children into a chore brigade to handle all of her duties before she left. There was the cat box, the bathroom, the yard, the garbage, kitchen, clothes and their rooms. They were not accustomed to being responsible for everything, but she squelched any and all whining by grounding them. They couldn't go out for a week. When they came home from school, she was usually on the phone with Ethyl, laughing and talking bridge. Her only acknowledgement was to steer each one to a task, snapping her fingers to bring them to attention. They found themselves doing things they'd done the day before. Frustrated, they complained, and a few days before she left, their grounding had extended over the period she would be gone, and all three of them were in the doghouse that had only been in the house for a few weeks. At first they thought it was cute, but now they hated it.

The day before she left, she was completely frazzled with the kids and with Peter as well. "No one around here helps me. One time in my life I make an important trip, and this is what I get. You all really frost me." When she said she was frosted, they knew it was serious, but they had no recourse except to clean, but even then, it wasn't good enough for her. Franklin had to do the bathroom floor three times that day, and little Peter was crying on his bed that he didn't want her to go. "I can't wait to get away from you three," was her reply. "If I lose, it'll be your fault."

When she boarded the plane for St. Louis and eased into the seat next to Ethyl, Caroline was convinced she was going to win big, but Ethyl had become a liability with worrying about the possible consequences of continuing her fling. "Look," Carol told her, "just keep him separate from the game, OK? We're going to play bridge, that's all." Ethyl expressed her relief. "Jesus, you act like I'm your mother," Carol said sarcastically. She'd already made up her mind that she couldn't trust Ethyl in personal matters. Whatever else happened, she wanted to win, just as she wanted to be loved.

Being loved was a critical issue, and Caroline was torn apart by the question of love. She could never demand it from her parents. She'd hardly ever approached them, and discussions were not encouraged. At thirty, she sometimes wondered how she'd learned as much as she had since no one told her much about anything. Until she was married, she felt love as an unrequited crush and was always told it wasn't love and would pass. When real love happened, she would know it, she was told, but every time she thought she loved someone, she thought she knew it, but it was so much like what she was told wasn't love that she eventually gave up on trying to fight it or figure it out. There was no affection in the house, no hugs at night, no kissing. Seldom praised, she lived in the shadow of Annie and her two brothers, quiet and sullen traits for which she was often berated.

For Caroline, love was something out of reach, something not received, or a pocket of feeling in the heart that caused painful damage when someone was lost to her. She sensed that most when Annie died. The only way she could explain the despair and ache of loss was that she'd really loved her sister, that all the rivalry was a selfish form of having taken her for granted, a gloss that obscured what she really meant. After the funeral, she began to drive the point into her children, especially when she was angry with them, that someday she would be gone. "I'm the only mother you've got," she would scream, or, "You're going to drive me to an early grave." Soon love and death were intertwined in the children's minds. They were sick of hearing about it later in their lives, but as children they worried about showing their feelings, and showered her with affection. It often made her cry to hear it, and she would tell them how miserable she was as a child, that she was an "ugly duckling" and no one had loved her.

But the most common of all her interactions with the children was to remind them how they were just like everyone else in her life and did not love her. "We do, we love you," they would say. "I don't believe you," she'd answer. "You're only saying it to get out of trouble."

Their biggest mistake was not to buy her a birthday cake one year. They sang "Happy Birthday," to her that morning in unison and gave her little presents they'd made for her the night before. But she told them to go away. It was a school day, and when they came home, she was still in bed. She'd stayed out especially late the night before, had had a few drinks while playing bridge, and had a bit of a hangover the following morning. She'd been in and out of bed for one remedy or another and cried when she checked the mail. There was nothing from her mother or father, not even a card. When the children came home for lunch, she made sandwiches and remained distant and depressed. Chantal asked, "What's wrong mummy?" but got no reply. They kept saying Happy Birthday. At most, she'd say "Thanks a lot," sarcastically. Between the three of them, they must have said it a hundred times, but it had no impact. She felt totally miserable and

The Voyage of a Bean

found herself looking at her children as creatures spoiled by too much kindness. They were hindering her when they should be centered only on doing whatever they could to help her.

"Where's mumma?" asked little Peter who was the last to come in from school. "Still in bed," said Chantal. "I think she's sick." The three of them went to her door and quietly pushed it open. "Happy Birthday mum, are you OK?"

"Am I OK?" she mocked, thinking of her father with hate. "No, I'm not OK."

"What's wrong? Can we get you anything?"

"Did you get me a cake?"

"A cake?"

"A birthday cake. Did you get me a birthday cake?"

"A birthday cake? No, sorry, want us to go get you one?"

Caroline began to cry. "I can't believe you three ingrates didn't even get me a birthday cake on my birthday." They had no idea they were expected to do such a thing. There was no precedent for it. "You're more concerned with the school ending this week and being on summer vacation than you are for your own mother. Get out of my sight."

They backed out of the room. "What are we gonna do?" asked Franklin. "We have to get her a cake." And so they went off, walking the mile and a half to the food store to get their mother a birthday cake.

"It's too late. I don't want it," she said when they brought it in the door. "And anyway, you ran out of here without asking my permission to go to the store. And whose money did you use?"

"I had some money left over from my birthday, mummy," said Chantal starting to cry.

"If you had the money, why didn't you buy it yesterday? Give it to me!" They handed over the bag, and she took the cake out of the box and angrily crammed it down the drain. She turned on the disposal, and under the running water, crammed and ran it. It chugged and rumbled, vibrating the whole counter. Finally, only the clean hum of a clean drain could be heard.

She sent them to their rooms with no dinner. They heard the

phone ring when their father called that night. He was away on business. They heard her tell him they were ungrateful brats, and they didn't get her anything for her birthday. They knew they'd have a choice when he got home: the brush or the belt. The concept of gift giving, with all the attendant joys, no matter what the occasion, had changed forever in the house. They always remembered to buy a cake after that, but over the years this birth symbol reminded them with increasing significance of a moment in time when something natural in them started to die.

When their cab dropped off Caroline and Ethyl in front of their hotel, a little girl with red hair rode by on her bike, and Caroline remembered the time she'd been totally alive. She was back on her bike, pumping the pedals and racing in front of the house. Never was she more happy or free than at that moment. It was only a representative moment. Why couldn't she say she was happy until a certain point, say, eight or nine, instead of remembering riding her bike? Perhaps it was that she spent most of her time indoors, and there was always the fear of her father. No matter what memory came to mind, if it had walls around it, the threat of her father formed a cloud. The bike was a refuge.

She remembered seeing her father and another woman while riding one day. They were coming out of a coffee shop in the square. She rode up to say hello, and remembered the surprise and anger in her father's face. "Have you been spying?" he shouted.

"Which one are you," the lady asked, "Anne or Carrie? Oh, she's so cute Oakie." The little redhead blushed red.

"Shut-up and get in the car," he told her.

"Just a minute. Carrie, you don't remember me, but I was your nurse when you were born." Her father now pushed the woman into the car. She complained he was hurting her arm.

"You get home young lady and keep mum," he said pointing his finger at the little girl. As they drove away, she waved, and he stepped on the siren, which Carrie always asked him to do.

Not knowing what he meant by keeping mum, she thought it had something to do with her mother, and she rode home. "I came to

The Voyage of a Bean

keep you," she said. Her mother didn't understand. "He told me to keep you, mum."

"You mean he told you to keep mum. Where did you see him?" And Caroline told her mother what she'd seen. Only years later did she understand what she'd stumbled onto. The nurse was his mistress. What had started not long after she was born when her father met her, the nurse had supposedly ended. Now her mother knew different. Caroline remembered the scene that night, how he yelled and left her mother crying. As he went out the door he saw Caroline at the top of the stairs. "It'll be the chopping block for you," he called.

The next day was her mother's birthday, and her father didn't call or come home. Caroline was her mother's sole support and tried to bake her a cake, making quite a mess. Through her tears, her mother pronounced it delicious, then cried. Caroline wasn't sure if she liked it.

Looking back, she steamed that her father hadn't had the decency to keep his distance from the house with his floozie. Ethyl had to tap her to end the daydream. She hadn't heard a word and had been looking off in the distance. The little girl on the bike was gone now. Ethyl had paid for the cab but couldn't find any change to tip the driver.

"Being totally alive is just a temporary lie — this is life," she thought to herself. She even wondered at remembering those moments when she had no desire to go back to it. Childhood was just a time to play pretend and then get hit from all sides on a long process of waking up. What is real is eventually all that matters. The weapons of strength write history. The meek inherit the earth alright, not heaven and Santa Claus. She was already regretting letting the children think Christmas had any magic in it.

The phone rang. Ethyl motioned frantically that Carol should answer it. "I haven't picked it up yet, Ethyl. You don't have to use sign language."

It was Mark. "Hey, anyone up there from our neck of the woods?" he asked.

Caroline put her hand halfway over the mouthpiece and said to

Ethyl, "Can you believe he already wants to take me to the woods for some necking."

In the two rounds of bridge that afternoon and evening, she won, beating Charles Goren himself. Ethyl and Pat, and Carol and Mark were having drinks in the hotel lounge. Carol asked Mark to dance, and in a few minutes they started smooching, Ethyl nodded when Carol opened her eyes and winked. It was their prearranged signal to stay away from the room. But she wasn't quick to leave the dance floor, pressing herself against him over the next four numbers.

The mixture of adrenaline from victory and bourbon from celebration was like grease in the steering column. Carol was at the wheel. She pulled him first into the room and then over herself like a tarpaulin over a wet field. She ground into his every thrust, abandoning herself in ecstasy and exhilaration like riding a bike downhill. When he rolled off her, she deliberately questioned what she felt about adultery. "Very underrated," she thought. There was no guilt, no feeling about her husband and children other than she had to lie to them about her Christmas joy. If anything she was amazed that this was only the second penis she had touched, being so much bigger than Peter's, "A bigger peter than Peter's peter," she told Ethyl and couldn't stop thinking about it the next day. She even touched Mark between the legs on the elevator as they stood in the back. When he gasped in reflex and others looked, he said he had a cramp in his side. Later he said he wanted to have it out with her. "You mean you want to expose yourself? Fine, in my room." In what followed, Carol took the upper hand in criticism, calling him a cheat, liar and lousy lover who was trying to destroy her marriage. In the end, she was crying, and threatened to call his wife. He turned white. "Don't do that," he pleaded. "You see," she stood up fuming, "you love her and you do this to me. What did you do this to me for? You don't love me. Get out of here!" And he left.

After that, they never spoke again. "I want it this way," she told Ethyl. "Why should I be like you, worrying about every move I make, and I sure don't want him hanging around."

"What did you do to get rid of him?"

"Don't you know how to scare a dog? I sent him away with his tail

The Voyage of a Bean

between his legs," she laughed, "except for maybe a piece of it. I do want something to remember him by."

"What do you mean, you cut off a piece of it?" asked Ethyl.

"Yeah, right. Jeez, are you naive! Do you have to take it literally? Of course I didn't cut it off." She paused and looked at her friend, then smirked, laughed and said defiantly, "I bit it off."

Caroline was never located after she disappeared. The search for her stopped after two years, and what was known of her, locked in the memory of those who'd known her, grew distant even there as it was unpleasant to recall. Franklin tried to bypass her when she sprang to mind since she was too much for him when she did. She'd managed to prepare his mind almost as a stage where she would not only act out the past, but also take on new roles and lines according to the power and legacy of her spirit. Franklin spawned her out of hiding into daily appearances. She became a negative commentator for his life. At least in the old days she had only been real, but now she was the essence of evil perceived, the evil that drives some people to depression, suicide, or a murderous rampage.

But not Franklin. She would have laughed at him even as he was strangling her, only in the last instant of life giving way to a look of terrible confusion, which might have just been losing consciousness. No, someone else must have done it. She had so many enemies. He had strange dreams about her and looked within himself, but all he found was how much he was like her, which was also what people told him. He hated hearing it, but he knew it was all true. She had her hands around his neck, but he only suffered when he fought her. The more he let her run loose, the more she seemed to loosen her grip, and the better he was for it. He could only fight her in the persona of a weak son she easily controlled, even as a missing person. Franklin's greatest fear was that she would show up again, and, indeed, after three years, she suddenly reappeared. She had gone away to fulfill her dream and was insulted when they questioned her motives. She expected a grand welcome, for she had become a Life Master. The irony was not lost on Franklin, but all of that is a story that can wait for another time.

My Little Flower

When I loved Dahlia, she actually came to stay with my father and me. It was a strange arrangement where he stayed out of our lives and tolerated our intimacy because I promised I would marry her — a fact that brought her relief that she wouldn't be an old maid. Like her face, she had a wonderful disposition when viewed either from an advantageous angle or at the right time of day. In the morning, she was ugly. But she lived each day as if it were a life — dawn was childhood; noon was puberty; from late afternoon through early afternoon she asked life's questions; and later in the evening, spent, she drifted off course incoherently. Her babble carried the drift of her being, however, and I often learned more of what trends were foremost and of what to expect of her from following the poetry of her thoughts during these hours than at any other time of day.

Dahlia wanted marriage more than anything, and for what was for her an excruciating duration, I never made her happy, nor honest for that matter. She was religious, but even after I finally proposed, we kept putting it off and never went through with it. I'd influenced her to tone down her fervor for the church, and she wrote this down in the same indictment along with other crimes which convicted me to life in her prison until we escaped one another. She thrashed me regularly for one of them or another, the predominant felony being that I made her wait for nothing for so many years.

It was wrong to procrastinate, but I made it easier by talking to the child as a father in the morning. In the afternoon, I was patient with her distress over her hair, a pimple, an embarrassing odor, or

The Voyage of a Bean

her not having gone to Sunday school. By putting her on a couch and making long love, I'd make her sleep, and she'd wake at early evening, not to another morning, but to her distresses and crises. I was careful during these mature tirades not to offer myself as a solution. That was the sole criteria for getting through her presentations of the woman she was. Beautiful morning sensations, the frustration of hair that wouldn't hold, lovemaking — none of these had anything to do with anything important to her life during those hours.

She'd often read evenings, and I thought myself fortunate to miss the feeling that her fingers were trying to rearrange the fragments in my soul though her tears were for the jagged shapes in her own that needed to be thrown on a potter's wheel and formed to fill a function. But her readings were from books that gave her fury fire, her rage the base it needed. And so I trembled while she read, not daring to interrupt, wondering what part of me I'd have to hold down in the winds of not marrying her that she'd howl the following day.

But as the night wore on, she aged and entered second childhood, sweetly made me coffee and cake. She would come into the room needing a hug. She needed the same squeeze every night, regardless of my mood or condition. Then she rubbed my back and told me gently while she kissed me that I was a good man. This was the start of her ramble. It was a mix of all that passed in a day, a blend and a mellowing. These were moments to light a fire, for me to read out loud and put her to sleep.

That was when she spoke like one of the mythological witches who could see only when she held the artificial eye. If you have the eye, she will answer your questions. If she has it, she will put it to her head, then chase, catch and cook you. During the first part of our affair, she answered all my questions because I controlled the eye. But later, I let it slip from my grasp as I veered off course, and when she spoke from dozing, she'd already concluded her chase, and was roasting me over a fire. Though she slept, her words saw clean through me like the skewer on which I turned. Somehow, she knew what I was doing — that I was seeing other women.

I hadn't meant to disavow our vows and betray her, but I saw myself imprisoned by a woman whose goal was to become a rustic

My Little Flower

vase or jar, pleasing to God for being of use to others.

With friends as my guide (they were not actively telling me what to do — I just did what I thought they would do) I started seeing other women. My first liaisons were tests of virility. My fantasies, on which I rode to get there, were replaced by galloping nightmares which twisted and tore my head off, absconding me into an inner night. On these paths of insight, from above a numb and shredded neck, I looked from emptiness into lifeless eyes. As Dahlia snuggled close, I shuddered. I controlled all outward signs from within a dark cloud, reaching out to adjust the smile properly and put an acceptable degree of life into still lifeless eyes. She'd ask if anything was wrong. Inexperienced hands would rush out of the cloud. An excuse would have to be fabricated. The frown and lifeless eyes would have their links, and the hands in the cloud saw the universe might take a few more days to create.

As for the affairs, I kept going back and getting better. I took experience I'd gained into each new affair, and watched possibilities multiply as I became more adroit, or more numb. It was the same in front of Dahlia. I learned to use the excitement of a breakthrough in a new romance to seem excited over an occurrence in our lives. I became comfortable with cheating, but behind every feeling faked was the fact which gave the feeling its life. My vision of myself was always in twos, and it was exhausting to keep it in order.

After such escapades, I had no commitments, neither to people nor to concepts. I was free to philander, but after what that had done to me, it wasn't a lifestyle that attracted me. It had been a direct challenge to experience to show me the rich fabric of life, but it turned out to only show me the cheap stuff out of which I was made.

One night Dahlia started talking in her sleep about my double life. She said something about seeing shadows not cast by each way that I carefully moved. Then I was careless. I came to bed late. She didn't wake completely, but kissed me and commented that a woman put a mask on me. I hadn't washed my face. As comfortable as I thought I was, as numb as I told myself I was, I couldn't live that way. I thought I had traded my nerves and fears to gain control, but so much more went along and out of me that I can hardly begin to list the loss, but I would start the list with loss of peace of mind. That was gone, and I spent the rest of the relationship running from the beast and becoming it, alternating between the two.

It is comparable to spit on the sidewalk. In the summer, it evaporates quickly, or is washed away by the rain. When I started having affairs, each fling seemed to dissipate in light breezes. But then it became icy cold, and my experiences like frozen lumps littered the streets. Numbly hunched in the wind, I followed them everywhere like bread crumbs in a maze.

That night I dreamed that I'd been spending a great deal of time with Dahlia. I knew I couldn't see her much longer because I'd killed her mother. When Dahlia and I had started dating some months earlier, her mother came over to my house to object. One day she got me so angry that I swung the nearest object and killed her.

I'd been careful about cleaning up and knew I'd hidden the body well, but the memories were generally blocked as I tried to lead a normal life. Guilt came in now and then as I remembered what I'd done (like a recognition that I am going to die), but I forced the overwhelming sense of it out of my mind. Even Dahlia never brought up the fact her mother had disappeared. Our relationship continued as usual, though seeing her became increasingly painful as more and more of the memories invaded.

One day several months after the murder, my father and I were talking. We were in the bathroom at the urinals, and he said to me, "So, have there been any deaths you know of concerning you recently?" I gave him a funny look, zipped up and said, "That's a horrible question," and went my way.

But the memories began to invade more intensely than ever. I knew I had killed someone. I couldn't get it out of my mind. Everything I'd ever wanted was threatened if I were caught. I wanted to be free, but I'd damned myself by the deed. Now the dating was too intolerable to continue. Dahlia never mentioned her mother, and I wondered why she hadn't been missed, what Dahlia thought had happened to her. Then for the first time it occurred to me that the mention of her mother was conspicuous by its absence and that perhaps I was suspected by more than my father, and they were testing

My Little Flower

me. I hadn't asked about her mother either.

A few days later, my father called about fixing up his building. He wanted me to come over and see the place. He'd turned it into a restaurant, and he took me on a tour. Afterwards, we went out to the alley which was in front of the building. The tide was out. There was a door in front of the building that I'd never seen before. My father took out his keys. He said he wanted to show me something. He opened a lock and swung the door open. We stepped in a dark room, and he pointed to something in the corner and asked, "Recognize that?" Wrapped up in sheets I'd carefully tied was the body of Dahlia's mother. I'd dulled the sharpness of recognizing I had killed someone to the point that I had failed to arm myself adequately against discovery. He locked the door behind him, leaving me in the darkness with the body.

In mythology, the gods underwent growth, but managed to turn mistakes into natural wonders — blessings to the world. A young and wild god could blunder greatly, relative to the immensity of his power and desire, but he could turn a death into a song, an injury into a waterfall, a lover into a swan.

Even the greatest of the gods would ransack the world for experience, but might change form more subtly, and have planned the entire experience previously, including the miracle.

The world on which the gods walk might have fear of the unknown, but noting the results of interacting with gods following their desires, people might have reason to hope to meet one. The imperfect world could always use another tree. Why not gather all the sickness and imperfection in one lump and hold it up to heaven?

Perhaps a tiny portion will be touched by a deity and be changed forever, eliminating the weight of the great burden and replacing it with a new treasure. But man's own attempt to alchemize the waste increases it. Even as we hold our misery heavenward, it changes in our grip, streaming between our fingers into our face. And yet we credit heaven when we're to blame for what we heap upon ourselves.

She never knew that I'd been unfaithful. That I'd been incorrigibly so would justify categorizing me as in the evil arena. I felt that she'd put me there anyway, without knowing, and I resented the judgment. When I'd see her I'd ask if she thought I was terrible, and she would say, "No, you're a good man," and only for an instant I'd feel just the briefest sense of pleasure in praise which would roll over like a crystal beneath which worms were snuggling. I knew what I was, and I couldn't absorb her compliments. I wanted to cram the worms in her face — to let her know what was actually in me. But I couldn't. She'd smile. I'd think, "She doesn't for a moment think I'm any good" — only because my own guilt had too much imbued my senses to accept a compliment, especially from the one I'd hurt. And yet what she didn't know wouldn't hurt her. I'd begun thinking of her as just so many old bones, but I felt that she was such a good woman that the fact that she left, even though I drove her to it, was telling me I was bad. She didn't have the goods on me, so what made me bad? Sure, I was terrible, but what did she think I'd done?

When she touched me and said I was good, it was her revenge. It became better not to see or talk to her at all. Any meeting with her infected my mind with disturbances like those I'd learned well how to hide from her, but I began to show that I was disturbed, betraying a confused combination of wanting her worship in order to scorn it. Still, unable to fathom the patterns that torment the mind, she'd say how good a man I was. She knew so little of me. But in spite of all my evil ways, she had complete trust in me. She thought I was a good man. Still, I continued to deceive her. She called me good despite the truth; and despite her many lovely qualities, I called her bad.

As for the dissolution of the affair, Dahlia finally broke away. I wish that there were contracts one could make for only certain times of day. I'd gladly take her early joys and late insights over what I've seen of any other woman, but it's her night that sets her tone. I told her of my need to gain experience. I projected a semblance of what I thought was her spiritual profile, and I dove into an imagined sense of her purity, missing her real self in a lie as bad as one that drives another away. She sensed the growing gap and tried to draw me back, but I would not stop. So, it was a great sin to drink from the well of life according to her! I must follow my growing thirst to live, I told her, and added that we were drying one another out. "I leave you to your drink," she said and left.

When Dahlia moved out, she left behind a mask which haunted me for months. It sat in a box of odds and ends that she'd forgotten. Vivid in yellow and red glazes, it was alive with her sullen, unattractive features. It watched me until I buried it in the box. It had been made from her face, and it fit her perfectly.

The plants she once tended were overgrown in the window. They were becoming like me without her — pot bound, stunted, and bearing no fruit. When I met her, she was searching through the Bible, and was content. I'd taken her away from that. Just before she left me, I found her trying to glean meaning from poems and novels over her head, and I found myself explaining things to her without success, until all she could say was her feelings had changed. It was as Pascal said, Literature must be understood in order to be loved; Scripture must be loved in order to be understood.

The more she got to know me, the more she learned to explore my privacy. The contents of my cellars and crawlspaces she searched and documented. Added to the bright, warm and open sides that she loved in me, the dark corners clouded the view, frightening her until at last she frantically headed for the high ground, shaking off the spiders. She thought she never had found anyone so able to warm her. After her inventory, she'd never met anyone with such fearful and dangerous recesses.

Another way to explain the dissolution of our love — things had a way of creeping out when she'd go out. Before her return, I used to have to stuff them back in their jack-in-the-box slots. I lived constantly on edge, wondering when something would pop out to scare her away. After nearly five months after she left, we weren't even talking to one another. She'd moved to another part of the village, and walked a different way to the same job she'd found when she'd decided to live with me.

During the first few months after we separated, things she'd left behind seemed to grow like mushrooms on the sides of trees in the closets and the cabinets, and I'd cut them off and fill boxes that she'd occasionally come to get, taking the mushroom salads away with her. These meetings were curt yet somehow tender. When she

The Voyage of a Bean

came to harvest the final mushrooms, the last two boxes I'd collected for her final visit, they seemed to wither in my eyes as she walked away. The plants in the window overgrew and screamed for release. Then weeds of my bachelorhood grew over and engulfed me.

My father told me once that when the right woman arrives, it's a call to recognize the whole experience, not just fulfillment of desire. He said that the arrival of such a woman puts you where you stand in the whole perspective, and getting along with purposes is an essential necessity of the soul. On the other hand, I'd always thought of women as soldiers who wage a war to put their flag into a man, claiming them as territory. I'd cleared her off my soil, but had become a desolate landscape.

As the weeks passed, I missed her, but when I tried to see her, I sensed she'd long before outgrown me. So much time had passed since we'd first met. Even the crabapple orchard where she made an indication that she wanted me to come closer had been removed.

Dear Dahlia,

I am not writing to undo what has already been done — too much has been undone to be done again. This letter is just a way to clear up a few details that I don't feel can be resolved by other means. It is irrelevant for you to attempt to respond to any of this since it is just a summing up of how I feel about what has happened. It would be futile to think it is within anyone's power to alter these perceptions.

During the years we spent together, though I loved you very much, I winced as many times as I rejoiced in our love. I think the seeds were planted when I first found aspects of you both irresistible and impossible.

Remember when we first met at my father's concert, when I walked you home and you stopped and took my hand, pointing out the crabapples growing on those small trees? I stopped to look at you, not those crabapples. You were exuberant and alive, but you had fixed ideas of the world. You were filled with an almost religious sense of all that was surrounding you. Those apples merely catalyzed this spiritual sense, and I was no more a part of your worship than a branch. I felt worthless and empty. For me, you were like a beacon that might fill me with life for all the life you revealed in that walk through the tiny orchard, but I felt dead

My Little Flower

by comparison, without a shred of hope that I might stir any reverence in you for me. From that moment on, it seemed in the early part of our love that I continued this tradition. Every time I was near you, I felt judged and odious compared to what you had going within that heart of yours.

Do you remember when I used to come visit you? You would be baking bread in the kitchen, bustling about with a seeming angelic enjoyment of every simple thing, even to crumbs of flour and yeast. Mundane tasks like cleaning up while lumps of dough were rising seemed to have a force of music you could hear. Your every effort seemed attuned, responding as a dancer flows interpreting the harmonies, the rhythms, the spirit of the whole piece. I watched your dances from the chair. All I could do was pretend that I was reading a paper. Nervously, I faked being relaxed. I was out of step with songs. It was dead silence for me except when you were in the room, and when I watched you stirring eggs in the bowl, hands white from having kneaded great balls of dough, pressing out great choruses of a yeast civilization, it was as though you were shyly saying you felt my eyes on you, as though you knew I detected the dance, even if you stopped in embarrassment that I still could hear its emanation from the sink like sparks flying out of the birth of total oneness with everything here and beyond.

I wanted you to take me into that spinning force of fire and make me feel it with you. I yearned to have a chance to feel that force as naturally as it filled you. But as I said, I was like silence and death on the chair and could no more impart more music to you than a flame can add pages to a book when its flames begin to dance in the contents. What I wanted was to be engulfed in you, but what would happen is what did. By degrees, I was able to draw you into trust that my sense of you was exactly what it seemed to you to be. That shyness that you felt, when lifted, saw me as I saw you because I'd learned displays of dance though I had no steps or music of my own. So when we came together, though I felt the song and the fire and was drawn in, it was a semblance of all I'd dreamed could be, but in the morning, I was left again with the same despair of being what I am. With it was the sense of doom that since you'd not implanted wholeness that I'd watched for months in you, I had rather filled you with the seed of emptiness, and that in time you'd come not just to see me for what I was but grow to see what I had done to you.

Why should I have felt so much despair in attaining what had been my

The Voyage of a Bean

only goal? In you I saw every chance to reach what I'd wanted to be in life. You certainly never needed me in your universe to have a sense of wholeness yourself, so I wanted you to see me, for that would mean somehow that I fit into the overall scheme of things, that I made sense and was a part of the universe. But when you accepted me, it was as if you were giving up that oneness with everything else. You were giving that sense of life up for me. Don't you see that I was irrationally concluding that you were weak to prefer me to your religion of existence? How could I fit into something so wonderful, and how could it be so wonderful if it wanted me? You could only remain perfect in my eyes by refusing me, but that refusal made me seem so base to myself for feeling that I had to have you. As soon as I did, that perfection was gone because I'd tainted it, and I could not forgive myself for that though now you loved me.

In time, I reached a point where I couldn't be myself with you. It was impossible to suddenly hide in a friendly facade after parading myself feelings naked before you, but it turned out that all those feelings that you'd seen parading naked, seeming to have music, seeming to know how to dance, were the mere signs of thrill at being around you, and when they faded or receded as the real aspects of myself came forward, I was angry that you could see me as I am. It became too difficult to fake. I was tired of not being able to show you a kind of perfect worship all the time. Even your songs began to play less often, and I felt that I'd corrupted someone who'd been fine without me. Your growing disappointment with me proved to me that you were able to see through me, and though I know that you had never taken me for anything less than a friend, I felt more and more like a fool, and behaved like one, slowly abandoning your trust and withering into utter hopelessness.

It started from shame. There was nothing I could call my own. Everything in my life had been given to me. All the external reality was due to someone else. The house I had lived in, owned by my father; the clothes I was wearing, bought by my father. You were the only thing that had come to me on its own, but what could I offer in return? I was even afraid that you might love someone else. I was paranoid that my father secretly loved you and that by degrees you'd find in him what you'd hoped to find in me. Though none of that was happening, I was blaming you for it already. As far as I was concerned, your departure was a foregone conclusion. You

My Little Flower

were already abandoning me though sweetly kissing me. Though you were swearing love to me forever, in my sickness I felt as if there was something greater you had to cherish because your heart just had that element of focus, and that sooner or later you'd detect it was nowhere in me and that you'd find it, wherever it was.

The fact is that it all happened as my demented fears projected it. You grew tired of my stall tactics and detected my concealed disgruntlement at what might have been the finest thing that ever happened in my life. It was as if I knew I didn't deserve to be accepted in the club so I burned down the building in revenge. I let you go, and I made it painful for you. It became too much for me to face myself for never facing you. I'd no hope of being unable to stand up strong with you. You needed to get out of my life so I might change my life to be worthy, but once you were gone, I was back where I was in empty frustration knowing that you had given years of solid devotion that I'd paid back with betrayal. I can never take back what I did to you. Some say that love can always find a way, but in this syndrome, I don't think it can ever navigate the labyrinth to me, though I often pray that I could cut the string in the heart of the maze that drags me back to be lost in the center every time I reach the outside entrance like the Minotaur that looks out to see and knows that you are somewhere across the waves. I hope you can dance again and that what I have done has not injured you, though I imagine you have the strength to make even a limp seem part of the overall design.

I take a regular, heavy beating for losing you. I sit around and curse you for one thing or another for something that happened during those last few months, but overall, I don't blame you one bit. There was so much leeway that you gave me. There were many things you wanted me to do that I couldn't have done in a short time, but you never expected major changes overnight. I never knew there was such a well of tolerance. You were willing to give me a long, long time. It's just that I didn't think at the rate I was going that I'd ever really sit down and be an open husband with you. I let too much water go under the "bride."

I would try to reel you back, but I am still too broken up. I told you people could change, but at the time, I wasn't doing much in terms of changing myself. I am trying to do that now. I have known being weak, but having survived losing you, I know that I am not a weak person.

The Voyage of a Bean

> *Finally, for you who finds it so easy to be friends, I won't ask you to remember me, but if it is not too difficult, I ask rather that you forgive me. Since for me remembering you is most difficult, if you had the power to grant my wish, I'd ask that you help me to forget you. I know there is no longer a small orchard where you could show me all that life offers in the form of one simple thing like a green crabapple, but I cry for the fact that my fingers will never again feel the warmth, the touch, and the strength of the charge of your hand.*

I never gave her the letter. I suppose I thought it wrong to admit so much and reveal such feelings of guilt. It might have made an impression, but I selfishly thought I'd a better chance of winning her back not by showing such weakness, which in fact she might have seen as a first sign of strength, but in continuing to posture that if she wanted me back that she'd have to come crawling. She never knew that side of me willing to admit that I had been so wrong, but as I had always feared and probably caused her to detect by thinking about it constantly, she knew enough to leave. At the same time, the letter only scratched the surface of admission and fell far short of any kind of confession. I also feared the added shame of not having come totally clean and what might happen if she thought well of me because of the letter.

Had she returned at any point during the years that followed, I'm sure she wouldn't have been surprised to discover that I continued my traditions of seeking gratifications for every desire that slowly wasted me to my present state reviewing how I quenched my thirst with sands that parched my throat and made a desert of my empty present.

I did have the satisfaction of feeling her healing touch one last time, but I was too ashamed to speak or even look her in the eyes. When I remember those first, wonderful days with her, I think that if we dig with the tools the Lord gives us and dig where He has placed us to dig, we'll find enough to live on, and surely, live well. I might have known such peace with Dahlia, but for some reason, I had to look elsewhere. I couldn't capitalize on a great gift, simply to stand by it to give it the air and light God promised to everyone that there should be growth. My trust was to attend, to just watch, but instead I threw darkness over it that spilled all through me in various forms of discontentment. How could either one of us grow in that environment?

She was everything I ever wanted and was all that I would ever need, but I couldn't handle the prosperity. I never felt clean with her, and I never came clean after she left me, because I wasn't clean to begin with. Whenever I remember Dahlia, I ask myself, what is it that possesses us to drift further into disorder even when it's peace we want, which we let drift further out of reach?

Who knows, and who can explain what happens in the mind after such a loss? In my case, I had one long, horrible nightmare of murder. Dahlia was dead, and I was guilty, and when I woke up, it took quite a while before I could shake the sense that it wasn't a dream. It really felt like I had actually had killed her.

This was a night filled with disparate images of Dahlia. First I killed her and put her body in a canvas bag and dumped it into a pond. I nervously returned to the pond the next day and found my father swimming there. Somehow, he was Dahlia, only he was still also a young boy. I told him to get out. He started for the shore and made a sign that he had discovered something. His feet were touching whatever it was, and he beckoned me to help him. I knew that I should have been showing excitement, that I should have been asking him to describe it, to hold it, keep track of it and not to lose it, but I kept trying to call him off as if it were nothing. Torn, I thought I woke, but I was still dreaming, and I felt like I really had committed a murder because the feeling of having done it was so real. I was also afraid of going back to sleep. The pond was just outside my bedroom window, and rather than to deal with such images, I went out to stay awake, and I saw a police car was following me.

They picked me up and took me to a building with a number of murder victims. Dahlia was one of them. Because of this, I was filled with the sense that I was somehow the murderer, but I was not sure just what I had done, or how and when I had done it. The corpses were upstairs. There were no signs of violence, but many legs and arms were sticking up. I saw Dahlia in the corner smiling at me. Her eyes were open, and she seemed to be staring at me. I looked away.

The Voyage of a Bean

There was a woman there as well. The police were arresting her. From her glances, I could see she was interested in me. I had crossed to the other side of the room, and as I looked over to Dahlia, it was as if the eyes had followed me. They were still staring. As they started to lead the woman away, an officer suggested that I quietly go along and try to get close to her so that she would tell me everything. I agreed, and something else — I was not surprised by the suggestion. In fact, I was rather relieved to be going to jail.

Once in jail, I was chosen for the lead in a play Dahlia was directing, but I didn't know the lines. I was given contact lenses to wear. My lines were to be written on the wall, and I would be able to read them with the contacts. As the play opened, the contacts started to grow. They were painful and too big to wear. I was afraid that I had broken them, but rather than take them out and be asked what I did to them, I faced the wall and tried to read. My eyes were watering, and I could only see that there seemed to be text, but I couldn't make out any words in the blur. The play went on around me as I squinted for what to say, not knowing what anything meant. Somehow I suffered through the embarrassment and carried scars with me off stage, only to learn later that I had given a masterful performance of a part Dahlia had written especially for me.

The steps led me out of jail. The chase was on, and I took refuge in a coffee shop where no one had heard about my escape. They were discussing Dahlia as if she were alive, describing events so recent as to make me wonder if I might have failed in killing her.

I stole a car and drove onto a bridge. Strangely, I was looking at the back of my head from the back seat. A shot rang out. I saw myself look to the passenger side and heard myself say, "Ah well — it's only a small caliber weapon." I heard another shot and saw it rip into my head. I slumped to the wheel. I saw the ground fly by, the car going out of control. I was somewhere on the bridge behind it when it crashed through restraints and plummeted into the chasm below.

The water revived me. I wasn't dead. I had a key to Dahlia's apartment in my pocket, and the next thing I knew, I was there. I walked in to find her making love with someone else. I left. Later, I returned, and she was reading in bed, alone. Her body language called for me to climb in bed. It was incredible that I was with her again. That thought alone relieved all my stress, and I knew I really did love her. As we lay there, afterwards, another Dahlia entered, and merged with Dahlia in bed. I was somehow not confused and saw it as the spirit from the Dahlia I'd killed being restored to life. But after that she changed. She was suddenly more aware of me than before. Her spirit roaming around brought full knowledge of my activities back, and this informed Dahlia was quite angry. No matter how I tried, I couldn't calm her down. I had thoughts of killing her again, but it was more about separating her from the true knowledge of me than really wanting to hurt her. Even though what I wanted was for her to love me, I had done so much damage that I had only the choice between a dead soul that didn't know anything about me or a living being that knew everything about me. I could only deal with Dahlia the same way I always had. I needed full control. I knew it was all a lie, but I needed her undying devotion and trust even if it meant that she must die, so in this craziest of dreams that I've ever had, I ended up killing her again. I watched the spirit go off sadly into the night. I carried the body out to hide it. I purposely did not say it was lifeless because I couldn't believe the look of absolute trust after what I had just done. Beams of love and admiration for me were pouring out of her eyes.

She smiled so sweetly as I put her in the trunk of my father's car. As I closed it, there were tears in her eyes, but they were of love and forgiveness, and it made me so uncomfortable that I ran away from the car. From behind me, I heard it start, and I turned in a panic and ran after it. I didn't even know who was driving, but how long would it be before someone would open the trunk? It wouldn't take much to tie the murder to me. I went straight for where my father lived.

When I neared his house, I was first disoriented, then distracted. I couldn't seem to find it. Where the house had been, there was a store. I entered and found it was filled with pornography. I quickly forgot my purpose and started browsing the magazines, amazed at the depths to which pornographers had sunk.

The cover of one magazine was unspeakable. I wondered how anyone could have produced it. The other publications were almost as

The Voyage of a Bean

bad. It angered me, and I was drawn to as controversial. It was just another step in a regression but I had the comfort and discomfort of not being alone. There were many people reading the magazines as if they were used to them. I had vowed never to accept such things, but I looked at them anyway. I was shocked that some of it was exciting, and though aware of having compromised myself, I wanted to see more. While looking over this garbage, I maintained a sense that I was still a good person. Then I recalled that I was a murderer and had some kind of business to attend to, which I remembered only vaguely. On my way out of the store, I saw a young lady in a one-minute photo booth. Her smile was so familiar that I approached her. Our conversation was so natural that my inhibitions melted away, and she invited me into the booth with her and closed the door.

As I kissed her, I wanted to pass on this sense of well-being, to convey my profound sense of trust. Intoxicated, I felt our soul strands wrapping us into one neat little ball, never to be undone, but as these feelings were shooting through me, I wondered if she was feeling them as well because she was not very responsive. I also had the feeling we were being filmed. A picture was developing slowly in my mind. As the resolution became more clear, the enveloping blanket of security unraveled, and I remembered the body in the trunk. How foolish to think I could find or offer any kind of peace! I suddenly began to recognize features of the booth. It was my father's car. I was in the trunk. I felt the engine start. My heart raced. I tried to pull away. Her arms around me were suddenly so tight. "Don't leave me," she cried. I pushed up with all my might. Thank God, it opened. Filled with guilt, I clambered like a crab out of the sea, not as a scavenger but as a clawless prey. As I popped outside, I was blinded by the flashes of many cameras, each making an exposure of one of the horde of confessions pouring out of my mind. The records would be compiled and stored where I could be reached by the inquisition when it arrived. Then the drama shifted from me to the trunk, where not in flashes, but under a bright, steady light, a single flower had grown and was withering. It was my Dahlia. I woke with so much fear and guilt, I knew the verdict was in, deep within.

This dream was one of an endless stream of disjointed scenes

My Little Flower

which I remembered not in pieces but whole. For days I was filled with those images, wondering why I'd had such a nightmare. It took away my peace of mind. I lost the sense I had of feeling whole. Despite the span of real experience with Dahlia, my sense of her was replaced with this series of disjointed images which hardly made any sense. There was no window through which my numbness could be reached and taught to feel. For a long time, I felt as though I'd really done something to spiritually kill her. I knew she was somewhere out there, but I believed she must be scarred from knowing me. I often wondered about her, but over time, I finally moved on. For many years I hardly thought about her until after going through some old pictures one day, I just couldn't seem to get her off my mind.

It was hard, but I called her. I was afraid she would be upset to hear from me, but she was quite happy. She had married and had several children who had grown up quite well under her care. I told her I'd always thought she would make a great mother. As for myself, I had never married. She was right that I would stay a bachelor, but we did not talk about such things. We laughed and reminisced about the good things, and I was surprised how much she remembered, and how she longed to remember more. I even started to think that she might still be holding a torch for me, that her marriage might not be a good one, and I got off the phone and entertained the thought that she might want to come back to me, that all I had to do was something proactive to set it in motion. But she still knew nothing about me. The truth was still locked away, suffocating me in a trunk.

That night I had a dream. I was with her thirty years in the past. I had full knowledge of the future, and it made me want to kill her, but her only crime was being happy without me in the future, and she didn't know this. She only wanted me, but I was so filled with anger that I was effectively hating her during the time I supposedly loved her. I woke realizing it was not only about the things I'd done but what they kept me from giving to her. Her resilience was what hurt me most. What did it mean that she looked past my essence, unaware of the hidden truth, yet didn't require me to sustain her? What it meant was that I would always be alone, dreaming of my little flower following the light and surviving in the darkness.

The Good Host

After the Second World War, a group of real-estate developers bought a large parcel of pasture and designed a village that would occupy this land and be a good host for its people. They placed schools, churches and parks strategically and a shopping plaza in the center. Schools and streets were named long before any construction actually began, and only when the entire plan was complete was ground broken for model homes.

Hundreds of GI's and their new families flocked to survey the plan and pick out a spot for a reasonably-priced, single-family home that was built almost as quickly as an airstrip on a remote Pacific island by a dedicated corps of engineers. Within a few years, the entire village had been largely sold with construction completed for every promised convenience including police, fire, city hall, swimming pool and library. An aerial photo taken in the early 1950s looked very much like the architectural drawing that had been used to sell lots early on.

I was born at this time and within my first five years of life walked up to a simple doorway to a house on my street. It was at the end of summer, and my mother had taken me to this house and left me on the doorstep while she went inside to talk with a friend for a few minutes. As I stood in front of the screen door, I couldn't see very much inside because it was so bright outside, but I could hear everything. There was my mother in the kitchen laughing, and the sound of a television. There was a football game on at the time. A boy and his father were watching the game. The boy was my age, and his father was teaching the game to him.

The Good Host

I did not know it at the time, but I was standing in front of something other than a house where a friend of my mother lived. The screen door was actually just the covering for a large radio speaker, and the house was the radio itself. The people inside including my mother were the tubes. There was a field behind the house that was used as an ice skating rink every winter. Wires went from under the house and drew power from cold cells under the field.

It was a one-day-and-for-my-ears-only broadcast. The signal was encoded so that I would only be able to unravel and understand its meaning after many years. It was a time capsule placed within me bearing an imprint of itself, not just as a radio but as the entire place at the time so that I could bear it out later when it turned me into nothing more than a housing of tubes drawing energy from cold experience while buried memories kept another light burning inside.

And so I broadcast that moment exactly as it was planned by the founders. There is a door into a house. The screen is vibrating with voices. There is a game being played and two conversations. The conversation in the foreground is between a father and a little boy about the game of football. My own father never taught me the game. The one in the background is between two women. It is about the game of bridge. My mother preferred leaving me outside than have me next to her. Suddenly there is a power drain in the house. The television signal fades momentarily, and the light in the kitchen dims for a second. At the same time, there is a discharge that bursts from the doorway onto a little boy waiting on the front step for his mother. The burst is absorbed and reduces itself to a little seed tucked away obscurely in a corner of the boy's mind. It will have its time in the distant future. For the time being, he is fascinated and happy with everything happening around him.

Now we get to hear the message. It is about any era's general placement in the ages. It is a reaction to hundreds of years of London, Paris and all places of rich history that are recognized as cradles of human thought and history. The burst from that single moment of my experience has ripened to demand equal time and permanence on the stages of history. I demand that my home town

The Voyage of a Bean

be recognized as having been a place where thousands of souls enjoyed the seasons where there was plenty of parking and a responsible effort to give children the proper facilities of both education and entertainment. It was a bastion of humanity with form and function — a dignified posture after a horrible war won for the sake of freedom. It should be remembered in the proper annals as a platform of stability on wavering seas. Though every trace of it be finally washed away, it should make some kind of mark on minds living at any given time.

Unfortunately, as any temporary structure made for a specific purpose is discarded when it has been used, the great village where I grew up has been largely abandoned, but it should still be greatly remembered, but not as founders would have hoped through any implant in a boy. They have their reward, far beyond any hoped-for historical mention, for there has been an unexpected crawling outward of their prefab principles that they never could have foreseen. In fact, in the over fifty years of replication, their ideals have already caused a national retrofit in strip mall after strip mall. Some say it may not be long before the whole world has been redesigned by the generation which happens to have been nurtured in places such as my home town.

But as for the impact of my experience, the little boy who once stood by that door doesn't exist anymore, and surely no one wants to hear the hidden agenda in the words of a grown man. My praise for the solace received in the village that cradled me is tempered by an understanding that a part of me was doomed from the start to become obsolete. There really isn't time for too much indulgence in a child, and the day finally comes when it's as if the little one left in us were a dread implant meant to be extracted.

The paradox is that if we must evolve and rely on energy derived from the cold truth of experience, it comes at a cost: it uproots innate faith and speeds up the process of slowly dying because it makes everything appear to be crumbling. While it won't kill me to keep it alive, and though it cannot sustain me as when I was utterly ignorant of the meaning of a lie, it's the only point of access for real faith to take root, emerge and endure.

A Siren in the Woods

I'm not out of the woods yet. They're more wet than lovely, dark or deep. I'm walking along a river bank, and I can hear sirens in the distance. Who knows what it is? Maybe it's a system test. Perhaps it's some kind of calamity, but someone will take care of it. I'm just trying to get away from it all and listening to sirens does not contribute to my enjoying an afternoon walk in the woods.

My path merges with an instructor who begins to expound on the history of the region. We reach a large clearing, and she takes up a position indicating that she is used to addressing large groups. But even though it is possibly due to all the rain, no one else has showed up for her class. Still, it was not my intention to be part of her lecture in the first place. I try to be polite and listen, but I soon grow bored and start to feel the need to slip away. At some point the realization hits me that I am in no way bound to stay. There is no obligation of any kind, but it still feels embarrassing, and my sympathy goes out to her. I know I have no reason to feel embarrassed, so I pick a moment when she looks down for a moment, and I turn and walk away at a brisk pace. I can still hear her speaking as I disappear into the woods. I wonder what she must be thinking at this point. Is it out of professionalism that she continues? Does she do it in order to receive full payment for her services? Is she bound to be there and instruct regardless of whether or not anyone attends her lectures?

Then, suddenly she stops. There is complete silence. I too stop walking, and without the crackling of stems breaking under my feet, for the first time I can hear the birds. Then I hear her say quite loud,

The Voyage of a Bean

"Now I an going to sing," and all at once she breaks into a most beautiful aria. The woods fill with the sound of her serene voice, and somehow I feel like I've gotten a message, learned a lesson as it were. It seems an inspired and perfect reply to the situation for a soul in tune with itself, and I feel I must go back to her.

But I couldn't find her. Her voice was fading in and out in the winds. I strained to hear it better, stopping to listen for the direction, but I couldn't tell where it was coming from. I had wandered to the point where I was lost, but as long as I could hear her voice, I didn't feel any fear. I wouldn't call and break her from singing, and continued to search. If I couldn't find her, I knew she would not receive me well should I be able to find her given that I had abandoned her, and I knew from her song that she didn't need anyone, and this made me want to know her more.

No Hand

Someone I used to work for comes over for a visit. He's still in the emotional throes of a nervous breakdown. He's crying, and he holds me as I try to leave. He won't let me go. He hates everyone for abandoning him, and yet he hangs around the phone waiting for someone to call with some ideas.

Then I go to see my old girlfriend. She too has been emotionally stricken. I thought we'd be alone, but the room is crowded. Her parents have hired a Japanese guitarist and Turkish zither performer to entertain. They stink. Quite uncomfortable, I decide to leave. She follows.

She's changed the color of her hair and has lost weight. She doesn't even look the same, and comparing her state to the one I knew when we were together, it isn't even the same person. I complain we didn't have any time alone at her house. She says it was recommended for her sake that we not be left alone. "What?!" I cry, "Am I a threat? Would we necessarily fight if we were alone?" We are alone, and we are fighting. It wasn't always like this. She says she loves me. My guts and heart twist inside. Tears well in my eyes. "I don't know," I cry, and covering my face I turn to leave.

What I always used to do, I do again: inside I hesitate, hoping she'll follow. As I run, I see her shadow overtaking me. She pulls me to a stop, pledging her undying love. We continue to walk together, churning inside. The way has become extremely arduous with undulating, steep sidewalks with no stairs. I expend enormous physical energy trying to walk around with her. She shows no signs of strain and offers me no hand.

World of the Small

Marcus Jenkins became sensitive about his height as a boy when suddenly he was left behind by his growing peers and looked to be about two grades behind when with them. He was the last picked to be on any team in sports, and gradually gave up his athletic aspirations and instead turned his mind to academics.

There was a point in college where he decided to pursue knowledge over everything else. He'd held various menial jobs through high school and at the university, and as graduation approached and the job market beckoned, nothing really interested him. The corporate world seemed all too stultifying to be excited about, and he couldn't relate to all the enthusiasm at the job fairs. How could anyone be excited about working for a defense contractor? It was beyond him.

One of his professors in the history department had approached Marcus about graduate school. Getting a Ph.D. was more appealing than getting a job, but after a few years, he was disillusioned with school. He'd become nothing more than a teacher's assistant. He graded papers mostly, and taught a few introductory undergraduate courses. What his life would become were he to stay in the university environment became all too clear to him. He became keenly aware of the politics of the history department, the drive for tenure and the abuse of graduate students as a kind of slave class. What he'd wanted was a place to unravel mysteries in private, but he'd struggled with advanced studies. The riddles of what hidden dialectic or gyres guided events were beyond him. As the day of his dissertation approached, he wondered what the heck he was doing in school and what he would do with a Ph.D. in history in the real world. He knew he would never add anything of importance to the discipline. The riddles were beyond him, and the mysteries of corporate life which not so long before had seemed so pedestrian now beckoned him with promised simplicity. He couldn't wait to get out and find himself a cubicle somewhere. He bought a new suit for the next job fair and bought a book that gave him a good answer for a nagging question: Why did you major in history?

He agreed that looking at history was to take a grand survey of the whole picture, and then to live was to apply the general truth on a smaller scale. He was better equipped than most people to endure the confines of a single day, week, year or life because he'd absorbed the sense of what it has meant to live not just one life but generation after generation; culture after culture; through wars and famine; summer and winter; morning, noon and night. He didn't get the first job, but someone finally bought it. He kicked the dust of the library from the bottom of his feet when he left.

He got the cubicle he wanted, but a heavy dose of unexpected politics awaited him. His boss began berating him almost at once, questioning his ability to rise in the organization because he was so short. Marcus let it go. He was prepared to prove himself by his work. Everyone in the office wondered how he could put up with being berated incessantly, but Marcus kept his focus. He also met a short woman named Judy and began to date her. They were married and put down a down payment on a small, single-family home, and Judy became pregnant.

Nothing bothered Marcus as he prepared for the child, but in her seventh month, Judy fell down the stairs and lost the baby. They were devastated, Marcus especially. He withdrew from the world to the point that he wouldn't even go out for a walk. The grass in front of the house went unmowed to the discontent of the neighbors, but he ignored the sarcasm occasionally spoken over the fence or from across the street. The world of his mind became more vivid than the world around him, and as the months wore on, he became increasingly interested in small objects. Anything that was intricate and beautiful that was also tiny was fascinating to him.

The Voyage of a Bean

First it was watches. He spent a month's wages on a Breitling and then bought several more until his wife said enough was enough. Japanese netsukes became his next preoccupation, but they proved to be pricey as well. Gradually he became interested in puzzles, in anything that boggled his mind for a time. He moved from three-piece rings to Rubik's Cube, and finally to the proofs in geometry. He'd hated the study in high school, but one day he picked up a geometry textbook in a store, and the theorems made good sense to him. His wife didn't understand his interest. One day she suggested that maybe one of the famous ancient Greeks lost someone or something, and new knowledge began to float freely down and out through the traumatized mind. She told him that he might be in line to make an important discovery in one of his studies, and that he should on the alert in case the sky opened up and distributed some new knowledge in his mind. Markus asked her what in the world she was talking about. She didn't know. Marcus told her that he wasn't developing anything new. He just seemed to want to hold a little magnifying glass over a tiny insect, or scrape a tiny paint spot off an antique figurine to make it perfect again. She told him that he should think of what he might do to benefit mankind, that great things come from helping others, and he was only hurting himself, and it was time to move on and maybe try to have another child.

What she feared most was that all of his activities were devoid of human contact. In taking comfort with his various diversions in the world of the small, he'd cut out most of whatever it was he had in his relationships with other people. She didn't object too strenuously at first because he'd truly intensified his focus on her particularly, but gradually his isolation affected him emotionally, and he had begun to vent his frustration at her by overreacting to little things. She wouldn't grind the coffee as fine as he liked it, and he would scream it was too weak and refuse to drink it, then after making it himself, he would retreat to listen to musical variations by Bach, Beethoven and Brahms. Later he would come out to offer his apologies and remind her that his days of outward reaching were behind him. What the great composers had done was to center on a single theme and stretch it into great aspect. It was like a great snake with coils forever unwinding from a center. It was like powder coming off a butterfly and filling a whole room with snow, or like a room with beautiful drapes blowing inward from a windy day so beautifully that one would be mesmerized to stay at home. She willingly received his love, and when she became pregnant again, they were cautious and considerate of every particular, and he was the proud witness when she bore a beautiful son.

Without truly being aware of it, Marcus had undergone the benefits of a natural process of grief, and the sudden good fortune, tempered by previous experience, set in motion a delicate machinery of his mind that had been painstakingly put together over a long period of time. Marcus had become a master technician in his job. He was beyond reproach, but that did not stop his boss from putting him down constantly. If anything, Marcus did his job so well that it made his boss look good. When he did not get the credit, he did not complain because he did not care. It was not what was important to him. He was making plans to do other things, perhaps even to return to the university to teach — he wasn't sure.

And he wasn't thinking of leaving his job because his boss called him "shorty" all the time. It didn't bother him even when three years later he was still at the same job, and he was still taking insults. His boss told him he was a little man, that he wasn't important and would never amount to anything. He told Marcus that anyone could fill his shoes though their feet would kill them to try to squeeze into such small loafers. He never missed a chance to call Marcus a good-for-nothing loser who had him to thank for everything, but it never bothered Marcus because it was like the weather: an outside environment, something he couldn't change if he tried. He learned that from studying history. And he was damned if he was doomed to repeat it.

Before he lost his first child, his boss had been able to get under his skin, making him feel worthless, but while Markus was grieving, he had learned to ignore it, and then, after he his son was born, he accepted the abuse as part of the job. Marcus knew he'd discovered the nature of majesty in little things. He knew his boss was not a player in the grand scheme, being far too small-minded and petty to

The Voyage of a Bean

understand the wonder of how everything manages to work together, and his kind of smallness was its own punishment. He liked to remember the young Julius Caesar demanding respect for his power as a birthright. He thought it was strange how the world was cruel, but that those who chose to be cruel in the world somehow received punishment, as if the world somehow had a just heart as well. Like the pirates who had kidnapped Caesar were later killed by Caesar, Marcus felt that there were forces that his boss did not adequately respect, forces at the heart of the world that were readying themselves to devour him for his actions. And when Marcus began looking at the canopy of history again, and the universe as well, not as something great in size but wonderful in miniature, inherently no different from anything simple and beautiful, he felt ready to contact universities about teaching positions. In the meantime, he stayed at his job, taking abuse as usual, but like a Christian seeking the safety of the catacombs, he never brought it home with him, and when his son ran up to greet him at the door, he always did the same thing. He kneeled to the floor, looked into the eyes of his intricate, little boy and told him he was somebody — somebody important, somebody loved — and that it was a wonderful world.

Mr. Pepperdale

This is the story of a modern man in a consumer society. The birth of Mr. Pepperdale signaled the baby boom to begin. His toe was immediately tagged with digits that would mark the beginning of his toeing the line of the state. No one knows whether Mr. Pepperdale's crying in the nursery was a response to this, but later in life, he was always heard to wail on the subject. It was during the sixties, those crazy political times when a whole generation connected ethereally and exerted tremendous influence, then was slowly absorbed into the system in which it had hardly made a dent. Now Mr. Pepperdale was entering his sixties. He was on the verge of being seen and seeing himself as an old man. The sixties were way behind him, and staring him in the face. His dreams were far off while he was beginning to feel the force, the involuntary desire of yawning before the deepest sleep of all. Something was pulling him back though, keeping him awake. He still had some of the anger of youth, but there was no chance of participating in a movement. New generations of young people had each in their turn connected ethereally and exerted some kind of influence, whether it was in music or fashion. But in the end, it was just another decade to wait for its day to be a degraded by the networks into a family sit-com.

Mr. Pepperdale knew he'd always been a little cranky, but now it was beginning to look like it was due to his age. It made him angry that his best qualities were forgiven because he was young, and the same qualities were again forgivable because he was old, and somehow these qualities had made no difference during his middle years when he did not especially exert them because he had to hold down a job. He felt superior to most people, but had to climb the ladder like everyone else, and he suffered the same emotions of watching younger sons of people better connected than he was, promoted over him. But he was no longer connected to others ethereally, through ideas and experiences. Now he was really connected as a part in a machine. He could drop out, certainly, and another part would be found to replace him, but he chose to remain and deal with his anger by solacing himself with the belief that one day he would have his day, that good things would come to him. But they really didn't, and so he developed an inner life of anger and depression, where he absorbed the blows against him in the world without complaint. He rose only so far in his job and was not generally noticed. But sometimes, in his dreams, he was the better person.

One of Mr. Pepperdale's dreams started with his friend Austin insulting a Russian librarian. Calling attention to himself as the superior literary intellect, Mr. Pepperdale asked to speak and remarked that he knew his friend Austin to be calm, that this behavior was unlike him, and that no ideas would be recognized. Rather, they would be swept away with personal attacks, but if the personal attacks were removed, both would grow in an exchange of ideas. Yes, he was a peacemaker in his dreams. Awake, he was more like his friend in the dream, believing his opponents to be inferior.

One of Mr. Pepperdale's pet peeves was the way in which the media's treatment of events became the perception of the era, and the general history totally missed Mr. Pepperdale's experience. Vietnam was not just a war, it was an era, and Mr. Pepperdale lived through it, but all the documentaries of the time and reinterpretations centered on and exaggerated newsier aspects like platelets and missed the atmosphere, the *zeitgeist*, like plasma, almost like calling attention to a few fish and missing not only the saltiness but the fact that there was a great sea. History missed the atmosphere, the real passage and feeling of an era, but even Mr. Pepperdale was hard-pressed to know how to communicate a nuance like this. He was just perturbed that movies about a period became part of the memory of a period, even though they were way off the mark.

His own depiction of he era would exclude millions of others'

Mr. Pepperdale

experiences. He only knew he was included in the general exclusion, that all but a few were left out. But in the long run, it was no more of a disaster to history to lose the experience of an entire generation, and be left with only a few movies, than to have layer after layer of fossilized extinct trilobites to look at. The crime was in the future's taking the misinformation as fact. No one could do anything about it anyway, and who would have the time to digest *Who's who in America* in 200,000,000 volumes later on? Mr. Pepperdale thought, "It is just ego." On the other hand, if it were just ego, and it were big enough, he might just be able to expound his history and pass it off for the greater edification of mankind, with the proper treatment, that is. It must have integrity. On the other hand, didn't it boil down merely and exclusively with utmost intention to wanting to make a buck? If he had to spend the time away from his work to make a living at this, wouldn't he have to dive into the media stream? Wouldn't he become just another polluter with his "interpretations?" Wouldn't the same piranha he was one of chew him to pieces for his effort? If they were right, would it be enough that he might be able to laugh his way to the bank? Could he become a big shot without getting shot at big time along the way?

On another hand (as many hands as the Buddha has, it would seem), all regard for the moment is an afterthought, where the afterthought becomes the truth because the moment is lost. You can't change the moment or bring it back for scrutiny, but you can change people's minds or reach a few among millions who have scarcely thought about it. The media is like a great political disposal system anyway, one with a political agenda, and by making the world watch it, it improves its chances to destroy what it deems wrong, improper and the like. A great deal of sympathy is generated. Dead ends and frauds have made millions of dollars and have become part of the national experience, thanks to media exposure. The media reaches millions who respond with the proper moral outrage, as if the media were on the side of the silent majority. But the media sees it only as feeding a giant, hungry blood sucker to stay alive. The bloodier the piece, the more succulent; yes, the more it appeals and appeases the monster. The really moral see the media

The Voyage of a Bean

as the monster, for seeming to take a stand while remaining the greatest intellectual polluter with its barfing smokestacks of simulated outrage and self-righteousness, driving many of the frauds to seek media attention because it's such good business, so self-sustaining, so narcissistic, the natural and national repository for the sin of personal and public pride.

Oh, it's necessary for the press to be free in a free society, but like the police force attracts all the town bullies when they grow up, the press attracts those who are hiding something, the liars, who take great pleasure in focusing attention on anyone but themselves for a chance to shine in the same focus and really not be seen for what they are. Mr. Pepperdale was tired and had a headache. He put down the newspaper and dreamed of a daily column he might write. He had a thousand topics, just no soapbox on which to stand.

The story of Mr. Pepperdale's life, from the vantage point of its high water marks, the mark on the bottom of the soapbox on which he never stood, is that he lived in an era that bestowed its meaning upon him. The times of greatest influence were long past, but that was the meaning he hangs on to. He loves to watch programs that recount those times that really explain his life, but he was never actually a participant in the main events, and so he's left feeling that there's a whole part of that era that he lived that has not been put down in history, and he was going down the tubes without ever having been discovered by the mainstream view of that period known for a few brief moments like Woodstock, the Vietnam protests and the Chicago democratic convention, but the way that he lived it and the effect of the thing with the long hair, the music, the protests, the sense of connection to one another, all of this made him feel there was something more to say. This could be the first in a collection of columns he would never write, but that being the case, why should anyone else? The soapbox on which he might have stood will one day be his coffin. Like the depressed millions who complained incessantly and never did anything, his epitaph will be that the sixties died in him and that by his sixties he was already dead inside.

The Sixth Room

It had been years since I'd been home with all my relatives, but I was finally back in the old family homestead. I'd made the trip deliberately to look into the old books and papers in the family archives. My father was the key contact. He knew all about my reasons for being there, but the initial emphasis was placed on the excitement of my being there after so long a hiatus. I was getting the royal treatment, laughter and hugs all around, as well as a complete tour of the house filled with its familiar smells that connected me like a dream to my childhood and the last times I really ever smelled it. I kept looking for a bookcase wondering where the collection was, and so after what seemed to be a complete tour of the residence I asked my father, almost sheepishly, where the book collection was.

He answered as if it were already understood, but at the same time divulging a long-held secret, sharing it with me for the first time, a sacred trust "why, they're in the sixth room of course," whatever that meant, and we were just at that point apparently, although I have no real idea of how it came to be known as the sixth room unless it had something to do with the original six rooms in the house. But then a sliding door opened before me, and another whole area of the house appeared. Inside was the bookcase I came to see. It was completely intact, exactly as I remembered it as a child, and another flood of memories cascaded as I reached the stairway to see after all those years the blue spines of those glorious illustrated books completed by my ancestors and shown only at special times within the family, but otherwise hidden away.

I gazed at the bookcase and scanned the collection. There were

The Voyage of a Bean

so many things to look over, so much wonderful work ahead of me that I filled up with an airy sense. It about lifted me off my feet. Here it all was, intact, and I would soon be doing what I wanted with it. I couldn't wait to begin, but I was just on a tour for the moment.

Within the sixth room there was another room on the side with a few children drawing. It was as if they were practicing for the day when they would make a contribution, and they had incredible talent drawing hats and shoes and calling it the "I am for" collection for sports teams. I am for a given team; I supported a given team; that sort of thing, but then they were all about four, and I thought maybe they misspelled the word, but it surprised me to see anything so commercial when I couldn't remember the archives containing such things, even in the sketchbooks.

I was led out, given a room, wined and dined, and finally went to bed. The next morning after breakfast when I went back out to see the main collection, ready to dig in, I saw in shock that all the essential books, the one's with blue spines, were gone. Someone had taken them away. The bookcase was decimated. There was hardly anything left, and everything there was now quite commonplace. My spirit sunk, and I asked why they were taken away so suddenly? What had happened to them? But they all just lied to me, and I was so aggravated. Wasn't I one of the family? Why wouldn't they tell me the truth? There were strangers here guarding the archives, making decisions to do things like this. Who were they compared to me, an heir? Hadn't my father given a long-burning green light by opening the place up to me? And I resented the fact that it was obvious that my looking at the old texts posed a threat to the old ways of handling and long traditions of keeping them.

I might bring them into the open. No, I would most certainly seek to publish them. Why should such wonderful material sit languishing in the dark or in a secret room only because in their own day the great works may have been rejected and overlooked? Even if I pretended I didn't want to resurrect and bring it forward, they had seen to it that I would never get the chance to see the books again. I got into a vicious argument with the young caretaker, the librarian of sorts, as to why the books should be brought back to me.

The Sixth Room

I said they were never conceived by their authors to merely sit on a single shelf but for duplication and enjoyment by as much an audience as possible. They were for the general attention and appreciation of anyone who might come along. And this young man was working hard in that room too, and what I was saying slowly began to affect him as I could detect from the strong emotional changes in his face. Gone were the cold stern looks. Now there were tears and terror in his look as he was coming closer to betraying one trust for another. He showed me the book he'd been working on. Its main character was named Wendy, and it was not bad for a start, and I praised his work and indicated that I could bring his work forward along with any other archives entrusted to me. I promised that I would handle all the originals with the utmost care.

But at the beginning of the argument, at the moment of the most heated exchanges, I had heard noises upstairs, and now, while I was so close to winning, down the stairs came two back ups, strange people who descended in costume as if ready for a Halloween party and glad to be so disguised. A look of terror grew on the boy's face, and one goon took him away while the other held me. I heard voices and screaming, and I could tell that he was rejecting their orders that this was his last chance to get back to the program. They were threatening his life, telling him that he must remember that the books had become a working library, a foundation for all they had going in life, something to be protected at all costs from any invasion, that not even one book at a time could be trusted on loan anymore than someone would borrow just your liver for a time, and my being connected to the family by blood alone meant nothing compared to all the decades I had been gone. I was coming as a usurper against traditions long-established in my absence. My blood claim was void in that I would happily copy and dilute the books in the vast waters with no plan other than to share. What of my foundation? The will of the past? My heritage? Who was I to think of ideas with no plan but my own profit?

They told him to think, but it was too late for that. He had a new idea of seeing his work in the open, just as I now had for revealing the secret location and the way in which all ideas from a soil that is

The Voyage of a Bean

fertile have an exponential value in the mind if withheld. They were ordinary men who drew them, slaved over them, and in the end, would be lost on other shelves with boundless other volumes. Here they were centered and powerful. I wanted to get my hands on them, but I would be prouder to see my works with blue spines as well protected, free for the regarding to the self-appointed chosen few, but locked away forever from all further view. And I would join the men and help them to preserve it and live with them in quarters that I came to call the room next to the dead, which was the room above the sixth room.

The Room Next to the Dead

I dreamed I was lost, trying to find my way with no memory of landmarks to guide me. This is just a landmark marking a page in my dreams.

The room next to the dead is this room. The dead are all around me, but they are in the next room. It is clear to me that I spend much of my time knocking on the wall for someone or something to respond, but there are no answers — at least none that come from the dead.

Something odd happened. I had an insight into who and what I am that explained a good many things to me. The insight broke me into separate personalities or beings in a procession. It was like breaking bread into its primary ingredients and knowing then what makes bread what it is. There was something strange in the parade though. It seemed hung up by a straggler. All these sides of me were moving along as one would expect, looking and acting as I would, but a particular part of me was pulling up the rear, making no effort to stay with the rest, absorbed in forms and shapes. His head was the shape of a crystal through which his head could be seen, and he was examining crystals of the same shape as his head, and plodding along very slowly. Perhaps the rest of his selves could have broken through the ice and knocked the cubes out of his hands for the sake of sense, but they had their backs turned to him, although their pace was determined by his. They were all in front of him, but his regard for them was very little. All in all, this parade was my very soul broken into parts for me. I know it was my soul because of the straggler and what he was doing. Since I had that insight, I often visualize the

The Voyage of a Bean

parade. I believe the straggler is a priest of some sort, in robes at an altar behind a disinterested congregation looking for a way out of the church, into the room where the dead are destined.

The walls of this room are thin, as thin as veins, and the pounding that we do on them is as necessary as a pulse. Don't veins break and collapse? It occurs to me that I am a clot on a mission, riding the rhythmic surge.

In this world I must communicate that I have the background to say what I feel about being alive. They look for my degree, the color of my belt, father figures, and then scrutinize my insights as if bringing the ultimate test to bear on it when the insight is an attempt to simulate an approximate scratch on the surface of a great teasing itch we all armless want to get after. Trees don't beg for water, and there is no great watering can campaign. Yet we all look after one another in the daylight for weaknesses, as if our dreams the night before weren't wild and unexplained, half-remembered shadows like characters marching off the tattered edges of a dead-sea scroll. No, I will say what I feel, not tell my background. Turn your lights on to burn out the imperfections and the germs you are immune to, and see only a grave stone carved with these words. Take a rubbing if you can't take a hint, and don't hold back when my heavy pounding finally takes me to the other side. Come to my funeral. Say that you appreciated my imperfect attempts to understand, that isolating the room next to the dead was misunderstood in its time, that it contributes to our understanding our ourselves. The sea of stones at your feet should do more to get you started on your own, though overall it's as much deafness as it is deadness that will help you put it out of your mind.

This is an examination of limitations, imperfect. There are already enough stories, enough markers pointing the way to the right stories, toward understanding, but we go alone. If I say that two and two are four, someone will leave, looking for spelling class, making me go over and over the equation wondering what went wrong. Somewhere the point I am trying to make is lost on deaf ears, misunderstood, lost in translation. It isn't a story, someone complains who doesn't want a lecture, who doesn't want a story either. But if I honestly believe that all the stories have been told, and one more just clutters up the road, how will I track my trail as I go, sum up my steps?

I prayed one night for clarity in body and mind, but the words came out in transmutation, *muddy and bind*, which is what they are in reverse without the clarity I prayed for. It gave a certain degree of clarity in itself. The mind is muddy, the body bound. One doesn't arrive at degrees of wholeness by ascertainment of the fractures in each portion of the greater fragmentation. Insensitive, I wait for difficulties and ignore the pain I cause. I look out the window to the city and see tiny caravans on the rooftop. The caravans represent tragedies in other homes far away, those who are dealing at this very moment with the very painful ultimacies of life and death. The rooftops are filled with them, but I can no more see the actualities and affect them anymore than I can really see the tiny, imaginary caravans slipping off the shingles.

There are those who must reach out and touch the elephant for themselves, and those who are satisfied with the reports of blind men. Tired, and at a great loss for what is happening in my life, my mind spins nervously with confusions of the week. They are at first what they are — individual and circumstantial, fraught with ironies and stresses. But as I begin to tire further, their definition softens into a new focus. They become metaphors of themselves, symbols with new edges. Suddenly I see them as if removed from them like earth from the moon. They are crystals spinning around, beautiful and destructive. Have I become that one-step-behind self? Is this what they actually are, or is everything reduced to such distances at the point of removal? I only know they are gone now, flung off like galaxies with a red shift, and that my examinations were too fanatic. Their final shape is a natural evolution like disease follows a bacterial salve.

All is habit and addiction, regimen possibly destructive, but cycle nonetheless. The great dead end is trying to point out the way to others. The great task is to tame the silences within and master the night. It is the ultimate end in itself, and there will be those who follow the compelling projections like children running after the

The Voyage of a Bean

sound of the march. They will be adult prepared and armed by the time they reach the front.

It eases the pain during the great sacrifice.

There are two possibilities for the location of the room next to the dead, or rather, two interpretations: 1)The room next to the dead is nothingness, non-existent. When we die, there is nowhere to go, meaning that the dead are with us, we occupy the same space. 2)The room next to the dead is a real invisible place where we pass. In the first scenario (no room) we are the dead. In the second, we are alive, but due to the passage, must accept a degree of being dead to the world.

We make one of two choices in our lives for what the room means, and vacillate between them as if caught in a hallway between two chambers. That the two points of view are mixed together makes the choice itself difficult as there is resistance to being dragged either way. Whatever the answer is, it exists. We must accept that we cannot know what it is. We sit and wait for a lifetime under the influence of fear of being wrong in the choice. Either way, there are penalties.

The dead form a middle ground, a line. If there is nothing beyond them, then the room next to the dead is this room where we live. If there is something else, then it lies next to the dead, and we are close to it. As it is, only the dead know, and in this room next to the dead, we press our senses outward and inward for inklings of the other room next to the dead, though the dead themselves have a way of driving us back from the pursuit.

Dying Visions

Those old people sure have a way of getting it done, don't they? We look to them for any information they might have uncovered or have been able to ascertain on the matter. We wonder if they've been contacted in any way, or how they feel as they face death. We want to know what they've learned. We want to experience the benefit they have derived from knowing what they know. They stand on the precipice, and we look to them for comfort. That is the strange truth of it, but more interesting is how they seem to be able to deliver.

Tish lived until she was a hundred years old, and she had what everyone who knew her said was the sharpest mind in Eastern Kentucky. In his nineties, Grandpa Ken's hearing was still as sharp as Tish's mind. You could whisper in the living room, and he knew what you were saying all the way out on the porch. Early in the 1940s, when the northern lights made it all the way down to Martin County, many people didn't know what it was. Ken said he thought it meant that the world was about to come to an end. When the auroras dissipated, he concluded that the world wasn't ending, but that it did mean war was coming. A few weeks later, the Japanese bombed Pearl Harbor.

A few years before she died, Tish dreamed that she and Grandpa Ken were out looking for water. She woke up thirsty before falling back asleep into the same dream where she saw him on a hill in front of a fountain, and she said, "You've found it," and he answered, "Yes, Tish, I've found the waters of life." Tish woke believing that Ken was going to die first, and eventually he did.

The Voyage of a Bean

Grandpa remembered when his mother was on her deathbed that she wouldn't eat anything but was making motions as if she were, moving her hands to her mouth and such. So he asked her, "Are you eating, Mother?" She answered, "Yes, I'm eating milk and honey." She was talking about getting it from heaven, and soon afterwards, she died. Ken had no doubt that she was getting milk and honey.

Meanwhile, Ken's oldest grandson was upset that his mother was planning to remarry only a few years after his father had died. Grandpa Ken, on the other hand, had been married several times in his life, and while he had experienced only failure in love, he still believed in it, recommended it, and would have done it again for the chance that it might work out. So he was happy that his daughter was tying the knot again.

But his grandson didn't like the idea even though his mother was in her early seventies at the time. Shortly before the wedding, he had a dream that he had rabies. He was about to attack his mother, but he cut off his own head so that he wouldn't be able to bite her. The head rolled away into the corner, but he could see it there, watching her, waiting to get at her. He woke up thirsty and could not go back to sleep. He did not attend the wedding.

Train Trance

It seems that being on a crowded train puts me into a strange mood. It makes me observe the world from a perspective of a rather defiant but helpless individual. I am aware of the fact that I have no choice in the matter, but that I'd like my life to change. I can sense that everyone around me feels the same, and that they like me as little as I like them. All we want is to be off the train, for it to take us where we are going so that we can leave it and all its inhabitants behind us. I tune them out and go into a kind of trance.

The mood the train puts me in begins when I stand on the platform waiting. Sometimes I've had to wait for hours. Sometimes after waiting, a train will come but not stop, or one will stop but it is too full to board. The train is a drug, a shot in the arm of a juice that affects me the same way every time. I stand and think distant, strange thoughts. Once I am off the train, the effect wears off quickly, but when I board a train later, I drift back into the same worn track. It is as if the experience repeating itself hundreds of times a year has trained my senses as a comb trains the hair, and I bend with it as it twists and turns, screeching through tunnels and over the city. I am a part of it like a seat. Take one if you're lucky enough to find one, or hold on.

I missed a train tonight. It was below zero. As I was climbing the stairs, I heard it coming and started running. When I paid, it was waiting, but its doors closed in my face, blasting me with warmth from within when I rushed onto the platform. Waving my arms in frustration did nothing, and when it pulled away, it was the

The Voyage of a Bean

smoothest train I ever saw.

Now that I am riding an older, decrepit train home, nothing is right. It is crowded, the heat is not working, and every stop is a chore. The first train is miles ahead by now, flying across vast free stretches with its light load of merry riders. It was a new train — well-lit, fully-heated and half-empty. The few riders there are less weary than the crowd packed against me. They were able to leave work early. They are better managers of their time. They are healthier overall for having more room to breathe, and being more intelligent, are able to discuss interesting subjects with strangers. They will be fresh when they reach their destinations, absorbed in new concepts and sensations.

All I hear is sniffling, wheezing, coughing, sneezing. I hide my nose in my coat. It is running. I sniff and get a dirty look. A man behind me coughs uncovered into the back of my head. I relinquish my seat which is besieged by three human wedges which lock against each other to form a Roman arch. They dispute the claim in subtle pantomime, each unable to reach the chair. The entire scene passes in an instant, but can be broken into intricate elements and described. It boils down to two giving in to one who takes it. I am resented for not having chosen a successor. The looks of the other passengers ride down cold noses on skis. Everyone's above that sort of thing, especially anyone who has a seat. The floor is frozen with the litter of icy glares.

The driver of the first train must have seen me. But it wouldn't be the ride it is if he'd waited for me to board. One or two at every stop will change the quality of a journey as an extra word or two will alter style and flow and tone of a poem. Our driver waits for people miles behind. They run and wave, and we wait. They hide their heavy breathing on arrival, and avert their eyes into the judgment handed down noses into the cold and jagged gloom.

At home tonight, will I hear on the news that the other train broke apart in the distance because of pressures applied to keep it going? In such an event, I'd be fortunate to have become a part of this train. Suddenly, I no longer resent it. Actually, given the chance to meditate and make a choice, I would pick this slower one.

Train Trance

Had I boarded that other train, I'd have learned to fit its elements well and would have become mesmerized on a ride straight to hell. How easily such poor fools ride there. The doors wait open day and night. For them, there's no greater fullness than the certainty that nothing is beyond them. But none have pockets quite so empty.

I ride the hot train to the city and stare out the window thinking, "I don't want much. If I were to buy a car, having to pay installments would take several more years, and yet I'm not going anywhere. But it would be one more thing weighing me down, and I want mobility." The train skirts the last fields, and I see the first ugly signs that a city is imminent. I am thinking, "I wouldn't want to move into this pit. I wouldn't enjoy the congestion, the lack of outdoor life, and besides, I don't have a car. What I could use is a country estate with a lake just minutes from downtown."

Street after street of tenements, then factory after factory, then dozens of warehouses and large parking lots whiz by. I imagine the faceless forms filling them all. It occurs to me that people are trapped like candles in an oven. They are melting slowly — the heat exposing long wicks never to be lit. How frightening to expire never having lived the purpose. They have payments to make, and so many shoulders squeezing them in that emotions are choked to the breaking point. There is no proper passage, and there are constant explosions in the city of nerves, like bolts popping in submarines gone too deep. The sirens sing. The husks litter the shore. The dead and maimed are carried away. The stew stays on the stove.

The train arrives at the station. The darkness outside and the light in the car turn the window into a mirror. I catch myself in a trance. There are lines on my face. I get up to stand in a long line. It occurs to me as I wait to get off the train how blind the surgeon is who swings the blade. We grow, and we're lopped from the branch. Our nerves falter. Once the plums of our mothers' eyes, we turn to prunes.

I'm soaring with other souls homeward. Today differs from the past as a buzz saw differs from a pitchfork. The third rail flashes a shadow of the train on the dark walls, and naked bodies cry out in

The Voyage of a Bean

relief, frozen between the windows. I look at the patterns of statues that grace these high boxes and find it remarkable they are even there at all. One building has a line of lions just at the base of the second story, and these roaring busts stretch the entire length of the face. I have only a moment to watch them, and they pass as if to cry out how quickly the world went through the jungle, leaving these markers on markets with rails running between them. There aren't even a few wild strays left to remind us anymore, and these were only carved, roaring in cement with steel rings in their noses. The only jungle left roars within.

I look about me on the train. What do I feel? This train might as well be a horse-drawn cab. It only gets me home faster than a century ago. We race through the frigid air. How? More conveniently? Are we better off?

These faces, shapes harboring souls that dare not roar, are cemented in rows waiting to get home. How far I am from being able to reach anyone! What would I say? What could I learn? Each one is as dense as I am on what all life amounts to. Just look at this lot, huddled, not daring to touch, not even casting a look. Life has such privacy, as though everyday we were trying out the boxes, practicing lying six feet deep and separate for eternity.

I wonder what these thoughts mean to me. Do they frighten me? No, and they would not scare a soul here. I only scan them to see if they might hold some quality that links each of us to the other. I rank those thoughts high, though knowing what binds us together never brought us closer, but who knows what we'd be without some sense of what we have in common.

The train screeches to a halt before another bend. One last look at these faces I'll never see again. If there is an answer, one thing to shout and make it all clear, quite frankly I am numb to it. Those days are gone when I plotted ways to bring the divorced back to marriage, and fill others, so miserable, with the joy of which there was too much to run short. Where did it all go I wonder? All I notice is the cold does not bother me. The train shivers and complains. Only the lions are serene as if, while their habitat disappears, whole new jungles are being born.

The Grafting

By the time they found them, months had already passed. Someone had been hiking through the woods near the highway and just happened to catch the glint of the sun in a shard of the broken rearview mirror. The car had gone off the road in the middle of the night. It was a drop of about fifty feet to the ground. The car went through several trees. The girl was thrown out of the car with such force that her bones actually penetrated the tree. Her father was trapped in the smashed car, but he had pulled himself free at a great cost. He had to leave a leg behind. He tended it as best as he could but only lived for a few days. His body was found next to the tree, close to his daughter. She watched him die and waited herself to die. She could not pull herself away from or out of the tree. There was no phone to use. Her father fell asleep at the wheel and went off the road without leaving any marks to follow. They did not break through any railing. It was just one of those clear situations where there was no indication that anything had happened.

The hiker thought it was just a junk, not an undiscovered wreck, but then he saw what was left of the body in the car and was about to run when he heard the voice of a young girl. "Can you help me?" she asked, and he turned and saw her in the tree. Then he ran.

Before the time medical services got there, his story was thoroughly gone over by several police. They finally sent someone out who went through the woods with the hiker. Arriving on the scene, the cop called in the various services, and within an hour, the woods were teeming with the authorities and the area taped off.

What they could not understand was how the girl was still alive.

The Voyage of a Bean

She seemed a little slow, but she told them that her father had saved her life, and she felt like she was becoming a part of the tree. Trees around her had to be cut down, and they brought in X-ray machines and took all kinds of samples. They even tried removing her at one point, but it proved too difficult. Before they started cutting, they wired her with a variety of sensors, and she registered pain, and she screamed when they started cutting into the wood around her. Experts reasoned from the samples and data taken that to remove her would be to kill her, and the only thing to do was to leave her there. They thought it was just an amazing serendipitous event; that her blood type somehow matched genetic sequences in the tree, and the two of them just symbiotically joined and facilitated one another's healing. The girl told a different story. She said her father was a medicine man, that he knew plants and had an instinctive knack for recognizing properties and applying them. She said that after he wrapped his own leg, he had crawled around the woods gathering leaves and roots, which he had applied to her and the tree. He made her eat certain mixtures. Others he applied directly to the tree. They wondered at how he could have performed so miraculous a feat to save her and not kept himself from dying with only a severed foot. She insisted that he was only thinking of her, that he had gone into as deep a trance as she had ever seen in order to save her. They gathered what evidence of this that they could from the base of the tree, dried leaves and blood samples, and they scoured the woods for evidence of any plants having been cut or ripped out of the ground, but they never indicated that they believed her story, nor did they manage to duplicate anything that he had done in any of their experiments.

For a few years, the girl was never lonely as there was always someone there studying her. They thought of removing the tree entirely, but eventually decided against it when she spoke about it from the perspective of the tree. She seemed to know what the tree thought about it, and they listened and continued their studies.

They eventually let her family visit her after properly prepping them. The girl's mother couldn't stop weeping. The girl was able to comfort her. Scientists were astonished that sunny day to detect

The Grafting

movements in the branches that were not caused by the wind. It appeared that she was able to provide more shade to her mother where she was standing. The family was able to visit more often, and they liked to have picnics under her shade, and she would enjoy it, but she wasn't able to eat human food of any kind. They noticed over time that she appeared a bit more slow. She seemed a bit more remote as well and slow on the uptake.

The experts determined that it wasn't that she wasn't healthy, but that she was becoming more and more a part of the tree. Blood samples were more sap-like than before. Her skin was beginning to take on the look and feel of wood. They said that the tree lived at a different speed, so to speak, and that it might live for hundreds of years. They said that it was very likely that she might live for hundreds of years as well, but that ultimately her sense of things would be slowed down to the level of the tree. It took the family some time to accept this, and year by year, they knew they were losing her by degrees.

After a while they stopped visiting her as frequently. Years passed. Her mother grew older, but her daughter seemed to still be young in the outline of the tree, and despite being distant and slow, still had complete command over the branches, which moved quickly at her approach much as a dog wags its tail.

Over the years, the area became a kind of nature preserve since eventually it became a huge attraction. The state bought the land and built a visitor's center, and an exit was added to the highway, which took cars off the road at the same place where her father had originally left the road. The ramp was made to form a graceful arc descending around the grove. There were paved walkways around the tree, drinking fountains, vending machines, and a guide to answer questions and engage the girl in conversations to demonstrate the remarkable abilities of the tree. One day a week, the park was closed so that scientists had private access to continue their analysis. They continued their work, but they were unable to show a link to explain how it happened, nor were they able to duplicate it with any of their experiments. They even tried adding car exhaust as they considered what may have been present that day that may

The Voyage of a Bean

have been a catalyst. The park also had to be cordoned off and guarded due to groups that threatened to destroy the tree as a freak of nature. Some people denied its existence, and one religion banned its followers from visiting the grove. Others made a pilgrimage to honor her, and many felt that she deserved a continuing connection to people in order to preserve her humanity, which seemed to be ebbing away.

One spring a branch grew out of her, and a leaf appeared on her finger. She was growing more rigid, but she was still able to move her branches, and she always had a nice smile on her face. The souvenir shop sold wooden figurines of the tree exactly as she appeared. The years passed. Her mother died, and then her brothers, and soon she was a presence in a new age that looked at her as a strange vestige of the past, much as an Egyptian mummy in a museum. There was still much life in her, but she had the tree's sense of time. Every fall, people gathered the nuts as they fell. The trees that grew from them had branches that waved without wind. These were classified as a new species with a latin name, not connected to the girl or giving any credit to her father for what he had done to save her, but to the scientists who had studied her and looked for answers using only methods consistent with their way of thinking but in the end came up with nothing and could do nothing to bring her back.

The Nail Scrum

For my first assignment, my editor told me to visit Dr. Heinrich Von Kleist and write a "formula exposé" on him and his machine. I asked what that was. He insulted me for being green. "Formula exposé," he explained, "you know, as in if you're writing on behalf of a guy you're trying to say was innocently put in jail, then you say the cops in the interview denied his request for a lawyer, put names of other people on the confession. You write it up like an episode for a television crime drama. So you expose the professor as a quack and do it in a format everyone's heard a thousand times. That's what they want to hear, so we give it to them. Now get out of here."

I really did plan to move to a more reputable paper when I'd gotten experience, but I was already feeling that the work I would do would hinder me from working for the legitimate press. I drove to Dr. Von Kleist's expecting some huge castle with dark clouds and lightning over it, but it was just a quaint brick Georgian with lots of trees. There were no bats and no moat, and he answered the door, not some hunchback from South Bend, Indiana.

Dr. Von Kleist actually seemed very professional and intelligent to me. He recognized that I was not from one of the big papers, but he said that we all had the same vendetta. I tried to defend myself, but he waved it off. "It doesn't matter in the end what you say or do. The machine speaks for itself, so I'll let it do the talking. Would you like to write about it as the others have, condemning it on appearances, or would you like to be the first to take a test drive?"

I couldn't believe my ears. I'd already read about it in all the Sunday Supplements. Could it be true that the writers just sat where I

The Voyage of a Bean

was and talked to the doctor, then wrote nothing but lies? "Well, Doctor," I said, "I must admit feeling a bit of trepidation to be strapped into your 'mind melder,' as one reporter dubbed it, as the stories I've read tend to portray it as a quick way to a bad headache, but I am intrigued somewhat by your offer. It won't hurt me will it?"

"You are thinking of doing it for the scoop, aren't you," he laughed. "Well, first, even if you do and get it right, who will believe you. You're working for the sorriest rag that ever blew up against a chain link fence in a red light district. I'm guessing you've already been told to give the public more of the same lies. Change the minds of the believers before society as we know it goes down the tubes, that sort of baloney," he effervesced.

"Not at all, sir," I lied. "I know how it looks, but I just started at the paper. I just graduated last fall. My father warned me I would have to pay my dues, and I knew I might have to write some positive stories about advertisers, but I hope you don't think I could sell my soul in the first week on the job."

"Actually, that's probably why you've been given this job," he said. "They want to get your hands dirty right away. Oh, it doesn't matter to me, mind you. I just hate to see a young man such as yourself thrown to the wolves like this." Then he laughed again. "And it's the wolves that are doing the throwing, to transform you, and to throw you here, of all places." He got up from his chair. "Yes, I think you should be the first. Come, come," he motioned, and I followed him through a door into his laboratory.

There were no elaborate experiments of colored water bubbling with dry ice. There was, however, a chair with straps and wires, and something for the top of the head. I cringed. "That," he said, "was sent to me by a colleague after he read the first story about me. Over here is my machine." As an apparatus, it was no more intimidating than having your blood pressure taken while listening to music on headphones. Its effect was another story.

As he was attaching it to my arm and head, he explained to me how it was going to operate. I simply had to choose some basic anomaly about the world, something that I did not understand, and the machine would basically put me to sleep and give me a vision

The Nail Scrum

that would explain it. It was not a dream, which would be different in each individual. No, the vision provided by the machine would be seen and felt just as real as if it were happening, and in that sense would be like a dream, but it would be the same in each person. "Except for a few key interactions," the professor said. I did not understand. "In order to come out of this with any understanding of the anomaly, you will interact in ways that will help you understand how you fit into the scheme of things. You may think you are part of the solution if you are a doctor and you ask about world health care issues, but in the end you may be surprised to discover through my machine that you are in fact part of the problem. You will therefore find yourself in a position of having to make a few key decisions. The vision is general, but the outcome does vary depending on how you participate. Don't worry about it. Just be yourself."

As far as what anomaly to choose, I had always felt particularly confused by the Problem of Evil. But not only by the Nazi death camps and such horrors as people inflict on one another; I was just as confused by Pompeii and Herculaneum where thousands die in a natural disaster. It wasn't evil per se, but the lack of intervention from an outside force in those instances leaves us wondering whether or not God exists, and it paves the way for lunatics like Hitler to believe there's no moral force standing in their way.

So I told the Doctor this, which made him scratch his chin. "Already you will alienate many readers. They want to read about movie stars having affairs. Maybe you should consider the anomaly of money and corruption. No? Alright, then the nail scrum it is." I asked what that was. "Oh, that's the vision you'll be having," he replied. "I said that these visions were preset. You will experience the vision of a nail scrum to help you understand your questions about the Problem of Evil and the silence of God. It may not make a good story, but at least you will have an experience to help you see where you stand in relation to it. So, we begin." And without further ado, he started the machine, and within a few seconds, I opened my eyes in another place without any sense that I was having a vision, and I already understood most of what was happening going into it.

I was in a large open area standing in front of great field with a

The Voyage of a Bean

fence around it. The whole village was about to have a nail scrum in the circle. Everyone had put their holdings into one lot, and they were having the nail scrum in order that one of them might win it all outright. This would be the survivor. Inside the fence they had laid out tens of thousands of nails. At the appointed time, everyone would go through a gate into the field and begin the scrum. They would fight until only one of them survived to reap the benefit. As they lined up, some of them asked whether I was in or not. I said I was just going to watch. Someone said I would still lose everything I owned if I sat out. I could only have something left after the scrum by taking part in it, in which case, if I survived, I would have everything. I realized this, and was making a conscious decision to merely witness the event. There was considerable pressure against doing this, and I was clearly only one of a very few, and they were throwing rocks at us. "You won't get away unscathed," they shouted. "Here, taste some of this," they screamed, picking up apples and shoving long nails through them and hurling them our way. I dodged them and stood further away. I had to keep on watching what they were doing. Everyone's adrenaline was running high.

Then a horn blew indicating that it was time for the scrum to begin. The gates opened, and people started shoving their way into the circle. Some had picked up nails and were already stabbing people around them to thin the ranks. As they poured out onto the field, the air filled with the roar of their rage. Whatever anger they held inside was coming out. I recognized some of the faces and saw neighbors attacking one another for what I knew to be petty grievances between them. As they pushed and fell, they were skewered with nails on the the ground. Within minutes, it looked like a battlefield. Most were standing, but there were already many lying dead or dying, but everyone had nails sticking in them, covering them like pin cushions. People were pushing bodies against others, using them as weapons, and I thought I saw balls of people rolling around picking up nails, but it was just the living, bloody scrum pushing itself around, throwing off as many as it could, degenerating toward the inevitable last one of them to declare itself the undisputed last entitled survivor. I even saw children, babies separated from their dolls, crying with nails in them. It was appalling. I turned away, and that's when I saw them walking in my direction.

There were two women, both of them quite beautiful, and I knew them to be the organizers of the event. I was starting to remember it now. Watching the scrum, it didn't occur to me to consider what force had made it necessary that the village do this. There had to be something that was driving them. It would have to be that all of them would starve, or that someone died and others had to pay. In order for this nail scrum to have any kind of explanation, they had to have a reason to do it, and that's where these women came in. I knew that they were responsible, but I didn't quite know how, and it made me terribly angry to see them, and it only would get worse.

They came right up to me and asked why I wasn't in there with the rest of them. I said I had chosen not to go. They said it was no matter, that I'd be dealt with as the survivor. The whole town was being cleansed, and it's assets seized. One of them pulled a gun and would have shot me except I was able to grab it away. They ran for their car, and I followed. I just stood there as they started the engine and looked back at the scrum. There was very little movement now. Just a mass of bodies in a wretched, bloody stew. I shouted for the women to get out of the car. I could hear it going into gear, and I jumped on the back as it rolled forward into the field toward the scrum. The one woman was driving as close to the fence as she could, turning the steering wheel quickly back and forth in an effort to get me to fall off into the nails. I held on and started shooting at the tires, jumping off when I succeeded and watched the car go through the fence into the scrum. It hit bodies, rolled over and blew up, killing the women inside. From all that I could see, I was the last survivor. From all that I had seen, I did not feel like living, but a briefcase had blown out of the car with all the assets of the town converted into negotiable bonds. I was rich. For a brief moment, I had a sense, despite the madness, that there was a God, and that I had been granted this great gift to do some good. Then all at once I felt the ground shake, which opened up and swallowed me whole.

It was then that I came out of the vision and found myself back in the Doctor's laboratory. "So," he said shoving a cup of coffee into my hand, "now you have returned from the nail scrum. You understand the Problem of Evil better already, yes?" I was not quite ready to discuss the matter, but quietly accepted the coffee. "So, what do you think of the capabilities of my machine, and that nail scrum is really something, isn't it? It wasn't a death camp, and it certainly wasn't anything like Pompeii, but it explains a lot, doesn't it?"

I sipped the coffee and thought for a moment before trying to speak. "Why wasn't there anyone there trying to stop the thing? And why were there no indications of there being any help on the way. I didn't hear any police sirens at all."

"Did you try to go to a phone and make a call?" Von Kleist asked.

"No," I said. "The way the world was there, no one would have answered. They were all in on it. It was a great conspiracy."

"Easy for you to say from here, but how could you know that from within the vision. The thought of calling anyone never crossed your mind because you were too intent on watching it happen." He was right about that. And I didn't know what the political situation was away from that field. "And how did you handle Beauty and Truth?" I didn't know what he meant. "The two women in the vision. They represented Beauty and Truth. They were the elements that corresponded to your freedom within the vision. Were they your mother and sister, for example, or your wife and daughter, or were they perhaps the ruthless organizers of the event?" I blinked. "Ah," he nodded, "and did you destroy them and walk away the winner? You should be proud of yourself for imbuing them with qualities you saw fit, and then justifying the means by the ends."

"I think this is dangerous machine, Doctor," I said finally.

"Oh yes, but of course you do, for what it reveals about you to yourself. You cannot know the good that the machine might have found in you where Beauty and Truth were more like the ideas to which you pay lip service; and you would have to deny that another might have the same vision of the nail scrum and somehow with their help, by the way that they are seen from within the self of that individual, find a way to stop the scrum from happening. You see, my son, history is driven by what resides in the heart. Wouldn't it be better for us all if we could put thousands to death or save them all with a machine like this, rather than to play out the problems of evil within ourselves, problems that we so quickly ascribe to others, on real fields where real people shed real blood for our false ideas?"

"I believe I have enough for my story, Doctor. If I may, I'd like to leave and get started on it right away."

"But of course, of course," Von Kleist said, putting his arm around me. "One thing I'd like to mention though is that I did stretch one point at the beginning of our interview that I'd like to clarify. Actually, each one of your fellow journalists had an experience on the machine. They did not choose the same anomaly, but they did have an experience. I am sorry to say than none came away feeling good about it. I am starting to wonder whether anyone can come away with good feelings regarding visions that explain anomalies that confound us. In the end, there is something intrinsically disturbing about them that emanates from within ourselves. It can be enlightening, but first, it must be thoroughly disturbing." As he opened the door of his house for me, he continued, "You go and write your story the way you see fit, and when you have your audience up in arms to come and destroy me, don't forget to tell them to bring their torches, and remind them as well that they don't just come for me, but for the monster that has already been released among them. And while they may be able to stop me, there's nothing they can do about it. You'll tell them that, won't you?" he asked, patting me.

I drove back to the office thinking it all over. The editor looked up from his magazine just long enough to see who it was, then said, "So what have we got?"

"I think I got an angle or two on this mad scientist thing that the other papers didn't cover," I said.

"Crazy, is he?"

"Completely."

"Did you try the thing out?"

"No way. It's some kind a mediaeval contraption that couldn't possibly work. He's made a monster he claims will make us more human. It's ridiculous. He even compared himself to Frankenstein."

"Too true!" he said. "Run with it, and if you can work in anything about bloodsucking vampires, that'll make it even more beautiful."

A Little Croaking

Harry was an oddball among oddballs, speaking only as highly as one could about him, naturally. To know him was to expect something strange would happen during any encounter. As soon as you saw him coming, it wasn't like trouble was on its way, but as many troubles as he had, you knew they were coming along with him for the ride. I was one of the few who let him come through the door. I sensed he was disturbed, and I did not feel he was dangerous, and he did have a certain charm, but behind the smile and smooth veneer there was something of the con-artist who always had to be one step ahead of you as well as get all the attention, such as the time he stepped in with tight pants and no underwear to play the ukulele for my wife and I. At the time, it just boggled our minds, but when he came back the next day with a hundred empty gallon milk jugs and a few months of dirty dishes, I thought being short on shorts wasn't the problem. The question was how many marbles was he missing.

If you look up Edwin Cayce and have an open mind, you'll still have a hard time believing the stories about him unless you alter your sense of what lies betwixt heaven and your philosophy. Cayce could see auras, and in one of his trances would tell people hundreds of miles away where to find a cabinet with a certain medicine to save the life of a dying boy. I had to admit after watching a story about Cayce that the witnessed events were hard to dismiss, but I have also always been a normal person. I do not hear voices, I do not see things, I am a reasonable man, but there is this thing that's bugging me, because when Harry came the day after he played

A Little Croaking

ukulele and brought the water jugs with him, I could hear bull frogs in the distance. I didn't think anything of it at the time.

I met him at the van and helped him unload the empty plastic jugs, which we took over by the hose and started to fill. My wife came out and took the pans of dishes in and started filling the dishwasher. What we learned was that this was how Harry lived. He said he used a half gallon of water a day to bathe and kept enough water for a couple of months. You're kidding. No, he wasn't. Why would you do that? He had no money, and there was the ongoing divorce he was still fighting, and I started to feel sick about it, at which point I started to hear the sound of frogs in the distance, like they sound when they just come out of winter hibernation, only it was late summer, and they're usually pretty quiet then, especially around where we live as the habitats have all been drained for construction. In fact, the only time I ever heard frogs was when I was out on an errand at least a few miles from home, so I asked Harry if he heard the frogs. "Oh, I bring them with me when I fill the jugs and do the dishes."

Well that threw me, because I almost believed him despite my better sense to believe he was crazy. I knew that already, and I could hear them, and he said it without so much as blinking an eye.

That afternoon, after filling all the jugs and storing them neatly in the van, we sat in the house while my wife did the dishes and talked about things. Harry was a firm believer in a woman doing all the kitchen chores, and he had no problem with my wife spending three hours running loads of dishes for him. He also didn't mind it when she stayed out of the room to let the men talk. "Between you and me," he said in a low voice when she was out of the room, "She's a damsel fly."

"What's that supposed to mean? What image is a damsel fly supposed to conjure up? Does this have anything to do with your frogs?"

"If it weren't for people like your wife, you wouldn't hear those frogs at all," he replied.

"I thought you brought the frogs?"

"True, but you wouldn't hear them, and I wouldn't have them to bring, if it weren't for her graciousness."

"And yet you apparently believe that her job is in the kitchen

The Voyage of a Bean

with your dishes. I just don't know if I can handle this frog and insect thing, Harry. It doesn't make any sense to me."

"It is what it is. Anyway, it's just a little croaking." he said. We talked some more, and when the dishes were done, he left.

Harry disappeared after that. He never came back for more water. I heard he moved away, and I forgot all about him over the next five years. Then one day I was picking my son up from school when an old homeless man walked by. He asked me for money, and I said no and walked on to the school. That was when I heard the sound of frogs in the distance. It was another case of it not being either the season for frogs or a near a place where they live, and I had a very strange change of heart and retraced my steps immediately to give the old man some money. He thanked me, but then asked me something extraordinary, which was whether or not I knew Harry. "I heard his frogs," he said, "as soon as I saw you, so I knew you'd help."

Now I know I don't have the power of extra sensory perception, and I don't envy those who do for the Cassandra complex or similar feeling of frustration it must give them; and I've never heard of anything being "assigned," as in the sound of these frogs, but now I actually fear them. I went camping in the woods this spring, and it was normal that the frogs should be there making lots of noise, but it bothered me a great deal. I felt like a damsel fly on a lily pad, except that I knew that there was a tongue ready to lash out and carry me into the darkness. Then I heard a splash and a scream. I was getting gear out of the car, and I ran to the campsite and heard more splashing from the pier. I ran out and jumped into the water awkwardly, hitting my head on a post, but managed to help my wife back to shore. She said she'd been looking into the water and had suddenly felt overcome with a kind of vertigo and didn't remember anything else. I cut the trip short. At home there was a message on my answering machine from a friend who had heard that Harry had died. Somehow I felt he had reached out for my wife and pulled her into the water. I don't know why, but now I hear the sound of frogs all the time. My doctor says it's tinnitus caused by the head injury, and I only think it sounds like frogs. I wouldn't begin to try to convince him otherwise.

Chartres

I want this story to begin with the image of the Cathedral at Chartres, France — the masterpiece of the middle ages that took several hundred years to build. It still stands today, hundreds of years later, beckoning man toward God.

The cathedral had nothing to do with the story, but now it is everything. My son was due two days ago, and I am waiting in stress for my wife to give birth. For weeks now, I have been planning charts for him — that is what made me think of the cathedral — charts. My charts are made up in response to situations that my son encounters in my projections. One incident or another leads to my having to explain something, to make a comparison, to teach a lesson, to explain the ways of the world to him, and out comes a chart. I envision setting him down and making a clear case via my visual aids, and now he is late, and I look toward the cathedral.

What would my charts mean to him in the long run anyway? What explanations of the world are left from any father that stand up to the Cathedral at Chartres? What God gave man made man build cathedrals to point to God. I should hope to make my son understand the enormity of a three-hundred-year undertaking, to make him feel the planning, the engineering and the beauty. He isn't here yet, but he is just as beautiful to me, and I begin to fear my charts will be desecrations, graffiti on the temple. I was going to list my ideas, but a cathedral came to mind, along with the thought that one day I could take him to see it, and it would be just another building.

What we reach naturally means most to us, and yet we tend to try to bring others around by force. How will I make my son behave to

The Voyage of a Bean

my liking without giving of myself? How will I explain the other side of the heart? I don't have a chart for what I hide within myself. I have yet to draw a picture of the siren who stands at the entrance of a cave. She is inert, a statue, until I approach her, whereupon she becomes beautiful. She beckons to me, inviting me in, but as I get close, I recognize her as the carrier of all the diseases of the ages. She is not alive but rather a kind of living death. I am filled with curiosity as to how she operates, and yet I understand intuitively that the key to her mechanism lies in me, and the better she functions, the worse I become. I ask myself how the extremes of terrible, unwanted things that should have been eradicated ages ago have instead been cultivated to lie dormant, and offered so that each person ultimately makes a choice whether or not to go with her. I see that she is actually hideous on closer inspection. There are ridges on her skin that seem more like waves of the ocean, and her face has the appearance of a nylon stocking stretched over it, not so much masking it as revealing how years of erosion have softened her features into an empty scream. She is there night and day for my needs, ready to bring me into the dark chamber, to the same death she brought to ages gone by. How do I warn my son about her when she is the manifestation of the afterthoughts, the guilt, and all that would follow if I went through with it. I will say to my son that I stayed away, but I did go through with it. We all do, and so will he, and none of us can help it, and she is not the one to blame, though in the end, neither are we. It is all part of the plan somehow, that we should fall and learn to look for what will save us, to find that which serves our greater need.

She is only the bearer of the fruit of the tree, and I had to learn what it was. I tasted it, and that began my demise, and that is what we keep from our children. We do not properly prepare them for the depths of despair. We only teach them the solutions that don't make sense to them at the time, for they have no sense of the corresponding, great need that will come along, all in good time.

It occurs to me that there are probably graves near the cathedral, and my son and I are carrying in our minds the same information that would be supplied by the charts of the dead, those they made

Chartres

while living, if they could show them to us, though we're hundreds of years apart and separated by death. There is an imprint on the heart that grows deeper by living, and no father is able to impress those ideas by a crash course. Even dead fathers have their influence on unborn sons. We all carry match points, winning ideas that will be ruled ineligible by minds we try to engage. Of what importance are the connections that we sense that cannot otherwise be grasped without delineating them with not only the logic but the experience that helped to create them? And what about the ways in which we change as we go, altering slightly from the ocean to the altar, and reaching a point where we say to ourselves that we don't understand why something was so important, and we don't even want to bother to attempt a reconstruction? Perhaps it is because we finally come to realize that even if anyone is listening, the waves crashing on the beach are saying something more profound, and we are the ones who have not been listening.

A line from a poem by Paul Valery comes to mind. *La mer est plus belle que les cathedrals.* What does he mean that the sea is more beautiful than cathedrals? The sum total of all the walls and windows of the greatest of all cathedrals is a monument to what man can do. The ocean peers within and pierces. Even my prayer-induced calm ripples at the thought of my bones being bleached. I cannot put into words this sense of awareness that even the lumps of flesh that live in shells might still have after crossing the threshold. The sea feels like it holds something for us. Before it we have a sense that the dead belong, that somehow in the roar of the ocean there is an explanation and a promise that this sensation will be verified. This is a beautiful but transient insight, a brief glimpse that defies translation, escapes retrieval even in the mind that just bore it as a thought. When I get there, my son will know what I mean as he thinks of me while watching the swells beyond the breakers, for a second, now and then. This perhaps will serve him better than my ethics class.

My wife heaves a sigh that another day passes without a live birth. I kneel at the gateway, then turn my back and build sand castles to pass the time. My tributes are washed down to ruins, then

The Voyage of a Bean

erased completely. The sea is more beautiful because no chart can contain it. From high altitude, it resembles skin that stretches under the fabric of land, where cathedrals cling long after we've been brushed away. We raised them, and so we may raze them, and our structural side is satisfied that we make improvements as we deteriorate, make the world better as we give up on trying so hard to change it. A walk on the beach would be nice about now. It is night, and I would build a fire as a tribute to being here in the void. I could use the straightening out of the perplexing anomalies that come from the sea's low roar and abounding light breezes. I cannot detect the design of the tapestry on which I walk, but needled into magnificence, I may be able to lay down a contributory thread, a stitch for a banner, as I walk along the beach. The cathedrals are beautiful things in themselves, but they still need us to lovingly decorate the stone cold walls in the same spirit that we are delivered out of the cold stars by the embers that fly up as we stoke God's fire.

The Dirges

I've finally narrowed down the process of selecting a church, and it has mostly old people in it. The pastor himself is not an old man but in his late afternoon, the *dirges*, if you will, and very welcoming. As I step in, I see his sick son on a cot. He looks pretty bad. Obviously he's not in very good shape, and it's just sort of a sad moment.

Anyway I get into the church, and the organ starts to play, so I find a pew and start looking in the bulletin for the page number of the first hymn to begin singing. Some start early, and others like me are still leafing through their hymnals, and the pastor goes to the front of the church and turns on his microphone. He tells the organist to stop playing, apologizes, and says that everybody in the church needs to be on the same page and for those who aren't there yet to raise a hand until they find the page. When all the hands are down, the organist begins again, and the pastor stays put to direct the beginning of the hymn. He says, "When I lower my hand, you start," and then he lowers it, and those who sing start at the right place, but actually, despite all the attention to detail, all the effort to keep people together and involved, very few people actually are singing.

I look around and see that there aren't actually that many people in church either. But those who sing do manage to fill the sanctuary in a way, and when the hymn is over, the pastor stands up and begins the announcements, and he speaks directly to people by name, and asks people to get up and speak to the congregation themselves, and in every word he speaks, there is a certain ring of warmth and sincerity and care.

At about the halfway point of the service, just about when the

The Voyage of a Bean

sermon in about to begin, it is time for me to leave, but rather than get up during the sermon, I slip away during the last verse of the hymn. The same people are singing. As I go by the back of the church, I pass the pastor's office and see his sick son again. He's on a cot right outside the office. I ask him how he's feeling, and he only looks at me. Something in his eyes tells me this is not a good time to talk. A woman comes out of the pastor's office and thanks me for noticing him. I say of course, that it's only natural, and she says that very few people have acknowledged the boy, and he's been there all morning, for all three services and was there earlier when his father came in to prepare. I just say that I hope that the hymns have been inspiring and relaxing for the boy, and say good day to her.

Later in the afternoon, when my business is concluded, I go back to the church to turn in my membership papers. It is just starting to get dark, and the boy is still there on his cot. The pastor comes out to greet me. He's been there all day as well, and I start to think that he is the most dedicated person I've ever met, if not overly dedicated as indicated by the fact that he's putting his son through a kind of torture. I remember hating the after school church programs that were a part of confirmation. For some reason I could not imagine that this boy was happy even when he was well.

The pastor started telling me that this was the time of day that his late wife used to call "the dirges," and that he thought of her most often during these darkening moments of the afternoon, as it turned quickly to evening. "This is my worst time of day, when I question everything that I do, everything I stand for, and see nothing but suffering and pain in the world," he told me. "Please forgive me in advance for what you might experience here." I told him that absolutely I forgave him, and that this must just be a passing thing, that I had a strong sense of his inner peace that wasn't just perceived but obvious in his expressions of joy to everyone around him.

"So you're really that blind, are you?" he asked. I was a bit stunned by the question. "Let's put it aside, shall we? All the nice reactions and respect for the collar and the place where we are, just for the moment, as it happens to be my private time when I stand before the shrine of my wife that I have built in my heart, and now

The Dirges

I have my son here, who as you can see is having difficulties, to say the least, and I have to bring him here with me all day. How do you think I like that, having him out here on a cot all day for everyone to see, when all day long I tell people about faith and healing, and he just keeps getting worse and worse?"

"I'm sorry," I said. "I came at a bad time."

He was infuriated. "You see! You don't really care. You would walk away and call it respectful rather than to make a heartfelt connection here. I know, because it's too hard for you. There's all this, this baggage, this pain, this suffering; not to mention the fact that what we're here doing is teaching the removal of all those things through God. So we have to keep up appearances, except I don't have to all the time, do I? Do I? Don't I get my fifteen minutes in the day to explode? Who's here to help me? I don't have anybody. I'm not saying I'm going to lose my son. Don't get me wrong. I'm not asking anybody for anything. The doctors are telling me he'll be fine, but after watching my wife die when they said she'd be OK, I just don't know. I just don't know. I pray and pray, and I know that God's will is just, but I want there to be a long stretch without any pain, just as those ten years with Mary. God, how I loved her. Maybe that was my long stretch. I just want it back, and I know that ten years go fast, and if I get another ten years of peace, I know the end has to come. I just wish it weren't this world I was in but the next one. I want it all over and done, or perfect, as it should be. But I accept my station because I know I'm doing the right thing. Again, I'm sorry for troubling you, and I'll cash in that forgiveness chip you gave me before I got into this. Really, I'm fine."

I noticed it was now dark outside. He seemed to quickly slip back into the pastoral persona and asked me to help his son up to walk around. I could see in doing so that his son was not in such bad shape after all, and that there was a hand-held video game visible under the covers as we got him up. It gave me a lot to think about as I left because I know we all have troubles, but there are lines we draw. On the other hand, we need of something like these dirges, a kind of honest, neutral ground where we can absolutely share the truth we feel at times when it may be quite far from the absolute.

Square One

A man is having problems with his wife after building up his career for a number of years. He lives in a six-story house, and he continues to be a workaholic.

One day he gets a call from his wife that she is leaving him. He rushes home in his car through a torrential rain and hears on the radio that the bridge on the river is close to being washed out. He gets to the bridge and runs through a police blockade and tries to cross. The bridge is swaying precariously, and suddenly he feels it sag and buckle, but somehow he makes it across. He races home and runs up the five flights of stairs to their penthouse suite. Already he is filled with frustration even at the prospect of dealing with her — he knows how she gets — and that it will be impossible to talk her out of it. But he must stop her.

But as he gets to the top of the stairs, the floor between the last stair and the closed door is gone. There's no way he can bridge the gap. Through the door he catches glimpses of her. She is carrying packed bags and hurrying the children along. Then he calls to her over and over to no avail. She's ignoring him as he expected, and as he spends his last cry, it is silent, and he can tell she's left him alone in their mansion.

That night he seeks the counsel of a friend who hears him out on all her faults as her husband sees them. His reaction and advice come unexpectedly. His friend first tells him that the taller the building, the more critical that it be engineered correctly. Short things will stand against the laws of physics, whereas tall things prove the laws. Even on the inside of the soul, the further the

Square One

attempt to structure thought, the harder it will fall if faulty. And he points out that while his wife was keeping house and raising the kids in the penthouse, he was either at the office or working in the basement, wasn't he? Yes, it was true, but there was so much to do to support the lifestyle, and he had just started to redesign the basement into a studio where he could relax to get away from the office, or the kids if it became too hectic. His was a world of great stress, and relaxation was necessary to offset it.

Then his friend made a confounding leap of logic — the floor hadn't been removed by his wife, but by him. With all his attention focused on the basement, a corresponding void above was formed so as to remove the floor at the top of the stairs. He thought it ridiculous, but took the explanation as metaphorical. "And as for yelling, and your wife not hearing you," his friend said, "have you ever been at the back of a boat at top speed and tried to talk to a person up front?"

"I see what you're getting at — all that anger and unreachable focus exuding from her is like a great wind that was impossible for me to get through," he answered.

"No, more like a wind tunnel into your heart — a gravitational force like a black hole around you, based in selfishness. No matter how hard you scream for someone, your words cannot go further than your own mouth because there's so much inward flux."

"Then how can you hear me?"

"I'm not looking for love from one incapable of giving it."

And that was the end of the interview. He thanked his friend to keep his opinion to himself and stormed out. As he drove home, he vacillated between fury and confusion. He rejected out of hand everything his friend had suggested, but he was going home to an empty house, and his psyche was doing everything it could to thwart even the slightest degree of blaming himself.

His entire attitude was that she was wrong. He would not budge. She had to change, not him. Never once did he think along the way of what he might have done to her, what he had contributed and what she might have to say about the whole thing. To even entertain her feelings would lend them a degree of credibility. No, it all needed to be met head on — that is how he became successful — he was a strong adversary who took calculated risks, stood his ground and counted his winnings.

On the other hand, he'd never been very good at relationships. His wife was the first woman to stand his domineering ways this long. He'd become relaxed in it, somewhat, and maybe then, even less flexible. No, he mustn't think that way — it was her personality. She was blockading him. Well then, let the battle begin. Still, there was that emptiness, like a storm had taken all he had away and left him peering out of a basement, the contents sucked out except for him. She took his heart and soul away, leaving him in an empty foundation.

He battled to think in concrete terms about the road and the trees, all he could see flashing by, and not sink into the jaws of some vision. Damn his friend for starting the intuitive processing! Now the car was suddenly floating in a vortex. He picked up his cell phone and gave his friend a call.

"Is there an attendant?" was his counsel's first question.

"What do you mean, an attendant. I'm swirling in a tornado!"

"I mean a hired hand. Your grass grows higher when it rains for days, doesn't it?"

"Yes."

"But you don't yourself mow it, do you?"

"No."

"And when you've had a party and the guests leave, you don't help clean up, do you?"

"No, the servants do."

"Those are your attendants. Now, in this vortex you're spinning in, do you see anyone in front of any controls, anyone standing as if ready to hand you a towel or a bar of soap or ready to shine your shoes?"

"No, no, none of that — just clouds and a violent wind throwing me around at an incredible speed."

"No attendant? Then I'm sure I'm right to say you're managing to go straight down the tubes without anyone's help but your own."

"How do I get out of it?"

Square One

"If you had the choice to visit a show boat or a casino, which would you pick?"

At that, the automobile landed with a soft thud on soft grass outside a group of office buildings. He got out of the car and walked toward them. On the way, he passed a pond with a half-sunken show boat in drastic need of repair. In the small village, he entered the central building and found an information booth. "May I help you?" asked the attendant.

"Yes," he answered nervously, "I just passed the broken-down show boat nearby, so I suppose I want to know if you can tell me how to get to the real show boat."

"The real show boat, sir?"

"Oh, I'm sorry, I said I just passed it, didn't I? I guess I'm looking for the casino. Is there a casino around here?"

"Certainly, sir." He then proceeded to give him extended verbal directions that he did not quite grasp although he nodded to keep up the appearance that he did.

As he wandered aimlessly then, he noticed a men's room with a sign, "Attendant on Duty," so he walked in. Inside, it looked more like a casino than a men's room. There were so many strange machines and light-bulb bedecked gizmos that he couldn't tell where to relieve himself even if he'd wanted to. He looked around trying to guess where the urinals, toilets, hand dryers and paper-towel dispensers might be, while an attendant, the same man who just had answered his questions in the information booth, eyed him suspiciously. Loitering was not allowed. There was a sign right above the attendant that said so. Finally he asked where the urinal was. The attendant stood up, opened a door, pushed a button, whereupon hydraulic gears began to hum. The machinery expanded, and a self-encased, high-tech urinal appeared. The attendant took a huge bib and began to tie it around his neck, but he fought it off.

"I don't have to go," he said, "and I want to leave."

"I'll need a coin to close up," said the attendant.

He gave the attendant a silver dollar which he inserted, pulled a lever and the whole urinal system closed up and concealed itself flush against the wall.

Embarrassed at having to leave a men's rest room in this way, he marched out, walked past the pond with the sinking show boat, all the way to his car still mired in the mud from having fallen out of the sky. He took his cell phone out, called his friend and explained the situation.

"The various buildings are the floors of your mansion all broken up, and you're wandering in the spaces between the original missing floor spaces between. The original missing floor space has expanded to a limbo at the base of the vortex in which you were swirling."

"I met an attendant this time. It was in a men's room that almost looked like a casino."

The advisor thought it interesting until he learned that the directions to the casino had gotten all mixed up, that he'd then gone into a rest room, and that the attendant had been the same person who'd given him directions to the casino in the first place.

"All that's bad," he said, "and when it gets this convoluted, I'm not sure I can make sense of it to you, but let's at least try to understand what's been going on here. You ask directions, miss them, being that they're quite complicated not to mention you're unfamiliar with the area, yet you pretend to understand and find what looks like it might be the right place. You do this with just one quick turn and happen to find the same person who gave you the directions who now is concerned you're loitering so you ask to use a john you don't really need to use? No, the place only seemed like a casino because of lights and gadgets, but you don't pay to play but to close up the place when you're finished. Am I right so far?"

"Right so far."

"And this all stemmed from my asking whether you'd choose to visit a show boat or a casino, right?"

"Right."

"But you really didn't make a choice, did you? You just happened to see a sunken show boat, ruled it out, and the first chance you had you asked about a casino, figuring you'd better take a look at that as well to complete the picture, right?"

"I guess so."

"Yeah, well, why did you do that?"

Square One

"I don't know. This is confusing enough as it is."

"Confusing, and you expect me to figure it out? It's happening in you, you idiot, not me."

"Look, don't get mad, just help me out of here, will ya?"

"Yeah, OK. Is the show boat still there?"

"Yes."

"How's she floating now?"

"She's derelict, listing badly."

"Did you notice she's not in a lake or on a dock, but landlocked in a small pond like some old restaurant?"

"Yes, now that you mention it."

"Well, my guess is that the casino is in the show boat, and if you don't want to settle in for the long haul, you'd better get in there and take your chances on the big wheel. Either way, you're starting out from square one."

"What do you mean?"

"You're in your own center and you're lost. It's an island you're on, and you're not supposed to isolate yourself like that, and look at yourself, you're calling out to me to help, and I don't know if I can give you directions home. You're going to have to take it from here. Is any of this having an impact?"

It sure was. By then, the buildings had vanished, and the pond had turned inside out. The show boat was sitting on land, and water was suddenly lapping up on shore on four sides all the way around him.

It was all he could do to clamber up the side of the show boat as the water rushed at him. The tide had surely turned. He climbed in a broken window and recognized the floor of the deck. It was the one that had disappeared that kept him from reaching his wife. In the center of the room was a wheel alright — a ship's steering wheel. He was on the bridge. There was a lever in front of him to power the engines. This was the gambling device, he thought, for he didn't know whether it would work or where to go. He thought he would try to just get them going enough to help the water lift her out to float on her own. He waited for the water to rise for a few minutes, then pulled the lever to "start engines."

"I'm at square one, and the next move is mine," he thought. He wanted to go back to his broken home and set it right, but wasn't sure of his bearings. Again, it was a gamble, and he just started to steer. Dark clouds were on one side. On the other it was clear. He chose to steer right into the thick of it. He was thrashed on violent seas that nearly tore the ship apart. It rained for days, and when he finally saw land, he recognized his building. The water was still rising and already up to the fourth floor. He sailed up to it and eased her in so that the deck became the top floor. He then pushed the lever to "all stop." He felt the last bit of energy leave him, and he collapsed.

He didn't know exactly how long he slept when the ringing of his cell phone woke him up. He was in his car on a small island in the middle of a raging river. He felt totally drained. He picked up the phone. "You made it!" his friend shouted. "We're so proud of you!"

"We? Who's we?" he asked.

He heard the sound of a helicopter above him and went up to the roof of his building. "I've got your wife and kids here," he said. "They want you to come home. I'm sending a ladder down."

A ladder was tossed from the door of the helicopter, and he climbed up carefully until he reached the door and was pulled in by his wife and oldest son. As he looked down, he watched the car being swept away. It rolled over and over in the moil of silt and water and disappeared.

The Voyage of a Bean

A few days before my father died, I was going through his papers when I came across some words he'd written about me. "I taught him courage," the note said, but it didn't elaborate. I pondered that while he was in a coma, so I couldn't ask him about it, but it stuck in my craw. First, I didn't feel like I had any courage at all, particularly regarding our relationship. He had never been around much when I was growing up, we never had heart-to-heart conversations, and he overshadowed me with the expectation that I would follow in his footsteps. I had disappointed him there and chosen another field, but he had been a disappointment to me as well, and I couldn't understand the note about teaching me courage unless the plan was that I would understand better and better the more he travelled, becoming an expert in courage through the pain of not having a father in the normal sense of the term.

It's funny what we remember in stressful times though. He was never around, and I swore I'd never forgive him for that, but while I watched him gasp for air through the oxygen mask, I recalled the first time he read *Jack and the Beanstalk* to me when I was a boy. When he was finished, I complained, "But the beans didn't talk." I'd misunderstood the title as *Jack, and the Beans Talk*. He laughed, and it hurt my feelings, but he made up it for by explaining the story in an interesting way. He said that we were like little beans going on a voyage, and that the stalk took us up and out, bringing us safely into the world; safely, that is, unless the world itself isn't safe. In the case of Jack's world, there was a giant that had essentially made the world a desert, and through the magic beans, Jack was transported out of his world unnaturally and into a position to destroy the giant. In doing so, he had made his world safe again. My father said that every age had its giants to be brought down, or we had our personal giant to deal with, and that it was our duty to make some kind of pilgrimage, a voyage, as it were, to the kingdom of the giant and fight him. We would not know ourselves or life's purpose for us if we ignored this duty or failed to have the courage to face it.

I didn't know at the time why he had given me this complicated explanation of a fairy tale, but it definitely stayed with me over the years. I thought of birth being a bean riding on a stalk until it was ripe enough to reach the world, whereupon it would grow and learn how to talk. This is what differentiates us from all other forms of life. And I thought of life as having a purpose of discerning the evil giant and finding a way to deal with him, for one's self or for the world, and that this would be one's defining moment.

But I never thought I had any courage. Without my father to guide me much further than a single comment on a children's story, I was pretty much left to my own devices. My late mother tried to make up for it, but it wasn't the same. To me courage was about taking a calculated risk, but it was still a risk, and when I was five, one of my friends died. We called him "Little Al," not because he was small but because his father's name was Al, and this was their way of avoiding calling him junior. He was six, and the day after he died, I stood near his driveway looking at the hearse filled with flowers. All I wanted was to become an adult and know what it was like to be fully grown. I knew that childhood was only a stage, that I was young and limited in understanding of the meaning of life, and I wanted safe passage to maturity to be able to realize whatever it was that one would understand by living a whole and complete life. In that defining moment, I always felt that a part of me had chosen the route a coward takes because I knew to make it safely into old age where I would know the meaning of life, I would not be able to take many serious chances. It wasn't that all this was conscious, but looking back at how I avoided military service and marriage, well, the death of Little Al looked more and more like a defining moment in my life. The problem was that I thought life was going to lead up to some kind of fulfillment or wholeness, and what I've found instead is that the world is filled with ignorant, broken people. If my father had done something he thought would instill courage in me, perhaps it had just died on the vine or like Little Al, for some reason just didn't get its chance to live.

As I stood by my father's bed in the hospital, watching him gasp what looked to be his last breaths, I cried. I had this idea of myself that I would not, and it was based on the sense I had from a film I'd seen that each person reacts in a specific way in witnessing a single death as they do to death in general. Some are repelled by it, others take it by the hand, while still others are shattered by it. I thought my reaction would be more contemplative, especially as I had given the matter so much thought over the preceding days, but now I just seemed to lose it, and it didn't do much for my self esteem. I couldn't bring myself to hold his hand, yet I wanted him to wake up and give me an indication of confidence that he was going to a better place as well as some last words of comfort and advice, perhaps, and what my course of action should be. I'm afraid it had always been a disappointment to him that I hadn't found and conquered any giants. What he didn't know, or perhaps he did pick up on it, was that he was always the giant I'd never confronted, and even as he was laid low, I was still looking for something from him, some clue or tool, something I could use to wend my way in life.

I felt that all my life I'd only been going through the motions. With the sickbed and the grave somewhere in the distance, are not all the things we do just meaningless diversions from the truth? What if we were to isolate all of the right precepts, the proverbs on the nature of living. Wouldn't those ideas be an obfuscation of reality, which is that I am going to die? Pascal said all of the truths had already been defined, and that all that was left was to put them in motion in our lives.

What else though can we do but live? We do not choose the era or the circumstances of our lives. In this ultimacy, we try to build a safe refuge in which we can see enough safe days ahead to calmly forget the ultimate reality that we face, and so we go about our lives — through the motions — getting caught up in the era's trends, in

The Voyage of a Bean

what we perceive as being important to others. Intimations of immortality may exist in childhood, but they evolve into delusions by the time we are adults.

Personally, my biggest problem is not being honest with myself. This carries over to others, who I never really face as I am because I've never really faced myself. What they get is a blurred version of what I should be. I have a constant sense of the disparity.

It is interesting that much of this stems from the privacy of lives around me. Due to the nature of individuals, each with his own insecurities, fears, hopes, doubts, experiences, there is raging caution and superficiality; and not much possibility of deep connection with any others.

I would say that to truly connect with anyone, I'd have to sit down and spill the beans, but it would be like tipping a cornucopia — endlessly pouring forth its immeasurable hoard, which is my cycle of delusions. Who could love me for that? And so, for fear of not being loved, I act in order to gain confidence.

Once any connection is made, it must be fed and fortified with new lies, such that soon I feel no great gain but the pain of having deceived. It is by then too difficult to explain how it all happened, and because even at that point I am concerned with how I seem, I find a way to end the relationship consistent with the role in which I have falsely portrayed myself. The irony, though it may seem cynical, is that very few people escape this kind of syndrome; only they do not feel despair in the disparity.

I have tried to make sense out of the syndromes that force us into such modes. It is frustrating when I feel I need to be with someone, to not be able to find anyone with whom I can feel comfortable about being totally open. People just don't want that. The manners we must adopt in socializing make us dupes. Once we set out in such narrow ways, the stage is set to nearly eliminate broadening and turning back. We become the creatures of customs which make us neurotic, but the customs are the opium from whose grip we cannot withdraw.

The sickness is that there is comfort in the shallows, in strangers that listen with interest to our exaggerations and watch in awe as we show them the high water marks of our experiences which are really no more than a finger dipped in a thimble. We turn our backs to our own recognition of our own base aspects just as we run full circle far from those who uncovered our lies right into someone new on whom we can spill our endless, fabricated stream. The motions we go through are of diminishing reliance on spirit and truth. We supplant feeling, communication, and honesty — thinning our lives to what society expects of us — with dissimulation and lies, and plow our hollow souls through our day and age.

My father couldn't give me anything now, and what I would do if he gave me some last minute advice would be to reject it, probably. I remember when I was a teenager that I woke him up to tell him I loved him, and he threw a fifteen minute fit about being awakened out of a sound sleep, how it would take him hours to fall asleep again, and what a stupid reason it was to wake him up. I always had trouble telling anyone I loved them after that, and then I remembered when I wasn't only going through the motions in my life.

My father always complained I didn't have anything in my immediate sights, that I never aimed for anything in particular. I used to be able to put his criticisms out of my mind when I went away to school. In my college days I had lots of goals and ambitions, and when I remembered Corinne, my depression changed immediately to a feeling of happiness as my old sense of self flickered into mind. She had been the love, and the confusion of my life, and was the only one with whom I had ever been so close to having a whole life. Shouldn't I call her and let her know about my father? Perhaps I was only thinking of myself. It was terrible being in that hospice room alone with him all day. I sat on the couch. My head felt clogged after crying. I thought I might try finding Corinne later, but I was so tired, and I nodded off into a dream where I was close to being dead and gone. I was talking with this woman I hadn't seen in a long time. I used to see her all the time in college, but she seemed only to only remember my friends at first, which bothered me. I kept telling her incidents until finally she remembered me. I don't quite hear her questions, but I answer as if I did. Then for some reason she asks me about my gravestone. She recalls that I was always working on it when we'd known one another. I tell her it is finished and in place except for the date of my death. This prompts her to leave. I am somehow not surprised and think of the spot where I'll be laid to rest not far from where I'm sitting alone. For a moment I think that I'll be in this nice grove off trees, then I realize I don't know where I'll be, and wherever my body may be, I won't be with it. I'll be gone, or somewhere else, but people will know where I am and be able to come and visit. Then I say to myself, just before waking up, "Nobody calls me now." Just then I hear what sounds like a phone call, only it's more of a muffled ringing, and it woke me up. It was my father. His breathing had suddenly gotten very congested. It sounded like gurgling. I got up and went over to him, and after another breath or two like that, he was gone.

For fear of the strong memories the experience might leave, I'd secretly hoped that he would pass when I was out of his room. Later that afternoon, when I left the hospital, the gurgling was still in my head. On my dresser was the note he'd written about teaching me courage. I chuckled that it was a fresh message, his last words to me, and that I'd know in time what I'd learned from watching him die. Somehow I didn't think it would be courage. I put on Brahms' second piano concerto, which Corinne and I loved, and memories of our days together seemed to flood out of the notes! Soon I was searching for her on the internet and was amazed to find that she was in the city, so I wrote down the number and grabbed the phone. My chest felt suddenly heavy. What would I say? I'd already forgotten the news. But she really didn't know my father anyway. She wasn't the overly sympathetic type, and would probably read my call as needing to cry on her shoulder. I released the phone, but I had to call someone. There was just a deep need to speak to someone that had been important in my life, even if it was someone I hadn't seen in over two years, not to mention the unspeakable thing she had done to me.

I did what I could to purge myself of all the various thoughts going in circles in my brain, and I just dialed her number. After three long rings, she answered. "Allo?"

"Corinne, this is Ben."

"I'm sorry?"

"It's me, Ben." That's when it turned south.
"Oh God!" she mourned. I cannot begin to describe the sound of the disappointed surprise in her voice, nor the wave of hurt it sent through me. "Are you in town?" she asked.
"No, I'm home, but my father died."
"I'm sorry. Look, I'm just on way out, but I'll be home Sunday."
"OK, I'll try then."
"I'll look forward to it." Then we said our goodbyes.

I knew she didn't want me calling her back, and I got a bottle of scotch and had a few drinks to my father. I think what I'd wanted to say was something I never would admit, that there was such a dullness of spirit surrounding me in those I knew that I just really missed her bright soul. She would not have understood a comment like that, and I was never one who expressed that kind of need for another. She would have seen it as weakness, and in all fairness, that's what it was. I felt weak without her at that moment, but I really hadn't been eating or sleeping very well for several days, so I was not feeling myself as it was, and drinking was not the most intelligent course of action. I got fairly drunk rather quickly, and then my stomach felt upset. I went to the bathroom cabinet, but I couldn't find the right bottle in the clutter. In the hall closet, too, there were so many kinds of medicine it took me a while to find what I was looking for. I drank some of it and went straight to bed.

The next morning I knew there was something seriously wrong with me. It was more than just a hangover from a couple of drinks. I realized that whatever it was must have started coincidently while I was having a drink, because the reaction was just too violent. I'd really never gotten to sleep, but as many times as I had to get up, I must have been close to being dehydrated. I knew I would soon need to start liquids again, yet I couldn't get up at all. That evening I called an ambulance, which brought me to the hospital, and there I remained in intensive care for five days, in and out of fever. I don't remember much except that I thought about Corinne, not in the present sense. It was more a case of reliving the past.

They had me on antibiotics, which the nurse said had finally kicked in when they thought they were about to lose me. She said I was lucky to be alive.

I didn't like the way it had all transpired, this life threatening disease of mine. In imagining what it would mean to die, I always held to the very strong belief that much of the meaning of my life would become more clear to me as the life ebbed away from me. I thought that I might die rather slowly and come to all kinds of bright ideas as to how life should be viewed. It wasn't like I felt the need to pass it on to anyone. I considered that the value of any kind of revelation or enlightenment about the meaning of life might be quite personal, and that I would be unable to share it with anyone due to my condition. But the way I had almost died left me with a sense that death could be quite swift and leave me with no time to have whatever thoughts I might think would come at death. I might not have the experience of realizing my life.

This made me wonder what my father had experienced in his last days. I knew that he had told others that he was not afraid. I knew that in the days before he went into the hospital he had lots of time to consider his demise, and yet he made no overtures to speak to anyone about what he may have been thinking. He did not see any priest or hospital chaplain, and as far as I knew, left the world without any intellectual incident if I can put it that way. I mean that there was no ripple in the cosmos, not that happened within him, nor one he had made that would have any affect on others; except for me of course, since I felt that it was just another slight, another way of not talking to me or giving me anything even at the end.

Now it was me in the hospital, except I was feeling sorrier for myself than for him. I was alone, and whatever impact I felt or might cause from my thoughts on death would die on the vine, right there and then if I were to go, though it can be safely said that I did not have any major revelation about my life or anyone else's.

But there was some reason why I thought so much about Corinne, however, which I found curious in how it started. One of the nurses had come to give me a pill, but she dropped it on the floor, and it rolled under the bed. I was transported back to when I first met her in college. She had a big sheep dog and used to walk it around. I used

The Voyage of a Bean

to see it pulling her around long before I met her. It just seemed to not be one of those perfect pairings of dogs and masters. Whatever training she had given the dog, it didn't seem to have retained either, as it was all over anyone who stopped her to talk.

I happened to meet her one afternoon through friends I was visiting in the same building where she lived. She was abrupt and unfriendly, and her dog jumped all over me as we were going out. I was friendly to the animal, more "fending" it off, but in a nice way, and I introduced myself. Corinne wasn't very friendly, but she certainly was beautiful. I went out of my way on several occasions after that to say hello to her and let her dog jump all over me. I just made sure to keep it short so that she wouldn't feel that I was interested in any way. Then I happened to be walking home from class and saw her without the dog and just walked past her, saying only a bland hello. I then paid more attention to the dog on the next several occasions, and then one afternoon she called to me as I was coming out of class. I ended up walking her home, and I learned that she had issues with men due to one very bad experience with someone who had humiliated and nearly raped her. It was then that I realized the dog was her protection and letting it jump on people was a kind of jamming of the potential predator's mental airwaves. She would be the one choosing her friends, not the other way around, and I thought, fortunately for me, she seemed to be interested in me.

We learned that our families lived relatively close together, which gave us a chance to give one another a ride home on weekends when it happened we'd both be planning to make such a trip. The first time we did this, she said she would drive, and she picked me up with the shaggy dog in the back seat, and it nuzzled up to me all the way to my house. But what was significant was how she dressed. She wore a buttoned shirt with a button missing just below her breasts, and she wasn't wearing a bra. I thought it might be another indication of liking me, but since she didn't trust anyone, I thought it was probably just another test, so I ignored looking into the opening as much as humanly possible for my age at the time.

One weekend, I drove her home, and her mother invited me to come back early that Sunday for dinner before driving Corinne back

The Voyage of a Bean

to school. Corinne smiled, nodding that she approved as well. I accepted. That Sunday I drove to her house in the late afternoon. It was still early in the fall then, sunny and warm, all in all a beautiful day. I hadn't really met Corinne's parents yet. On this occasion, her father was out of the country. They were French, and they went to France quite often. Her mother had a strong, but I thought very cute accent. She said "eat" instead of "it," that sort of thing, but after a few glasses of wine and my looking into the bowl of beans she had made and saying, "How have you bean," she also started calling me "Bean" instead of "Ben," and eventually Corinne picked it up during dinner, and I began to find it a little irritating after a while, and the presence of beans on the table just seemed to exacerbate it. As is my custom, I ate rather quickly, and to my misfortune, a bit too sloppily, because Corinne's mother pointed out I had a bean in my beard. "How long has it bean there?" I joked. I was even doing it to myself. I felt the area and found there was juice there as well, so I excused myself to the bathroom, and her mother suggested I might take the time to use a razor and shave my beard off as well, and be a "gentleman" as she put it.

I took that ill, but was used to such comments, the times being what they were. In those days, it was all about how young people looked and dressed. In the bathroom, I cleaned off my beard quickly, and while holding the bean, I opened the cabinets and found an incredible assortment of pills of all kinds. I figured it had to have accumulated over many years, little knowing that her mother had a condition, and right in front of my eyes was a bottle of small brown pills. I opened it up and dropped the bean inside. I still don't quite know what made me do it. I thought it was a harmless prank.

But the next day her mother found the bean in the pills, and the moisture from it had damaged the medicine in the bottle, so she wouldn't take it, and this caused her to be sick, Corinne told me, though she was able to get a new prescription filled rather quickly. Corinne had a fit and reverted to her distant self, and she may have even trained her dog to attack me, or perhaps she had a way of conveying to the dog how it should behave with various people, because from then on, it growled while trying to jump on me, and

The Voyage of a Bean

whenever Corinne took steps toward me, so I was constantly backing up while trying to apologize. I did my best to make up for it, and the way I succeeded was to take my three years of college French and write a letter to her mother that I had my French teacher correct before I mailed it. I signed it, "Bean," and her mother was fine with me after that, but her father formulated his prejudice of me from the story reported to him on his return from abroad, and I never quite made it into his good graces.

Corinne and I dated after that until we'd both finished school, and we were well enough acquainted with one another's foibles that we talked about getting married. This is where her father really stepped in to interfere. I didn't know how much it was a cultural difference, but I thought the French were relatively liberal in general, and it wasn't that I was another denomination. But they were Catholic, not even church-going Catholic for the most part, but he nevertheless stringently objected to my being a Lutheran. I asked Corinne if this might be some kind of enmity left over from the war, some residual hatred for Germany. I also thought it was about me. Perhaps he was just looking for an excuse to unload his rabid distaste for me. It didn't matter. What mattered is that Corinne cared that they cared, which I found even more alarming because we'd really never talked about religion, but she answered this by declaring that before any marriage could take place, some things were too important not to consider. I did realize that it was already having an impact. I just thought, given that it was from an outside source, we should be able to surmount it. She did not consider her parents an outside source.

I reached my limit during the final discussion about this issue. I pointed out that it couldn't be about differences in faith that we hadn't been living, but about the belief in one another that had already kept us together for so long. I asked how could I win a fight against her religion when I didn't share it, and yet I wouldn't convert either, for my own reasons, so I understood something of the strength, but it wasn't as if this really made a difference. These were denominational difference. I wasn't going to argue against the bishops and the pope or the mother church with all its pomp and circumstance. All I could sell was my love, that it wasn't for the ideas of the church to separate two people, to put your heart down in favor of ideas where love is at the center. "Well let's examine that," I said. "What do you really want to do here, please your parents or state your theology? Do you want to spend your life with someone who fills gap in your life or deny yourself the happiness for an idea you don't even follow? If we get married we have a chance to knock down the things that are standing in front of us — the ducks of convention — all the things that squawk at us when we walk by. We could knock them down and force a free path. But we've already got enough of these things squawking at us, and what, you're going to throw religion into the mix and use that as an excuse? We're together because you still have feeling for me, and who's going to say that's wrong ultimately when it's what you want? If they love you, they'll want it for you, but if they need to have control, they will just try to exert that control, just to make sure they still have it, even at the expense of your happiness because they don't know when to let go. They're not sure of the transition. All they know is that you are their little girl, and they don't want to lose you. Faith and the religion have nothing to do with it because they're not pulling us to God in this sense. They're just trying to keep us from doing something they deem wrong, save themselves from whatever they are not quite prepared to experience because they still think it's about them, that we don't yet have lives. But we understand the bigger picture. We've grown up past that and we know the reason we're together is bigger than them."

"But is it bigger than God?" she asked me.

I didn't want to do battle with God over this, but to me it was more about the world. "God said what He had to say," I told her, "and we've muddled it up to the point that we have groups of people believing it differently as if it could change from different angles. It's more about what people think than what God thinks! Why would they insist that we can only be happy if we abide by conventional faith as modified by men over the centuries? Is the spirit really moving them in this? Let us have our lives, make our mistakes. Yes, they save us from making them if they keep us apart, but that may be the biggest mistake of all."

I continued in this manner rather passionately for some time, even to the point of delivering the ultimatum that it was either the church or me, at which point Corinne started to cry, which brought her parents out of the house to get her as they'd been listening from an upstairs window. I had not considered that they might have been eavesdropping, but that was just my typical luck.

We did continue on after that. But her parents won her over on one thing, which was to go out with the son of a French family of whom they approved. His name was Claude. I never knew much about him, only that he was a few years older and a professor, apparently quite the brain. I lost Corinne for more than a year and got my own career started, but out of the blue she called me and wanted to see me again. Claude had gone home to visit his family in France and met someone else. Corinne only found out about it after his return. He came back and acted as if nothing had happened for a few weeks. Then the woman followed, and there was a confrontation, and Claude went with the other girl. I felt like a second choice myself, but I was happy we were together again, only Claude had given Corinne a venereal disease, which she unknowingly passed to me. I experienced symptoms quickly, and she thought I'd been fooling around, but she discovered the truth when her appendix burst. The venereal disease had only made matters worse, and she had herself a case of acute peritonitis.

My staying with her and taking care of her during her operation and recovery went a long way in reassuring her as well as her parents regarding the condition of my soul. In time, ideas were not the main concern. I was accepted as an honorary Catholic, I suppose, and even attended Mass with them on the important holidays. Her parents allowed that we might try living together, which I found ridiculous though I never said anything. After all that rigmarole over religion, and here they were rather blasé on a crucial point. I thought they were hypocrites, but I thanked them gratefully for their kind understanding. In short, I dissimulated my rear end off.

But the relationship didn't go very well. Within a month, it all went terribly wrong. I happened to find a letter Corinne had written.

The Voyage of a Bean

I picked it up off the floor and unfolded it. It wasn't in an envelope, so I didn't know what it was. All I had to see was the salutation, "Dear Claude,..." and I closed it up. When Corinne came in, I held it out to her and said, "I'd appreciate it if you wouldn't leave your old letters to Claude lying around."

She lunged and grabbed it from my hand. "Where did you get that?" she yelled. I was for a moment taken aback as her outrage seemed a bit out of keeping with the situation.

I said, "All I'm saying is I don't feel very good about finding connections to him on the floor. It was just lying there. You must have dropped it. I'm just asking for normal consideration."

She still was fuming over the incident, and it slowly came to me that this was not some old draft of a letter that she had written to Claude. And he would presumably have any letters she had actually mailed to him. No, her emotions told me that this was the discovery of a secret letter she was writing him, and now it wasn't about whether it was the first, or whether she would actually send it. It was about the fact that she was carrying a torch for him even after all that he had done to her.

It was more than I could stand, and I set in motion what turned out to be the longest separation from her to that point. She was not happy about it, but I did not give her a choice.

I moved out and got on with my life. I kept touch with her parents for a while. Corinne's father still maintained an air of distrust, but I could detect that he had taken a bit of a shine to me. I believe that it mattered to him that I behaved within normal parameters, that I was good for his daughter, and she was the one with the tendency to bring problems on herself. He didn't like the men that she tended to choose, and why she didn't seem content with someone who treated her right was beyond him, and me, except that she was just one of those people who seem to only be themselves when in direct connection with something that demeans or destroys them.

I eventually stopped seeing her parents altogether when my career took me to the west coast. Five years went by, and I happened to be in the area on business. I saw my father, but that was boring. He took me out to dinner and hardly said a word. He was not in any sense interested in my success as he said, "You've only been at it a few years." But I did find the time to stop by Corinne's parents to find out where she was living. I must say they seemed terribly relieved to see me. It was almost like I was a godsend. I could almost hear them saying, "Please, you've got to help her," in their effusive excitement that it really was me at the door.

What I didn't tell them was that it was really about some music that I'd inadvertently left behind. I remembered it shortly after I'd moved out, but I was too angry to confront her again, and I thought I could live without the music. But at the time, it was going to be expensive to replace it, and I knew she wasn't fond of it, so I wanted to get it back. After seeing her parents, I was a bit concerned about what I might be getting myself into, but having done relatively well for myself, and having been "deClaude" as I put it, I wanted to show her something, and I hoped if not to pour any salt on her wounds to at least have the satisfaction of some closure or rise in self-esteem for myself.

I thought her parents might call to tell her that I was coming, but I caught her completely by surprise. She betrayed a degree of the same enthusiasm I'd seen earlier in her parents, then hid it behind a cool exterior. As we went up the stairs, she told me she'd gone back to school and had been getting her doctorate in philosophy. I said that was nice.

Upstairs, there was a man in her living room who was not happy with my being there, whoever I was. He set out to make me as uncomfortable as possible but was one of those types with whom I am quite at ease either ignoring or exchanging barbs. I was the only one totally relaxed in a tense situation, and I quickly gathered that I had walked in on an argument in progress.

Corinne went to get my music, and I engaged in light chit-chat with her friend. I remained standing and wandered around the room looking at what was on the shelves. That is when I noticed that there was a special area reserved for memories related to me. She had all the little things I'd given her as well as some things I'd made, all together in the central area of the shelves. It wouldn't be obvious to the casual observer; only I would be able to recognize the care

The Voyage of a Bean

she went to in order to preserve a link to me. I realized too that this other guy had the same difficulty with such a link as I had to the one she had kept with Claude. He got up and left the room. I could hear them talking.

"So that's *the* Ben you've talked about? What's he want? Hey, I like that music. You're not giving it to him are you? Well what's the statute of limitations on music these days?" It was that sort of conversation, and she was getting louder and more defensive in her replies. I decided to use the bathroom, and I heard them return to the living room. Corinne said something about him making me leave. He said something like, "Good riddance."

Corinne said she couldn't believe I'd just show up like that and leave without saying anything. She wondered if I'd left a note and started looking around. This upset the fellow. "What do you need a note for? He obviously got the message that he wasn't welcome, and he left!"

"What do you mean, not welcome? This is my house!" She yelled. "He's welcome if I say he is, and what right do you have to make him feel unwelcome?"

I began to feel uncomfortable listening behind the door, so I flushed the toilet and made my appearance. "Sorry," I said with a smile. "I just had to use the facilities. I hope that's not a problem."

That's when Corinne blew up at me. "What did you come here for, anyway? What do you think you're trying to do?"

"Sorry," I explained, "but I came for my music. If you want, I can just leave my address, and you can mail it to me at your convenience. I also was looking forward to catching up with you. It's been such a long time. Well, then," I said slowly, waiting for an answer, "I guess I'll be running along."

"No, please," Corinne objected. "Don't go like that. Stay and have a drink or something."

"Hey, what are you talking about? A drink? Let him go if he wants to go," the guy blurted.

They started to argue, so I said, "I'll just call you sometime," and as I turned to walk out, I saw her run into the bedroom.

The guy followed. "Hey, what are you looking for?" I could hear her rifling through drawers. "You're not looking for the gun, are you? OK, Corinne, this has gotten out of hand. You've got to settle down here. What do you think you're going to do. Look, I understand he's just an old boyfriend. Just let the jerk go. You don't have to hurt him. Leave the gun alone. Just let him go. He's not worth it."

I felt a wave of panic that I might have gotten myself in way too deep, so I went down the stairs as fast as I could. I fumbled with the door as it was unfamiliar to me, and heard what sounded like someone stumbling on the floor above me. Then I heard incoherent shouting. Then it struck me that she really might try to kill me. I got the door open, and heard yelling and screaming on the stairs above me. When I was halfway into the street, I heard the gun go off, and I started to run. There were a couple of shots in the stairwell, and then the door flies open and her boyfriend burst out running, and Corinne comes out behind him shooting in the air, shouting after him as he raced down the street, "And don't come back!"

During my recovery, these memories came to me with an unexpected clarity, and the incidents that seemed to connect without the gaps made sense to me for the first time as one thing instead of a group of experiences. By the fourth day in the hospital I was told I was out of trouble. My memories of Corinne were only intensifying.

After she chased her deadbeat boyfriend out, Corinne caught up with me on the street, and we started communicating from a distance, laughing for the first time at what had at one time seemed so serious. It was actually fun to call and talk with her. I found as I was getting a little more experienced that it's easier to resume long-term friendships than keep new friends. I knew by having known Corinne before, that even though we hadn't spent any time together over several years, I could more easily relax with her again at the outset and enjoy a conversation. We didn't have to "feel one another out" as it were. And that was how we got started seeing one another again, and we were both grateful for a time that the other had not found somebody else who was more compatible during that long hiatus. We each felt that we had each been through so much that we had grown beyond the influence of our family, and despite the history we had of not getting along, we also felt a certain trust, and it made it easy for us to be companions without feeling that we might be getting involved again too quickly.

But Corinne's parents were still in the picture, and while they behaved more as an older couple that happened to be our friends, when the four of us were together, I felt their influence at times. They had money for one thing, and this gave Corinne and I a chance to go to Europe together, but we essentially were tagging along with them because they still had a little cottage on the ocean. Corinne and I were only too happy to accept the arrangement because we planned to rent a car and see some of Europe together. We told them that we just wanted to take advantage of the opportunity, which they thought was a good idea as well. We decided to go to Italy because we both wanted to see Rome.

The trip to Europe, in the end, was an unpleasant experience for me, and I wasn't feeling well in the hospital thinking about it. I had a high fever, was sleeping quite a bit, and certain ideas cycled through my mind over and over, or one thought would just dominate my thoughts. It was something very irrational, a nonsensical repetitive task, for example, where I would be doing something with bottles and a tall building, only the building would be in the way, looming, and it would turn out to be a headache on waking.

Then I opened my eyes and realized it was a migraine. I could hardly see. I wondered if I'd had a stroke. I was full of high energy, blind as a bat, more mish-mashed vision, feeling I'd broken through, or, like a bubble on a vein, formed an eddy that could burst, swirling with last ideas from God and wiggling my fingers to make sure it wasn't a blood clot. After a few hours it passed. What was left was residual, the hangover metal plate of selected pain across the back of the head, napping and popping up with ideas out of nowhere, more like a dying fire, the occasional crack beneath the embers though the flame itself is gone. At the same time though, it was beyond clarity like something opening up saying nothing is forgotten, everything is today, but you want to get back to the numb state, plod along because the heightening is too frightening, because I felt like I was going to break. The nurse gave me codeine, and I quickly

The Voyage of a Bean

fell into a dream where Corinne and I were in a car with my dog, which Corinne had told me not to bring because she didn't like animal smell, but I was determined to keep the dog between us, so I'd had it washed, and the car was not a convertible, but had a retractable sun roof, and the dog kept putting its paws on her to stick its head up through the roof, and the wind was blowing its hair all over because the cleaning and the wind through the car had accelerated its shedding, and the hair was thick in the car. Corinne was livid, and I was laughing, and the car was filling up with hair. Soon we were just two heads sticking up through it all, and the dog was nowhere to be seen, but there was the sound of a baby crying, and I started digging to find it, and Corinne couldn't find the wheel, and the car went off the road, and I woke up, a tall building still looming somehow over my mind and worry I was losing my hair.

We did take a car trip to Italy, but there was no dog. It was hot, and the air conditioner broke, so we were driving with the windows down. It was so humid, but it was worse when we had to stop. We spent a few days in Rome, touring the major sites, and on the last day, Corinne wanted to visit the Piazza di campo dei Fiori where the philosopher Giordano Bruno had been burned at the stake for heresy in 1600. She briefed me on the story, which is fascinating given the forces at work in those days. It was also very pleasant to hear the tale in our air-conditioned room where I would have been happy to look at pictures of Rome for the duration of the visit. Bruno believed Copernicus was correct in his view of the heavens and was wanted by the inquisition, but he did not seem to fear it. The exact grounds for his condemnation are not clear because his file is missing from the records, but he also spoke openly on the infinity of inhabited worlds. He'd been a monk, but gave it up and lived in Germany where he spoke. At one point, he accepted an invitation to speak in Venice where he was finally nabbed. They held him for eight years, until finally, they burned him at the stake after he refused to recant, saying to those who had sentenced him, "Perhaps you, my judges, pronounce this sentence against me with greater fear than I receive it." As the fires burned around him, and he was dying, someone held out a crucifix, which he pushed away. In 1889, a memorial was erected on the spot where he died, which is now a marketplace.

Corinne was quite excited about actually being able to visit the memorial, but I was a bit sullen that morning. My exotic dinner from the previous evening was still with me, and I couldn't seem to get my systems running normally. She waited for me at our hotel room door, stressing that we didn't have all day, and she obviously was not interested in how I felt, so I did not tell her all the details. When we got to the lobby, I looked at the line of people waiting to check out and saw a man fall over backwards onto his head. He had been outside in the heat, and he just keeled over. Someone rushed to give him CPR. We walked right on by and out the door.

The marketplace in the Piazza was rife with shoppers. In my haste to leave the room to appease Corinne, I'd forgotten my sunglasses, and it was one of those days where the combination of heat and light almost distort what you see. I didn't seem to be able to take it all in for some reason. I wanted to sit down, even jump in a fountain, but Corinne kept pulling me along, describing the scene.

"Over here is where the gallows used to be, and there was a horse market over there. Did you know this place wasn't even paved until the fifteenth century?" I didn't understand her particular fascination with this quarter, and I was ready to go back to the car. I started wondering what I was doing in Europe at all. Suddenly the states felt so far away, and I wanted to be back in my own bed. If I collapsed on the spot, how could I be sure I'd wake up with both kidneys as I didn't speak a word of Italian.

Corinne detected my disinterest and impatience, and did not seem to associate it with my physical state. I tried to bear up and had not been whining to her, so I had little reason to expect her to be sympathetic. I was just feeling sorry for myself. We stopped and bought a couple of cold drinks, and for some reason, that and sitting down a moment, brought me back. I started thinking about the modern age, how it had already been more than a hundred years since Bruno had been exonerated. I looked around at all the people, and down to the statue and thought about the history. Then it struck me how the world had really changed. I said to Corinne, "You know what's amazing? Back then, all Giordano Bruno had to do was

The Voyage of a Bean

speak his beliefs, and he was at risk. Unless one was part of the system, one was against it in a way. I mean, consider that most people had no ideas and were kept under the thumb of the church. If you were intellectually minded, you might know many things that held society together, but you couldn't really question any of it. Now we can say anything we want. I can't think of anything I couldn't say if that memorial to Bruno were a soapbox that I could stand on and shout. I could denounce the Pope or the President. I could speak out for gay rights. I might be able to marry a man in this square. Even with whatever controversy I could generate by being as outrageous as possible, we are all so numb to all the ideas that nothing would surprise or threaten anyone. I think that's a kind of enlightenment, don't you? I mean, we've come so far, don't you think?"

I was angling at that point for her acquiescence because she was glaring at me so. She looked like she was ready to lash out, and yet there was a tinge of overall annoyance to it, as if she thought I were an idiot for my comment.

"Alright," she said calmly, and turned on the bench, spreading her legs and opening her arms. She laid her head back and closed her eyes under the sun. "Just make love to me me right her and now and see what happens." She sat up and lit into me. "You think the world has changed, do you? You think we're past burning people at the stake? That's just an outmoded way of execution, but we continue to kill people. We just have better ways. I can think of a thousand things to say to get me in trouble. It might not be that the Vatican Guard will march in here and take me away, but we're at a crucial point in history, actually. I think of it more as the eye of a hurricane than anything else. We look at Bruno, the middle ages, the second world war, from our vantage point and think it was all stupidity, but it spans hundreds of years. What do we actually have but a time of relative peace, and there have always been those between wars. Our age of ideas isn't so great either. I mean, consider that we are in Rome. Just two thousand years ago they were throwing people to the lions here; just a few hundred years, burning people; only sixty, Mussolini was in power and in cahoots with Hitler. You couldn't have stood here without getting shot because you're an American.

The Voyage of a Bean

"It's like we're in the eye of a hurricane right now. Pretty soon, maybe only a few years, maybe a little longer, there's liable to be another five hundred years of chaos. Look at the signs. Behind us are all the centuries of chaos we've already had. The current state of the world is ready to blow. Look at what we're doing to keep the lid on. In politics, we still have millions of people suppressed all around the world. How many people do you think are starving to death on the planet every day? Some age of enlightenment. Are you talking about religious freedom? What about the fact that five hundred years ago, Pope Alexander the sixth, at least when he was a cardinal, was father to Lucrezia Borgia, famous for probably poisoning her husband. Is the Pope really infallible? Is it possible that the current push in the church to make Mary a co-redemptrix with Christ will succeed? How many more items would Luther object to if he returned in our age? Did Mary ascend into heaven where she was crowned queen of heaven and earth? Do you think that the Muslim view of heaven with all its virgins is true? Could Mohammed really be a prophet when he says Jesus was not resurrected but that he and the disciples were good men, and then forbid the reading of the Bible? Are the Jews any better for what they've created over the centuries, letting the words of those considered to be the greatest rabbis contribute to a text, which is studied like scripture? Have you read the introduction to the *Book of Mormon* where an angel returns several times in a short time to repeat his words to Joseph Smith? Is there really any evidence of the societies depicted in what some consider to be a second testimony of Christ?

"Now put them all together and ask yourself this: can they all be right? No! They cannot all possibly be right. On the face of it, there have to be ideas that would be immediately dismissed in light of the truth, and there's the rub, for they are all acceptable together as long as whatever the ultimate truth is remains in the shadows. Now, get up and shout all of that. Say that Islam is crazy, that Mohammed is a false prophet, that it is ridiculous that heaven should be believed to be a place where martyrs are rewarded with an endless supply of virgins, and see how far you get. Go to Salt Lake City and declare the Mormon Church is fraught with false teaching. Paint a swastika on the nearest synagogue or make a racial slur, or denounce Catholicism here and now, and see if your life stays the same. We're in the eye of the hurricane, and Bruno may have thought it was safe too, but obviously, one voice can shake things up, and it is your duty to do it if you see the the truth. And what may seem true may only be transient, like the Woodstock Nation, but when you stand for the things that change people, make them whole and able to control their own destinies, you will be a dangerous man. Even attacking totalitarianism, which still controls millions of people, and takes the place of religion, is dangerous. All these ideas together form the current fabric of the world, and while it is true that they cannot all be right, they are currently holding societies together.

"And if I understand you correctly, you've adopted the liberal view that it's better to allow all the ideas in the world than make the world think about ideas that it allows. The politically correct view shrinks from a schism, maintaining that all are true, and worst of all, in fact, that there is no truth, so nothing can be ultimately brought out to force one to decide on the matter. Government goes on, and people are out there, working and following one another like sheep, and the truth waits for anyone with the courage of Giordano Bruno to give their lives rather than give in. Galileo, great as he was, will be remembered for recanting to appease the cardinals. In the end, when the eye of the hurricane passes, who knows what winds of change will blow. A change of power may lead to a happy gathering to pull the statue of Bruno down or burn it down. That would be more likely." She stopped and sat back, deep in her own thoughts.

"That's all very interesting, Nostradamus," I started, and Corinne started laughing. She took my arm, and we got up and started walking out of the Piazza. I looked at the statue of Bruno a last time in the distance, and it looked a little like smoke was in the air. I thought it was all that was left of what Corinne had done to me.

When we returned to France, Corinne's parents went off to Paris with friends for the last weekend, and we had the cottage to ourselves. I'd been anxious to test my popularity with Corinne, to see whether I was in her good graces, so that Saturday morning I was

The Voyage of a Bean

very affectionate, rubbing her shoulders, making her coffee, all in the hope that we might use the unexpected privacy we had to consummate the vacation. When we started kissing, however, and I led her to her parents' bed, she balked.

"Not there," she pleaded. "I can't do it on my parents' bed." I thought she was kidding, but she wasn't. At first I gently tried persuading her that it was no big deal, but I soon realized that there was just something about it being their bed that made it impossible for her to go there. Our alternative was one of the small cots that we'd been sleeping on separately, and this was a difficult throwback to the old days in college given the comfort of the big queen bed. But she would hear none of it, and rather than lose my temper and not be able to regain the moment, we used the cot in the shadow of her parents' bed. It was the one on which she'd been sleeping.

Afterwards, I wasn't as worried about expressing my opinion, even if there was a sense that an argument on the matter was a certainty. I accused her of being a Puritan. That was a stretch, except that her parents had often used the term in connection to any negative reaction I had to anything the French did openly that Americans did not. I once complained that a child was riding a potty chair in the kitchen while we ate dinner, and they said I was a Puritan, that sort of thing, but Corinne was certainly not a Puritan, and she ignored the comment, or rather, she let it in to simmer.

I went on to accuse her of being overly connected to her parents despite all the years that had gone by. I said that obviously she thought first of the principle and let it destroy feeling, which is how the poet Schiller defined the barbarian. She'd used it on me once or twice. His counter notion of the savage being one who let feeling destroy principle was also one of the things we had thrown at one another from time to time. Again, she didn't say anything. But I was reaching the point where I was again considering that I had made a mistake to get together with her again. I craved the shared culture of an American woman. This European influence was complicated and arrogant, and I was tired of being the amiable stranger. They still called me "Bean" rather than Ben, affectionately albeit, but I just wanted a return to normalcy, to dive back into oblivion

The Voyage of a Bean

and disappear without having to make a federal case out of a statue, and be torched in the process, or not be able to make love to the woman I loved because her parents had made a psychic imprint on the mattress that made it taboo. I was starting to blame them again. Remembering her eloquent tirade in the Piazza, I made the mistake of tying it to her shaggy dog, and I accused her of being one of those women who substitutes intellectuality for love and holds it out as a barrier to keep men from getting too close, for which she slapped me.

We didn't talk much that day, but went down to the beach to watch people collect mussels and net shrimp. I didn't hold her hand. We slept in our separate cots that night, and the next day quietly awaited the return of her parents so we could leave the country. Why we had to wait for them was beyond me. We might have met them in Paris for the flight, except we were connecting out of Nantes, and they had left all their bags because there wasn't enough room in the car. I was just arguing within myself over any little thing due to the silence between us. Everything was going smoothly except that Corinne had made love with me, and it wasn't good enough for me.

Her parents sensed there was a problem but did not interfere. The flight home was civil but tense. Corinne probably guessed that I would quickly go my own way once we were stateside. She didn't ask whether I'd call her. I just took my bags, thanked them for the trip and left them. For some reason I don't much recall getting home or what I did, but Corinne called me a few weeks later, and I received the call a little too coolly, I'm afraid. I think I was still waiting for her to relent and apologize for putting me on the cot, but she had news for me. She was pregnant, but she told me not to worry because she would have an abortion.

That was another thing about the French that I didn't understand, another reason to call me a Puritan, which they did, but they had developed an abortion pill, RU-486, that made it easy, and I was against it on principle that a decision like that should be difficult, putting you in mind of the direct connection with the life being taken by feeling some of the pain yourself. I had always wanted children, though I was somewhat disinclined to believe I would ever have them, and all the depth of my stand with her on the bed was rendered as petty and thin as it really was in my heart when I started trying to talk her out of it. She was very matter of fact about it. It was as if I was trying to talk her onto the bed again, and she was insistent about getting tied into the gurney. That little bed where the child was conceived was going to be the very place where she would give it up. I asked if her parents knew, and she told me they did not and not to say anything, or she would never talk with me again.

This was one of those rare moments when I remembered my father's words. In this case, what he'd told me about fighting giants came back to mind. Corinne was about to do something I had to fight against. She was the giant. Not long ago such things were illegal, but by gradually changing the law, society soon adapts to wearing every day what it would never have believed it would even try on for size. There was another side to the eye of the hurricane, which was what kinds of things we think we can get away with while the world seems a gentle, whole place experiencing a new renaissance. To me it was a ticket to hell, and I told her I'd fight her. I also said I was sorry for what had happened in France, that I just needed some time by myself, but that she had to know I would have called her because we always got back together. I said that her call was the beginning, that we could get married and have the child. She would have none of it. If she had a dog, she would have put it on the phone just to put something between us. I say that because she had the music up and full, and she wouldn't turn it down. She kept saying I really didn't want her to turn it down. She kept saying I really didn't want her or the baby. I told her it was my dream to share thoughts with a child, to help it grow into a confidence in the world, to perhaps make a difference, by believing in life and the voyage we all take through the world. I begged her to reconsider, but she would not listen. She said I sounded foolish. I told her about what my father had told me, about the beans talking, that we started life in that form and made our way through it, even to where we might wind up on a bed doubled over in the fetal position, but that life had purpose, that anyone can make a difference, and does, even in one person's life, and this child, whose life she was going to take, might be the very thing that would give her life the meaning that

The Voyage of a Bean

she was looking for, even if it was to be without me.

I went with her to the clinic and went as far as the waiting room, where I saw a father with five children whose wife was obviously aborting a sixth. The kids were so cute though. What harm could there be in another, to give it a chance to live? I was full of strange thoughts that day, of what life means when there is no meaning, heading for oblivion, versus the life that never gets a chance to live. It is like counting by fours to infinity, which is a smaller infinity than counting by ones. Dying before ever reaching the world where in the end there is only oblivion is just a different kind of oblivion. What did giants and Jacks matter at all in such a place where the fight in the end didn't make a difference? If oblivion is the ultimate truth, those who realize it are the smart ones, and they can do anything they want, even if it makes them unpopular. I was not going to buy any of that. I might lose the battle here, get kicked out of the giant's kingdom, but not without some kind of fight. I could even refuse a crucifix and hold to Christ in my heart. Bruno must have realized that Christ, as they were forcing it, was not Christ at all, and acceptance of a symbol would be a recantation after all. To hell with them, and judged properly, no matter how things may look on earth, we have to do what we think is right, no matter what the world has to say about it. Even exoneration is meaningless in a sense. What matters is what is in the soul at the time. I walked away from the abortion clinic without waiting for Corinne. There was a life within her and a life outside her. She was killing two at once, and it wasn't anything I was trying to convey. It was what I felt. I went back to my life, and watched my father slowly die. It was not a good couple of years for me to say the least.

As my fever began to break, I realized for the first time that the whole of experience is not about just living to the point of having a revelation or experiencing what could be termed "enlightenment," but about coming around to thinking the way that God thinks, or rather, to come around to the way of thinking of God. Enlightenment of that kind changes one's life if one lives, and helps one accept death as one dies. There is no greater kind of enlightenment

The Voyage of a Bean

as even if one were shown all that there is on the other side and became imbued with a full sense of the absolute truth, what one would write would take its place among similar texts and be bound to create a following of some kind, perhaps better, perhaps worse for the world as we know it. If you condemn the religion of the American Indian as being pagan, you take away something held dear to many righteous individuals. What we may have trouble discerning through the multiplicity of ideas may be easier seen through the adherence to the sound principles of the faith that we have learned. There are good reasons to stay true to the ideas we have learned from those who love us, and it is the obvious conflict of ideas, the innate contradictions that are more readily seen than the good that comes from living within a certain faith. The underlying beauty of the world is similar to what we find in the complexity of music when it suddenly becomes familiar to us. There is something beautiful that is fathomable only to the single mind, a mind whose wish is that others see it too. The problem with ideas by themselves is that no one readily shares them. Life teaches what ideas are true. Otherwise they are cold and inert.

But as I came out of my fever and reflected on all that I had thought about Corinne while I had been so sick, I suddenly realized that the music that she had been playing so loudly in the background was my music, the very music I'd gone back to her place to get that she did not like. Was she playing some kind of message. It just didn't seem right, but my mind was not playing tricks. I just hadn't realized it at the time.

The nurse brought me one of those terrible liquid lunches with jello that they use to start off a recovery, and as bad as it was, I still took it as a good sign, an indication that I was really going to be alright. She said that it had really been touch and go for awhile, and they had been in touch with next of kin, which I didn't understand because my father was all I had, and I explained to her that he had just died. She said that people had enquired, and indicated they were family, and they did not make any decisions or arrangements, but were standing by. I asked what that meant. She said that they would come visit when I was able to receive visitors. I said then let them know that I would like to see them.

That afternoon, Corinne's parents stopped by to see me. They had heard about my father's death, and they learned about me as well when they contacted the hospital about him and any arrangements after they couldn't get in touch with me. I thanked them for coming and said that I had done little else but think about Corinne since my father had died. They said Corinne had told them that I had called, and she was waiting outside, and would come in if I would see her. Corinne? Right there? Of course, please, go get her right away. Corinne's mother went out, and her father took my hand and said, "I think you're in for a leetle surprise, Bean."

I heard the whining of a young child in the hallway, and Corinne came in holding the hand of a two-year old boy. She had gone in for the abortion but hadn't been able to go through with it. It wasn't that they didn't put her out, but even as she was unconscious, on what I imagined was a gurney, the cot in the cottage, she was pulling off the oxygen mask and the intravenous tubes, to the point that they had to "abort the abortion," as she put it. They put her in a room, and she thought about what they had told her, and she said she felt that she had been given a second chance, and decided to not go through with it. But I had left, and she thought it was better to leave me out of it, but the boy needed a father, and the time was right for the family to come together, whatever that would mean.

I was all in tears. I had a son! "What's his name?" I asked. She said she named him Bruno after Giordano, which she didn't think would be a good first name, and I said, "That's so typically French to prefer Bruno over Giordano," but I loved it, and I looked at him as he hid shyly behind his mother's leg, wanting him to run out and play, to jump all over me. He looked like I did as a boy.

So we are back together again, for whatever that will mean, and I have plans to teach my son courage, and I'll teach him that beans can talk, that they can make a difference as they go on life's voyage, and I'll teach him not to fear giants, but to seek them out and fight them wherever they may be; and I'll tell him about the defining moment of my life, though exactly what that is will depend to a very large degree on exactly how one defines "moment."

ABOUT THE AUTHOR

Bruce Adam was born in Chicago. After graduating from Northern Illinois University with honors, he moved to Nantes, France where he taught and continued his studies. Returning to the US, he worked ten years in publishing before turning his attention to completing his own work. *The Voyage of a Bean* is his second volume of short stories after *Dreams of a Lifetime*, which appeared in 2004. A third volume is scheduled for early 2008. He also edited *In Search of Gold*, the journal kept during the gold rush by his great-great grandfather, John Fisk, and published by Ara Pacis in 2005. Forthcoming books include *Zen Death Poems and Other Stories*, which is slated for the second half of 2006.

www.ingramcontent.com/pod-product-compliance
Ingram Content Group UK Ltd.
Pitfield, Milton Keynes, MK11 3LW, UK
UKHW041416180426
11947UKWH00007B/159